Shyt List

Smokin' Crazies

the
Finale

a novel by Reign

PUBLISHER'S NOTE:
This book is a work of fiction. Names, characters, businesses,
Organizations, places, events and incidents are the product of the
Author's imagination or are used fictionally. Any resemblance of
Actual persons, living or dead, events, or locales are entirely coin-cidental.

Library of Congress Control Number: 2012935127
ISBN 10: 0984993002
ISBN 13: 978-0984993000
Cover Design: Davida Baldwin www.oddballdsgn.com
Editor: Advanced Editorial Services
Graphics: Davida Baldwin
www.thecartelpublications.com
First Edition

CHECK OUT OTHER TITLES BY THE CARTEL PUBLICATIONS

SHYT LIST 1
SHYT LIST 2
SHYT LIST 3
SHYT LIST 4
SHYT LIST 5
PITBULLS IN A SKIRT 1
PITBULLS IN A SKIRT 2
PITBULLS IN A SKIRT 3
POISON 1
POISON 2
VICTORIA'S SECRET
HELL RAZOR HONEYS 1
HELL RAZOR HONEYS 2
BLACK AND UGLY AS EVER
A HUSTLER'S SON 2
THE FACE THAT LAUNCHED A THOUSAND BULLETS
YEAR OF THE CRACKMOM
THE UNUSUAL SUSPECTS
MISS WAYNE AND THE QUEENS OF DC
LA FAMILIA DIVIDED
RAUNCHY
RAUNCHY 2
REVERSED
QUITA'S DAYSCARE CENTER
THE END: HOW TO WRITE A BESTSELLING NOVEL IN 30 DAYS

WWW.THECARTELPUBLICATIONS.COM

What's Crackin' Fam!!

I'm coming to you all with a heavy heart and mind as I write this letter. The end of an era...The "Shyt List" series. Seeing this series come to an end is truly sad for me. It was not that long ago when the first book, "Shyt List: Be Careful Who You Cross", was published. We were boosted, excited and thrilled, to say the least. Now we are on the last book of the series, "Shyt List 5: Smokin' Crazies The Finale" and I am jive sad! Although I realize that all good things must come to an end, I don't know what I'm going to do with myself now that the tales of Yvonna are done. Maybe just hope and pray that one day, Yvonna will make her way back to a book in the near future. But, in the meantime, get ready to read a finale that will go down in history! Remember, choose wisely ;)

But before we get into that, in keeping with The Cartel Publications tradition, we MUST pay homage to an author who is making noise in the literary world. In this novel we like to recognize author:

"MiMi Renee"

MiMi Renee is the author of several titles including, "Pretty Bright"; "Deadly Decisions" and "Deadly Decisions II". We had the pleasure of meeting and hanging out with this author and we had a ball. She is talented and sweet and we know she will take the industry by storm!

Aight peoples, I'ma bid you adieu so ya'll can jump into this classic! Remember, life is a blessing! Live it and love it to the fullest!

Be easy!

Charisse "C. Wash" Washington
VP, The Cartel Publications

www.thecartelpublications.com
www.twitter.com/cartelbooks
www.facebook.com/publishercharissewashington
www.myspace.com/thecartelpublications
www.facebook.com/cartelcafeandbooksstore

Acknowledgements

I acknowledge every Shyt List fan who has supported the series from the onset. Yvonna's world is wicked and to be honest, I'm not sure where the vision to create this series came from. What I do know is that I was saddened when I wrote the final word to this book. I guess with all good things, it must come to an end. I truly hope I did you proud.

Love,

T. Styles AKA Reign

www.facebook.com/authortstyles

www.twitter.com/authortstyles

www.youtube.com/tstyles74

www.thecartelpublications.com

Dedication

To Crazed Shyt List Fans Everywhere

ShytList V

Prologue

The doctors thought Yvonna Harris was unconscious. Thought she couldn't feel a thing, but they were wrong. This was a nightmare. She felt extreme pain as a scalpel sliced the flesh of her arm, to remove a bullet that pierced one of her arteries. It was the most excruciating pain she ever experienced in her tumultuous life.

Whoever shot her three times in the upper body, and once in the ear, wanted her dead. They wanted her stopped. And judging by the amount of blood she lost, they were going to get their wish. Yet a little girl by the name of Delilah, needed her to survive. And that same little girl, born to a woman plagued with a mental disease, would not understand if she didn't keep her promise, to come back to her in one piece.

Yvonna did enough dirt to see death row ten times over, yet as she lay on top of the operating table, she was asking the one with the final decision, to spare her the death penalty. In the past, dying was not a fear but that was before she experienced unconditional love.

Trying to get her mind off of the bullets occupying her body, her thoughts flashed to those she murdered. As if they were standing before her on a jury, she could clearly see their faces - Bilal Santana, Bernice Santana, Cream Justice, Sabrina Beddows, and Dave Walters. Sure there were more, but in her opinion, when she took their lives, it was the beginning of her demise. And then there was Bilal Jr, the innocent child whose life she destroyed, because of jealousy.

Remembering the prayer Pastor Robinson recited before she killed him, some months back, she wondered would it work for her. *Our Father, who art in heaven. Hallowed be thy...hallowed be thy...*

She couldn't finish the prayer because she was enveloped in pain once more, thanks to the relentless effort of the doctors. This time the feeling was so incapacitating, that she saw flashes of light under her closed lids. She tried to part her lips to speak once more, to let them know that they were making a mistake, but nothing on her body moved, not even her mouth.

Screaming from the inside she yelled, *I can feel you! Please stop! You're hurting me!* There was a brief pause before she felt the rest of her clothing being torn from her body. *What are you about to do now?* The moment the thought entered her mind, a scalpel ripped through her trachea. Suddenly, she whisked back mentally, to how she ended up in the predicament, which may very well cause her, her life.

3 Months Earlier

YVONNA

It was cold as a mothafucka outside. And Yvonna's crew was pissing her the fuck, off as they sat in the passenger seat of a stolen 1976 Monte Carlo, belonging to the late Pastor Robinson. She didn't know what possessed her to think that she could roll on a mission with Bricks, Swoopes and Ming, and everything would run smoothly. They fought nonstop and their personality's crashed harder than a drunken driver with his eyes closed.

"You don't think Robinson was lying to us do you?" Yvonna asked, as they sat in front of a large home in an upscale part of Maryland. She removed her red Prada shades and focused on the brick home. "'Cause we been casing this house for days and we still haven't run into Ron Max."

"It's a little too late to ask questions, Squeeze." Bricks said, polishing his bullets to remove his prints. "You killed slim right after he told us where he lived. In his church at that."

"That wasn't no real church!" She said with spite. "Robinson was just as guilty as the rest of those baby fuckers as far as I'm concerned. I just put him out of his misery."

"Well what the fuck are we waiting on then?" Swoopes asked, wondering why they couldn't just run up in Ron Max's house and start blasting. A black eye patch covered his left eye courtesy of the paint thinner thrown in his face as a teenager. "I know the mothafucka in there! We been watching this house for hours and ain't nobody come out yet."

Swoopes had his own reasons for wanting Ron Max and the rest of the pedophiles murdered. Just like Yvonna, he remembered having to do things to grown men, and sometimes women, that no child should be subjected to. 'Till this day, his dreams forced him back to those tender, terrible moments and were the cause of him being the sadistic killer he is in present day.

"We not going nowhere until we make sure this is the right place." Bricks quarterbacked, as he looked back at him. "I'm not fucking with you on no bullshit today, nigga. I'm done wit' your shit."

Swoopes leaned forward in his seat. "Nigga, you ain't got to fuck wit' me at all."

"That's exactly what I'm saying." Bricks bucked back. "If you wanna go shoot up a bunch of niggas for no reason, don't let this mission stop you. The door is to your left, it opens."

Just like the others, Bricks had his reason for staying with the cause. For starters he was in love with Yvonna, and secondly, he didn't trust Swoopes alone with her. Because of him, they'd been involved in five mini wars with random dudes due to his unmotivated temper. Although they were always able to put each matter under wraps, sometimes having to bust their guns in the process, his rants still expended energy they couldn't spare.

Yvonna slithered down as far as possible in her seat, when she saw someone walking out of the house. "Somebody coming." She whispered. She wiped her shoulder length hair out of her face and peered outside of the frosty window. Following suit, Bricks, who was driving, along with Ming and Swoopes, who sat in the back, also tried to conceal themselves.

"Now we got action," Swoopes said, rubbing his hands excitedly together. "This what I been waiting on all night."

"I was thinking the same thing," Ming grinned. Her red leather jacket exposed the tops of her breasts, despite the weather being frustratingly cold outside. Ming was still ride or die for her friend, even though she secretly hoped that her new crush, Swoopes, would look at her as something other than a *fuck at night'* buddy.

Bricks pulled the 9-millimeter from his brown leather jacket and in a husky voice asked, "Can you see his face yet, babes?" He cocked and loaded his weapon. "'Cause I can't see shit over here."

"Why you not ask, Ming?" Being the smallest of the gang, she was able to peer out of the window on all fours. "Ming has good view too."

Irritated with Ming's constant need to fit in, Yvonna said, "Shut the fuck up before he hears you. You been getting on everybody's nerves since we left the hideout."

Gabriella, who rarely left Yvonna's side these days because she wasn't taking her medicine said, "She just needs a little dick. And if you ask me, we do too."

Yvonna rolled her eyes and ignored her other half. She was no longer a rookie at hiding her illness and those in her life were unaware of the severity of the problem. She was getting sicker by the day and even resorted to relying on Gabriella for advice. Without people like Dr. Terrell Shines to force her to medicate, she was losing hold of sanity.

"Ming will not be quiet! I'm sick of the three of you leaving me out! Having meetings behind back and not telling Ming what's going on. I signed up for this job too." She looked at all of them, using the moment to voice her opinion. She had a strange knack of doing things at the wrong time. "You all must learn to respect Ming."

Swoopes shook his head. "This why nobody fucks wit' you sometimes. You too hot!" He grabbed his revolver out of the holster on his blue jeans, and removed bullets out of his grey tweed jacket. He was fully loaded. "You gotta learn to calm down."

"You calling somebody hot?" Bricks rebutted. "As much shit as you got us into?"

"Why you always feel it in your power to say something to me?" Swoopes asked.

"Do you see the nigga or not, Squeeze?" Bricks questioned, ignoring Swoopes. "My back hurting down this mothafucka."

Both Yvonna and Ming peered out of the frosted window again. When the man turned to the side, Yvonna was able to identify Ron Max, one of the leaders of the child sex ring. Although he had on a knit hat, his large pink lips protruding from his face, were a dead giveaway. She didn't remember him from the orphanage, but Swoopes did and would always seem uneasy when the four of them discussed a plan of action.

"Yes! Ming sees him!" She exclaimed, eager to alert the clan. "It's time to move."

Yvonna glanced down at the picture in her lap once more. "She's right," She looked at Bricks. "That's the mothafucka Robinson told us about." Although he was a small man on the totem pole, they were sure he'd be able to lead them to the big man. "I think we should..."

Suddenly the door opened and a cold gust of air entered the car and crept up their bodies. The three of them looked toward Swoopes and saw an empty seat. When Yvonna turned toward the house, she saw a blur quickly move past the window. In seconds flat, Swoopes was behind Ron Max, as he was preparing to lock the door to his home. Sensing Swoopes' presence, Ron turned around and was knocked in the face with the handle of his gun. His body plummeted before Swoopes unloaded into his white teeth making them red.

"I'm sick of this nigga!" Bricks said to no one in particular, as they all poured out of the car. "If we don't drop this dude, he gonna get us killed!"

Yvonna could predict how things would pan out. Bricks and Swoopes fought twenty-three hours out of a twenty-four hour day. They argued so much, she was certain that they battled one another in their dreams. No matter how hard she tried to reason with them, nothing seemed to work. It got to a point where they needed to hate one another just to get through the day.

"What the fuck is wrong with you, nigga? Have you forgotten we got mothafuckas looking for us?" Bricks asked as he steam rolled Swoopes. "We ain't got no time for all this *RA-RA* shit you bringing. If you wanna be on that..."

Unfortunately for Bricks' mouth, he was unable to complete his statement. He was met with all five of Swoopes' knuckles and he dropped in the snow next to Ron's bloody body. Since he only had two fingers on his right hand, he did what he could with the other, by way of body blows. As if he was never swiped, Bricks popped up and stole Swoopes in his good eye, knocking him to the ground. It didn't take long for them to be in the throws of a violent brawl. It mattered to neither that a dead man lie amongst them or that the world and Yao wanted their heads. At the moment, their only mission was inflicting pain on the other.

Turned on by the scene, Ming, having absolutely nothing to do with the matter, decided to jump in the middle of the battle, in the hopes of getting slapped around a little. Yvonna was so angry with all three that she felt like murdering each of them and rolling solo.

"I don't know why you just won't get rid of them." Gabriella said standing next to Yvonna. She dusted the shoulder of her red leather cat suit. "They're going to get you killed or locked up. Unless that's what you want."

"Leave me alone, Gabriella." She didn't care if they heard her or not. In her opinion at the moment, they were crazier than everyone claimed she was. "I got one thing on my mind. Killing these mothafuckas and getting on with my life."

While the three of them tussled in the snow, she lifted the keys to Ron's house and dawdled inside. The moment the door opened, a strong scent of Pine Sol and cigarettes smacked her in the face. The aroma instantly made her queasy, as it brought up memories from living in the orphanage. The staff members would make them clean with it, to hide the smell of blood and death that constantly ruled the air. She held onto her stomach contents, by taking a few quick breaths, and continued through the house. When she was calmer, and remembered they couldn't hurt her anymore because she was in charge, she refocused.

Taking a few seconds, she observed her surroundings. From where she stood, she scanned the foyer, and the living room and everything seemed bland and lifeless. Not how she expected a pimp to live for sure. When she spotted a portrait above the mantel of a family, she walked slowly toward it. The picture was of Ron Max, a woman and two kids. Of course she knew who Ron was, but what fucked her up was the woman with him. Up until that moment, she wondered what happened to her and now she had her answer.

"I remember her," Swoopes said as he, Bricks and Ming drug Ron's body into the house before dropping it in the foyer, like dirty luggage. He stepped over it, wiped the blood off the corner of his mouth from the fight he was in, and moved toward Yvonna. While Bricks busied himself with the contents of Ron's pockets. "Her name is Ebony or some shit like that, right?"

Yvonna turned around to look at him. "Oh so what, the three of ya'll finished fucking already?" She turned back around to examine the picture. "I'm so over the fighting shit. I just want to take care of these mothafuckas and go on with my life. And you should too."

"So I don't want this to be over?" Swoopes countered. "You not the best of company yourself, Tootsie. Don't get it twisted, bitch, the moment this is done, I'm out."

"I hear you," she smirked, "But it seems to me that you more interested in Bricks than completing this mission."

Bricks stepped forward at the mention of his name. "Don't get hurt, Yvonna." When he stood up he noticed his side was sore, so he gripped it and pushed past Swoopes, knocking him a few inches forward. "You knew me and this bamma was gonna be at war when you signed him up." He mugged him. "That's why I'm still trying to figure out why he's here."

"I know you betta watch where the fuck you going, slim!" Swoopes growled although he avoided charging him. Besides, he was still winded from their recent battle outside. He would wait until he rested up later. "This nigga stay wit' my name in his mouth man."

Ignoring him Bricks asked Yvonna, "Who the fuck is Ebony?" He rubbed his side harder and hoped his ribs weren't fractured. "I heard you say her name when I was walking inside."

She rolled her eyes at him and said, "She use to live with us at the orphanage." She turned back to the portrait. "Before now, I thought she was dead. Now I'm finding out she shacked up with this nigga. After everything we been through."

Ming walked up to the picture and stood in front of all of them, just to be the center of attention. She wasn't as banged up as she wanted from the fight and Yvonna shook her head. Over the weeks, Ming had proven to be a little thirstier than Yvonna originally thought and she didn't understand why. It was like she was constantly looking for something from them, but especially Swoopes. "So he took her when she was a child? To have for himself?" She stared at Ebony's face which in her opinion, looked sad. "To make wife?"

Yvonna was about to respond when a stinging sensation coursed through the fleshy part of her ass. "What the fuck!" She jumped around, and rubbed the area repeatedly, hoping the pain would subside. "Who just stabbed me?"

When she turned around, Ebony was aiming a BB gun in their direction. She was about to shoot again when everyone rushed her. She didn't go down easily and they hadn't expected her to be so strong. It was Ming who was successful in knocking her to the floor, while Swoopes and Bricks disarmed her. When the situation was under control, Yvonna approached in attack mode.

With a murderous mien she inched toward her prey. Looking down at her she stated, "You must wanna die, bitch!"

"I want to know what the fuck you doing in my house?" Ebony combated, from the floor, although she was outnumbered. Her long brown hair was spread out on the floor and one of her fake eyelashes rested on the bridge of her nose. She was disheveled but still extremely attractive. It was apparent to all that she was being taken care of. "And what have you done to my husband?"

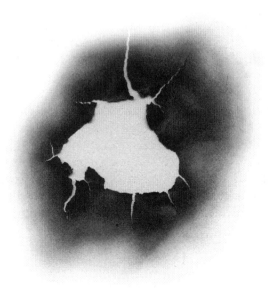

RUFUS DAY

Rufus Day, the worlds nastiest pedophile and pimp, stood his six foot seven inch frame slyly over his pulpit. He hovered slowly, as he lustfully searched the congregation for his prey. He just finished ministering to his flock and they waited desperately for his next word. To the weak he was God, to the strong he was the devil reincarnated.

Their cheers and praises rang in the background and he adored every minute of it. Although they needed the final word of the day, before going back to their miserable lives, he needed the perfect little girl to add to his stable. His droopy eyes, which always leaked due to conjunctivitis, scanned over several hopeful candidates again. Although he was an unattractive black man, in their eyes, he was as handsome as John F. Kennedy. His flowery words, power and expensive taste in clothing, did an outstanding job of concealing his immorality.

It didn't take him long to find the one. Her long black pigtails hung down her back, and were dressed at the ends with two pink ribbons. Her brown skin was light enough to show her naturally rosy cheeks, as she hid into her mother's shadow, texting on her phone. She seemed preoccupied and troubled, the combination needed for him to enact his scheme. She had to be twelve, just the age to start a career in the sex industry. So sweet. So perfect.

Once he spotted the perfect schlemiel, he imagined how her young body would look naked. With a wicked vision in mind, he flipped a few pages in his bible, mainly for affect with his gold ring covered fingers. He already had his marker on the page he needed to deliver his final message, but he was nothing without a performance. Raising his manicured hand, he weakly said, "Settle down." When the congregation didn't simmer, he raised his voice just a tad, "I love you too, but please, settle down."

When they were silent he vocalized, "Before you go home, I want to read you an important scripture." He stuck his index finger, which blinged with clear nail polish, on his pink tongue, before flipping a few more pages and stopping. "If we can turn to First Thessalonians, chapter five, versus twelve to thirteen." The sound of flapping paper filled the sanctuary before fading away. "This passage shows how you," he waved his hand, "the members of AFCOG should treat your pastor." He pointed to himself. "Now, I all know you want to treat your pastor properly. Am I right."

The church sang, "Yes!"

"I know you do," he grinned. Bowing his head toward the bible he begin, "The passage reads, *'But we request of you brethren, that you appreciate those who diligently labor amongst you and have charge over you in the Lord and give you instruction.'* He looked at his victim and her mother to be sure they were paying attention. They were. "Let the church say, Amen."

"Amen!"

When he was done, he closed the bible. "What that means is this, I am your Leader. I am your Master, and if you don't trust me and my words, I can't lead you to the Promise Land." He looked at everyone before his eyes settled back on the child. "Do you hear what I'm saying?" They nodded. "As much as I would like to, I can't walk with you to meet the Lord thy God, unless you trust in your Master. As a matter of fact, you have to trust me above all things, even above the man known as Jesus Christ." He knew his request was heavy, but he mind fucked them so long, that he was sure they were ready to surrender. "Ya'll not ready for what I'm saying."

"Yes we are!" They cheered.

"I hear you, but I need for you to make it clearer." Staring at them with penetrating eyes he continued, "So I ask you again, will you follow me?"

There was brief silence before they said, "Yes!" Their palms faced him as if they needed to feel him. Needed to be near him. Needed to smell him. "We will follow you!"

"I said, will you follow me?"

"Yes!" The church erupted in thunder.

"Then get on your knees and bow your heads." At first they looked at each other, in confusion. But when the first person dropped, no one wanted to be the last one standing. In less than two minutes, everyone was on their knees...the choir included. He succeeded what most pimps would give their lives for, the creation of a clan.

Smiling slyly, Rufus stepped down and walked toward the middle of the church, touching members on their heads softly as he passed them by. "I am your master, and I will never lead you astray." People wept because they believed he was as close to Jesus, as any of them would ever see in their lifetime. When his ego was fully fed, he said, "You may rise."

Then he made his way to Marge David, the unemployed black waitress and her twelve-year-old little girl that he'd been eyeing all morning. Marge was so star struck as he moved toward her, that she could've sworn he had the power to take the breath from her body. The other women looked on in envy at the attention he was preparing to give the new member.

"Sister Marge, right?" His clammy hands reached out for her warm ones. When he had them in his clasps, he held onto them tightly. "What a pleasure."

Marge unconsciously teased the brown wig she wore with her fingers, which looked like it fell off of one of the *Supremes'* heads. "Reverend, I can't believe you know my name." She blushed. "I feel so special."

"You are special. Which is why I wanted to talk to you. I received your letter and have chosen Tyisha, for my *Get Them On The Right Track* program." Although the word track was hopeful to Marge, in the pimp world it meant the stroll, a place where young girls and sometimes boys, sold their bodies for profit.

Marge submitted a letter to him a few weeks ago, after she learned about the program from a friend on the street. All they knew was that Rufus awarded prize money to single mothers, to help them get on their feet, and honestly, that was all she cared about. "The competition was thick, Marge, but my decision is made." He softly touched the top of the child's head. "Congratulations."

Marge's eyes widened as if she was just accepted to Yale, while Tyisha stared at him with suspicious eyes. "Say thank you, Tyisha!"

"Thanks." She responded flicking the buttons on her phone again. She was uninterested in anything that didn't have to do with boys. "I 'ppreciate it. I guess."

"I know you do, child." He eyed her again and licked his lips. "And you'll be perfect. Of course she'll have to spend the entire summer at my home. In order for it to work I have to be with her most hours of the day." He softly touched her head again and she pulled back. She hated the man already but he wasn't phased. "There she'll learn the bible fully, along with the fundamentals necessary to be a leader. And because she's selected, she'll receive fifteen thousand dollars." Marge's eyes widened. "I'll have my secretary draft a check up right away." The money was just enough for Marge to get out of debt and back on her feet. She couldn't believe the amazing opportunity he provided. "I offer the money to single mothers who are having a hard time. I hope you can use it." If she accepted, he was essentially buying her daughter's soul and once it belonged to him, he would not let go.

Overwhelmed with gratitude, Marge said, "I can certainly use the money! This is awesome! Praise God!" She raised her hands to the sky again. "Praise his name!"

He gently tugged her chin and looked into her eyes. "Don't praise God, Sister Marge. Praise me."

Shyt List V

BILAL Jr.

The small bedroom was pitch dark as Bilal Jr., pretended like he didn't hear his older brother Laser, fucking the dog shit out of his girlfriend Owl, on the bottom bunk. He faked sleep on the floor to hide his cowardice. He would kill himself before he let either of them know that he was weakened by his brother's indiscretions. Besides, Owl, who earned her name because of her smooth dark skin and wide eyes, was a freak. He knew it the day he stepped to her at the corner store.

"Turn over," Laser whispered to Owl in the darkness. "I wanna hit that back hole for a minute. You know how I like it." They had been fucking nonstop since Bilal, Jr. met her six months earlier.

"No, that shit hurts." She responded coyly. "Anyway, what's wrong with my pussy? I want to get mine off too."

"Your cave is lovely, ma. I been told you that. But I wanna do something a little different tonight. So stop fucking around and turn over."

"Shhh, you talking too loud, Bilal. gonna hear you." She giggled, as she rustled with the covers. Bilal, Jr. widened the slits in his eyes to see if she complied. Because of the murkiness of the room, all he could see was the white sheet shuffling and bodies moving beneath them. "You never were good at keeping your voice on the low. Wit' your loud ass."

Laser was growing impatient with Owl. Although she was good for a decent nut, she played too many games before he got what he wanted. "Shut up, bitch. That lil nigga know I'm fucking you already. Stop tripping."

Prior to that moment, Bilal, Jr. assumed that Laser believed he was sleep whenever she'd sneak over the house late at night. Now he felt like a gump, who was too afraid to fight back. But when it came to his twin brothers, particularly Laser, he felt inferior. They were bigger than him and in his opinion that made them stronger.

"No he don't, Laser. You always lying and shit." Owl's voice was heavy with embarrassment. It was cool to play the freak when she thought it was behind Bilal, Jr.'s back. Now she wondered if her actions were being made public without her authorization. Perhaps they were videotaping her freak-whore ass. And if that was the case, she had to perform properly for the cameras, by denying that she was loose. "If he knew I was here, how come he ain't say nothing?"

"Cause he's a fragile lil ass nigga at best. That's why. Plus he know if he say something out the way to me, I'ma turn his teeth to sand," he chuckled, "now grab them ankles, so I can bust right quick. I'm almost there." Owl was suddenly aggravated and the springs on the bed screeched loudly, indicating that she'd gotten up and off the bunk.

"I'm leaving. You gotta get somebody else to be a freak with." Her feet slapped against the wooden floor. "My mamma ain't raise no fool. I know what's happening in here."

Whatever, bitch. He thought. Irritated he said, "You know I don't game, Owl. Especially when I'm trying to fuck."

"Well that's what you trying to do to me now, run game." Her statement seemed all over the place. She thought she was his little secret, like he told her all the time. "Trying to smut me out in the family!"

"You the one creeping over here in the middle of the night. Don't try to act like you don't know what it is." Laser spit. "You ain't nothing but a wet hole, you got me fucked up."

"Like I said, I'm gone! Ya'll not 'bout to tell everybody I put out to both of ya'll."

"Bitch, you not going nowhere!" Laser's feet shuffled against the floor and because it was dark, he accidently stepped on Bilal, Jr.'s forearm because he couldn't see him, nor did he care. Although it was certainly obvious that Bilal,

Jr. was awake now, he remained as still as a corpse in a grave. "You not gonna come up in here and play games with my dick like that." He forcefully grabbed her arm and she could've sworn he was preparing to rip it out of the socket. She heard that Laser was one visit away from being confined to a mental institution, but now she had living proof.

"Nigga, fuck off!" She pushed him to the floor and opened the door. A blast of light from the living room, spilled into the space, as she stormed out wearing only her panties. Her sweaty ass cheeks moved up and down in pursuit of the front door. Not bothering to get dressed, her clothes were balled up and stuffed securely in the pit of her underarm. She lived a few houses down the block but the real kicker was that it was cold as hell outside, but at the moment, loose booty didn't give a fuck. She wanted out. "Red niggas trying to play me."

"Make sure you lock that door, girl." Easter, one of Bilal, Jr.'s aunts screamed at Owl. "I'm tired of your little whore ass running in and out of here fucking my nephews anyway." Owl slammed the door and her feet trekking over the snow-covered grass could be heard outside, before finally fading into the night. "Don't let that bitch back in here!" Easter continued. "I don't trust that young girl."

Treyana, who was Laser and Uzi's mother, had six brothers and sisters. Their names were Gabe, Hall, Easter, Tabitha, Tahir and Oakes. They were the epitome of everything wrong with the hood. In fact, they were so over the top, that if you took the first letter of their names in that order and put them together, it would spell GHETTO. Before she died by the hands of Yvonna Harris, Treyana was just as unruly.

When Treyana was murdered by Yvonna, Laser and his twin brother Uzi were placed in foster care. Originally the government wanted to place them with family, but when the six of them showed up for court wearing 'RIP Treyana' tshirts, with the words *'FUCK THE POLICE'* on the back in red, the courts decided they would be better off in the system.

Laser and Uziya aka Uzi lasted all of three years in foster care. The first year they did well, all things considered. Even though they lost their mother and Avante, who they believed was their father, they made a way. Everything changed when one day after returning home from school, they were met by their social worker. In no uncertain terms she told them that because of their natural good looks, their foster father was growing uncomfortable with having them in his home and around his lovely wife.

Laser and Uzi were growing into young men so attractive, that an insecure man would rather have them executed by hanging, than to have them anywhere near his spouse. Although the social worker pissed Uzi off with the news, he knew where his foster father was coming from. He saw how Denise, their foster mother, gazed at Laser as he played handyman around the house. The twin brothers spent no less than two hours a day in the gym, and they both were physically fit and sexually active. If their foster father did anything *but* get rid of them, without a doubt, Laser would be fucking the shit out of the man's wife by the end of the year.

The second and third foster homes were murder on their spirits as well. They constantly fought to prove that just because their hair was curly, it didn't mean their dicks didn't get hard, or that they wouldn't defend themselves and each other. Before long, no foster family wanted them around, no matter how much the checks were. So the twins decided that it was time to find their aunts and uncles, and that's exactly what they did. Although the four bedroom home in Washington DC couldn't comfortably fit them all, they'd made it work and had been living with them ever since.

When Owl stormed out of the house, Laser flicked the light switch on and stood over Bilal, Jr. His toes were inches from his nose and he let them remain to taunt him. Although the light's glow peeked through Bilal, Jr.'s eyelids, his body remained in the fetal position, as if he were still sleep. He didn't want to face Laser because he didn't know what to say. Not only was Laser fucking his girl consistently, he could care less about his feelings.

When Bilal, Jr. continued to play possum, Laser tapped him softly on the nose with his big toe. "Get up, nigga. I know your bitch ass up." Out of both of the brothers, Laser was the evil one. There always seemed to be something dark moving him, and guiding his actions. When Bilal, Jr. didn't budge Laser stomped on his face hard. His wet lips smeared across the bottom of his foot. "Lil nigga, I said stop faking and wake your bitch ass up! I saw you move when that bitch bounced." He stood over his body preparing to crack his jaw, if he didn't stand up within fifteen seconds.

Sensing danger, Bilal, Jr. popped up and stood in the middle of the floor. His white t-shirt was wet with sweat because the heat was on too high. And the large blue cotton boxers on his body hung to the left, exposing his hip. "What's up, man?" Bilal, Jr. said, trying to appear tough. He took his fist and rubbed his left eye to add to his performance. "I was knocked out." He could smell his brother's cruddy toe dirt under his nose.

"Your punk ass ain't sleep." Laser walked to the bottom bunk and flopped down. Next to him was Owl's pink bra. When Bilal, Jr.'s eyes roamed toward it, Laser picked it up and pressed it firmly against his nose. His eyes remained fixed on his little brother. He wanted a reaction. Inhaling deep he said, "Ummmm, that bitch smells so good." He threw it up to his face and it dropped to the floor. "To be a young nigga, you sure did pick a good bitch. She can take dick like the best of them, but you probably wouldn't know that." He winked. "Hopefully we can keep her around if she calm down and then you'll find out."

Before Bilal, Jr. could respond, his other brother Uzi, Laser's twin, walked through the door and up to the closet. He had four large brown paper shopping bags in his hand, which he placed down. "What ya'll in here doing?" He took his coat off and hung it up. He snatched the navy blue Washington Nationals hat off of his head, exposing a mane full of black curls, like his two brothers. When nobody responded he turned around and asked, "I'm talking to myself now?"

"We not doing nothing," Laser said, eying Bilal, Jr. "I was thinking about hitting this jay with BJ before you walked in. You wanna fire up?"

"Later for that shit," Uzi opened one of the two shopping bags. "Try these on, lil nigga." He threw Bilal, Jr. five pairs of blue True Religion jeans. Four of them smacked against the floor but he caught the fifth. "I wanna make sure they fit before I pay this nigga shit. And check the inseam to make sure they real too. He'll try you on some fake shit if you let him."

Bilal, Jr.'s face lit up, when he saw the gear his brother purchased for him. Uzi always looked out when it came to keeping him fresh. When he left the foster home he was staying in, he didn't have anything except the clothes on his frail body. So having his older bro keep him together was a blessing. He didn't know what Uzi did to make a living, but he knew he was on his mind in the process.

As Bilal, Jr. slid the blue jeans over his boxers, Laser eyed him jealously from the sidelines. He had a fucked up sense of entitlement and hated the spotlight being off of him for one moment. "Why you always buying this nigga shit?" He fired his blunt and pulled. When the smoke exited his lungs he pointed at Bilal. Jr., "Before he came, you use to buy me stuff. Why that change?"

Uzi laughed at his twin. "You an able body mothafucka just like me. I think the shit I use to do for you when we were kids made you forget that. You not younger than me, Laser. We the same age." Uzi loved him with all his heart but sometimes Laser acted like he was his father and that fucked him up at times. They slid out of the same pussy, on the same day, so what was wrong with his hands? He didn't have anything to do with Laser choosing bitches over money, which in his

opinion made him weak. "If anything you should be looking out for your little brother too." Uzi playfully hit Bilal, Jr. in the chest. "At least until the pup can stand on his own paws."

Laser gave Bilal, Jr. a vengeful look, which Bilal, Jr. chose to ignore. Focusing back on his gear, he tried on the other jeans too. Thanks to Uzi, in less than a week he had accumulated a new navy blue North Face coat, a new pair of Foamposite's along with two pair of retro J's and a pair of leather Ugg boots for men.

"Fuck that little nigga." Laser stood up. "Just like I'm able bodied, he is too. Just cause his nuts dropped some years after mine, don't make him no charity case. And you need to stop treating him like that."

"You serious?" Uzi asked with a penetrating gaze. When he spotted the way he eyed his baby brother he stepped into the line of fire. Whatever heat he was giving Bilal, Jr., he wanted on him instead. "I think you need to adjust the fire you throwing at little B."

"What that mean?"

"It means I hope you remember he family. Or do I gotta remind you?" Laser was vicious but Uzi had him in every category. He did things in the dark that Laser's weaker heart could only imagine.

Backing down Laser said, "Yeah...whatever. If you want to set this nigga up and play daddy, then that's on you. When he turn out to be a punk, don't say shit to me." He trooped out the door and slammed it, leaving the tension in the air.

Uzi proceeded to take the clothes he bought himself out of the bags. "Sooner or later, you gonna have to stand up to him, B. Even if it means going to blows." He peered at him to be sure he was receiving the message. "I know him, and he's not going to respect you until you give him a reason."

Bilal, Jr. leaned up against the wall and looked at the floor. His brothers were so complicated. "I do stand up to him." He said under his breath. He picked up the sheet on the floor from the makeshift bed he slept on and folded it. "I don't know why he always coming at me like that though. I don't understand why he hates me so much." He placed the folded sheet on top of one of his bags, which was the substitute for dressers. "I'm confused."

"It don't matter why he hates you." Uzi walked over to Laser's bed and sat down. He wanted to speak hard to his brother so he could understand, but suddenly he was distracted by something pink. Picking it up he asked, "What's this?" Bilal, Jr. remained silent and Uzi got his answer. "You let this nigga fuck your girl in the bed again didn't you? While you slept on the floor and faked sleep."

Silence.

"That's what I'm talking about. You were supposed to put it to him the moment he violated. He's testing you, B. And that means any bitch you bring around is his for the taking, unless you put an end to it now. I heard him last week telling somebody how he be banging her back out and you know what people ask?" He shook his head no. "Where were you?"

It made him uncomfortable to know that Laser took to telling the world, but what was done was done. "She a freak anyway. I don't even give a fuck no more. If anything," he convinced himself, "he doing me a favor. I don't want to be with nobody like that on a one on one basis."

"I bet you all the bitches you dealt with carry it like that."

"Not all of them." He looked at the floor before gaining the strength to lie to his brother. "My last girl didn't carry it like that." Bilal, Jr. thought about Rozay, the cute little girl he was seeing with the Chinese bob and fast mouth. Things were good until the nigga he sold drugs for, broke her fingers after she came at him sideways. That one event resulted in the beat down of a lifetime on his body from her brothers, even though it was not his fault. It didn't stop him from thinking about her and it didn't stop him from looking for the same thing in an-

other girlfriend. He like high-class girls, with pretty faces and wet pussies.

"I gave you some real advice and hopefully you'll take heed." Realizing the conversation was over, he stood up and moved toward the packed closet again. "Fold your clothes and put them in your bags. You gotta make sure you keep your shit fresh."

Bilal, Jr. proudly folded his clothes and placed them neatly in one of the four trash bags in the room, until he remembered he wanted to talk to Uzi about something. He'd been waiting for the moment to speak to him in private, but Laser was always around. "Uzi," he said in a low voice, wrestling with the bags. "Did you know our father? I mean…our real father?"

Uzi sat in the chair next to the door and took off one of his boots. "Naw…I only remember Avante, my mother's husband. I didn't know *Bilal,* who you was named after. But our tios and tias said the three of us look just like him." He removed the second shoe.

"What are tios and tias?"

He laughed. "Tios means uncles and tias means aunts in Spanish. Which is part of our heritage."

"Oh."

Leaning on his knees he said, "Why you ask? If I knew our father?"

Bilal, Jr. held his head down and picked his pillow up off the floor. "I guess I miss him."

In a stern voice he said, "How you miss a nigga you ain't even know? It don't add up."

"I guess I always wanted a father." He sat on Laser's bed. "And since people say we look like him, I wondered what he was like. Everybody on my pops side of the family is dead, except you and Laser."

Uzi shook his head again and said seriously, "I got about five homies. I'm talking about real niggas who would kill for me. Out of those five, not one of them can honestly say they have a family like ours. You got six tios and tias. You got me, and you got Laser. So you don't need a father or another family. Starting from this point on, I want you to forget him and move on. Living in a past that never included you makes you feeble."

Just when he said that Laser bolted through the bedroom door. He had a deranged look on his face and Bilal, Jr. and Uzi jumped up because his energy spelled danger. "You got anything on you, man?" He looked at Uzi. "If you do get rid of it now, because the cops are here!"

"For what?"

"I don't know!" Laser walked further inside and bumped into Bilal, Jr. as he placed his shoes and coat on. "I think that bitch called them when she left earlier. She probably lied and told the pigs I hit her or some shit like that. Young bitches will make up anything."

Uzi knew the answer but he asked, "Which young bitches you talking about, Laser?"

With humiliation he looked at Bilal, Jr. and mouthed, "Owl." Bilal, Jr. felt his stomach juices swirl. It was about to become public information that his brother was fucking his girlfriend and he was sick about it.

"Fuck!" Uzi stomped around the room. "I told you, you didn't have no business fucking that dumb bitch in this house." He pointed in his face. "Now you got heat over here unnecessarily."

From the living room they heard Easter cursing the cops out for blood. "You need a mothafuckin' warrant to come in here!" She paused just to catch her breath. "Wait a minute! What the fuck ya'll think ya'll about to do? Ya'll don't live up in here!" Her threats didn't slow them down because Bilal, Jr. could hear the stampede moving quickly toward their bedroom.

A few seconds later, six cops hung in the bedroom's doorway. One of them stepped close to Laser and asked, "Which one of you are Laser Pliers?"

Shyt List V

Laser quickly pointed at Bilal, Jr. and said, "He is!"

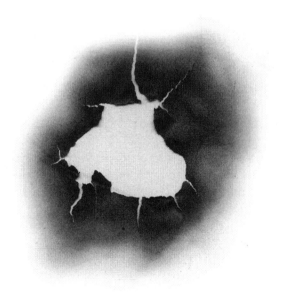

YAO

Yao lay on his living room sofa with a glass of Glen Livet XXV scotch in one hand and the head of a nineteen-year-old whore in the other. The two hundred dollar bottle did little to ease his mind or relax his murderous spirit, but the tongue of a professional rubbing against his asshole did. Still, he was in shit. Deep shit, unless he could bring Yvonna to answer to the murder charge of the heavyweight champion in Vegas.

"Does it feel good?" Roxie asked, flicking her tongue in and around his hairy hole. The gold wig looked oddly out of sorts next to her pretty chocolate skin. "I can make my tongue stiff and go deeper if you'd like."

"Deeper." Naked from the waist down, he bent his knees so she could get at the target. Although some may have assumed the act meant he was a closeted homosexual, Yao was anything but. He just enjoyed a good bout of freaky sex, especially when he was worried. "You're doing good." She grinned and proceeded to work her tongue like a drill.

As he received his service, Yao thought about his attorneys who were doing everything they could to prevent them from implementing him in the murder of Urban Greggs. Because of it, he could not run his drug operation because eyes were on him at all times. Thanks to Yvonna, who actually murdered Greggs in his suite, after he attempted to kill her, Yao was having to fiend off investigators daily.

Not only was he dodging the police, his mind and heart was heavy. Sure he'd never thought about falling for a black woman, but now that he found Yvonna, he didn't take kindly to losing her before making her his wife. His devastation was infused with rage when he learned that Ming, his niece, had run away with her, even though she was valuable to his drug operation. What was it about Yvonna that made people lose reason? There was nothing left to do, he needed to put togeth-

er a team that knew the circles Yvonna moved in, so she could be brought to him. In one piece was good, but dead would work also. He did enough research to locate five people.

He was still getting his asshole popped, when Onik, his most trusted warrior, knocked on the door. "Sir, you have company."

"Bring them in, in five minutes." Yao responded.

Roxie wiped her mouth with the back of her hand and stood up. "Want me to leave?"

"Not yet."

Yao placed his clothes on, sat in a leather chair accented in gold and Roxie opened the door. Three members of the Mah Jong Dynasty poured inside to guard him, as he awaited news from the three men he recently hired. A few seconds later, Onik returned with Growl, Rook and Mike...all members of the YBM (Young Black Millionarz). The members of the YBM feared Yao, which most men having done business with him did.

"Sit," Yao advised, pointing to a couch while Roxie massaged his shoulders. The three men examined the other Chinese men present. They were very intimidating although they said nothing. "Over there."

"You must have information for me at this point." Yao stated, as he lit an expensive cigar. Grey smoke circled his head like a halo. "You've had enough time to come up with something. So I ask you, where is Yvonna?"

Growl grunted a little and said, "We haven't come up with anything....but we..." The flesh on his neck split open like a banana stepped on, as Onik fired a bullet into his throat. Roxie jumped and covered her mouth in horror. Growl placed his hand over the wound, at first due to shock, but later to slow his death. It didn't work.

Earlier Onik was given the orders to kill Growl if he came back empty handed. Yao wasn't fucking around with them. All week they'd been calling him, promising to deliver the goods. But first they needed money for a car and then they needed cash for room and board, as they chased Yvonna around town. He knew what they were doing, trying to milk him dry, but he never stopped the money's flow. He decided it was best to let them hang themselves before he attacked and that's exactly what they did.

Growl's blood was splattered over the walls, soaked into the couch and drenched into the carpet. Mike and Rook went for the weapons on their hips, before they remembered Onik relieved them of their hammers at the door. "Sit." Yao was calm. When they didn't move he said, "I won't say it again." Then he looked at Roxie and said, "Finish." She ran for his shoulders and massaged them like keys on a piano.

Rook quickly obeyed Yao's order while Mike hesitated. "Sit where? On the couch?" Mike's eyes widened. "I mean...you just slumped my man." To save his life, Rook pulled the back of his coat, forcing him to plop on the couch next to him. Blood immersed the back of Mike's jeans and the side of Rook's left leg. Yet they remained still.

"Let me say this clearly. I am Yao...a man who doesn't do excuses. I'm not..." he cleared his throat, "how do you nigga say it? To be fucked with." He checked their eyes for understanding. "Now you took my money, which means you've been paid in full. I want this bitch brought to me like yesterday. Do this, and there's one hundred thousand ready for you in the end. If not," he looked at their dead friend, "well, I don't have to say anything else." He examined Rook, which meant he was now in charge. "Do I make myself clear? Or do I have to kill somebody else to prove my point?"

YVONNA

Yvonna stood over Ebony as she lay face up on the floor. Now unarmed, she perspired like a pig as she considered her fate. She had every right to be frightened; after all, she just hurt one of the craziest bitches alive. Yvonna also wondered what she was doing with any of the members of the sick organization.

"You must've lost your fucking mind shooting me, bitch."

"I'm sorry, Yvonna." Ebony moved but was stopped in mid squirm, when Ming stole her in the face. Licking the blood from the corner of her mouth she said, "I deserved that."

Ming grinned, stood up straight and looked down at her. "We already know that."

Ebony frowned. "Who the fuck are you? You don't know shit about me, chink!"

Ming was about to hit her again until Bricks blocked her blow. "That's enough for now." Ming stepped back, folded her arms and waited for her to fuck up again so she could have another chance.

Ebony's eyes adjusted back on Yvonna. "I didn't know who you were when I first saw you." Ebony pleaded, before her eyes roamed over the others. "All I saw was people in my house! I was scared. It's not everyday you find somebody in your home who's not supposed to be there. Please don't hurt me, Yvonna. I have a family."

Gabriella stood next to Yvonna. "She knew who you were when she fired. That's why she aimed at you first. Why else would you shoot a bitch, when there are two niggas in the house too?"

"I don't know, but I'm going to find out." Yvonna answered herself.

The crew looked at her and Bricks said, "Who you talking too, Squeeze?"

"Nobody." She hunched, having slipped up once again when talking to Gabriella in front of others. Focusing back on Ebony she asked, "What are you doing here, Ebony? With a pimp?"

"I don't understand what you asking. I live here."

"I know that, bitch. I mean...why are you with this nigga in the first place?" She pointed at the corpse on the floor. "After everything he did to us, I'm not understanding why you would get in bed with this dude."

Ebony looked up at the ceiling and tears rolled out of her eyes and onto the wooden floor beneath her. She didn't need Yvonna to make her feel guiltier than she already felt. Not a day went by when she didn't ask herself why she was with a man who exploited children. "He took me away, Yvonna. He took me away from the things I hated about myself."

"He also took your pussy and sold it to anything wit' a buck!" Swoopes yelled, the lines forming over his eye showed he was seconds from snapping. Yvonna hoped that whatever he planned would wait until after she had answers. After that she wouldn't stop him. "If anything you a fucking traitor."

She gazed at him as if she wanted to slice his throat. "You don't think I know that shit? You don't think I remember everything we been through at that orphanage?" She paused, hoping they were apprehending everything she was saying. "But when you have a chance to get away, you don't ask questions! You do what the fuck you have to!" She hoped their judgmental eyes would soften but they didn't. Growing slightly angrier she said, "Anyway, I don't remember you staying around either." She looked at Yvonna. "So don't point the finger at me unless you point one back at yourself."

"FUCK THAT!" Yvonna screamed. "If anything you handle this mothafucka the moment you get a chance." She pointed to the portrait on the wall. "Not pose for a picture and start a family with this dude!"

"That's right...unleash on that bitch," Gabriella cheered. "She's all the way outta pocket."

Ignoring Gabriella Yvonna continued. "You don't know how it was to be considered a *favorite*. To always be picked when you wanted to be left alone. You don't know how it felt to walk around with shit in your panties, hoping you'd smell too bad and they'd pass you over. Knowing that they'd wait the extra minute for somebody to wash you, so they could fuck you anyway." She recollected the awful time in her life and rage crept up her body. When she was like that, there was nothing anybody could do but step back. At first Yvonna didn't remember the past, but as life went on, she started to recall things she wanted to forget. "You made a weak move when you married that mothafucka, Ebony!"

"You ain't shit but a slut!" Swoopes said, thinking of what he endured under Ron Max's leadership as well. "You probably liked having multiple dicks in your ass." He looked at Yvonna. "If you leave this bitch breathing by the time I come back, I'ma kill her myself." He stormed off.

"That nigga gonna make me like his ass!" Gabriella admitted. "He has a point too. You should get rid of her. Now! Don't play with snakes."

Yvonna's head begin to thump. Part of her understood where Ebony was coming from. But the other part, the little girl who stayed inside of her, felt she sold out. "Bricks, put her over there." She pointed to the couch in the living room.

Bricks grabbed her body and threw her down. He remained in front of her with a loaded .45 in case she got slick. Yvonna moved to sit in a chair across from her, but the moment her ass touched the cushion, she leaped up. The pain

from the wound Ebony caused rippled up her body. "Fuck!"
She rubbed her ass.

"I really am sorry." She looked up at the three of them.
"Please don't kill me."

"If you knew who I was now, Ebony, you'd be surprised you are even alive."

Ebony held her head down. "You'd be surprised how
much I already know about you."

"Fuck is that supposed to mean?"

Silence.

"Yvonna, if you are going to kill me, can you please tell
me what you're doing here first?"

Refocusing she said, "I need to know what you know
about this organization."

"I don't understand."

"The leader. What's his name and where does he lay his
head?"

"I don't know what you're talking about," she lied.
"What organization and what leader?"

"So you still want to play games? Even now?" Ming
asked, stepping closer. "We came here because we already
know you're involved. So stop fucking 'round."

"Robinson already told us where to find your so called
husband, Ron Max." Yvonna added. "You might as well kick
the shit down and save your own life."

"Don't end up like your husband." Bricks said, stepping
closer. "'Cause we can make that happen if you desire."

Ebony wiped her hands over her face and looked up at
all of them. "Can I stand up?"

"No." Ming said, folding her hands over her chest and
leaning back on her right foot.

"Please...I want to show you something." She put her
hands up in the air. "You see I'm unarmed."

Yvonna reluctantly said, "Let her up." Ming snatched
her by the hair forcing her awkwardly forward. If she were
taller, Ebony would've been on her feet. Instead she fell to her
knees and Bricks helped her from the floor.

Embarrassed Ming said, "The bitch can walk. No need to help."

Yvonna shook her head at her over the top friend and focused back on Ebony. "Go ahead. Show me what you want me to see. But I'm warning you, don't try anything swift. If you do, you'll be on my shit list, and you don't want that."

Trust me, what I'm going to show you will explain everything you need to see. Ron didn't know I knew where the information was," she seemed to ponder what she said, "or maybe he considered me too weak to do anything about it."

Ebony walked toward the back of her house with Yvonna and her clan hot on her heels. When Ebony opened the door to a huge room, the scent of Pine Sol was heavier than before. "And what's up with the fucking Pine Sol?" Ming asked. "It makes Ming stomach sick."

"He huffs." Her voice was low. "Well…he use to huff before you killed him."

"Fuck is huffing?" Ming inquired.

"Sniffing household products and stuff like that to get high." Ebony clarified. Not only was he a pedophile but he was also a huffer. Everything about dude spelled weird. "He did it so much that he was loosing his hearing and starting to have spasms in his body. Just by living here, I would catch a contact."

"Well that's stupid," Ming offered. "Why would a grown man sniff Pine Sol to get high? What's wrong with cocaine? Or heroin? Ming hates cheap ass people." Yvonna shook her head. Ming was her best friend but she was getting on her nerves. They spent so much time together, that she was starting to desire her own space.

When Ebony reached the bed, she got on her knees and pulled out a black shoebox. Bricks rushed her and snatched the box out of her hand, to examine the contents. "its just papers." Ebony advised. "I'm not dumb. I know ya'll have guns on me ready to blast. And my kids are at my mother's. The last thing I want is not to see them again."

Bricks continued to shuffle through the box until he was satisfied no weapon was inside. When he was sure it wasn't he looked at Yvonna and said, "It's clear." He handed it back to Ebony so she could explain what was inside.

"Yvonna...can you come sit on the bed next to me? I want to show you something." Ebony got off her knees and sat on the king size bed. She pulled a stack of papers from the box. Yvonna walked close enough to read what she wanted her to see, but she remained standing. When it was evident that Yvonna was not sitting down she begin. "The organization you're talking about runs under a name called *Adults For Children Of God* or *AFCOG*. It's a national company that I'm sure you've heard of before."

"Wait a minute." Bricks said scratching his head with his hand that held his weapon. "I remember seeing a commercial awhile back about AFCOG. They were advertising some shit about Africa. And sick kids."

"Yeah, they're everywhere. They portray themselves as Christians, but they are pimps." Suddenly Ebony's shoulders drooped and she seemed desolate. "Yvonna, you don't know what you getting into by going after these people. They're worst than the mafia. They're worst than any entity you can imagine."

"Don't tell me I don't know what I'm getting into."

"It wasn't meant as a slight, it's meant as a warning. I know who you are, and I know what you're capable of."

"And how do you know that?"

"People talk, Yvonna. But I also know that you're about to make a bad mistake. You and your friends should turn back while you still can." She looked at the three of them. "I wouldn't tell you this if it didn't need to be said."

Yvonna frowned and stepped closer. "You don't know shit about me or what I'm capable of. If I was afraid of dying, I wouldn't be in your face right now. Now these mothafuckas are not allowing me to have a life and that can't happen anymore. On my name, I will not rest until this shit stops, even if I have to die in the process."

"I don't know about all that, but I do know if you have anybody you care about in the world, anybody at all, you better walk away and leave this shit alone. Unless you're a millionaire, you don't have the money or the resources to fight AFCOG. You can never stop this because prostitution is only a portion of what these people are into. There's too much money involved for anybody to allow you to blow up the spot. When you have the kind of money these people do, you can make anybody disappear. Including you...your family...and friends." She looked at all of them intently. "Turn around and walk away while you still can. Please."

"You don't get it because you're a coward. These mothafuckas have taken everything from me. *Everything.*" She said slamming her fist into her hand. "They took my body, my mind and now they want my life. I might not be able to stop this shit all the way, but I'm going to do everything I can to put a dent into it. Believe that."

Ebony sighed. "I might be a coward but at least I'm alive. And if you care about Delilah like I think you do, you'd better turn around now."

Goosebumps covered Yvonna's skin when Ebony said her daughter's name. "Who told you my daughter's name?"

"I know more things than you think I do."

"Kill this bitch!" Gabriella instructed. "Now!"

On instinct, Yvonna rushed Ebony and placed both hands around her neck. Ebony tried to fight by clawing at her arms. Bricks and Ming attempted to pull her away, but there was no stopping her. Reason was thrown out of the window because the chick brought to attention Yvonna's worst fear that someone was after her only child. Delilah was the reason she was putting her life on the line to begin with. And the traitor had the audacity to judge her and better yet, say her child's name? When she chose to lay up with a man who had a thing for underage kids?

"Squeeze tighter," Gabriella cheered. Without Yvonna's medicine, she was becoming more impulsive. The feeling she derived in the past from killing was heightened. She was remembering how she enjoyed it. Remembering how she loved the sound of her victims' pleas for mercy. "She's almost gone, Yvonna. Don't let up until she's dead." Gabriella continued.

"Squeeze, if you kill her, we might not find these mothafuckas." Bricks was trying to reason with her but it was difficult. "Let her go, babes."

"I'm going to find, Swoopes. Maybe he can help." Ming said, rushing out of the room.

"Squeeze," he said placing his hand on her shoulder firmer. "We didn't come here for this. We came to find out who we dealing with. Think smart!"

When Ebony's eyes rolled to the back of her head, Bricks was finally able to snatch Yvonna away. He rushed up to Ebony and placed his fingers on the vein in her neck. There were no beats. Just as he predicted, she was gone. Suddenly sane, Yvonna flopped to the floor and cried her eyes out. At the moment Ming returned to the room and consoled her by rubbing her back but Swoopes was not present.

"They're going to kill her." She said to no one in particular. "What am I going to do without my baby? If she dies, I don't have a reason to live."

Yvonna knew where Delilah was but she chose to let her stay. Bradshaw, who was Delilah and Ming's son Boy's father, had her with him. He kidnapped her awhile back and he thought Yvonna was dead. Since he wasn't a killer, although he tried, Yvonna allowed Delilah to stay until things cleared up. In her opinion she was safe. She drove past his house on many occasions and hung in the background. Each time Delilah appeared happy and at peace. Now she wondered if it was a mistake.

"Ming knows you miss Delilah," she said softly, rubbing her back. "Ming misses Boy too."

Yvonna shook her away, stood up and dusted off the back of her pants. Weakness amongst the crew had to be kept to a minimum. If she were seen as inadequate to carry out the mission, she would lose respect. "You don't know what the fuck you talking about, Ming. This bitch jumped out the window when she mentioned Delilah's name. She don't know shit about her and that's why she not breathing." She walked to Ebony's bed, pushed her to the floor and sat on the part of her ass that didn't hurt. Going through the box she pulled out several stacks of paper. Scanning them quickly she saw a list of names and addresses. "Ming, get lost. You don't need to be in here anyway."

Ming tried to bite her tongue one time until she said fuck it. "One day you gonna wish you didn't talk to me like that. All Ming does is try to be there for you. That's it. I'm your friend, Yvonna. All I want is a little respect."

Mad at the world she said, "The only friend I got in life is me." She looked her in the eyes. "Now bounce."

"Ming goes to find Swoopes. At least he listens to me." She disappeared from the room.

"You mean at least he lets you suck his dick!" Yvonna yelled, although she was already gone. She focused back on the papers in her lap. "That girl gets on my fucking nerves, Bricks. She thinks everything we do is a game! She don't know nothing about what me and Swoopes went through with this shit. I think I'ma ditch her ass before I have to hurt her."

"First off you can't do that." He said seriously. When he looked at things in a broader perspective, he realized he and Ming were in the same boat. If she was expendable then so was he. "I don't know what you been through either, but I'm here because I want to help you. And I love you. She does too."

"But you my man. You gotta be here."

He thought her comment was cute. "And Ming is your best friend. That girl has given up everything to help you…including her kid for the moment. Stop looking at her like an irritant and remember that she don't have no reason to be here if she didn't care about you."

"You don't understand. You think this some stupid girl shit."

"I don't, but I hear her spending a lot of time in the bathroom crying. She misses her son but she gave that up for the moment to help you see this shit through. She deserves more credit than that."

"And I don't miss Delilah?"

"I ain't saying that, Squeeze. All I'm saying is you gotta think about shit before you move so quick to X people outta your life." He rubbed her leg. As if he had a better idea he said, "If you get rid of anybody, let it be the nigga Swoopes. If anybody's jeopardizing the operation it's him."

"Naw…we need him." She was still thinking about what he said about Ming. She didn't agree with him at all. "He knows weapons and he's fearless."

"And I'm not?"

"Don't play with me, Bricks."

"I asked a question." When she didn't respond out of left field he said, "I think the nigga wanna fuck you."

"Ain't shit about him attractive to me. Don't forget, at one point in life I wanted to kill him." She looked into his eyes. "Remember the history and know my heart."

Ming suddenly appeared in the doorway interrupting their conversation. "Ya'll gotta come downstairs." Swoopes hung in the background. "It's important."

"Why what's up?" Yvonna asked.

"Ming can't explain. You must come see for yourself."

BILAL, Jr.

Bilal stood confused in the doorway, as his brother fingered him for a crime he didn't commit. Although he was sure he didn't care for him, he would've never thought he'd stoop so low.

When his sibling misidentified Bilal, Jr., the cop stepped closer. "Is your name Laser, young man?" He question, his right hand hovering over the handle of his weapon.

"I want you mothafuckas out of my house right now!" Easter yelled, adding gasoline to the fire. She was flailing wild arms in the background. If she hit one of the cops, the situation would surely escalate. "You don't have no warrant to be up in my house. Ya'll think ya'll can do anything you want in people's houses! Well I know the law!"

"We have something better than a warrant."

Easter stayed in front of the TV watching the *First 48* so, she figured that made her knowledgeable of all aspects of the law. Hands on her hips she asked, "What's better than a warrant?"

"Probable cause!" He yelled, forcing her back a few inches. "And if you don't step the fuck back, you'll be going downtown too." When she didn't move, one of the other officers grabbed his handcuffs. Embarrassed that her law education failed her, she retreated to the living room and slumped on the sofa. But not before yelling, "Fuck you, Uncle Tom ass cops!" On the way to the couch.

"Tia!" Uzi yelled to his aunt, fearing the last insult may have pushed the limit. "We got it. Just sit down and chill." She rolled her eyes and crossed her legs.

"Officer, I don't know what my brother is tripping off of," Uzi said, bringing them back to the problem at hand...his twin's lie, "but Laser Pliers is me. Not my little brother Bilal,

Jr." Uzi accepted full responsibility like a G. "Now can I help you with something? Because it's obvious that there's been a mistake."

The officer was skeptical. "If you are Laser Pliers, then why did he say it was him?"

Uzi moved toward Laser's dresser and the officers rode his back like a coat. They were afraid he was going for a weapon and they would not hesitate to fill him up with lead and take a few weeks off with pay while the department sorted it out. "Freeze!" One cop pointed his department issued .9 millimeter at Uzi.

Uzi threw his hands up in the air. "I just want to show you my identification. That's all."

"Tell us where it is. We don't want anybody getting hurt." He was mainly talking about himself and the other cops. He could care less about any injuries Uzi sustained.

Knowing where Laser kept his wallet Uzi said, "It's in the top drawer. Next to my socks."

Bilal was stunned silent. Nothing was making sense to him. Not only was he not Laser Pliers but neither was Uzi. And then there was the thing with Laser lying. He couldn't wrap his mind with understanding why he would throw him under the bus and pull off. Finally there was Owl's freak whore ass. Sure Laser disrespected when he grabbed her arm, but did it warrant the cops coming to his house?

"Go check for the ID, man." One of the officer's said to his partner, while the others kept their guns on the brothers. "I want everybody's hands in the air." When they didn't move fast enough he yelled, "NOW!"

When the officer happened upon the wallet in the dresser he opened it up and flapped through the dividers until he saw the license. When he was in the right place, he examined the picture. With the exception of the small birthmark on Uzi's earlobe, which the officer didn't notice, the picture on the driver's license matched Uzi perfectly. After all, they were identical twins. "You see what I'm saying officer? I'm

Laser Pliers." Uzi verified. "So it could not have been my little brother.

"That's fine with us." They hoisted Uzi by the arm and
rushed him outside before he could dispute. Upon seeing him
being escorted out of the house like a garbage can, Bilal, Jr.,
Laser and Easter piled behind the cops. When they made it
into the cold night air, from the backseat of the police cruiser,
Bilal, Jr. saw Owl with her arms folded over her breasts. He
wanted to talk to her and ask why she'd go so far, but he
knew it wouldn't make a difference. Had he been man enough
to stop Laser from fucking his shawty from the gate, none of
this would be happening.

The officer pushed Uzi toward the car. Looking down at
Owl he asked, "Mam, is this the man?" She knew before Uzi
even reached the door that it wasn't him. "If not, there's another one over there who looks just like him."

Owl was sick on her stomach when she saw the birthmark on Uzi's ear. Uzi was a good dude who despite how he
felt about her, never kicked a bad word in her direction. But if
he wanted to eat the bullet she prepared for his twin, she
would gladly pull the trigger.

Owl leaned up and peered out the window. Her eyes
rolled from his feet to his eyes. She was doing this mainly for
effect and to make the real Laser sweat. After dragging it out
longer than an R&B singer at a wedding, she sat back and
without an ounce of remorse said, "Yeah, that's him." She
looked straight ahead. "He the one who tried to rape me!"

"Rape?!" Uzi shouted, before looking at Laser. Not for
him to step up, knowing the police would haul them all to jail
for interfering with the investigation, but because he wanted
to be sure his brother wasn't that foul. He focused back on her
when he got his non-verbal answer. "Why the fuck you lying,
you dirty ass bitch? Fuck wrong wit' you?" He felt like strangling her.

With her confirmation, Bilal, Jr. watched as his brother was placed into another police car. He hated to think selfishly, but after this shit, he couldn't imagine his family allowing him to stay with them now. Although everyone else went inside the house when Uzi was carried away, he stayed outside until two cars pulled in front of the house. Upon hearing the news that one of their nephews was arrested, the other five uncles and aunts returned home.

Once parked, they piled out of the cars and moved toward the house. "Fuck just happen?" Tabitha asked, approaching Bilal, Jr. Like Laser, she didn't care for him but luckily for Bilal, Jr., she was the only one out of them who shared her view. "What you do to him huh? Why Easter telling me that Uzi was taken away on some shit to do with your girlfriend?"

"Tabitha, get the fuck off that kid!" Gabe said. When she didn't move he yelled, "Now!" Tabitha hock spit next to his foot and walked a few feet away, although her eyes remained planted. "Let's hear what the fuck happened first! You all ready to jump on him without knowing the deal." Gabe looked at Bilal, Jr. "What happened earlier?"

Bilal, Jr. was stuck. If he told his family that Laser tried to frame him, Laser would most likely take his life. "I don't know, Uncle Gabe. I was in my room with Uzi and the next thing I know the police were here. I think Owl lied on him, saying he raped her or some shit like that."

"Raped!?" He yelled. "That's your girl right?"

"I don't fuck with that skank like that." Bilal, Jr. hoped he was making Laser proud by disowning the girl. "We just do what we do but it was never nothing serious."

"Well if the bitch starting shit like that, sounds like you made a good choice." Hall said. "Easter, get on the phone and see if you can find out if Uzi gonna get bail. We can't leave him in there."

"And what the fuck we gonna do if he does need bail? We ain't got no money."

"Speak for yourself," Tabitha said. "I keeps me a little change for rainy days."

"Well what you keep for the days the phone bill due?" Easter placed her hands on her hips. "'Cause I show remember asking you to put in last week, when you cried broke. Now that Uzi need rescue you got bread?"

"The phone bill ain't no rainy day. Anyway, don't nobody talk on the phone but you. If anything, that should be the one bill you always hold down."

Tabitha and Easter was at each other's necks within a minute flat before Oakes and Gabe pulled them apart. Before long they were discussing shit that didn't matter. "Let go of me!" Easter screamed. "I'm tired of her eating all the food and not putting in on shit. She ain't nothing but a mothafuckin' freeloader!" Instead of leaving the matter alone, she decided to go at her like she was a bitch on the street. "You ain't nothing but a dusty bitch who be passing out STD's like club flyers. I'm so sick of your shit."

"Well if you sick, bitch...die!" Tabitha retaliated, perfectly willing to go another round. "I don't know why you think you the boss of this family because you not. I mean, what were you doing when they took our nephew out of here? Huh? Probably running your fucking mouth on the phone as usual!"

"Fuck all that shit ya'll spitting." Gabe said, "let's go in the house and sort shit out. The family way. I'm tired of niggas being in our business because ya'll don't know how to handle shit civilized.

Once they were inside Laser said, "I'll get the money! Just give me a minute." He patted Bilal, Jr. on the shoulder and said, "Come with me."

Bilal, Jr. with his chest on swollen followed his brother into their bedroom. He felt proud that he would be included in the money making plan. He figured Laser inviting him to the board, meant he did him good outside. Hopes for praises went out the window when the moment the door was closed Laser knocked the wind out of his lungs. He violently fell to the floor as he tried to gasp for air.

Grabbing a fist full of Bilal, Jr.'s curly hair, Laser asked, "Why you let him take that bid? I gave that shit to you to handle and you dropped the ball!"

Bilal, Jr. didn't know if it was the severe pain his body was experiencing, or the trouble he was having breathing. One thing was certain and that was that he was perplexed. "I don't understand. What did I do wrong?" He asked rubbing his chest hoping his ribs were not fractured.

"The moment your brother took that charge, you should've manned up and set the record straight. But you ain't do that shit and now Uzi going to jail. Get up and grab your coat. We going to that bitch's house."

Bilal, Jr. pulled himself up, trudged toward the closet, snatched the coat Uzi bought for him and slid into it. The sounds of his aunts and uncles yelling in the living room carried into the bedroom like a fog. He felt to blame for all of this shit, and contemplated running away from home.

"Here, put this in your coat." Laser handed him a nine, before putting his coat on, with his .45 already tucked inside. "You know how to use it right?"

Bilal, Jr. saw many times on TV, how gunslingers would pull back the slide to get the bullet into the chamber. He attempted the same move, and when it snapped back, it grabbed a piece of the skin on his finger too. "Awwwww!" he screamed, dropping the weapon. Luckily for him it wasn't loaded but blood oozed from the wound.

Laser slapped him on the back of the head. "Fuck is wrong with you? Why would you drop it? If it was loaded you could've shot me." He could've shot himself also but Laser didn't care. He picked it up, placed the magazine inside and slid it to be sure it was loaded. He made it look so easy, Bilal, Jr. felt foolish. Handing it back he said, "Now you can just point and aim. Hopefully you know how to do that."

Once outside, the cold air rushed up Bilal, Jr.'s nostrils and stung the back of his head. He rubbed it several times causing it to run. He didn't want to look like a snotty nosed kid, so he wiped the mucus on his jeans and stroked it five times so it would disappear into the fabric.

When they made it to Owl's house Laser hung back and said, "Go knock on the door."

"What you want me to say?"

"Go knock on the door," he repeated, no explanation or further instruction given.

Bilal, Jr. knew better than to buck, so he climbed up the steps and knocked softly. Owl swung the door open. Placing her hands on her hips, she said, "Yes?" With a neck roll she added, "Fuck can I help you with?"

Bilal, Jr. looked at his brother and back at her. He felt a strange sensation when he saw her face. He thought about the sounds she made when Laser was inside of her and how she gave him her boot to kiss whenever he asked to do so much as finger fuck her. No longer thinking straight, he blacked out and stole her in the face so hard, she dropped at the threshold. Once down, he dragged her by her hair outside and into the front yard. Owl's brother came outside and Bilal, Jr. caught him with a bullet in the thigh. Laser didn't know what he expected from the young one, but he certainly could not have imagined Bilal, Jr. carrying shit like that.

With Owl's brother screaming to the hood gods on high, Bilal, Jr. aimed at him and said, "Shut the fuck up before I give you one in the gut." Then he faced Owl. "You lied on my brother. Why?"

"Please don't hit me again!" She sobbed, covering her face. "I didn't do nothing. Please!"

Punching her in the gut he repeated his question. "Why you lie on my brother?"

"Because Laser tried to rape me." She wept. "I was scared. So I told the police."

"Bitch, ain't nobody try to rape your bitch ass!" Laser said, his gun now trained on her brother. He finally decided to show up to the party. "If your ass wasn't in my house, trying to give up the pussy, none of this would've happened."

Bilal, Jr. ignored the dispute between them because he wanted answers. Thoughts of being run over constantly plagued his mind and weighed on his heart. He even thought about not having parents all because of the legendary Yvonna Harris. Although he wasn't the only person in the world with problems, he damn sure had his share.

"It's like this…you gonna go with me to the precinct and you gonna drop the charges on my brother."

"I tried already, but they said it was a criminal matter now so they were involved." She was crying so hard her abdominal muscles cramped. "Please…I'm sorry about all this. Everything is all my fault." She said, as if he weren't aware. She wiped the tears off her face before they froze against her skin. "I'm sorry for cheating on you too, Jr. I really do love you."

"You said you went down to the precinct," he said, ignoring her call for endearment. "How much was bail?"

"They saying fifty thousand. But all you gotta do is pay ten percent for a bails bonds man and they'll let him go."

"How much money you got on you?"

"Only twenty five dollars."

Bilal, Jr. dug into her pocket, relieved her of the money and stuffed it into his coat. Turning around to face his brother he said, "What you wanna do now? She saying she tried to drop the charges already." If he would've given the word, Bilal, Jr. would not have minded killing her.

Laser couldn't help but look at Bilal, Jr. differently at that moment. Something took over and he wasn't sure if it was for the better or worse. "We gonna go to the dude my brother works for. His name is Yao, maybe he can come through."

YVONNA

Y vonna, Bricks and Ming were downstairs in the basement looking at what appeared to be a small, frightened family. There was a man, a woman and a child. They weren't wearing anything but underwear and the baby had on a soiled pamper. The smell of feces and old food loomed in the space. There were also twelve cots and a white sink with ten washcloths thrown over the edge of it.

"What do you want?" the man asked, stepping in front of the woman and the child, as if Bricks' .45 wouldn't penetrate him and anybody else he desired. "And where is Ms. Ebony? Did she send you to..." he was choked up as he looked at the baby, "did she send you to take him away?"

"What's going on down there?" Swoopes asked from upstairs, interrupting the moment. He didn't come down because he had a fear of basements, after being abused in them so much as a child.

Not liking Swoopes' unexpected phobia, Yvonna ignored him and focused back on the people. "Who are you? Do you live here?" As she waited on a response, her heart rate increased because it looked like the dungeon she was kept in as a child.

"My name is Elika," the male said nervously, "and this is my sister Tata and our baby Martin."

Bricks frowned. Having limited knowledge of how sick the AFCOG really was, he couldn't move past the relation between them. "Wait a minute, you telling me this is your sister but this baby is both of yours?" He paused, hoping he was wrong.

"Yes." He said with shame.

"So you fucking your flesh and blood?"

Elika held his head down. "Yes. We were forced together, to produce. Our baby will be leaving in a couple of days." He softly palmed the little boy's head. "It's going to be a rough couple of months when it happens but we're use to it now."

Yvonna grabbed a chair against the wall and sat down. Bricks and Ming chose to remain standing to cover her in case things got wild. "How long have you been in this hellhole?"

"We've been here all our lives," Elika said, as Tata remained silent. "We were born here. Are you here to take him from us? Normally they allow us to keep the child for at least six months…because of the breast milk. To be sure he's healthy. That way they can get the best money."

"We ain't here to take no baby!" Swoopes yelled from upstairs, trying to make it known that he was still involved. "Ya'll niggas can roll out for all I give a fuck."

"Any nigga too scared to come downstairs, shouldn't be allowed to say shit!" Bricks yelled up at him. "So just shut the fuck up and fall back. We got it down here!"

"Come up here and say that shit to my face, bitch ass nigga!"

Bricks was about to take him up on his offer when Yvonna rose up and grabbed his forearm. "Baby, not now." She paused, pointing at them. "Please, we got business."

"What did he mean when he said roll out?" Elika asked Yvonna, stealing back her attention. "Does that mean we can leave?"

"Yes, it also means that we not here to take no baby from you." She briefly looked over the child and was amazed he wasn't deformed, since they were brother and sister. "Have any of your kids been warped?"

Knowing what she meant he said, "Yes. Two. But we've had over ten."

"What happens with them when they come out like that?" Ming asked, flabbergasted.

"They throw them away, wait a little while her to heal and force us to have sex again until she's pregnant."

Yvonna shook her head and her temples begin to throb. It was modern day slavery at its finest. "We are not the enemy. You are free to move on with your lives if you want to. It's over."

Elika looked at Tata and asked, "But what about AFCOG? And master Ron Max?" His heart could be seen rocking in his thin chest. "I'm confused. Are you in charge of us now?"

"No." Yvonna took a few steps back, the smell was killing her. "You don't have anybody to rule over you anymore. You're both free to go on with your lives. But if I were you, I'd do it as far away from here as possible. Until the leader is dead, it's not safe."

They were about to walk back up the stairs when Elika said, "Tata, do you hear what they're saying?" He gently touched the sides of her face. "We are free to leave. We don't have to be afraid anymore! Our prayers have been answered! It's what we've always asked for."

Tata's body began to shake uncontrollably. She gripped her baby so tightly to her breasts, as she eyed them suspiciously, that she was in danger of suffocating him. "No, don't listen to them." She sobbed, shaking her head. "You can't leave, Elika. I'm afraid."

He pleaded with her to calm down. "You don't have to be afraid anymore."

"Don't tell me not to be afraid! It was I who nursed your wounds, when the master beat you badly the last time you tried to get help. Remain loyal to AFCOG, like they told you. Like they told us and everything will be fine. And they'll let us keep each other. That was the deal." She smiled oddly and touched his face. "We'll be okay."

All of them were floored but Bricks was taken aback. He didn't have a clear picture of the monsters they were dealing with until he saw the fear in Elika and Tata's eyes. His respect for what needed to be done, to the members of AFCOG, grew tremendously in that moment.

Yvonna on the other hand, did not respect Tata because she felt she was a coward, just like Ebony. After all, who would have a chance at life, and refuse to take it?

Seeing how distraught Tata was, Elika gently took his child away from her, rubbed the tears off her face and kissed her softly on the lips. Bricks walked over to the corner and vomited. "I'm going upstairs, Squeeze. This shit too sick for me."

Before they left he said, "If he is really dead, can I see the body?" He nodded at Tata. "For her sake?"

"We'll do better than that," Yvonna added. "We'll show you both of them."

One Hour Later

For the first time in their lives, both Elika, Tata and their baby Martin was allowed upstairs to eat in the kitchen. The first thing they did was bathe and take some of Ron Max and Ebony's clothing to cover their naked bodies. When they got out of the tub, the ring around it was so dark it looked as if it were spray painted black. And at last count they vacuumed down five bowls of cereal and eight sandwiches between them. It was obvious that they hadn't eaten good in days.

With a mouthful of food Elika said, "The thing about AFCOG is…the entire operation is extremely organized. More organized than you may already know." He swallowed the food in his mouth and put down the spoon. "Not only do they sell girls, but think of five superstars right now who had children recently, and I guarantee at least two of them were purchased from AFCOG."

"How? Most superstars who have children are pregnant first." Bricks inquired.

"Fuck is you talkin' 'bout, slim?" Swoopes interrupted. "You don't make no sense." He was trying to appear hard again, since he suckered up with his basement phobia.

"I'm talking about the fact that they have bellies and all." He gritted on Swoopes. "So how could they fake a pregnancy when they seen in the media with bellies?" Nobody but Elika understood where Bricks was coming from.

"It's all an act…and AFCOG facilitates the entire thing." Elika continued. "You have to remember, they make pregnancy props all the time for actors and actresses in movies. With the right make up and props, you can easily make a woman look pregnant who's not."

"Question, if you stay in the basement, how do you know so much?" Bricks inquired.

He beamed and said, "They didn't know, but sometimes I come upstairs. I'll sit in the living room and turn the TV on for an hour. Tata would be too afraid to join me." He softly touched her hair. "I'd watch everything I could and come back downstairs before they get home. Mostly all I got to see was entertainment shows."

"Well why didn't you run instead of watching TV?" Yvonna asked. "

"Because they'd catch me and I didn't know where to go." He shrugged. "I mean, we heard of a man, who was a former drug dealer turned reverend. His name is Reverend Dynamite. Apparently after his daughter ran away from home and was forced to sell her body by a pimp, a john in an alley murdered her. So he vowed to turn his life around. Now he owns a large home in Virginia, that's a safe haven for people forced into the business, but I don't know where it is."

"He's right." Tata added. "Elika has tried many times to run, but he can't leave me. So he stays." She looked at him lovingly. "AFCOG is notorious, a very dangerous group. And selling kids was second nature and they were able to get away with it, until recently."

"What happened recently?" Bricks inquired.

"The Great One started causing havoc and bringing attention to AFCOG." Elika continued. "And if they hate anything, attention is it. They're able to do more under the veil of darkness than they can in the spotlight. Anything else spells trouble."

"The great one?" Swoopes asked. "Where can we meet this nigga?" Tata giggled at him and wiped the milk off her mouth with the back of her hand. "What the fuck is so funny?

"The nigga you speak of is a girl."

"Well what's her name?" Bricks asked. "If we can link up with her, maybe she'll help us out. We'll take any info we can get at this time. Especially since everybody claims AFCOG is so thorough."

"I think her name is Yvonna." Tata advised. "If I remember correctly."

Yvonna thought she was hearing things at first, until Elika said, "Yeah...Her name is Yvonna Harris."

Yvonna felt as if the room was spinning. And Ming thinking the entire ordeal was hilarious said, "Wait, you're talking about this bitch?" She pointed at her angry friend. "She is great one?"

The spoon dropped out of Tata's hands and the sandwich from Elika's lips. Both of them stood up and looked at her as if she were a profit. Forcing the baby into Ming's hands, they fell to their knees and kissed Yvonna's black Prada boots.

"We've prayed for the longest that God would lead you to us!" Elika sobbed heavily. "But we never thought we were worthy of such a visit. Never thought he heard our prayers. But as sure as we're black, you are here! You're really here!"

Seeing their worship in action, Yvonna backed up and looked at everyone in the kitchen. This sort of attention made her uncomfortable and she wasn't sure how to handle it. She was trying to calm down but it wasn't working. "I don't understand what you mean. Why am I called the great one? What is this shit about?"

They both stood up and moved slowly toward her. They could tell she was spooked, so they decided to adjust their actions to soothe her. "Ebony, our female master, wasn't always so mean. We didn't realize that until late, but when it came it was like a breath of fresh air. She seemed to be able to identify with us."

"That's because she was sold into slavery too." Swoopes informed.

Both Elika and Tata seemed surprised. "We didn't know that," Elika continued. "I do know out of nowhere she started giving us fresh food and new clothes to wear. Ron never came downstairs unless there was new product in camp, so she was able to get away with it. We got a new teenager once every two months. They'd find them on popular social networks, at bus stops and things like that. Most of their parents had written them off because they were considered troublemakers. Anyway, when a girl hung herself after not being allowed to go home, Ebony told us a story we'd never forget."

"At first we thought it was a fairy tale, something to give us hope that things would eventually be better." Tata interrupted.

"But we soon found out she was serious." Elika continued. "She said Yvonna Harris was the only person who got under AFCOG's skin. The only one AFCOG was afraid of." They gazed at her again, with grins on their faces. "Anyway when Ron found out Ebony was getting closer to us, he banned her from downstairs. So we would tell each other the story, to keep it fresh in our minds." Elika looked at Yvonna. "And we never forgot your name."

Tata added. "You're a blessing from God. And now you can help the other young girls! There are so many. We think thousands."

"I didn't sign up for that shit!" She frowned, looking at them seriously. "If you knew me, you'd know how ridiculous you sound. I can't be responsible for no shit like that even if I wanted to. That's not what I signed up to do."

"But why? They'll believe in you. We believe in you."

"Well you shouldn't!" Yvonna screamed. She didn't feel worthy. "I don't give a fuck about nobody but myself and my baby!" She looked at Bricks and he walked out of the room in disappointment. Holding her head down she said, "This is all too much for me right now. I don't need this kind of stress." Tata pleaded with her eyes, for her to reconsider. "Look, all I'm signing up to do is kill these niggas who are after me and my child. So we can have a life without worry. I know you know how important that is. I saw how you looked at us when you thought we meant to do you and your family harm. I'm no superhero nor do I want to be."

"But you are a hero! Whether you want to be or not." Tata retaliated and Yvonna grew frustrated at her persistence. Downstairs she was as silent as a mouse and now she couldn't shut her up if she cut her tongue out and fried it.

"You have a duty." Elika added.

"She doesn't have a duty to help anybody! You mothafuckas should have been strong enough to fight for yourself instead of electing to play victim." Although Yvonna's mouth was moving, it was Gabriella who was speaking. Turning to walk away, she stopped short before leaving. With her back faced them she said, "Stay away from her. Stay away from both of us. Or you'll be sorry."

RUFUS DAY

R ufus sat in his office, in his leather chair, that was dressed with two tilted silver crosses. The crosses were unique to the church of AFCOG. Years earlier, they received flack from the Christian community because the crosses were not straight. But after explaining that the tilted cross represented the way Jesus carried it on the day he was crucified, the symbol was widely accepted. Although the Christian community backed down, they were on to something. Because the crosses were actually Rufus' attempt of knocking religion in replacement of his own.

"You love that phone don't you?"

"I guess." She shrugged. "But I probably won't have it long. My mother pays the bills for a few days and she can't afford it no more after that. So I don't give my number out most times."

"I bet you hate that. A pretty girl like you, not being able to speak to your friends when you want. So sad." He grabbed a few pieces of yellow tissue from the silver holder. Dabbing the corners of his drippy eyes he asked, "You like candy, Tyisha?"

She swallowed and said, "Yeah. Some of 'em."

He grabbed the top of the silver candy dish on his desk and said, "What about Peppermints? They're my favorite." The grin on his face reminded her of Mr. Grinch.

She nodded and he extended the dish. She took one, plopped it in her mouth. He placed it back on his desk and leaned back in the chair as he watched her suck the candy. "I think you're being different around me."

"Different?"

"Yes." He threw the tissues he used earlier for his leaky eyes in the trash. "Now I've heard you speak more than what you're doing now, when you're playing with your friend in Sunday school." He rocked harder in his chair and she wondered if it would fall backwards. "So why is that?"

"I do talk." She played with her phone again. "Sometimes."

"Good. Because I would like very much to hear that pretty voice of yours. So if you're going to speak to me, I'll need you to do it now. Okay?"

She was preparing to nod her head again, until she remembered his request. If there was one thing the master didn't like, insubordination was it. So parting her lips with the candy dancing around on her tongue she mouthed, "Okay."

He clapped his hands together. "Good. And as a matter of fact, come over here and sit on my lap." He slapped his thigh once. "Because if it's not too much to ask, I'd love to hear you sing. I heard your voice in Sunday school a few weeks back. I said then that you sounded like a star."

There was something about the man that felt off kilter to young Tyisha, but she was too naive to decipher. And her mother hadn't given her the tools necessary to know a creep when she saw one. She was too concerned with money and what everybody else thought about her. So instead of going with her feelings, Tyisha stood and traipsed toward him. When she reached him she smelled two things, the scent of the scary leather chair and the stench of his sweaty penis. Although it was not hanging out, he wasn't wearing boxers, which allowed the unsavory fragrance to roam.

Rufus hoisted her onto the top of his lap and she could feel what resembled a roll of dough under her bottom. "Before you sing, I wanted to ask you something."

"Okay." She was beyond skittish as she wondered what was about to happen. "What is it, master?"

"I wanted to know if you're as excited as I am, about spending time with me in my program." He moved her slightly back and forth over his penis, without her knowing what he was doing. "Because I am. I know when you see the room I have for you, you'll love it. You like dolls?"

"Yes."

"Good, because I have plenty of them for you. So tell me, are you excited?"

"I am." She presented him with a half smile and his watery eyes scanned over her body as if she was naked. She turned away. "But I'm also scared." She placed her cell phone on his desk and looked at him. "Like real scared."

"About what?" He looked at her suspiciously. Normally the kids he molested wouldn't know what he was doing at this point of his game. "There's never a reason to be scared around your master."

"I'm scared I won't be able to do what you need me to do. And I want to do a good job." She admitted, looking at the floor. "As long as it doesn't hurt."

Her response intrigued him. "Why wouldn't you do a good job? And why would anything I ask you to do hurt?"

"I don't know." She shrugged. "I was just thinking it."

"You have to know, Tyisha. You said it." He grabbed another tissue to dab his wet eyes again before throwing it in the trash. "After all, you know how important it is to please your master. And if you stay in tune with everything I ask you to do, and follow through, you'll make me happy and that's ultimately what you want right?"

"Kinda."

He smiled although her insolence was troubling. "Why do you say *kinda*? I'm getting tired of these short answers. Now tell me what's going on, before you see a side of me you won't like."

"Well, I don't want to do other stuff that I hear you make little girls do. I think my mommy would be mad at me if I did. I'm not old enough yet."

Rufus' body felt as if it was splashed with hot water. Normally the children would be too afraid to talk about anything he didn't initiate. And at first, it seemed like Tyisha was that scary too, which was his reason for selecting her. He steered clear of mouthy little girls in his congregation and took care to pick the right ones. The ones he could manipulate. The ones he could teach and the ones he would ultimately put on the stroll. Yet it appeared as if this time, he made a mistake.

He wasn't sure if he should ask the next question, but decided to anyway. "What have you heard about me, Tyisha? Tell me everything and leave nothing out. It's very important that I'm aware what's being said in my congregation." She didn't answer. "Don't be afraid. As long as you're honest, you can do no wrong."

She played with the zipper on her jacket. "There are some girls who don't go to church here. They play with one girl who does. She's like my best friend." She looked at him until he frowned. "The girls told my friend, that you play under little girls dresses and stuff like that. And that sometimes you make them touch your privates and put stuff in they mouth. And they say you make them do stuff with other men for money."

Silence.

Although a smile lay upon his face, it wasn't in order like he thought. Instead, he resembled a clash between the Joker and Freddy Kruger. This did nothing but make her more nervous. "Well what did you say, when she told you that about me?"

"I told her to stop lying. And that our master would never do anything like that. But she told me I'm stupid and that you were going to get me too." She looked at him hoping he would put her at ease, but he didn't. "That's the only thing they said." She raised her right hand, something she saw on TV. "Honest."

He could tell by the look in her eyes, and her stiff body mechanics, that he was in control of her mind. But, there was still the matter of the children. "Tyisha, I want you to give me the name of the little girl who told you that about me."

She didn't want to be a tattle tell but she reluctantly agreed. Knowing that it would be the end of her friendship. "Okay."

"Did you tell your mother?"

"No, because she won't believe me. One time I told her that her boyfriend came into my room to kiss me in the mouth, nothing else and she got mad."

Those words were music to Rufus' ears. If there was one way to get to a little girl, her irresponsible mother was it. He knew that the majority of girls he was able to put to work, came from the homes of mothers who didn't care. From the homes of mothers who were selfish, or too busy to pay attention.

"Well I'm happy that you told me what your friend said, but I'm also saddened." He tried to appear saddened. Although it worked on the child, an adult in her right mind would've seen right through his shit. "And I would never think you'd make me feel this way."

"What did I do?"

"You should have never participated in the conversation. And the moment she told you that, you should have come to me. But you didn't. You came late and had I not asked you to sing for me, I would have never known. Do you know how sad your betrayal makes me, Tyisha? Do you have any idea of how you make me feel?"

"What's betrayal?" She was trying to hold back her tears.

"Betrayal means to be hurt by someone you love and trust." He paused and softly touched her chin. His fingers smelled dirty, like he'd been digging in his ass all day. "Before now, I loved and trusted you and now I'm thinking it was a mistake."

"But Jesus said you should love all people. And forgive them."

The words she spit were like venom to his ears. She was too smart for her own good. He started to back hand her but held back. "I'm not talking about the man you call Jesus! I'm talking about me! And the fact that you should never repeat a lie. I don't care who tells it to you. Repeating a lie is the same as telling it yourself. Do you want to be a liar, Tyisha? Because if you do, I'm not going to allow you and your mother to be a part of this church anymore."

The look on Tyisha's face was priceless. Just like so many of his other members, the church was their world. "I don't want to be a liar! And I don't want you to be sad because of me."

"It's too late. The damage has already been done."

"Master please don't kick me and mommy out of the church. She loves it and I do too."

"I just want you to know, that whatever happens is all your fault." He pointed to the chair. "Go sit back down, over there. I'm going to call your mother." He had an idea and her reaction would determine if he could still use her or not. Everything was a game with him.

Tyisha hopped down off of crazy's lap, gripped her cell phone and dawdled toward her seat. She felt weak and this was more pressure than she'd ever experienced in life. Rufus picked up the phone to call his secretary, while he gave Tyisha another dispirited look. "Kelly, call over to the Woman's Ministry and have Marge brought to my office right away. It's important. Thank you."

He hung up, pulled his bible out and thumbed through the pages. He wasn't reading anything. It was just his way of reminding the child, that he was a holy man, who should not be questioned or mistrusted. And since she'd done both by his standards that put her in a bad way with him.

The little girl trembled so badly, that he thought she would spontaneously combust. Five minutes later, Marge walked into his office with a heavy look on her face. Being called to Rufus' office wasn't necessarily a good thing and she knew it. Quite a few people were fired after digging too far into his personal business and she hoped she wasn't about to be ousted too.

Closing the door behind herself, she looked at her child and then at him. "Is everything okay, Master?"

"No, unless you believe your daughter participating in rumors is okay."

"Of course it isn't!"

"I didn't think so, which is why I'm very upset with her." He closed his bible. "You know, when I initially selected her for the program, I thought she would fare well. I thought she was a child who was respectful, and could appreciate what a great opportunity this was, and now I believe I've made a great mistake. And this is terrible considering how many children applied for this program." He looked at Tyisha and then back at Marge. "Hundreds, and I chose your daughter, but it doesn't look like you'll be getting the scholarship."

She already spent the money in her mind so this was totally unacceptable. "What...I don't understand. You're throwing her out of the program?" Her eyes alternated from him to her. What was she going to tell everyone she bragged to, if Tyisha was no longer selected? "Maybe there's been a mistake, Master. Tyisha is a child but she's far from a bad one."

"There's been no mistake, Marge. I know what I heard." He looked at Tyisha. "Has there been a mistake, young lady?" Tyisha was as still as a mannequin.

"Well what did you say?" Marge nudged her shoulder when she didn't open her mouth. "You hear me talking to you?" The way Marge was acting, you would've thought that the freak was Tyisha's father instead of a phony pastor. "Master, what did she say? I'm sure whatever it was, was a misunderstanding."

"Ask her yourself."

"Tyisha, what did you say?" Silence. "Tyisha, do you hear me talking to you? What did you say?"

That was the fourth time her mother asked her what she'd said, and each time she ignored her. His plan worked. After he told her that a lie shouldn't be repeated, she refused to repeat it even to her own mother.

"You know what, Marge, judging by the look on her face, I think she's learned her lesson. I'm so sure that I've decided in this moment to give her a second chance. But if she messes this up, she won't get another."

Marge's eyes remained on her daughter but she could feel something off in the room. There was a thick veil of deceit and maliciousness, but she loved money so much, that she would let it pass. So instead of going with her intuition, she decided to sell her daughter to the devil for a small price. "Okay, as long as you're sure, Master. The last thing I want to do is fail you and I know Tyisha feels the same way."

"I know you do." When the line leading to his secretary rung he picked up the handset. "Yes, Kelly?" His eyes moved over Tyisha's lips and her small legs. He was going to have so much fun with her, he could feel it. By the time it was all said and done, she'd be one of his top earners.

"You have a call, Master." Kelly explained.

"Well I'm busy right now. Have them call back later."

"I tried to but she said it's important."

"Who is it?"

"Her name is Yvonna Harris."

Rufus was stuck. He was realizing that it wasn't so much fun when the rabbit had the gun. Originally he thought for sure that Gabriella and Penny would be able to kill Yvonna, which is why he dispatched them to Vegas. But when he found out they were all murdered by Yvonna's hands instead, he realized he had to take her seriously. Things got worse when Pastor Robinson was killed a few short months later.

"Sir? Are you there?" Kelly asked, after a long period of silence.

He was there but he was trying to quarterback the situation in his mind. He didn't even know where to start. And how had she gotten his office number? He knew she had his cell phone number, thanks to Penny who left it in her coat pocket the weekend of Vegas, but he changed that a long time ago. And nobody but his circle had the office line. "Give me one second, Kelly." He looked up at Marge and Tyisha and placed his hand over the handset, "I have to take this call, but I'll be in contact." When they left he said, "Patch the call through."

He took a deep breath and tried to take charge of the situation. He was Rufus Day, the world's most wealthy pimp and evangelist. Why should he be scared of some girl who was too stupid to realize by fucking with him, she was signing her own death certificate?

With as much confidence as possible he asked, "What do you want, Yvonna?"

"Now is that any way to speak to someone?" Yvonna said coyly. "Especially to someone you have a past with?"

"I don't have time for games."

"When did that change? Because the last thing I remember was me telling you that I was coming for you, and you saying that you'll be waiting. Is that still true?"

"Where are you?"

"We'll have our time soon enough, Rufus, but for now, I just wanted to know how my favorite pimp was doing?"

He tried to remain calm, but the fact that she knew his name, and had his new number, meant she was closer to uncovering more about AFCOG than he wanted. "I never told you my name. How did you know it?"

Silence.

"What will it take to make you go away?" He asked, opting to reason with her. "How much do you want?"

She laughed. "You don't have enough money for me."

"I doubt that, Yvonna. Everybody has a price."

"And you couldn't afford mine."

"I doubt that very seriously."

"You shouldn't doubt me. And I'm sure if Ron Max could talk, he'd vouch for me."

Chill bumps formed over his skin and he felt the strong urge to vomit. "You don't even know what you're doing do you? If you did, you would run away while you still can."

Click.

"Hello?" He looked at the handset as if he could see where she'd gone. Placing it back to his ear he screamed, "Hello!" When he didn't get a response he slammed it down. He needed to think and he needed to think quickly. Picking back up the handset he said, "Kelly, get Ron Max on the line."

"One minute, Master."

As he waited, his nails click clacked over his desk. It seemed like forever waiting on Kelly. He looked at his wall and all of the pictures from the celebrities he met in his lifetime. He wasn't prepared to give up this lifestyle and trade it for prison or the grave. He would see to it that she was killed, even if he had to do it himself.

It took two minutes for her to return to the phone. "Master, I'm sorry it took me so long but…"

"But what?"

"I kept calling Ron Max because every time I called someone would pick up the phone and say…they would say…uh…"

"What is it?!"

"To tell Rufus Day to go fuck himself."

The pressure in his body reached heights causing him a severe headache. He didn't want to make his next call, knowing things could get out of hand. But considering his current status he didn't have a choice. "Kelly, get Charles Bank on the phone right away. Tell him I need his services as soon as possible."

SWOOPES

All of the drama had Swoopes' mind wrecked. Having to relive the memories of what he endured as a child made him understand more that AFCOG needed to be taken down, but also that he would never live a normal life. The mission had become his everything and he often thought about his life after they finished, he didn't have a plan.

Since Yvonna and the clan decided to stay in Ron Max's house until morning, he decided to shower. When he walked into the guest bedroom's bathroom, a soft steam cloud touched his face and when it cleared, he was looking at Yvonna's naked body. She had taken a nap earlier and he thought she was still sleep.

He knew her to be crazy, but what he didn't remember was how beautiful she looked wearing nothing. "My bad." He averted his eye a little to offer her respect. Never moving anywhere without his black eye patch, the other was concealed. "I thought you and Bricks was using the master bathroom. My fault."

She grabbed the blue towel hanging on the rack, wrapped it around her body and tucked it in the front so it would stay in place. "We are, but since he's taking a shower now, I decided to grab one real quick in here." She walked past him and their arms touched lightly. "It's all yours now."

Before she left, he tenderly grabbed her hand. Realizing touch wasn't something they shared, he quickly released his hold. "Sorry 'bout that."

She cleared her throat. "Not a problem, but what is it?"

"I wanted to ask, what was up with you earlier today? On more than one occasion, I caught you talking to yourself. And then when we were in the kitchen with Elika and Tata, you was talking like you was somebody else. I mean, I remember hearing that you had mental issues, but I can't lie, I ain't see nothing like that shit before."

"So what?"

"It got me noid that's what, especially since you 'spposed to be in charge of this shit."

"I don't know what you talking about, Swoopes." She saw her clothes on the toilet and grabbed them. "And as far as me handling this mission, if you don't like how I run shit, bounce."

"I'm so tired of you and that nigga of yours giving me an ultimatum. Trust, if I want out, I know how to move."

"Just as long as you know."

Originally he hadn't meant to upset her, but since she was carrying it like she didn't give a fuck, he decided to match her mood. That was until he saw a raised scar on the back of her shoulder, with several names on it. The name that stood out the most belonged to him. "Hold up, is that my name...On your back?"

She turned her head slightly to look at the back of her shoulder, as if she didn't already know the deal. Still full with attitude, she said, "Don't worry about what I got on my body. Because anything over here don't concern you." Remembering how he eyed her nudity earlier she completed her statement with, "And that means my pussy too."

He threw his hands out in front of him and chuckled. "I don't know what you mean by all that, 'cause you got me fucked up if you think I'm coming at you." He looked at her seriously. "Now you still haven't answered the question, what's up with my name on your back?" With a serious stance he added, "And who are the other people?"

Frustrated she let out a puff of air. He wasn't going to let the matter go and she didn't feel a need to hide. He already knew she hated his fucking guts at one point in life, so it was best to keep shit real. "As you already know, I couldn't stand you and you couldn't stand me. That's when I added your

name on my back. It was a long time ago, Swoopes. Nothing for you to get all un-smiley-faced about."

He scowled and for a brief moment, was mentally taken back to the days when they were at war. "What is it...some kind of list...Of the people you planned to kill?" She turned away from him. "You might as well keep it real."

"What you think, Swoopes? We were never fucking. Unless you consider the time you raped me, sex." His body mechanics told her that he was ashamed of what he'd done. "So why else would I have your name on me?"

"I never got a chance to tell you, but I'm sorry about that shit. Everything we went through as kids had me mad at the world. And to be honest, I don't even remember that night, just what the YBM members told me. I had to get drunk just to do that shit to you. I like rough sex, but I don't have to rape nobody."

"You could've fooled me." She paused, with her hands on her hips. "And am I supposed to feel better that you fisted me and fucked me raw and didn't remember? Let's not even talk about you letting the dog fuck me too." She exhaled and shook her head. Hearing the past reminded her that they had no business being in each other's company. There was too much pain and too much hurt.

"You not 'spposed to feel better, Yvonna, but I just want you to know that I'm sorry. On what's left of my life." He stepped out of her space and said, "So you had my name on your back 'cause you was gonna kill me for what I did to you that night?"

"First off this is old," she said, tapping her shoulder with one finger. "And don't act like there wasn't a time, when you didn't want to kill me too." She looked at him and rubbed her hand over the wet sink, just to have something to do. "You would've killed me quick if you could've found me."

"Well I guess it's over. But tell me this, how do you feel about me now?" He paused. "I don't want to have to worry about you stabbing me in the back when I close my eyes."

"What are you asking me, Swoopes? Just come out with it."

"I'm asking can I trust you?"

"Why you in the bathroom questioning my bitch?" Bricks said walking up to him. He didn't know if the conversation was pleasant or disagreeable...nor did he care. Yvonna and Swoopes remained silent as they looked at one another. "You heard me, mothafucka!" Swoopes' eye settled on Bricks. He was sick of him stepping into his space. "What's up with that shit?"

Swoopes sighed. "One day you gonna realize you don't run me. You better hope when the day comes, you crawl away from the situation alive." Swoopes stepped out of his path and turned the water on in the shower to get the right temperature.

"So you threatening me?" He said to the man's back.

"Baby, come on." Yvonna said pulling his hand, hoping he'd leave with her out the bathroom. Outside of the slight movements her tugging caused, the man didn't budge. "Please, Bricks. I'm tired and all I want to do is get some rest." Hearing the hurt in her voice he relented. Bricks gave Swoopes one last look, before they both walked out, leaving Swoopes alone.

"Bitch ass nigga."

Unaccompanied, he closed the door and placed his gun on the back of the toilet bowl. He wondered at that moment why he didn't smoke Bricks and be done with him all together. Bricks was a killer no doubt, but Swoopes had done things most grown men couldn't fathom.

He eased out of his grey sweats, turned the shower on and allowed the warm water to roll from his head to his toes. Placing both hands on the wall before him, his chiseled body under the showerhead looked like an ad for Polo, eye patch included. Remembering their conversation, he tried to shake the way Yvonna's body looked out of his mind. There was no denying that although he'd never admit it to another living soul, he was attracted to her. After all she was his equal.

When he pictured her perky breasts, he lathered up his dick and jerked himself slowly back and forth. Running his thumb over the tip, he made quick repeated motions in the hopes of bringing himself to a good nut. The roundness of her breasts. The way the beads of water trickled down her back, on the path to her ass, as she reached for the towel, had him done. Evil or not, Yvonna was the truth and suddenly honesty consumed him. What he wouldn't give for one real night alone with her, just as long as it would be forgotten in the morning.

He was almost about to cum, when Ming knocked on the door and walked inside without an invitation. From the outside of the shower she said, "Swoopes, can Ming join you? Ming was waiting for you to come to bed, but you've been in here so long." Ever since the clan had gotten together, Ming had been actively pursuing him. Although he'd fuck her from time to time, that's as far as he wanted to go. Ming on the other hand had visions of a long-term relationship dancing in her head.

Swoopes wiped the water beads out of his eye and in an irritated voice asked, "What are you doing in here?" He looked at the closed blue shower curtain. "I'm busy!"

"Come on, Swoopes! Let me suck and fuck that dick. You know you like how Ming does it." She paused to let their past fuck sessions vouch for her credibility. "Don't be alone when you don't have to. Girls need love too."

Silence.

"You're quiet, so Ming is going to take that as an invitation." She slid into the shower and stood behind him. He wondered how she got naked so quickly. She eyed every muscle in his perfectly formed back. Instead of attacking his masterpiece right away, she opted to wrap her arms around his waist. Because she was short, her face rested right above his ass. "This feels right. Doesn't it?"

Unable to deal with emotion he turned around to look at her. His body change broke her embrace. Bending his head slightly to address her cute face he said, "I thought you came in here to get serious."

"Ming just wants to hold you, Swoopes." Her eyes were filled with pain. "Everybody forgets that I'm here. That I need attention and that I'm lonely too."

"What are you talking about? Bricks and Yvonna the only people in a relationship."

"Not true."

"What you mean?"

"You have Bricks and you have Yvonna."

He laughed and was five seconds from throwing her out of the shower, by way of her hair. "You tripping now, hard." He turned back around, grabbed the soap and started lathering his body again. "I knew I should've locked the door."

"Ming is serious. You argue with Bricks everyday so you and him have a relationship. It might not be nice, but it's a relationship all the same. And you and Yvonna are bound by what you went through as children. Who do I have? I'm alone and I miss my son. I miss home. All I want is a little love from you, Swoopes, even if it's not real."

"And I told you I don't wanna relationship. And as far as missing home, you can go back anytime you want," She tried to hold him again but he was able to slither away from her. But like an octopus, she managed to get her arms back around him and at that moment he had to admit, she felt good. "Ain't nobody saying you gotta be down with this AFCOG shit, Ming. I don't even know why you here anyway."

"Ming can't turn around now." She pulled away and he turned around to look at her. "What is it about Ming that you hate? Am I'm not sexy enough for you? It's okay to be honest. Ming prefers it that way."

"Listen, before I met you, I never thought about being with a Chinese bitch. Since then, I have to say you are the

baddest chink I ever met in my life. But a relationship is not something I'm looking for right now."

Ming considered his *chink* comment extremely racist. She forgot that she said the word nigga more times than the old rap group NWA. "Chink bitch? Ming ain't just some chink bitch. Ming is woman, whether you know it or not."

Swoopes dick was now so soft, it looked like a deflated balloon. Had she not burst into the bathroom, he would've gotten his shit off already. "Look, I just want to take a shower and do me. How 'bout I get up with you when I get out."

"Are you gonna sleep in the bed with Ming tonight? So we can finish what we started?

When the bathroom door opened and the lights went out before closing again, Swoopes heart beat thunder. Until Bricks whispered, "Be quiet...we think some niggas in the house," he thought his life was over. "And turn the water off. We don't want them to know we in here."

Swoopes turned the water off and tried to remain in goon mode although he was naked. He eased around Ming and reached for his weapon on the back of the toilet, but it was gone. He was about to go off, until Ming placed it softly in his hand. Feeling his way in the dark, he eased out the shower, grabbed his sweats and Ming followed by wrapping a towel around her body.

"Ya'll doing too much fucking moving," Yvonna whispered. Swoopes didn't know she was there until she spoke.

Swoopes took the moment to activate the slide on his weapon. Bricks irritated with him as usual said, "See this why I don't fuck with this nigga. He don't listen. Didn't we just finish telling this mothafucka to shut the fuck up?"

"You the only one doing all the talking. I'm gearing up instead of hiding in a hovel waiting to get fucked." Their conversation was ceased when from the outside of the door, they heard footsteps moving down the hallway in their direction.

A few more seconds of silence passed before they heard, *"Who are ya'll?"* It was Tata, and Bricks felt guilty that he couldn't alert her and Elika that they had unwanted company in the house. *"And what are you doing in this..."*

Two bullets rang out followed by the sure sound of a body drop. Moments later, a second set of rushed footsteps could be heard coming from the basement. Elika's voice cried out in anguish and it was obvious that he saw Tata. *"What have you..."*

Three bullets muted his sound and the tension in the bathroom was heavy.

"Who the fuck are these niggas?" Bricks asked, praying they wouldn't open the bathroom door and murder them next.

"I don't know why don't you go outside and ask." Swoopes fired back, angered at what he considered to be dumb questions.

"Where the fuck you think that bitch at?" the intruder said. *"They said she was in here."*

"They must be looking for Yvonna." Ming said, her words trembled as they left her lips.

"Just 'cause the nigga looking for a bitch, doesn't mean he's looking for me.

"I don't know where she is, but Yao said that his niece called to check on her kid from this house." Everyone looked in Ming's direction, although they couldn't see her face in the dark. She was warned about calling home and her insolence may mean their lives.

"I'm sorry," Ming whispered. "I missed Boy. It was just one call."

"Wait a minute," Swoopes said in a harsh tone. "That...that sounds like Rook and Mike."

"Who are they?" Bricks asked although Yvonna knew.

"Niggas from the YBM. Let me go talk to them right quick." He moved around in the darkness for a second.

"Please don't go, Swoopes." Ming sobbed. "They'll kill you."

He placed his lips against her ear and she seemed to calm down.

Focusing back on the group he said, "Ya'll stay in here. I might be able to get us out of this shit alive."

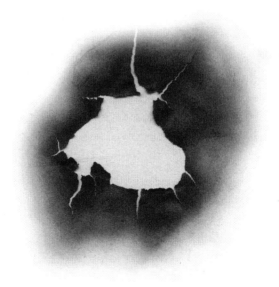

YVONNA

The bathroom seemed too hot as the three of them waited on the verdict. "Yvonna, I don't trust this nigga. I'm telling you." Bricks whispered. "I see how he talks to you sometimes he got larceny in his heart. This dude should've never been near you or me. I wished you listened to me. Whether you like it or not, I'm gonna start taking the lead in this shit. If we make it out alive."

"We gonna die," Ming sobbed softly. "I don't wanna die."

"You should've thought about that shit before you called Boy." Yvonna responded. "This is mostly your fault."

"Don't take this out on her," Bricks defended. "You should've gotten rid of the snake when it crawled out the bush. This is as much your fault as it is hers."

While Bricks passed the "*I told you so's*" out, Yvonna wished he could be more optimistic. The more time they spent together, the more she didn't like certain things about him. The bottom line was they didn't have a choice, they had to trust Swoopes.

Earlier that evening, when they heard the niggas rushing into the house, they dipped into the bathroom without their weapons. Had they went for their heat, they could've possibly crossed paths with the intruders. Opting to live another day, they took the best route, which was the guest bathroom. Since Swoopes was the only one with the gun, they were defenseless and at his mercy.

"I don't have a choice but to trust him right now, Bricks. None of us do."

From the bathroom they heard Rook ask, *"Swoopes, what you doing here, man? We been looking all over for you."*

"*I'm trying to find this bitch.*" He lied. *But what ya'll doing here, Rook? How did you know she'd probably be here?*"

"*Since we ain't getting money with you no more, we got up wit' this Chinese nigga, Yao. Seems like the whole world want this bitch dead, Swoopes. When I saw the paper he was laying, I figured you were on to something the whole time.*" He paused. "*But hold up, how did you know she was here?*"

"*I been on her trail for the longest. Seemed like every time I got closer she shook me. I was waiting for her to come back tonight, when the next thing I knew, I saw ya'll niggas. I just got here too.*"

"*Well where your shoes?*" Rook asked.

Silence.

"*Yeah, man, why you ain't got no shoes on?*" Mike added.

"*I took a nap in the bedroom. I found out she went to see her kid, so I figured at some point she'd come back. It was just a fifteen minute nap. Nothing serious. If anything, Yao should've hired me to get at her. No offense, but if anybody knows everything about Yvonna Harris, I'm it.*"

"I don't got a good feeling 'bout this, man." Bricks whispered. It was evident to Yvonna that Bricks kept saying he didn't trust him for his good not hers, because it wasn't helping anything. "I don't know how I let you talk me out of killing that dude."

As he spoke to himself, she thought about Yao. After everything she did for him, all the murders she committed in his honor, he still wanted her dead. "I can't believe this shit." Yvonna said as she felt around in the darkness for the toilet bowl to sit on. The tenderness from the BB shot bothered her momentarily before she pushed it out her mind. It seemed trivial since she might die in minutes anyway. "Yao won't leave me alone. Why can't he just leave me the fuck alone?"

"How do you think I feel?" Ming said, "I'm his niece and he never showed me an ounce of respect." Her voice trailed off. "Or love."

"So when did YBM get with Yao?" Swoopes asked.

"'Bout a month ago." Mike replied. *"This bamma paying niggas heavy. We can finally get put on like we been wanting. And if you act right, you can too."*

"And what the fuck do you consider acting right, Mike?"

"By telling us where that bitch at for real. That's how you act right."

"I already told you. I'm waiting for her to get back from visiting her daughter."

"And I'm saying we've known you for too long, man." Mike announced. *"You half dressed. You would not be loungin' & loafin' unless you knew something. Come on, Swoopes. Keep it right and tell us where she at."*

"The nigga Yao gonna give us a hundred thou to bring her alive. We couldn't make them numbers up if we prayed, man. You help us, and we'll give you a cut." Rook said. *"It'll be just like old times."*

"It's that simple. So where she at? What's the address?"

"The nigga 'bout to give us up." Bricks whispered. Sweat poured down his back and tickled. He hadn't been this nervous ever. He wanted to cut the lights on to see what he could use as a weapon but knew it was futile. "I didn't even get a chance to get my son right before I died. I was gonna give him some paper and set him up and now it's too late." His statement sounded like blame in Yvonna's direction, but she was done with him anyway. "I can't believe I'm gonna die without setting Chomps straight."

"You ain't the only one with a kid." Yvonna advised. "We got children too."

"Come on, man. Be real with us. Tell us where she at." Mike persisted. *"I know you got your own reasons for wanting her dead, but let's make this money together."*

There was twenty seconds of uncomfortable silence before Swoopes said, *"She's in the bathroom."*

"I told you." Bricks slammed his fist into his palm. "If we get out of this shit, maybe then you'll start trusting me."

Quick footsteps moved toward the bathroom and Yvonna popped off the toilet. This was it and she felt weak at the knees. When Swoopes opened the door, Bricks rushed him and connected with a fist to his nose. He fell to the floor and he was able to land a few more in his mouth and good eye. Yvonna walked out slowly while Ming stayed inside, hidden in the bathroom, out of harm's way. Yvonna wished it was something she could do to help Bricks, but guilt weighed her down. She wasn't thinking straight.

"Fuckin' traitor! I should've known I couldn't trust your bitch ass." For fifteen seconds the two men were in throws, each promising to murder the other. "I knew you was a snake!"

Finally Mike and Rook hoisted him off of Swoopes. They held onto him as he tried to wiggle away. "Hold him, ya'll." Swoopes said giving him one last hateful look. "I'ma handle the bitch first." Swoopes wiped the blood from the corner of his mouth and walked up to Yvonna. His eye told her he couldn't hate her more if he tried.

Out of nowhere, he recited the poem she'd written Tree in jail, some time back.

"You are I.
And you are what I want.
I am her who can't live without him.
You are my heartbeat.
I'd rather be raped.
And.
I'd rather be tortured.
Until I say when.
Because it's.

Not going to do me any good at all.
I said.
That until it's all said and.
Done.
That you are what I.
Want.
You…not him.
When you left I felt killed."

The hairs on the back of Yvonna's neck rose when he was done. The fact that he remembered the poem, she used as a means to have him raped and killed in jail by Tree, meant he never forgave her. To some the poem would seem meaningless. But if you took the last word of each line, you would receive the message she gave to Tree.

"What does the poem mean, Yvonna?" Swoopes stepped so close to her, she could feel his rage. "Tell me."

"Get the fuck outta her face, nigga! If you got so much to say, say it to me!" Bricks bravely yelled from the sidelines despite being outnumbered and out-armed. "You better not hurt her either!"

Swoopes turned around to look at him. "My man, you ain't in no position to give orders." Focused back on Yvonna he said, "What does the poem mean, bitch?"

Reluctantly she said, "It means, 'I want him beat, raped and tortured. And when it's all said and done, I want him killed.'" Swoopes gave her a sly smile. In her opinion, he just justified his reason for betrayal.

"I knew you should've killed this mothafucka when you had a chance," Gabriella said, appearing next to her. "Now you're about to die and there ain't shit you can do about it."

"Shut up, Gabriella!"

Swoopes frowned.

"Who the fuck is Gabriella?" Rook asked, maintaining his hold on Bricks.

"Nobody," Swoopes laughed, "Just this bitch's way of trying to throw niggas off, by talking to herself."

She thought about Delilah, and how she didn't get the chance to see her again. She looked at Bricks and thought about all his warnings. Had she allowed him to lead, none of this would have happened. She loved him. In her own way, but she loved him all the same. What she wouldn't give to go back to the day, when she held the gun to Swoopes' head in the garage, when they were all alone and she just shot Gabriella. Had she pulled the trigger, the world would be free of him.

Looking at Bricks, she felt it was her duty to get them out of the situation, even if it meant pouring her heart out. In a low murmur she said, "Please don't kill us, Swoopes." She finally looked up at him. "Please. I have a daughter and Bricks has a son. Don't hurt us. I saved your life."

"You so fucking weak." Gabriella taunted. "I can't believe you're doing this shit."

"Don't kill you?" Swoopes repeated. "After everything you did to me? Bitch, if I don't do nothing else in life, it'll be to kill you." He spat. Taking one step back from her, he said, "After I get my money from Yao."

"Now you talking!" Rook cheered behind him.

"For a second you had me worried too." Mike added.

"Naw I didn't forget the paper." Swoopes looked at them. And then looking over Yvonna's shoulder, toward the bathroom he said, "Buck them niggas."

Out of nowhere Ming ran out firing in Rook and Mike's direction. Since they didn't see her coming, or knew she was in the bathroom, they were caught off guard. Rook tried to reach for his piece but he trusted that Swoopes would handle business and because of it, he wasn't quick enough. He paid for his slowness with his life because Ming caught him quick, with a hole to the throat. He fell backwards and placed his hand over his neck as blood poured out of his body and between his fingers. When Mike tried to reach for his gun, Bricks stole him in his jaw and watched him plop to the floor next to his fallen comrade. Together, he and Swoopes drug him into the living room and threw him on the couch. While all of the action was taking place, Yvonna dipped into the bedroom to get her and Bricks' artillery.

"I don't wanna kill you, man," Swoopes said to Mike out of breath, "We go way back, but this shit here is deeper than you know about."

"I'm not even hearing you." Mike said angrily. "This the ultimate offense."

"You would say that, but I can't have nobody gettin' in the way of what we trying to do. Which is why I had shawty kill Rook. I knew he wouldn't understand why I can't let you hurt Yvonna but maybe you will." He was out of breath and leaned against the wall. He lied to Mike in order to try and pump him for info before stealing his life. "I'm sorry, man."

"I'm not understanding none of this shit! So ain't nothin' you can say to me. We YBM! Where's your fuckin' loyalty?"

"I know it may seem fucked up...but I got some people after me...some people who not fuckin' around. These niggas make everybody we ever came in contact with look soft."

"You forgot about one thing." He laughed hysterically. "Yao and the Mah Jong Dynasty. What you think he going to do when he find out you involved?" Without waiting on a response he said, "I watched him kill Growl before he could finish a sentence. I sure hope that bitch is worth it."

"You right. Yao does carry heavy weight. And I don't have time to be worrying about him. That's why you gotta tell me his plan."

"Fuck you, you bitch ass, gimp, punk mothafucka!" When a bullet flew between Bricks and Swoopes and split the flesh of Mike's leg, Swoopes and Bricks jumped out of the line of fire just in time. When they turned around they saw Ming holding the gun she was given by Swoopes in the bathroom.

Swoopes stomped toward her, snatched his shit away and said, "Gimme my shit! You almost hit me. That's why I was skeptical 'bout handing it over in the first place."

"You shoulda let me in on the plan." Bricks said, using the moment to get a few things off his chest. "Handing it to a female was a sucker ass move." Prior to him telling Ming to bust the gun, he thought Swoopes was stabbing them in the back. Although he was relieved to be alive, he didn't like being wrong. "I was better equipped to handle business than her."

"You sound crazy!" Ming said. "Ming was trained by the Mah Jong Dynasty! The best!"

"Naw...you probably would've turned the gun on me instead." Swoopes interrupted talking to Bricks. "You don't trust me, and I don't trust you. And we never will." He paused, taking the moment to reload his hammer. "Plus it's my bird. If you wanted to protect yourself you should've had your own." He laughed as if he was considering a few more things. "If niggas were trying to kill my bitch, best believe I would've taken the necessary precautions. You slippin'."

Hearing the insult, Bricks saw blue. "Fuck you mean!?" He stepped closer to him and they both forgot about Mike being on the couch. "I ain't take care of my shawty?"

"You gotta answer that question for yourself, B, now don't you?"

They were just about to go to blows, again when Yvonna walked back into the room. "I'm sick of ya'll with this shit." Bricks and Swoopes stepped back from one another, but the hateful stares remained. Slowly she walked up to Mike who was trying to stop the blood from pouring out of his body by a hand press. "What is Yao's plan?" When he frowned instead of answering her question, she raised her weapon and said, "The next one going in your head. If he didn't find me here, where was he going next?"

Mike looked up at her and said, "I don't know what his plan is. I do know he got his eyes on some niggas named Uzi and Laser." He tried to adjust himself because the bullet wound was excruciating. "They were in a meeting we were in the other day. That's all I know."

"Uzi and Laser?" She repeated. Swoopes was already hip on who they were also. "Treyana's sons? What would he want with them?"

"Don't know who the fuck Treyana is." He threw his head back because he was in so much pain. "All I know about is a Uzi and Laser. And I also know I wanna get out of here before I die from losing all this blood. Can I please leave?"

"We can't even talk about you getting out of here, unless you answer my question."

"Like I said, I don't know shit else!" he barked. "Just what I told you already."

"Well I guess you no good to me then are you?" She raised the weapon and punished him with a bullet to the forehead. The blast spit blood in her face and she smeared it off with the back of her hand, leaving blood tracks over her face. She was done with all of the games. If they wanted to get Roman-Like, by making everything bloody and gory, so would she. When life escaped Mike's body, she turned to face her crew. They all wore looks of disbelief because of the way she handled his death. "I thought you sold us out." She said to Swoopes. "Thank you for proving me wrong."

He grinned, looked at her and then at Bricks, "I wouldn't do that. Not with all this beef with AFCOG anyway."

"So what you gonna do after that?"

"Come on now, you and me both know we got a war to attend when this shit is all over." Swoopes countered. "I guess I'll see you there."

"You can count on it!"

"We gotta leave." Yvonna interrupted.

"You telling me something I already know." Bricks said, looking at the corpse on the couch. "Wait...where is Elika and Tata?"

Yvonna looked in the dining room and saw them dead, with their baby. Rook and Mike were so trifling; that they even killed an infant. As Yvonna looked at the bodies she said, "I'm so over all this." She looked at Bricks, and he tried to hold her but she shook him off. "I'm not asking for sympathy." She looked at the bodies again. "Just stating facts. All they wanted was my help. And now, because of me, they dead."

"You can still save more, young Yvonna." Swoopes said.

"And how's that?"

"Free the kids who caught up in the shit. Now it ain't about just smokin' crazies, we got a reason to fight back."

"When you took a nap earlier, Squeeze, we spoke to them alone." Bricks touched her softly on the back. "Let's go to the kitchen so I can run it down to you."

Ming, Swoopes and Bricks sat at a table with the box Ebony had earlier. Yvonna stood over Bricks to see what he was about to show her. "Elika told me how AFCOG works in a little more detail, when we looked over the things together in this box." Bricks took a deep breath and pulled out a chart. "The leader to this entire organization is Rufus Day, who you already know about. Directly under him are the *Four Captains of Pain*."

"What are the Four Captains of Pain?"

"They pimps. They all are. But they call themselves that because if the people under them don't follow the rules, they do what they have to, to set 'em straight. Whether it be violence or some other sick form of punishment." Swoopes contributed."

"Anyway, the Four Captains are Ron Max of Maryland, who we got already, Anna Livingston of Washington DC,

Ramona Cass of Virginia and Abel Pickling of Delaware. They run the fifty states. We found out Abel owns some creepy haunted house in Maryland called *The Pumpkin Face* and apparently, from what the papers show, she spends a lot of time there. Several meetings were held in that location."

"I think she stash her money there too." Swoopes added, although Bricks wished he'd go mute.

"Outside of them being somewhat hit men, they are also in charge of the Breeder Machines. Places like this which breed and house children." He looked at Yvonna to be sure she was still with him.

"Go 'head. I'm listening."

"Okay...under the Four Captains of Pain are the *Eight Secretaries of Tolerance.* They are supposedly nicer and slyer. Willing to work with people instead of being violent at first. Each Captain has two secretaries who report directly to them. Under Ron Max are Dana Kellogg and Elizabeth Hay. Under Anna are Charles Blaine and Heather Randolph. Under Ramona are Hillary Webster and Patricia Parker. And under Able are Toni Upshur and Susan Madison. We call them pimps too, but the world calls them evangelists."

"This shit sounds so complicated." Yvonna said, shaking her head. "When we got involved, I didn't know it was going to be all of this."

"You don't get to be in business as long as they have, sell children and avoid the law unless you're complicated. This organization sees a billion annually for sure." Bricks paused, to return his attention to the papers on the table. "Now...under the secretaries are the *Fifty Orphanages* which are located in each state. If they can't sell a kid, they send them there and that's where all the sick shit happens. Child sex orgies, bondage and some more shit. A lot of people pay money to fulfill their sick fantasies."

"When I was coming up, I think they had us in an orphanage." When she remembered the babies having babies she said, "Maybe it was both." She rubbed her head. "I'm so confused."

"I know, Squeeze." He softly pulled her hand and made a space for her on his lap. She sat down, hung her arm over his shoulder, and immediately felt at ease. When Bricks looked at Swoopes, Swoopes smirked and shook his head. Their little riff didn't go unnoticed by Ming, who once again felt like a third arm.

"Okay...one captain will breed fifty kids a year to be sold and they'll also recruit Outsiders to work the stroll."

"What's an Outsider?"

"A girl who is recruited on a social networking site or in a runaway hangout. She can also be from the home of a parent who is irresponsible. They dope them up and make them sell their bodies. Outsiders are *never* adopted out for money. They know too much of the real world and must always be watched." He paused. "Now the children who are bred, are adopted out because they are sold as babies or brainwashed if they're older. They are never at risk of trying to find their families. And it's the secretary's responsibility to oversee both the outsiders and the bred children."

"The bred children are like gold minds because they sing the praises of AFCOG, which encourages contributions and donations from people who are none the wiser. Baby, these mothafuckas are selling pussy, kids and getting donations because they operate as a church.

"How can we bring 'em down? It's too many mothafucka's involved. I wouldn't even know where to start." She was frustrated not because she was going up against AFCOG, but because if they didn't have a firm understanding of the process, she would never win her life back and be able to spend it with her child."

"It's easy...instead of going for the orphanages; we go from the middle up." Swoopes said, as he clapped his hands together. He didn't have to tell them but dreams of murder was on his mind.

"What 'Little-No-Basement' is trying to say is that we'll go after the Eight Secretaries of Tolerance, to the Four Captains of Pain and finally to Rufus Day." Bricks smirked and Swoopes gritted on him.

"Why can't we just kill Rufus? Why the middle men first?"

"Because any of the Four Captains is fully capable to run shit alone. And because the same may be true for the Eight Secretaries, it's best to kill them too." Bricks paused. "You bring down the heads of this shit, and everything else crumbles, including the orphanages."

She loved the plan and how her team came together. "How can we get to all of 'em?"

"According to this paper," he pointed at it, "there is a religious conference in a few days. The Eight Secretaries of Pain will be there."

"And we will too." Ming added.

"When we get them, we hit 'em quick and hard. Now it won't be that easy with The Four Captains because we'll have to put in a little more work for them, but at least Rufus will know we're not to be fucked with."

"He knows that now." Yvonna grinned. "And I love the plan."

When Mike's phone dinged, their conversation was interrupted. Ming walked over to him, snatched the phone out of his leather jacket and read the incoming text message. As her eyes moved from left to right, the color drained from her face.

"What is it, Ming?" Yvonna asked rushing up to her. Bricks and Swoopes were right behind her.

Ming couldn't speak so Yvonna snatched the phone to see for herself. The text read: *'Yao says let him know if you can't find her. He just located the address to her kid. We're moving there next.*

BILAL, Jr.

Bilal, Jr. sat in a chair in his bedroom, looking out the window for his brother Uzi, who made bail and was on his way home. He could smell burnt bacon from the kitchen, courtesy of his aunt Easter, along with her ranting on the phone and he was irritated. Wanting a little privacy, which he hardly ever had, he stood up, closed the door and walked back to the window.

Since Yao gave them the money to bail Uzi out, Bilal, Jr. wondered how Uzi would react toward him when he got home. He heard his aunts and uncles whispering behind his back. He knew at least two of them blamed him for everything and didn't want him there anymore. It was like his future was in Uzi's hands.

When a cab finally pulled in front of the house, Bilal, Jr. could feel his heart thump wildly in his chest. It seemed like it took forever for Uzi to step out and pay the driver. Bilal, Jr. was trying to read Uzi's facial expression, and unfortunately it didn't tell him anything he could decipher.

The moment the front door opened, Easter who was still on the phone in the living room, screamed as if Uzi was coming home after a twenty-year bid. "Bitch, I'ma call you back! My nephew home!" The sound of the phone dropping followed her random screams.

"You wildin' out now." Uzi said to his aunt. "It ain't been but a couple of days." He talked to her for a few more minutes before walking toward the bedroom. When the dirty white door opened slowly, Uzi's head peeked around the corner. "What you looking all sad for?" He joked. "Don't tell me you miss a nigga too."

Bilal, Jr. grinned because he just knew the reunion would end with him telling him to kick rocks. But the wide smile on his face told him that for now anyway, everything was cool. To say Bilal, Jr. was relieved was an understatement. Uzi, the main family member in his corner, could make or break his world. He was the big brother he always wanted, but felt he didn't deserve and the last thing he wanted to do, was let him down.

"I kinda missed you. But it ain't all like that."

"Yeah right?" He moved up to him and play jabbed him twice in the chest, while protecting his face with the other fist. "Don't try to fake now, youngin'. The look on your mug when I came in told me everything." He chuckled and went to Laser's dresser to rough his bag of weed and a blunt. Uzi sat on the chair across from him and got to work on the blunt. "You know you look just like me right? I never saw it before now but it's crazy. If I had any of my baby pictures, you wouldn't be able to tell the three of us apart."

"I ain't got no problem with it, if you don't." Bilal, Jr. smiled, sitting on Laser's bed.

"Don't sit on his shit." He yelled, pointing at the bed. He sat there all the time so he was confused.

"What?" He looked down at it, thinking something was on it. "I sit on it all the time."

"Well don't sit on it no more, mothafucka." He shot back. Uzi never spoke to him like that and he felt something was off. "Your bed on the floor, remember that shit."

Instead of sitting down on the floor, he leaned against the wall. "My bad. I was just trying to get comfortable."

Uzi shook his head. "I was thinking about what you said the other day, about you looking like your father. And it made sense at first until I thought about it in my cell. You don't look like him," he licked the edges of the blunt paper, "you look just like me." Bilal, Jr. eyed his brother's naturally good looks and had no complaints. "But we have some working on you to do. It's time for you to step up and man up." He looked him over. "Would you kill somebody if you had to?"

"I never thought about it."

"Well the time to think about it is now."

"I guess." He shrugged. "But it would depend on the reason."

"You should always be willing to do what you must. And you need to ease up too. I saw the look in your eyes when I came home. You thought that shit was going to keep me down. I'm tougher than that."

"I was worried about it. Since you answered for something you didn't do."

"I didn't have a choice. My brother can't handle jail, I know that. Grant it, he could've made a better move by not fucking that skank in the first place, but that's what brother's do, pick up the slack for one another. I'm just glad they dropped the charges since she wouldn't testify. And the hood told me what Laser did to her brother."

"Laser?"

"Yeah, he shot him. I knew that was going to happen when I found out she lied. You gotta be careful with him. He snaps." Bilal, Jr. was stuck because he couldn't believe Laser's deception. He was the one who shot the brother, not him.

"How's her brother doing?"

"They say he fine. The bullet didn't hit no artery." Uzi shrugged. "But who gives a fuck?" He paused and looked at him. "What would you have done if she showed up to court?"

Since he'd didn't get the credit for what he did to her brother, he gave a lazy response. "Whatever I had to do."

He smiled and when the blunt was completed, he pointed it at him and said, "Would you have taken the charge for me? If I didn't step up?"

Bilal, Jr. felt like he was testing him but he didn't understand why. He also knew his brother was serious, and that he needed to be sure before he responded. For all he knew, he would call him on it in the future. "Yeah...if I could, I would do anything for you. You my brother."

Uzi grinned. "Luckily for you I'm a grown ass man. And ain't shit them weak ass police can do to me, that I can't handle." He put the blunt on the dresser. "Be like me, not like your father, B. I heard he was part soft anyway." He stood up. "Any nigga that would deny his kids, like he did us, is part soft."

Uzi stood up, took his coat off and then his shirt. Balling the shirt up, he lifted his right underarm, wiped the perspiration off and moved to the left pit. When he was done he smelled the shirt and said, "Damn...I'ma have to wash these right quick." Bilal, Jr. didn't know what to do with his eyes, so he observed everything he did. On his way out the door he said, "Follow me, B. I gotta rap to you about something serious and I don't want to forget."

Bilal, Jr. did as he was told and followed him out the bedroom, past his aunt Easter who was eating bacon as black as tar, and into the only bathroom in the house. Uzi turned on the sink, grabbed his yellow washcloth and a thin pink bar of soap. Everything seemed to be a performance, like it was thought out. Lathering the rag up he said, "What you plan to do while you here? I been meaning to ask you but we never had a chance to get serious. Since Laser's not home right now, I think this is the best time."

Bilal, Jr. looked at a roach trying to make its way into the bathroom, so he stepped on it. Uzi picked it up with his bare hands, threw it in the toilet and proceeded to wash his pits.

"I guess I don't understand the question." He was talking to him, but looking at the roach that surprisingly, was still alive and fighting to reach the edge, to save his life. "I don't have a high school diploma, so I don't know."

"What you mean you don't understand, the question is simple enough?"

In Bilal, Jr.'s mind, this was Uzi's way of trying to put him out so he kept it real. "I don't have nothing planned I guess." He shrugged again, his favorite motion. "At least I haven't thought about my life that far yet."

"Everybody that stay here gotta work." Bilal, Jr. heard his aunt Easter's cackling voice, as she held the phone to her ear and wondered what her contribution was. "I guess I can find a job, if I try hard, Uziya."

"Never call me my government name again," he told him, pointing in his face. Suds from the washcloth touched his face and he wiped it away. "There's a reason I go by Uzi, respect it."

Uneasy about his tone he responded, "Sorry, man." Bilal, Jr. focused on the roach in the bowl again. If it swam just a little bit faster, it would probably make it out safely. "It slipped out."

"And as far as gainful employment, you gotta start thinking about shit like that." He washed under his arms and suds dripped down the sides of his body. "Matta of fact, you should always be thinking about how you gonna make paper. Always. Or else you not worth the balls hanging between your legs." He looked at him seriously.

Bilal, Jr. looked down at the floor. "I guess I plan to get a job...maybe at the grocery store or something like that. Unless you got a job for me to do."

"It's funny you asked." He grinned, pleased he walked into his trap. "Because now that I think about it, I do have something for you to do, to get your pockets right." He threw his drippy rag over the edge of the sink. "You remember that bitch who supposedly killed your mother and pops? I think her name is Yvonna."

Bilal, Jr. was immediately depressed. That happened whenever he heard her name. "Yeah...I can't forget her. She's in almost every nightmare I have."

Uzi contemplated what he said. "I use to dream about the bitch too." He turned around so he could see his back. "You see that tattoo?" It read, *'Don't Get On My Shyt List Again'*. "She gave me and my brother that when we were kids. It was the first time I experienced real pain." He shook his head. "Let me tell you how she got us. This crazy bitch comes to a play we were performing in at school right, and tells us that her name is Aunt Paris from Texas. We go with her thinking shit was straight."

"You got an aunt from Texas?"

"Don't be dumb." Bilal, Jr. held his head down.

"Anyway, I remember having so much fun with this broad until she gives us tattoos. That shit changed our life." He laughed to himself. "She was also the first bitch to give us alcohol. She didn't look like what we thought crazy was, which is how she got to us." He chuckled to himself as he remembered how gullible he was. "When we got home, we slept that whole day, because she brought us back drunk. But the next morning, Avante beat our asses for going with her. Said we should've been smart enough to avoid strangers." He shook his head. "I'll never forget that shit." He paused and checked it out in the mirror, as if it were his first time seeing it. "We use to hate the tattoos, but now it's our ode. Something we live by." He grabbed his black toothbrush and wet it. "Anyway the nigga I work for, Yao, offered us a lot of dough to find her alive."

The temperature of the conversation changed quickly and Bilal, Jr. frowned. He wasn't trying to murder anybody especially her. Something about Yvonna gave him the creeps and he preferred to be as far away from her as possible. "I don't know about that, we tried to get at her before."

"Who is we?"

"Not we, I mean Swoopes. You remember him right? He was the one who told me where to find you."

"Yeah...the nigga use to hang over here all the time when we were younger, so we thought we could trust him. Had us thinking he was good people and everything. The next thing I know, he takes our money and bounces. I heard he was on dope bad."

"Well he tried to get at her too but it never worked."

"Well he ain't me." Uzi responded seriously. "And he ain't us. Now I don't know why Yao wants us to do this for him, but if he asked, I'm on it." He put toothpaste on his brush and got to brushing. "To tell you the truth, I don't give a fuck what the reason is." He spit out a glob of paste. "But I can tell you this," he pointed at him with the brush, "he spending a lot of money to see it done."

"How much?"

"Enough to get us out the hood...for the rest of our lives."

"Well I never done nothing like this before."

"Don't worry, little brother, I got you." He turned around and flushed the toilet, taking the roach with it.

The sun was bright as Bilal, Jr. rode with his aunt Easter to the convenience store. Although the weather was nice, it didn't warrant the window being open like she had it. Easter was making spaghetti that night, her favorite, and she needed somebody to carry the bag since one hand was always holding the phone. Bilal, Jr. didn't feel like going, but she made him since Uzi had to meet up with Yao later that night, and Laser was over some bitch's house. He would not have minded riding, if he was able to hear himself think, but whenever he was around her, that wasn't the case. What bothered him the most about his aunt was that she never got off the phone and she insisted on subjecting everybody to her meaningless conversation. He wondered who she could be talking to, because they stayed on the phone so much, in his opinion, they could not have had a life.

"Girl, you gotta let me know how that shit is tonight! It's gonna be some fine ass niggas up in that bitch." Easter laughed, maneuvering down the street. "I wish I had something to wear because I'd take my ass with you."

Bilal, Jr. looked over at the scarf she was wearing and shook his head. All he wanted was to think about Yvonna and what it would mean to come in contact with her again. He didn't know if he wanted her dead or alive and he imagined how things would roll out, once she was in his company again. His mind was twisted with everything going on around him, and he would've given anything for five seconds of peace.

"Bitch, I'm not playing! I know you don't believe me but I would go." She laughed to herself hitting the steering wheel. "Okay, if I find something to put on, don't say shit to me when I step up in the place and kill the game." She scratched her scarf-covered head. "Because once I let my hair down, ain't none of ya'll bitches can fuck with me."

"Shut the fuck up." Bilal, Jr. said softly, before looking back at the road. "I can't think."

"Hold on, girl." She said, removing the phone from her ear. She took a moment to look at him because she thought he said something. But when she glared at him, he was staring at the road ahead, like he never said a word. "I'm here, girl," she said hesitantly, stealing one last look at Bilal, Jr. "I just thought my nephew said something."

When she focused back on the road, her face was forced out the window with a punch to the jaw. She tried to pull herself together wondering where the blow came from, but she was hit with another. The phone dropped out of her hand and the car veered to the left, sticking itself to the curb. While she was partially delirious, he wailed on her as if she was a nigga in the street.

When he took a break, Easter held her mouth and looked over at him again with glazed eyes. "Why you just do that..."

She couldn't finish because he hit her again, and again. By the time he finished with her, blood was splattered all over his body and inside the car. Realizing what he'd done, he looked at his bloody hands and her limp body. He fucked up now.

YVONNA

Although it was frigid outside, from his wheelchair on his deck, Bradshaw looked at his youngest daughter playing in the yard. The years had been unkind to him, and recently the doctors informed him that he wouldn't live more than five years, due to being paralyzed. Had he known he would never walk again, he would've cherished everything he was able to do on his feet.

When he saw Delilah throw her ball down, and prepare to take off her red coat he yelled, "Honey, don't take your coat off! It's freezing out here and you'll get sick."

She placed her hands on her hip, looked at him and said, "But I'm hot, daddy. If you could come out here and play with me, instead of sitting on your ass in that chair, you'll see what I'm saying."

He couldn't help but laugh even though her comment was cold. "Well if you stopped running, and sat up here with me, you'd cool down too." Then he looked at her seriously when he saw she was ignoring him. "I mean what I say, Delilah, don't take it off unless you want to come in the house."

"Daddy, you do realize I only listen to you because you're old. You can't catch me."

"Delilah!" he yelled, when he saw she was pushing his limits. "Do what I say."

"Okay, daddy." She continued playing with her ball.

As he watched her kick the ball back and forth, he wondered how she was able to move on with her life, with Yvonna dead. She seemed carefree and like everything in the world was great. With time, Bradshaw learned not to hate her even though it was her mother's fault, he couldn't walk. He still remembered the day he was out jogging when life for him changed.

The morning was beautiful, until he looked up and saw an old red Forerunner, with Yvonna behind the wheel, coming speedily in his direction, all because she was angry due to his deception. The next thing he knew he was paralyzed and in the hospital fighting for his life. Before the accident Yvonna thought he loved her, but when it was discovered that he was making a deal with movie producers to obtain the story of her life, she felt betrayed as Gabriella, sought revenge.

When he first entered the hospital, the doctor's told him he'd never talk or walk again. When he said his first word, he gave them the finger, and paid for round the clock care using the money he earned from the movie based on Yvonna's life. But lately his body was failing him and it was obvious that despite the money, he would not be turning around for the good this time. Lately he'd been finding it hard to breathe. As a result, he had to stay on a ventilator twenty hours out of a day.

All was not lost when it came to getting back at Yvonna. A smile spread across his face when he remembered what he did to her in retaliation. It took forever to get her alone the weekend of the Urban Greggs fight. But when he did, he was able to get her to an empty garage in Nevada, along with Swoopes and Gabriella, and leave her for dead. Bradshaw hadn't planned on taking his daughter that day, because he didn't know she was there. Besides, who would take their child to Vegas on a fight weekend? But when he found her, he couldn't leave her either. After all, she was his flesh and blood. It was a lot of work taking care of her; especially considering his eldest daughter was in her first year of college. He thought he was done raising kids but he was completely wrong. There he was, a father again, thanks to the craziest bitch he'd ever met in his life.

"Is there anything I can help you with, sir?" His maid asked, walking up behind him. She bent down, sucked his earlobe and groped his dick. On many occasions she took care of his every need, and it was her pleasure. "I can run you a bath, and play the kiss the snake game like you like while you bite my back. I know how much you love that."

Bradshaw frowned, lifted his neck and looked up at her pretty dark face. "What did I tell you about doing that shit in front of my daughter?"

The nurse stood up straight, looked out at Delilah playing in the yard and back at him. "I'm sorry, I didn't think she could see us. She's all the way over there."

"You didn't answer my fucking question." If he could've moved his arm he would have smacked all the shit out of her. Since he couldn't, he elected to hit her with one of the meanest looks known to man. "Now what did I tell you?"

She stepped back, grasped her hands and held her head down. "You told me not to disrespect. I'm sorry. I guess I'm so use to us living alone." She was doing everything in her power to get a part of his estate, when he killed over, so sometimes she acted prematurely. She already got him to will the Rolls Royce; he couldn't drive to her, that sat in the driveway. She figured if she sucked him a little more often, she'd make it on the list for some of his money too. "Please forgive me, Bradshaw. Sometimes I can be insensitive."

"Yes you can and let me tell you something else. *We* don't live alone, Nancy. *You* live with me." He focused back on Delilah. "Now get the fuck outta my face. I want to be alone."

She cleared her throat, "Right away, sir."

When Nancy scurried away, Bradshaw smiled when he saw Delilah doing a dance she saw from the old movie, *Sparkle*. Unlike his oldest daughter, she was quite content talking to her self, and didn't require company. There was no real need for friends. The way her pigtails bounced around was so childlike and innocent, it did his heart well.

He was just about to call her in for lunch, when he felt the maid's hand on his dick again. This time when he looked back, instead of seeing Nancy's face, he saw Yvonna and three barrels pointed at his head. "Hello, Bradshaw." Yvonna smiled, before squeezing his dick hard, forcing a yelp out of his mouth. She removed her hand and walked in front of him. She took a moment to look down at him, so that he would know who was in charge. "I bet you didn't think you'd see me again did you?"

He was so shocked she was still alive, that he almost killed over. How could she be alive, when he left her for dead? And when he saw Swoopes, who was also in the room with her, the night he left them in Nevada, he figured for sure he was dreaming. As far as he knew, they couldn't stand each other, so what were they doing together?

"What are you doing here?" He trembled. "I thought...I thought..."

"You thought you killed us." Swoopes said crashing his hammer over his head. More people were struck over the dome, with the butt of Swoopes' gun, than a judge's gavel slammed in federal court. "I can't wait to do a few things to you. To repay the favor in Vegas. I been waiting on this forever."

Yvonna was so tuned in to Bradshaw, that she didn't see her daughter in the backyard. Her oversight didn't stop Delilah from spotting her. "Mommy!" She paused, holding the ball in her hand, before throwing it down. "Is that you?"

"Fuck...I didn't see my baby out here," she whispered. "Wheel this mothafucka in the house and finish him off. When you're done, dump him where we put the maid." Ming hating him just as much as Yvonna, put pressure on the handle bars, so that the front part of the wheel chair went flying up in the air. Bricks and Swoopes followed behind them.

Yvonna, trying to prevent Delilah from running into the house, met her in the backyard as they ran toward each other.

"Mommy, is that really, really, really you? I thought you were gone! Forever!"

Yvonna's face was frozen with a smile as she jogged toward her. "Yes, baby. It is mommy! I can't believe how pretty you are!" When they connected, Yvonna lifted her off her feat and swung her in the air. This was truly one of the best experiences in her life. The little girl made her responsible. Made her think of someone else other than herself. And she was grateful to say that when she gave birth to her, she experienced true love.

After planting a million kisses all over her face, she placed her down and walked around her for an examination. When she was done she scanned over her fingers and her body to be sure she was unharmed. She'd been by enough to know she was good, but she wanted to be sure. When she was done she had to admit that although she was without her, Bradshaw did a good job of taking care of their child. "I missed you so much, Delilah. I thought about you everyday."

"I didn't think you were coming back for me. I thought you went to heaven, mommy. Daddy said I wouldn't see you again until I was a hundred years old and died too. But I didn't believe him. I knew you would come back because you promised to never leave me. You promised that no matter what, you would never give me away."

Yvonna was beyond irritated with what she just said, and if Bradshaw wasn't dead by the time she got to him, she would show him. "I'm glad that you were smart enough not to listen to him. That's why I came back, baby. Because I learned that everything your daddy says out of is mouth is a lie. So you not going to see your father anymore."

"You need to leave this little bitch where she is!" Gabriella said. "You can't do what you have to with her hanging on. She's weak and is only going to bring us down."

"Shut up!" She yelled at her. "Never talk like that in front of my child."

"Mommy, who are you talking to?"

"Nobody, baby, but are you gonna be okay with living with me now? You can't stay here anymore because..."

"Yvonna, we see somebody coming up the driveway!" Bricks yelled through the sliding glass door. "It's time to get shit started. Bring Delilah in the house so she can be safe."

Yvonna's heart rate kicked up. She just knew Yao was on his way, to do anything he could to hurt her reason for living by killing her daughter. Although she knew him for a while, she would've never thought he would stoop so low.

Yvonna bent down and said, "Delilah, do you have a special hiding place in the house? A place where grown ups don't know about?"

"Yvonna, the car gettin' closer," Bricks warned, "Whatever we do we gotta do now! So you gotta bring Delilah inside and stop wasting time!"

She stood up and turned around. "Okay, give me a second," turning back to Delilah she said, "Do you have a place, honey?"

"Yes. And it has a secret door too."

"Good," She responded gripping her hand, "take me too it. And when you get inside, I don't want you to come out until I get you. As a matter of fact, if I don't knock on the door, don't open it. Okay?"

"Got it!"

It. took Yvonna all of a minute to get Delilah situated. When she was done, she peeked through the large cream curtains in the living room, near the front door. Her .45 hung by her side as she waited for the first person to turn the knob. To her left, on the other side of the door, was Bricks waiting for his chance to fire if he had to. Toward the back of the living room was Swoopes and Ming was in the kitchen on guard in case they needed reinforcements.

When nothing happened, Ming whispered. "Where are they now? Ming ready to bust some caps."

Yvonna released the curtain, turned around and said, "Shut the fuck up! I'm not playing with you this time!" For whatever reason, Yvonna took to hating Ming more. "If you see somebody come through this bitch, you know its time to show and prove. Until then hang back and relax."

Moving the blind to the side again to get a better view of outside, she suddenly saw a familiar face. She heard that when you're about to die, people from your past are reintroduced in your life, to give you a reason to right the wrong. If this was the case, Yvonna would use the opportunity to take a few folks to hell with her instead.

"You see who at the door yet?" Swoopes inquired. "I heard somebody get out a car."

She didn't want to say who it was out loud, because she knew Swoopes would not react nicely. The man approaching the house also was none other than Tamal Green also known as Tree. He was the convict who she hired to rape and kill Swoopes in prison. He was unsuccessful on the murder but the rape he carried through. What she wondered was what business did he have with Bradshaw, and why was he at the house. Unbeknownst to Yvonna, Tree and Bradshaw had a plan to kill both her and Swoopes in Vegas at the time of the Urban Greggs fight. However, Tree got word that Swoopes was still alive and was coming to confront Bradshaw about what happened.

"Who the fuck is that nigga with the braces on his legs?" Bricks whispered. "I know Yao not stupid enough to send a broken nigga to do the job." He released the curtain. "It will be like killing a baby if this mothafucka comes through here."

"If the baby gotta a gun, we gonna blow his back out." Yvonna looked at Swoopes again grateful that he was not on the front line. "I'm just glad it ain't Yao. Maybe he's a friend of Bradshaw or something." She had to admit, the two of them connecting was not necessarily a good thing. She hoped whatever he was doing there, had nothing to do with her but she doubted it seriously.

Tree walked up to the door, and used his cane to knock heavily, before stepping a few feet back. The four of them gripped their weapons not underestimating anybody, not even someone disabled. *Go away.* Yvonna thought. The last thing she needed was the heat he'd bring in if he came inside. "Open the door, man! I know you're in there, your car is outside." After five more knocks, he said, "Fuck it! I'm gone."

Yvonna didn't exhale until Tree walked back down the stairs and got into his car.

"You should've killed his ass, Yvonna." Gabriella said softly, standing next to her. "Doesn't it seem weird that he and Bradshaw would even know each other? You just let a loose end live another day."

"You don't know what you're talking about. That's your problem, you talk too fucking much." Yvonna's clan looked at her, wondering whom she was talking to again. "Maybe it's a coincidence he was here. Stop tripping."'

Gabriella laughed. "All I know is, if you want a real chance to live, you have to at some point in your pathetic life, kill everybody who you ever fucked over. If you don't, everything you're doing is useless because they'll always come back. AFCOG is not your only enemy. Remember that shit."

"Who were you talking to?" Swoopes asked. The talking to her self was creeping him out even more. "You been doing a whole lot of that shit lately. It ain't sitting too well with me."

Ming came out of the kitchen and everybody awaited Yvonna's answer. "Nobody." She looked away from him. "I'm not talking to myself. Ya'll just hearing shit." Nobody was buying what she was selling, so she walked away from the window and sat on the sofa. "The nigga gone anyway."

Swoopes shook his head and asked, "You think he gonna come back?"

"Probably," Bricks volunteered. "But he don't have a key so it's obvious he don't live here. We should be good to hide out for the night at least. I rather stay off the streets as much as possible."

"I don't know about staying here. You saw what happened at Ron's house. Had it been somebody else, we could've been dead." Swoopes was about to look out of the window to catch a view of the departing car.

To prevent him from seeing Tree Yvonna said, "So you don't trust me? Or are you just trying to get us killed by looking back out the window?"

"I'm just going to see if the dude is gone."

"I told you he was." She turned around and looked at the TV that was not turned on. "Maybe you shouldn't touch the curtains."

Swoopes stopped in his tracks, raised his hands and returned to the living room. "So now what? Should we wait on Yao here and deal with the shit instead of running?" He turned the TV on. "Or do we do what we gotta do with AFCOG? I'm ready to move."

"I really think we good here tonight." Bricks said sitting on the couch next to Yvonna. "We need to stay low until the convention anyway. And if Yao does come here, we'll take care of him. It'll be like killing two niggas with one bullet."

"My uncle doesn't move like that." Ming walked closer to Swoopes just to be next to him. "He'll never do the dirty work himself. He likes to stay as far away from the trouble as possible. That way when they start passing out handcuffs, he won't get a set."

"I don't understand." Yvonna said to herself but looking at her clan. "If Yao isn't showing up here, then where is he showing up? The text made it sound like it was urgent."

"Maybe it's too early, Yvonna." Bricks advised.

"Maybe they had the wrong address."

"Like I said, we should stay here until they show up." Bricks advised. "We already got beef with AFCOG. We don't need to be running from Yao's people too." After the commercial for the movie on Yvonna's life went off, which she hated immensely, a news brief flashed across the screen, which caught all of their attention.

Swoopes pointed at the television. "Didn't that bitch use to watch your kid?"

Bricks answered for Yvonna and stood up to move closer to the television. "Yeah...her name is Quita. She use to watch my son too. What the fuck is going on?"

Upon seeing Quita's face, everyone approached the television. While the newscaster reported the story, Quita, was crying her eyes out, as she was taken from the house to an ambulance. The newscaster stated that some masked men ran up into Quita's establishment, looking for someone in particular. The police had no further information about the crime. And although no kids were hurt, one of Quita's assistants was murdered.

"I don't get it...why would the nigga show up there?" Bricks asked, eyes still glued on the screen. "Unless..."

"Unless she was the last person he saw with Delilah." Yvonna looked at them. "So Yao thought she was there. When I worked for him, I never told him about Bradshaw so he didn't know about her father."

"I'm sure he knew she has one." Swoopes responded.

"Don't be stupid!"

"My uncle has lost it now." Ming interrupted, shaking her head. "Big time." Spotting a full service bar in the corner, she walked toward it and pulled out a bottle of vodka and Hennessy. She raised one in each hand. "Ming doesn't know about ya'll, but she's going to have herself a drink. You're welcome to join me."

"Pour me one too." Swoopes said, stuffing his weapon under his shirt as he approached the bar. "Vodka and Hennessy, mix my shit together."

Bricks followed. "I'll take Hennessy, Ming." He looked at Yvonna. "You want anything, Squeeze?"

Still thinking about Yao she sat down and scratched her head. "Yeah...give me two of what Swoopes is having."

An hour later, the crew was drunk but still ready for war. And even though they were sure Yao didn't know about Bradshaw, they couldn't help but look at the door. Despite feeling inebriated, they went over their first plan of attack on AFCOG at the convention. They realized it was not a smart idea to take on Yao and AFCOG at the same time, so they decided to dodge him as much as possible, until they didn't have a choice. When the meeting was adjourned, they listened to music and went about the house as if they didn't have two bodies, Bradshaw and his maid, stuffed in the basement. It was the second house that became a graveyard, after a visit from them.

Yvonna just put Delilah to bed, when she returned to the living room. "Come on over here and sit next to me," Swoopes said to Yvonna, when she walked into the living room. Mixing Hennessey and Vodka, he was drunk and loose with the lips. "I been meaning to ask you some questions for a minute now."

"Why she gotta sit next to you to do it, nigga?" Bricks countered, before swallowing his Hennessy and pouring another glass. "I think you confused on who Yvonna is wit', player-player." Yvonna sat next to Bricks and threw her legs over his lap, while he massaged her toes. "I can remind you if you want."

Swoopes chuckled and with a glazed over eye said, "I know who she belong to, partner. You ain't got to keep telling me like I'm trying to get at her." He placed his glass down on the floor. "Anyway, I knew her way longer than you. So if you see the bond we have, take it for nothing more than a past. If you want," he smirked, "you can even call it a connection."

"A connection huh?" Bricks was trying to maintain his cool but he was Hennessey impaired, and caught off guard by his forwardness. "You act like you weren't the same nigga trying to murder her a year earlier."

"Well I'm not now. Things change." Swoopes reached for Ming as a consolation prize. She flopped sideways on his lap, and played with the elastic band connected to his eye patch.

"Swoopes, why do you keep bothering Bricks? You act like you want Yvonna or something." Ming replied. "Just let it go."

"Nobody's saying that." He picked up his empty glass and put it to his lips, although nothing came out.

"You don't have to." She paused rubbing his leg. "I wish you'd put half as much time into me, as you do with her."

"It ain't even like that." Swoopes countered. Focusing back on Yvonna he said, "So, Yvonna, tell the truth, did you think I turned on you back at the other spot? When Rook and Mike came through?"

Yvonna poured herself a glass of vodka and took a few sips before sitting it back on the floor. "Yeah, I told you that back at the house." She recalled. "But what I really want to know is this...did you consider turning on us?"

Swoopes looked at Ming and then back at Yvonna. "I'ma be a hundred wit' you. For a second it crossed my mind." He tapped is head with his index finger. "Especially after the run in with you and Bricks in the bathroom. But I remembered why I'm doin' this shit. It ain't about you, it's about finally being able to get at the people who ruined my life."

"See...I told you this nigga a bitch!" Bricks responded pointing in his direction.

"I'm not doin' it wit' you tonight, champ." Swoopes shot back. "Besides, whether I was going to or not, you still alive. Which means I didn't." He tried to take another sip of his devil mixture before realizing it was still empty. "If anything, you should be grateful."

"Grateful for what?" He smirked, leaning in to look at him closer. "That you was about to turn on us but you didn't? Now that I think about it, the only reason you didn't is because you probably want to fuck my shawty. You would love to know how it feels going inside this pussy wouldn't you?" Yvonna never told Bricks that he raped her, knowing he wouldn't be able to handle it. "I mean if we gonna keep it one hundred, let's go all the way."

Yvonna shook her head, at the way Bricks was acting. Lately he had become extremely territorial when he didn't need to be. When she first met him she knew he had the potential to love hard, but never thought it would be like this.

"You really consider me a threat don't you?" Swoopes asked handing Ming his glass to refill. He watched her sexy ass switch to the bar. "You know what, don't even answer that. 'Cause I can't even blame you. If I was you, I'd fear me too."

From the bar Ming asked, "And why is that?"

"Because it's obvious," he paused, "Yvonna's doin' something that's making him feel that way." He looked at the couple. "But maybe you should check your girl, instead of rolling on me about the shit every five minutes. As a matta of fact, let's put it all out there now." Swoopes looked at Yvonna. "So what's up, Yvonna? You sweet on me or what?"

Yvonna looked at him and said, "Whatever, boy. You need to put that liquor down. You way off now."

Bricks eyed her strangely. Focusing back on Swoopes he said, "You know what, I'm gonna let all that shit you spitting slide. If you ever thought you could get my bitch, you better adjust that eye patch, because you must be looking out the wrong eye." He paused to sip some more liquor. "What you need to be doing is thinking about your plan when this shit is all over."

"Why can't he come with us to the Philippines?" Ming inquired, with hopeful eyes. "I want him there with me."

"Well I don't." Bricks responded. "This is why it needs to be discussed. After the shit is all said and done, if everybody lives, he needs to be thinking of a plan."

Swoopes' entire mood changed. Although he didn't want to admit it, after everything was done, he didn't have a home in the states. Truth be told, he hoped he went out in a blaze of glory. "Don't worry about my plans. I'm good."

"I hope so. Because there is no way on earth I plan on looking at you for the rest of my life."

"Then close your eyes, nigga!"

"Whatever." He stood up and extended his hand to Yvonna. "Let's go to bed, Squeeze. I got some other shit I want to rap to you about in private."

"Later," Yvonna said, as Bricks led her to one of the six rooms in the house.

When the door was closed, they both slid out of their clothes and eased into bed. Yvonna's head rested on his chest and he rubbed her shoulder. "Squeeze, so what's the plan to get rid of Swoopes?"

She looked up at him and sighed. "I can't believe you called me to bed, to talk about another nigga. I thought we was about to fuck, not talk about Swoopes. Are you really being that lame?"

"It ain't about being lame. I was just hoping you started thinking straight." Bricks frowned. "I mean, even after you heard what the nigga just said, you cool with having him around?" he sat up straight. "Out of his mouth, he just told you that he was thinking about rolling over on us."

"You act like we paying him to be here." She sat up and rested her upper body against the headboard. "He's still here because he has just as much interest as we do, to get back at these mothafuckas. He's an asset, Bricks! Maybe you should start seeing him that way."

"You know I hate when you tell me that shit right? That he has just as much interest to see AFCOG fall as I do, because he don't. You are my woman and I care about your well being outside of this shit. That nigga could've cared less that you were running for your life, until he spent time with you in Vegas. Alone. You all he got, Yvonna. He ain't got no other family and that's why he's not making any plans for the future. You were his obsession and now he gets to be with you on a daily basis."

Yvonna sighed, and her temples started throbbing. "When I walked into the room that day, in Ron Max's house, and saw Elika and Tata lying on the floor, you know what I promised myself?"

"No."

"I promised to appreciate people. As a matter of fact, I'm doing what you told me to do. Remember the conversation we had?" She leaned closer to him. "You told me not to X people out of my life so quickly and I'm taking your advice. The dude saved our lives, baby. Rook and Mike were his friends and he chose us."

"And that makes him trustworthy?"

He had a good point but she would never tell him. "As far as I'm concerned, yes. And don't forget, he didn't have anything to do with Rook and them showing up to the house, but he chose. And guess what, we still alive."

"You so blind."

She exhaled. "I'm not blind! I mean yes...me and Swoopes had beef, but we also went through some of the most horrific shit you could never imagine." She turned on her side to look directly at him.

"Not this shit again."

"You brought it up not me. I can only wonder how you would feel, to have a man rape you every night, Bricks. So if the nigga is a little off, forgive him because he has the right to be."

She had some good points but he would give her nothing. "Why didn't you respond when he said you feeling him?"

She stood up and grabbed a magazine on the dresser. Her nervous movement didn't go unnoticed. "What are you talking about?" She flipped through the pages. "I did say I'm not feeling him."

"No...you didn't."

"Bricks, what the fuck is up with you? It seems like since we been together, you don't trust me." She was silent for a minute. Tilting her head she asked, "Are you trying to find a reason to leave? Or not to be with me? So you making up this shit about me wanting to fuck Swoopes or him wanting to fuck me?"

"You sound stupid!"

"No I don't. I think you're building yourself up to walk out. Well guess what, Bricks; you don't have to do all that. If you don't want to be around this, just go." She pointed to the door.

He stood up, snatched the magazine from her hand, and forced her eyes in his direction by way of a chin snatch. "Fuck you trying to say?"

"I think I made myself clear. If you want to leave, why don't you go? I never asked you to be a part of this, anyway. You invited yourself." She laughed. "People always tell me I'm crazy, but you know what? At least Gabriella never left me, she's the one person who was always by my side."

"Gabriella huh?" He looked at her with lowered eyes. "That's who you talk to?"

Silence.

Bricks looked at Yvonna long enough for an apology. When he didn't get one, he grabbed his pants and threw on his clothes. Without giving an explanation, he walked out the door leaving her alone.

BRICKS

B ricks walked toward the bathroom to wash his face before leaving the spot. His mind was twisted and he was beyond angry at how Yvonna tried to carry him. He was growing sick of her treating him like he wasn't a man. Like his dick didn't get hard and his gun didn't bust in her honor. She put him through more shit than an audit by the IRS, to prove his loyalty. All he wanted was to love her, but he was starting to doubt that it was even possible.

On the way to the bathroom, he approached Bradshaw's bedroom door. Immediately something came over him. He looked up and down the hallway to be sure nobody was coming. He had a lot of questions and curiosity was getting the best of him. He wasn't a sneak, but he had to know more about the only man, who in his opinion was able to domesticate Yvonna, because she gave birth to his child.

The moment he turned the gold knob, he was surprised to see Ming sitting on the bed on the phone. Her voice was low and she was turned away from the door. The moment she sensed his presence, she disconnected the call and jumped up. Ming was often missing for hours in a day, or found talking on the phone in private. Although they couldn't put their hands on what she was doing, she swore she wasn't reaching out to Boy, which could get them all in trouble.

"Bricks...I didn't...I thought..."

"Sorry, Ming, I didn't know nobody was in here." He stepped inside even though his original plan was foiled. How could he dig through Bradshaw's shit if the room was occupied? He was already embarrassed that he was interested in the life of a dead man anyway. "You not making calls are you? The last time you called home, they knew where to find us."

"No. I was just…I was just, trying to find a place to order some food." She was lying but he couldn't prove it.

"What you really doing in here?"

"I came in here earlier just to look around." If she was telling the truth, it meant they had the same idea. "You know, he was Boy's father too." She paused. "Yvonna never told you?"

"She said Boy and Delilah was brother and sister, but I didn't see past anything else. In the hood, it's nothing for a family to be extended, even if they don't share the same bloodline. I can't tell you how many play cousins I got out there." He laughed to himself hearing how ridiculous it sounded.

"I guess you're right." She looked around Bradshaw's room and then down at the floor. She seemed melancholy, like something was on her mind. "No…they actually have the same father." Her deep smoldering eyes appeared to avoid his, as she looked for something to do with them. "Well," she walked toward the door, "let Ming leave."

He respected her departure, until he grabbed her hand softly. "Ming, you have a second? I kind of wanted to talk to you about something."

He gripped her hand and the touch lingered longer than either of them wanted. There was so much sexual tension between the foursome that it was tough to deny. In that brief minute, without words, they shared recognition. Prior to this moment Ming felt like she was alone, but suddenly she could tell he felt the same emptiness inside. She felt like an outcast in the world of Yvonna and Swoopes and Bricks felt the same.

"I didn't mean to grab you like that." He cleared his throat and let her go. "I just wanted to rap to you 'bout something. It's jive fuckin' me up." He paused. "Have you noticed anything about Yvonna? That's different lately?"

Ming walked to the bed and sat down. She thought he was going to ask her about Swoopes. Because she was short, her feet dangled off the edge. When her leg softly touched his, he gave her some space, by scooting to the opposite end. There was something weird going on between them, and Bricks figured it was the alcohol, because he never looked at Ming in anyway but respectful.

"Not really. She seems fine to me."

He knew that wasn't the case and decided to be the one who jumped out there. "How do you feel about her, talking to people who aren't there? Does it bother you?" She shook her head, as if it was forbidden to acknowledge it out loud. "I'm confused." He stood up and walked toward the black ornate dresser with a large mirror mounted on top of it. When he got there, he turned his body around and leaned against it. It rocked a little. "I don't know what to do. I don't know how to handle this shit. Black people don't usually deal with mental illnesses."

"Ming doesn't understand most of it either." She shrugged. "Maybe it's not for us to understand. Maybe we just need to be there for her."

He looked down at his dry hands and back into her beautiful eyes. "I know this is heavy, and I don't even know why I'm asking you but I…" he swallowed, "I…don't know what to do. I mean…what can I do to help her? I'm her man and I feel helpless with this shit. Like all I can do is sit back and watch her take a turn for the worst."

In confusion, she pointed at herself. "So you're asking me?"

"Yes."

Since her opinion was usually disregarded in their fold, she was caught off guard. Now that it was time to contribute, for the health of the team, she was coming up short with something noteworthy to say. She had a few ideas, but what if she said the wrong thing? Would he seek her assistance in the future?

She slapped her hands on her upper thigh and rubbed them toward her knees before stopping abruptly. The motion seemed awkward but so was the moment. Stuck in place, she squinted and said, "Maybe you should call the doctor. The one who loves her." Going further she said, "Terrell Shines."

He frowned and got heated. He knew there was a reason he didn't ask her shit, she was too stupid. How could she even mention his name, when they found out a month back, he was consorting with the police? In his book he was tagged a snitch, and in the world of real men, they didn't have a place.

Instead of responding, he moved for the door and leveled a basilisk glare in her direction. "I'm out."

Needing to prevent his exit, she leaped off the bed. "Bricks, don't leave yet." He stopped. "Hear me out, please."

He slowly turned around. "What, Ming? Because you tripping hard now."

"Yvonna is sick. Ming doesn't need to tell you that because you already know." She played with the edge of the large white t-shirt on her frame. It was the only thing covering her naked body. "But it's serious. You only need to read the papers to see how she rolled in the past. This is dangerous."

Agitated he said, "Get to the point."

"Okay," her right foot shook nervously under her body, "I've known she was sick for a long time. And I'm ashamed to say, part of the reason I liked her was because of her illness. To me she was different." She walked closer to him. "Still, she's sick, the kind of sick that love can't cure. If you care about her," finally she looked into his eyes, "and I can see that you do, you need to get her help." She moved toward her purse and grabbed a phone. "It's clean. I bought it when we went into the store the other day." She scrolled through it. "Terrell's number is right here." She extended the phone but he didn't accept it. "Maybe you should call him."

Instead of taking the phone he scowled. Her insolence was pushing him to the limit. "You called this dude? After you know he ratted us out?"

"Yes, but it wasn't because I wanted to. I'm worried about Yvonna." She eyed the floor again. "Anyway, he wouldn't talk to me. Said something about me being responsible for her sickness. Because I won't call the police and tell them where she is, so that she can be admitted to some dirty ass hospital." She looked into his eyes. "I don't want to see that happen, Bricks. But just like you, without his help, I don't know what else to do. We can't go to the hospital; she's wanted by police. We can't go to a clinic, they may see how bad she is, and admit her right away. But it's up to us to help, if we say we really love her."

Bricks felt her heartfelt response and knew then, whether Yvonna realized it or not, that she loved her. Ming could be a little irritating at times, he'd give her that, but she did care about her friend. If she was willing to put herself out there to help Yvonna, he needed to put his differences aside regarding Terrell, and step up. Even if he and Yvonna weren't going to make it, because after the last fight they had in the bedroom, he couldn't be sure.

He walked toward her. "Give me that phone." She relinquished it and he dialed the number. To his surprise, Terrell picked up after the first ring. Bricks was hoping it lingered on for at least one more ring, so he could get a few thoughts together.

A flustered tone covered Terrell's voice. "What do you want, Ming?"

"It ain't Ming." He looked at her. "It's Bricks."

Silence.

"Hello?"

Terrell began huffing and puffing, as if he was trying to contain himself from jumping through the phone. "I'm here. But what the fuck do you want with me?"

"I know Ming talked to you..."

"She did!" He interrupted. "And just like I told her, I'm gonna tell you too, you're not helping Yvonna by being with her while she commits crimes."

Angry he asked, "So you help her by trying to get her arrested? I don't know if you ever been in a prison, but good health care is the least of their worries."

"The cops came to me!" he defended. "I didn't go to them. Either way, she wouldn't be admitted in a prison, she'd be sent to a mental institution. But you won't give her that opportunity because you're selfish." Then he paused. "Yvonna is a sick woman, and without her medicine she'll do nothing but get worse. God forbids she drinks alcohol too. You're fucking with fire and you need to do her a favor, call the fucking police!"

"Just like a snitch to make excuses."

"Call it what you want! But a man was murdered by her and...

"And what?" Now Bricks was angry. "You tell me what happened good doctor? Don't sit over there and act like you know what the fuck happened that night, when you weren't even there 'cause you were fucking her fake ass friend, Gabriella! But guess what, I was there!"

"I don't have to act like anything because when Yvonna is involved, I can predict the outcome. I was with her for years before you were even thought of, youngster. And you know what, I'm no longer a fool." He sounded like a bitch, even though he added an extra level of base to his voice. "I'm hip to what Yvonna is and what she is, is a monster."

"It's so easy for you to make the decision that she needs to be admitted now, but I gotta wonder, if it's because she's not wit' your ass no more?" he paused, to let his statement simmer. "If I recall, she committed a boat load of shit before she even met Urban Greggs, but it didn't seem to be a problem then. Maybe you never cared."

"I did..."

"Well if you say you loved her then why would you judge? She had to do what she had to do, to save her life. And I can vouch for her about what happened that night."

"Don't tell me about love!" He screamed, and his voice broke. At the moment he felt pain like Bricks could only imagine. Sure he fucked Gabriella, her friend at the time, the weekend of the Urban Greggs fight. But after he thought about it, he realized why he felt he needed to be with her then. It was his attempt to be connected to something related to Yvonna, after her constant rejections. "I have defended her on more than one occasion, even when it meant putting my practice on the line. If that ain't love I don't know what is."

Although Bricks didn't like him, for the first time, he felt where he was coming from. Putting him self in the man shoes, although he didn't like his style, he replied, "Look, if you love her like you say you do, meet up with me."

"For what?"

"To give me her medications. She doesn't have any and she thinks she doesn't need 'em. I know better, so if I have to, I'll force her to take 'em. She can't go to a doctor but none of us can take her right now. It's tough on us. We need your help, I'm asking you."

Silence.

"I'm going to report this number to the police. So don't ever call it again. And that goes for Ming too."

Bricks looked at the phone and slammed it into the wall. "FUCK!" Witnessing his rage, Ming jumped back to keep her distance. He looked at the damage he caused to her cell. "You need to get another phone anyway, the bitch ass nigga going to the cops."

She sighed. "So now what?" she was still hopeful. "What do we do about Yvonna?"

"For now we act like we don't see a problem. And hope shit gets better before it gets worse."

DELILAH

Delilah tossed and turned, as she lay down in her pink and cream canopy bed. Every available space on the lower wall in the bedroom was stuffed with a doll, her passion.

Confusion wrecked her consciousness and she didn't understand what was happening in her world. One minute her mother was dead and the next she was alive. But since she reentered her life, all she wanted was to be around her, yet her attention seemed to be focused on her friends. Sure she knew Bricks and Ming because she played with their kids, but who was Swoopes. And what did he want with her mom? Whatever happened over the next few days, she prayed that her mother would never leave her again. Those thoughts put her to sleep until her mother entered the room.

Delilah sat up in bed, rubbed her eyes, and turned on the pink princess lamp on the nightstand. "Mommy! I was just dreaming about you." A bright smile flashed across Delilah's face and she reached for her with outstretched arms. "It's amazing!"

Instead of coming in, she hung in the doorway, with a glass of Hennessey and Vodka in her hand. Now that Delilah could see her eyes, she noticed they appeared glazed over. "A dream about me, huh? Well why don't you tell me what it was about." She walked in and closed the door softly behind her. She took a sip, "I'd love to hear this shit."

Delilah's smile turned upside down and she dropped her arms to her sides. "It was a bad dream. You probably wouldn't like it."

"It can't be that bad." She moved the cream curtain hanging from the bed, and sat on the edge. "You had a high smile on your face when I first came in. So tell me about it."

"You won't like it, mommy." She assured her, with a few heavy head rocks from left to right. "It was that God took you away from me again, and I was really sad." She scooted closer. "If he does, I'm not going to like God anymore. I didn't like him when I found out you went to heaven either. But I especially wouldn't like him now. The devil might be nicer if you ask me."

"Don't worry…can't God or nobody else take me away. Anytime soon." A sly smile spread across her face. "I have so much left to do on earth."

Delilah beamed again and threw her arms around her mother. "I knew it! I knew you wouldn't leave me again."

Delilah was in heaven in her mother's arms, until her fingers were pried off and she was pushed violently against the headboard. Her head bang against the edge and a small knot raised in its place.

Instead of a warm smile, an evil glare took its place. "Listen here you little, bitch," she pointed her finger in her face, "you better never put your hands on me again! Ever! Do I make myself clear?"

Delilah was motionless.

"Mamma…what's wrong?"

She leaned toward her and averred, "Nothing is wrong with me, but a lot will be wrong with you, unless you listen to me." When Delilah backed away slightly, she snatched her toward her again. "Now…there's been a change of plans. In the morning, you are to stay with your aunt Jesse. This is not open for negotiation."

"I don't understand. I want to…"

Yvonna slapped her in the face. "Do you understand me now?"

Although she was fearful about what her mother would do next, there was nothing more terrifying than being without her again. Tears rolled down her face and she said, "No, mommy. I don't want to leave you. I don't want you to leave me. I can see aunt Jesse next time. Please don't send me away."

The girl was stubborn and it wasn't favoring well with Gabriella, so with extreme force she slapped her again. "I'm not your mother." She pointed in her face, and the child caught a whiff of the strong alcohol on her breath. "I could never have pushed something out of me as weak as you. So don't say it anymore."

She was confused. Her mind was swinging. She had plans to be the best little girl Yvonna ever wanted, just so she would remember how much she loved her, and would never leave again. It seemed like before she had a chance to prove herself, she was already displeasing her. "What did I do, mommy? I promise not to cry again. I promise not to do anything to make you mad. Just please...don't send me away. Don't you love me?"

"Love you?" Gabriella laughed heartedly. "I fucking hate you."

Delilah cried hysterically but Gabriella could care less. She was trying to even the slate and get Yvonna in a position necessary to fight AFCOG. Having kids hanging around would only complicate the situation and get them killed. "Now, you are going to tell me tomorrow morning the moment you wake up, that you want to go stay with your aunt Jesse. I'm going to probably ask you why, and you are going to tell me that you miss her. No matter what I say, you have to be with your aunt. Do you understand?"

She didn't understand. And if fighting for her mother would make her see how much she loved her, then that was exactly what she was going to do. Until Gabriella made her next statement.

"If you don't do what I'm asking, I will never talk to you again, Delilah. Do you want that? If you force me to do that, I will hate you forever."

Delilah finally understood. There was no reasoning with this person. So she wiped her tears away and said, "You are Gabriella...aren't you?"

Gabriela laughed. "Wow...you're smarter than I thought."

With anger Delilah said, "My mommy would've never hit me, or tell me she wouldn't talk to me again. She loves me too much. And you don't love nobody but yourself."

"Since we're not playing games anymore, you need to know this, if you don't do what I'm asking, I'll kill her."

"But you'll kill yourself too."

"Do you think I care?" She paused. Delilah's eyes showed her she wasn't sure. "Don't fuck with me, Delilah. You're a big girl, but you're not bigger than me. I'm the devil reincarnated, so stay in your fucking lane."

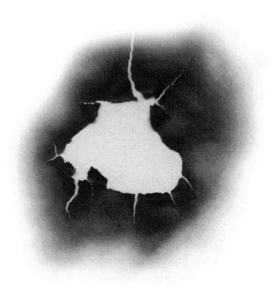

BRICKS

Bricks drove angrily down the street with Yvonna on his mind. He slammed his fist against the black leather steering wheel, every time her last words replayed in his head. As much as he hated to admit, Yvonna was right. He was trying to find an excuse to get as far away from the situation as possible. But it wasn't because he didn't want to ride with her or because he was a punk. His reason for needing to be sure she was the right one, had everything to do with Chomps and the promise he made to always be a presence in the young man's life. And every time Yvonna took up for Swoopes, he doubted her loyalty.

Removing his cell phone from his pocket, he decided to call his brother who had his son. He always checked up on them, but he needed to hear his son's voice more than ever now. The phone rang twice before Melvin answered. "What up, big bro?"

"Nigga...I been waiting on you to call," Melvin averred. "What the fuck it do, son?"

"Not a lot." He laughed.

"Well I hope you calling to tell me your 'Guys On A Mission' situation is over. You got me over here playing daddy and I gotta tell you, I'm not doing a good job." He laughed.

"I wish I was calling to tell you that too. But that ain't the deal." Bricks confessed, as he reached a stop sign. "On the real we just getting started bringing this to a close. It shouldn't take us too much longer though, we gotta plan now and we focused."

"You don't sound like shit moving in your favor. Everything cool?"

He sighed and tried to sound confident. He knew Melvin worried about him and he could only imagine what went

through his mind, while he was out there in the streets. "Yeah...I'm good sorting everything out. Right now I'm just trying to remain focused."

"I know you, B. You my kid brother. Now we may have our differences, but you have to know you can always talk to me. I don't want that to change, just because you signed up for a war, that in my opinion, ain't got shit to do wit' you."

This was one of the reasons Bricks hated talking to him. Although he called himself being nonjudgmental, Melvin was one of the most opinionated people he knew. But not having anybody to talk to forced him to open up. "It's Yvonna. I mean...I want to see this shit through wit' her. I gave my word and you know how I feel about that. But lately she seems to be tuning into the nigga Swoopes instead of me. They always on the same page, to hear her tell it and I don't understand this shit. Just because this cat was fucked by some other dudes don't make him smarter than me. And I ain't sure how I feel 'bout it."

"So he still riding?"

"Yeah, and I would've thought he would've fallen off by now. But the dude still going steady."

"You think she fucking him?" Melvin interrogated, heightening Bricks' perceptions. "'Cause if you ask me, he do seem to be a little too concerned with what she got going on all of a sudden, specially after we had to lay a few people down in his camp, when he was trying to get at her. Now all of a sudden they bosom buddies?" He laughed. "You don't need me to tell you what's going on."

"All this shit is dumb." Bricks admitted. "I just want it to be over."

"Well walk away, man. It ain't too late. Right now you only one foot deep in this shit. Don't bury yourself by adding the other foot."

"My pride won't let me walk away, Mel. Plus, if I told you in detail how important this shit is, you wouldn't ask me to give up. Kids gettin' raped, forced into slavery and some more shit. I knew it was bad, but didn't know how bad until I got involved."

"You not a Black Panther, Bricks. You a hustler who fell in love with the wrong bitch. Don't confuse the two."

Bricks sighed. "This why I don't talk to you."

Melvin was tired of faking with his brother. At the end of the day, they didn't have a father or anybody to lead them the right way. He had to play the father role and he accepted that position with pride for over thirty years. "I'ma put it out there, because I be glad when you realize you don't need to be bothered with this bitch. I'm telling you, Bricks, I have a bad feeling about this chick. If you don't get the fuck away from her while you can, she's gonna get you killed. And that goes for that Chinese bitch and the gimp; too. Walk away now, and let her sort the shit out on her own. It's her problem right now, don't make it yours."

"You can never be biased." He confessed. "First you tell me I can be real with you, and when I do, you bash. I might be your little brother but I'm a grown ass man first. You gotta start respecting that some decisions, are binding. And that goes for anything I pledge to do with my name."

"So let me get this straight, you take the crazy bitch's shit all day, but you hate to call your brother because he gives a fuck about you? That makes me wrong because I can't sleep sometimes, wondering if you still alive? I'm wrong for that?"

"You know that's not what I'm saying, Melvin. I just need you to understand that I made my decision and since I'm a man, I stand by it."

He sighed. "You know what, I'm not about to let you give me a heart attack." He paused. "All I know is, it's a damn shame that I'm in my late forties and playing father to a boy you said you would be there for. I fucks wit' the little nigga Chomps, but I ain't bang his mother out to have him. And you didn't either, so let's just put the shit out there." He paused only to catch his breath. "He the child of a man, you thought was a bitch, that ended up gettin' killed by the nigga in your little group. He's not our responsibility."

"So all this is Chomps' fault now?"

"I'm not saying that."

"You know what, after this shit, you don't ever have to say nothing to me! Now whether you know it or not, that's your nephew. Why? Because I took on the responsibility to be his father." Bricks' tone was serious. "Now I'm sorry I had to go on you just now, but know that I'm not leaving this situation until it's done. The only question is, will you help me or not?"

"Whatever, man." Melvin disputed. "Let me put little homie on the phone. I got a shorty over and the three of us were about to grab something to eat before you called. And since she give this little nigga more hugs than she give me, you already know it's not my kind of date."

"I hear you." When the line went silent, Bricks waited nervously to hear Chomps' voice. He couldn't say exactly when it happened, but along the years they'd spent together, he could honestly say he didn't love anybody the way he loved him, and that went for Yvonna too. It didn't matter that he was not his biological father.

"Daddy! Is that you?" Chomps said excitedly. He was the one person who was always thrilled to talk to him. "When you comin' back?"

"It's me, son. And I'll come back as soon as I can." He smiled hoping he could feel his love. "So how are you?"

"I'm good. We going to get something to eat soon." He paused. "But daddy, I want to go with you. Come get me."

"You can't, son. I told you that already. You gotta stay there with uncle Mel until I finish taking care of something."

Silence.

"Chomps?"

"But uncle Melvin don't like me. He spank me too much."

"See that's why the fuck I don't let you get on the phone sometimes! You too fucking grown." Melvin said. There was a lot of rustling around in the background and Bricks felt like a man on the edge of murder. The world already gave the kid a bad break. He didn't need Melvin adding to the situation, especially when he knew where the kid stood in his heart. Melvin was his brother, and he loved him more than anything, but if he fucked with his little youngin', when he knew what he was faced with at the moment, it would be along time before he'd ever talk to him again.

"Chomps...you still there, man?" Bricks pulled into a parking lot just to talk. "Chomps, you there?"

"Yes." He said in a shaky voice.

"Are you okay?"

"Daddy, please come home."

Bricks' heart cried out. This was not the plan for his life, to be without him. And for a moment he felt like stealing Yvonna in the jaw and breaking Melvin's legs. He blamed everyone for the kid's sadness including himself. "Calm down, Chomps. We gonna work on that, I promise. For now put Melvin on the phone. I gotta rap to him right quick."

A few seconds later Melvin said, "What's up?"

Bricks took a few quick breaths and tried to pace his words and calm down. "Do you love me, big bro?"

"Don't come at me like that."

"I'm coming at you real. Do you love me or not?"

"You know I do."

"Well be careful with how you treat my son. I know shit rough, and you ain't sign up for this. But believe me when I say if I didn't love little homie, he wouldn't be there with you now. I would've been sent them people, to take him and put him in the system."

"And you know I ain't want that for him."

"I know, man." He swallowed. "I know. I also know your life ain't about all this shit, but I need your help anyway. You hear what I'm saying?" he paused and his frustration could be heard and felt through the phone. "I need you, bro. If you had five kids, and had to complete a mission and needed my help, I would be right there for each one of 'em."

"And that's what I'm doing...but I gotta be real with you, I'm not feeling this daddy daycare shit. I feel like I'm missing out on life or something. You signed up for this shit not me."

"So what you saying?"

"I think you know, Bricks. This ain't me, man."

Bricks sighed. "Give me twenty minutes and I'll call back."

"So you mad now?"

With mostly disrespect, he hung up in his face and quickly dialed the number of his brother from a different mother. It rang three times before he heard his homie's voice. "What up, Kelsi?"

"Oh shit! Nigga, I been waiting on a line from you! Had me thinking you fell off the left side of the earth or something. What's happening?"

Bricks grinned after hearing the excitement in his long term comrade's voice. "You know I been around. Just trying to solve some things before I step back on the scene."

"Still attached to that chick?"

"Until we put this shit to rest."

"I got it. I got it. But what you need? Me to come through and help out or something?" This was why he fucked with Kelsi. He always lent a hand without asking what it was for. "If you do consider it done."

"Naw...I need you to do me a favor that you might not be feeling." He was dressing him for the situation. "Trust me, Kelsi, I wouldn't ask you to do this, if I didn't need your help."

"You can't be my best and give me all that first. If you need something, just say it. You already know, it's done."

He hoped it was true. In a low voice he proceeded. "You mind if my little man stay with you until I get shit together? I mean, I know you got your own youngin' now, since you just had a baby. And I know you run the club with your shawty, O and mama Janet, but I would really appreciate it." He paused to release some frustration. "Melvin acting like I'm five seconds from taking him to court for child support. Talking about he ain't sign up for this and that. I can't have my little man around me right now, but I would die if something happened to him. I need him around somebody who wants him there." Kelsi laughed. "What's funny?" Bricks inquired.

"You." He continued. "Nigga, are you asking me do I have a problem taking care of a youngin' who love me like an uncle? You sound like a fool."

"I gotta ask."

"You may have to ask, but you don't gotta ask me."

"I'm serious."

"Don't play games with me, Bricks. I'll be down by the end of the week to scoop him from Melvin. Just let him know I'm coming through. Tell him he don't even have to pack his shit. I'ma get the little nigga straight when he come back to the 'A' wit' me. So if that's your problem consider it solved."

Bricks felt the weight of the world lift off his shoulders. "You always come through."

"You already know what it is." Kelsi paused, when he heard one of his employees call him in the background. "And let me get up with you later, duty calls. But know that your kid is in good hands with me. Rest easy."

"One."

Feeling better about things, he got back on the road and parked at a convenience store, to get a new burner and a pack of cigarettes. Ever since he was involved with AFCOG and Yao, he'd adopted a new habit of smoking. Swaggering up to the counter, he was clueless that he immediately caught the attention of a customer, who walked in after him. Her blue jeans were painted on the way he liked them and her body filled them just right.

"Can I help you?" She grinned, anticipating if he'd smile back. "I hope the first thing you let me do is put a smile on that face."

He grinned, eyeing her body in all its splendor. "You work here?"

"I can get a job if you need help."

He shook his head. And when the real cashier stepped up he said, "Give me a soft pack of Newport's and one of them burners," he pointed at the wall at a bunch of cheap mobile phones. "Any one of 'em'll work."

When she walked away to fulfill his request, he caught another glimpse of his new friend's body, who walked away toward the chip aisle. An ass man since his birth, he couldn't help but be attracted to her. The way her natural brown hair touched the middle of her back, made her more appealing.

"Here you go, sir. Can I get you anything else?" The cashier interrupted, his gaze.

He cleared his throat and said, "Naw...but give me two one hundred dollar airtime cards."

The cashier looked around her area suspiciously and grabbed the two cards. When she was sure the coast was clear she scanned everything but the cigarettes and placed everything in the bag. "Here you go."

"You ain't ring everything up." He didn't want no problems on his way out the door. And where was the girl with the fat ass?

"Shhhhh." She placed her finger against her lips. Whispering she said, "That's from me to you. You do take gifts don't you?"

Bricks hit the jackpot. Not only did a girl hit on him on his way into the store, but the cashier also wanted to give him the business. He had been so caught up in Yvonna's shenanigans, that he forgot that he was one fine ass nigga. Where he came from, bitches fell over him and vied for his attention by the loads, and now he was having to compete with a dude with one eye and seven fingers.

He accepted her gift and said, "Thanks, I appreciate it."

"Anytime." She waved, going back to work.

When he turned around, Miss Big Booty was looking directly at him. What's your name, cutie?" He asked.

"Grey."

"Grey?" He simpered. "Well I can appreciate a unique name."

"If you really appreciate it, you'll join me for dinner, that is if you're not in a rush."

Thirty minutes later, they were at Mama's Kitchen, a soul food restaurant, enjoying each other's company. Bricks ordered country fried steak with rice while she picked over a Caesar salad with grilled chicken. Her conversation wasn't spectacular, but their temporary union wasn't about having an explosive connection. It was about feeling appreciated at the moment, and separating himself from the cloud of pedophiles and molested children that hovered over him. He was sure that after he fucked her, they would never see each other again, and that was fine with him.

"You are so handsome." She admitted. "And I normally don't tell guys how they look, but I have to tell you."

He raised one eyebrow. "Why don't you tell them how you feel?" he chewed a piece of bread. "Nothing is wrong with a woman telling a man what she wants."

"I know, but I find that most of them already know."

He laughed. "Well you should always say what you feel," Bricks advised, "even if it's a compliment."

"True," she agreed, placing her fork down. "I do believe that it's important, to tell a person what you're feeling. So let me start and then you continue. What I find interesting about you is that you don't even know what you're doing." Her facial expression suddenly changed and almost made her look like a different person.

Intrigued, Bricks placed his fork down and said, "Why would you say that?"

"Because you're walking right into fire." She grabbed the napkin off the table and wiped her mouth. "And because I like you, I'd like to offer you a little advice. That might save your life."

"Shoot." He responded.

"Hopefully I won't have too."

The hairs on the back of his neck stood up. "What the fuck is that supposed to mean?"

"Why do you help her?" She stabbed a piece of chicken with her fork and stuffed it into her mouth. "The girl with the multiple minds?" she chewed with her mouth full. "Don't you know that just by being with her, she'll have you killed?"

Bricks reached under the table and felt comfort knowing that his gun was in place. "Who are you?"

"Someone who needs to finish off Yvonna. Someone who has been waiting for the perfect time to kill her." She giggled which seemed to be out of place considering the topic. "I have been following Yvonna Harris for a minute and you know what, I can never seem to get my hands on her. Do you know why?"

He remained silent.

"Because of you. You always seem to be in the way, as well as the others." She placed her fork down. "Now I have the next best thing, you. I don't want you, I want her, so the question becomes what shall we do?"

Bricks looked around him to see if he killed her, how many people could identify his face. "So what was all that shit about in the store?"

"I still think you're cute, and so I'm giving you a chance to walk away. All we want is her, Bricks. You don't need to get caught up in all this shit." She reached over and softly touched his hand. "Tell me where she is, and I'll let you walk away alive."

GABRIELLA

S woopes was lying on the sofa alone, drinking the last of the Hennessey. And Ming had already gone to bed, after things didn't go her way, which was fine with him. She wanted to be alone with Swoopes and he wanted to be alone with himself, to think things through. Although he didn't say it, it fucked him up that he had to kill two of his closest friends. Swoopes was not the same since he went on a mission to kill Yvonna. Suddenly he was realizing that what he thought was important wasn't and he questioned the man he had grown into. He was bitter, hateful and abused a lot of people, in a pursuit to get over in life. Now it felt like it was all for nothing.

"What are you doing?" Gabriella said, sitting next to him on the sofa. "You look like you lost your two best friends."

He took one look at her, threw his head back into the cushion and closed his eyes. "If you think that's funny," he responded, referring to the members of the YBM, "it's not. Don't make me go off on you."

"Cut the tough guy routine. There's no need to be so up-tight. Learn to love life, like I do." She cooed placing her hand softly on his leg.

He sighed and shook his head. At the moment, everybody and everything was irritating him. "What do you want, Yvonna?"

"Company." She advised inching closer to him. "Where's Ming?" She looked around for her. "I'd think she'd be stuffed up under your ball sack."

"Somewhere wit' an attitude."

"So what are you doing all alone?" Her hand inched closer to his dick. "Because you know you don't have to be."

He looked at her hand, which seemed out of place on his body and closed his eyes again. "I'm thinking. And what are you doing, trying to set me up? Playing games? Whatever you're doing I don't feel like being bothered with."

"I'll give you a penny for your thoughts."

He sighed. "You gonna need more than that to hear half the shit in my head."

"Awww, now you've made me sad." She responded in a child-like voice.

Two quick laughs escaped his lips. "And why is that?

"Because I was hoping you'd say you were thinking about me."

Swoopes lifted his head off the cushion and looked at her. Immediately Gabriella began to get aroused. "What's up wit' you, Yvonna? Why you looking at me like that? When your man was here, you acted like you didn't have two words to say to me. Now you can't stop touching me? I disgust you remember?"

"I never said that."

"You were thinking it."

"Why are you asking so many questions, Swoopes? I know you want me. I can see it in your eye. So let's stop playing games because we don't have a lot of time. He may be back soon."

Swoopes hopped off of the sofa. He looked at the front door for Bricks and towards the back for Ming. If either of them came out and saw what she was trying to do, it could be problems for the crew. "Yvonna, I know you had a few glasses, but I'm not 'bout to go there wit' you tonight. It ain't even like that between us. You know that."

Gabriella stood up and moved toward him, as if it was dinnertime and he was on the menu. "Don't tell me I'm about to give you the pussy and you gonna turn it down." She kissed him softly on the neck. "This is the kind of offer that won't come around every lifetime. You better get it while its good."

"I hear you, but you not listening to me. Like I said, it ain't like that between us." For the first time in his life, Swoopes allowed another person to back him into a corner. "So I need you to step off wit' that shit."

"Stop fucking around with me, Swoopes." Gabriella grabbed his dick and ran her tongue along the side of his neck. "You been wanting this pussy for the longest. I can tell by the way you've been looking at me. Now what you want to do?"

Swoopes wanted her so badly it was tough to deny. Part of him desired to see what was so special about her pussy that caused two of his men, Bilal and Crazy Dave, to fall. The other part of him, the part that was just as crazy as she was, wanted to fuck her into submission. Wanted to see how their bodies gelled together, legitimately this time and not by force.

"Look, I don't know what this is about, but I'm not feeling this shit right now. Maybe if you came at me when you weren't drinking, I might've taken you up on your offer and my dick would've been in your mouth ten minutes ago. For now I'ma have to say we gotta take a rain check."

"A rain check?" She repeated, not believing his reason. "Did you actually just say that you wanted a rain check on this pussy?" She placed her hand between her legs.

"Come on, man."

"Take me up on my offer now, Swoopes. Not later. I'm saying I'm trying to fuck you and all you can say is if I wasn't drunk you'd be down?" She massaged his dick to a stiffness. When he was as hard as he was going to get, she dropped to her knees, released his dick and placed him into her warm mouth. "Hmmm, you taste so good."

"Oh my, God!" He looked down at her. The way her head bobbed and her tongue rolled was beautiful. If he could take a picture and refer to this moment as many times as he could, he could beat his dick for the next six months and be fine. "What the fuck are you doing to me?" He looked around to be sure no one was coming. If Bricks came back he would have to kill him if he saw this, he was sure of it. "What if your nigga comes in? You know this shit wrong."

With a wet mouth Gabriella looked up at him and said, "You thinking about shit you shouldn't be." She stuck her pink tongue out and eased it on the tip, eying him the entire time. "Let me worry about Bricks. You just enjoy yourself." When she said enough, she went back to work.

Fuck it! If she wanted to take care of business, why was he going to stop her? He wasted enough time begging with her to leave him alone as is. Had he went with the flow, he could've came by now. Swoopes looked down at her and couldn't wait to shoot his load into her mouth. "Keep it like that, bitch." He grabbed two fistfuls of her hair in the pursuit of her throat. When he found it, his head dropped back against the wall and he enjoyed the performance. "Damn that shit feels so good."

"I'm glad you like it." She managed to say as she looked up at him.

"I do," But when he looked at her this time, something came over him. He tried to close his eyes and not think about what he was doing, but the nagging feeling wouldn't go away. He felt no better than the men who took advantage of her, when she was a kid, and he didn't want to contribute to that type of lifestyle anymore. If she wanted to get it in when she was sober, he was game. But until that moment came, their little rendezvous would have to wait.

Reaching down, he helped her to her feet. "I can't do this shit." He zipped his pants. "Not like this anyway."

"Fuck you mean?" She wiped her mouth with the back of her hand. "What...you didn't like it or something? I can do it better."

"I'm saying I can't do it like this. If you want to see me, make it another time. When you ain't have so much to drink. Until then, I'll get up with you later."

YVONNA

Yvonna woke up in the bed, with Bricks not next to her. She knew they had an argument but they argued all the time and always managed to move past the dumb shit. When she sat up, the headache she developed from drinking like a sailor kicked her hard. For a second she lay back down, to let the pain subside as she wondered where he could be. Although she didn't remember going anywhere after Bricks left her in the bedroom, she felt like she only had an hour sleep. And there was blood on the edge of the shirt she was wearing. Had she hurt herself?

Twenty minutes later, she finally decided to check on Delilah. She realized it was insensitive to make her go another night without her, since she'd been without her for so long, but the past few days were wearing on her and caused her to be a little selfish last night. Guilt plagued her when she considered the reason she didn't spend time with her, was because she was drunk. She hoped that her irresponsibility was not a sign, that she wasn't fit to be a mother. Delilah was the one person who made her feel that maybe she was actually sane.

On her way out the bedroom she heard a voice say, "You killed Tree last night. You took Bradshaw's cell out of his bedroom and found his address. I'm not saying you're wrong, but I wanted you to know."

"Who is that?" She looked around the room. "Where are you?"

"I have to talk to you, Yvonna." This time when the voice spoke, it caused her entire body to tingle. She hadn't heard it in awhile, but that didn't mean she could forget it. Slowly she turned around and when she did, her first love, Bilal, was standing before her. But instead of excitement, she knew his presence meant death.

He was wearing the same thing he had on the night he asked her to be his wife, and the night she took his life. "You're not here, Bilal. You can't be. I killed you."

He grinned and walked over to her. She saw the tattoo on his arm that read *'LalVon'*. It was short for Bi*lal* and Y*von*na. The words were inside a coffin and it represented his motto that it would be he and she until death.

He grinned and ran his hand over his smooth black goatee. Since he was Hispanic and African American, it lay smoothly against his skin. "You did kill me, baby. But that's not why I'm here to see you. Miss me?"

Her heart told her he wasn't there, but that didn't stop her from melting. "I do miss you, but…what's going on?"

His hazel brown eyes twinkled. "I'm here for two reasons. For starters, I need you to do me a favor that only you can do. And secondly, I don't want you to be scared, but I'm here for you."

"What you mean you're here for me?" She backed herself into the wall but he followed.

"Yvonna, you already know what I'm saying." She shook her head in defiance. "You've gotten away with a lot. You killed some people you may have thought needed to die, and a bunch of others along the way." He pointed at Tree's blood on her shirt. "You don't get to live a life like that, without having to pay the piper." He placed his hands on her shoulders. "It's over, Yvonna. You had a good run."

She walked away and sat on the bed. For the first time in her life, she hoped she really was crazy. She closed her eyes and reopened them, but he was still there. "I know what this is," She smirked, rocking back and forth. "I'm seeing you because I took your life. Just like I've seen some of the other people I killed. It's all a part of my illness."

He sat next to her. "You're about to die, and before you do, I'm going to give you an opportunity to right some wrongs."

"I don't want to talk to you." She turned to face the door. Why did her life have to be like this? Why did she have to see people who others claimed they couldn't? The people that came to her in life were so real, that sometimes she'd think others were lying just to fuck with her mind. "Leave me alone, Bilal. Please. I'm dealing with a lot right now. I don't think I can handle all of this."

"I can't leave you alone, Yvonna. Not this time. But I wish I could."

Yvonna got up and walked out without hearing anything else he had to say. She was sure seeing her daughter was guaranteed to make her feel better. She knocked on the door twice and when she didn't get an answer, walked into the room. Surprisingly Delilah was up already and sitting on the floor, with three pink *Hello Kitty* suitcases next to her.

"Good morning, baby." Yvonna said, cheerfully. "What's this all about?" She pointed to the luggage on the floor. "Going somewhere without me?"

When she approached, Delilah jumped on the bed and sat with her legs folded closely to her chest. "Please don't hit me. I wasn't doing nothing. Please."

Yvonna backed up and tilted her head. "Hit you?" She frowned. "Why...why would I do that?"

"I don't know, but I want to go see my aunt Jesse, okay?"

"Sure." She nodded. "We can do it when everything settles down. But I can't take time out to drop you off now, there's too much going on. But if I'm going to take you anywhere, can you tell me what's wrong first?"

"I don't want to talk about it. I just wanna stay at my aunt Jesse's." When she started crying, Yvonna was startled. Her daughter was acting like she was scared of her, when she didn't have a reason to be. "Please...take me to see her, mommy. That's all I want. Okay?"

Yvonna sat on the bed and Delilah jumped off. She was doing a good job of keeping her distance and Yvonna was trying to figure out why. Just yesterday she couldn't keep her

little arms from being wrapped around her and now she acted as if she was contagious. "Delilah, come here, baby" she extended her hand and wiggled her fingers. "Please." She shook her head no. "Why, baby? Did I miss something?"

"No!" she yelled. "I just don't want to be here. I want to be with my aunt."

Yvonna took a moment to look at how frightened she was and it dawned on her. She heard all of the commotion in the living room last night and was nervous. She reasoned that Bradshaw probably did a good job of keeping her away from drama, so she wasn't use to being in fear. Yvonna knew she couldn't keep her with them while they fulfilled their mission, she just hoped they'd have a few more days together, before they parted ways again. Her living with Jesse was always in the plan, but not now.

"Baby, if you're worried about the things you heard yesterday, you don't have to be. I'll make sure you're safe while we sort things out, Delilah. You don't have to worry about anything. I will never put you in harms way."

"I want to live with my aunt Jesse!" She screamed, crying harder. "Please!"

The look in her eyes was filled with fear and pain, and Yvonna held her chest because she found it difficult to breathe. She reminded her of how Jesse looked at her, on the night Bilal was murdered. "Delilah, please stop crying. I'll do anything you want but I have to know." She felt the inside of her nose burn and knew she was on the verge of sobbing. She didn't want Delilah to see her in such a desperate way, but it appeared she might not have a choice. "I just have to know baby, if I let you go, will you ever want to live with me again?"

It seemed like she waited forever, for her to respond. "I just want to be with my aunt Jesse." She continued. "Please, mommy, take me to her house."

"Okay, baby, there's no need to," she felt tears coming so she made an exit and closed the door before she could finish her statement. There was no way she could hold back. She couldn't face her. After speaking to Jesse on the phone and getting over the chivalries, she explained that her niece would be coming to stay for an indefinite time and as always, she was happy to oblige. Now alone in the bathroom, she wailed harder. She didn't understand. If that little girl didn't want her, than there was no need to be anything other than pure evil.

"Do you realize that ever since I've known you, I've never seen you cry?" Bilal asked, sitting on the edge of the tub. "I must say, I love the vulnerable side of you."

The last thing she needed was to be bothered with him. She wiped her tears and said, "Bilal, please go away. I want to be left alone."

"I told you already that I can't do that. I'm here to take you with me. And, I also need you to do me a favor."

"Well since I already know that you believe you're here to lead me to death…"

"I'm here to lead you to hell."

An icy feeling ran over her. "Well, since you believe you are hear to take me to...to...," for some reason she couldn't say the word, "take me away, what is the favor?"

"I need you to check on my son. And you know you feel guilty for how you treated him, which is why you're here talking to yourself about it."

"You don't know what you're saying."

"I do," he laughed, "now that you have a daughter, you know how it feels to want the best for a child. So you can't help but remember what you did to him. And he's all alone and it's all your fault."

"First off what son are you talking about?" Yvonna stood up to turn the faucet on. She ran her fingers under the cold water and splashed it against her face. "You have three kids remember? Well, three that I know about. You were always good at sticking your dick into any and everything."

He didn't seem phased by her comment. "I'm talking about Bilal, Jr. The one you owe. You knew which one I was talking about."

"I don't owe anybody anything, Bilal. I'm not his mother. Sabrina was." She turned the water off and looked at herself in the mirror. She couldn't remember the last time she looked so rough. "Now either kill me or let me be."

"Not only do you owe him, you owe him big time."

"Why is that, Bilal?" She turned to look at him. "You slept with my best friend and had a child by her. I don't owe that kid shit but to leave him alone and let him live. Since you know so much, you also know I wanted to kill him to get back at you. So consider it a favor that he's still alive."

"You can't be serious."

"Dead serious. I wanted to put a bullet in his head. Which was my original plan. But everybody who would've cared is gone and unable to be hurt by his death."

"You still don't get it."

"Get what?"

"That the reason you are even having this conversation with yourself, because you *are* talking to yourself, is because you feel guilty about what you did to him. You realize that he didn't do anything but breathe on the day you chose to hate him. You despised him from the start and took everything and everybody away who loved him. His mother, me, and even my mother, Bernice. At least the twins had the love of Treyana and Avante until they got older. He didn't even have that." He stood up. "The bottom line is, you are about to die, and you have a chance to make a few things right. You need to check on him, to make sure he's okay. Do it for me, or do it for yourself."

"You sound like a fool!" She placed her hands over her ears. She didn't want to hear any more of his lies. Because she was getting sicker by the day, she wasn't realizing that

Bilal was in her mind. Holding her ears would not make him go away. She was falling further into insanity.

Bang! Bang! Bang!

Three hard raps on the door startled her.

"Yvonna, what are you doing in there?" Bricks asked from the outside of the door. "And who are you talking to?"

She turned around to look at Bilal but he was gone. She hoped Bricks didn't hear him. She certainly didn't want him to think she was cheating. "Nobody...uh...where were you last night?" She spoke to the door. "How about you start by answering some questions for me."

"Yvonna, I don't know what you're talking about, but I need you to come out here. We havin' a meeting."

"Give me a few minutes. I'm washing my hands."

After she got herself together, she walked out and into the living room. Ming was sitting on the sofa next to Swoopes and Bricks was standing up. For whatever reason, Swoopes seemed to avoid eye contact with her.

"We have to get moving." Bricks started, taking the papers from the box they confiscated from Ron Max's house. "I don't know how much safer it will be for us to stay here."

"Where were you last night, Bricks? And why didn't you come back here?" She paused long enough to allow him to respond with a short answer. When he didn't she continued, "Were you out cheating on me? If you want to do you, why worry about coming back?" Swoopes burst into laughter. "Fuck is so funny, nigga?" Yvonna questioned him.

"Are you serious?" He asked looking at her.

Not knowing she tried to suck his dick less than twenty-four hours ago, she placed her hands on her hips. "You see me laughing?"

He looked strangely at her again. "You know what, ain't nothing funny. Go 'head, man. Finish with what you were saying."

"Naw...let's not go 'head." Yvonna interjected. "I want to know where the fuck he's been all night. Where he's just seeing it fit to bring his dirty dick ass back in the house."

"Yvonna, ain't nobody got time for that shit." Swoopes said, for the first time coming to Bricks' defense, shocking everyone in the room. "He about to discuss business and you going at him on some other shit. Cheating is not what the meeting is about."

"I got it, Swoopes." Bricks said raising his hand and giving him a nod. "First off, I been in the house all night. You would've known, if you hadn't been out all night yourself, only to spend the rest of the time in the bathroom, doing God knows what."

She knew she supposedly killed Tree, but she was clueless on everything else. "What you talking about?"

Ming, Swoopes and Bricks all laughed. "We heard you fucking yourself in the bathroom, Yvonna." Swoopes continued. "You didn't come out until about an hour ago and then you took a nap. We been up all night going over the plans. When we heard you talking just now, we decided to invite you to the party. You're late, so let's get down to business."

"That's not true." She shook her head and stepped back. She eyed all of them in confusion. "I didn't leave the bedroom after you walked out on me. Remember, we had an argument about Swoopes." She was trying to convince herself she wasn't that far gone "You see I know what I'm talking about."

"Why the fuck were ya'll arguing about me?" Swoopes interrupted.

"It wasn't even like that, man." Bricks said before focusing back on Yvonna. "Squeeze, you were in the bathroom, for hours." He tried to approach her but she backed away. She was starting to favor a mad woman. "I wouldn't fuck around with you like that. We been up for most of the night going over the plan." He pointed at Ming. "Ask your girl."

Yvonna looked at Ming. "You were in there all night, Yvonna." She said softly. "Ming thought something was wrong at first. But when I knocked on the door, you told Ming to get the fuck away as usual."

Yvonna knew what was happening, they all were banning against her. Trying to make her think she didn't know what really happened when she did. Of course she was diagnosed with this or that in the past, but since she stopped taking her medicine, she had a clearer head. And she wasn't going to allow them to bring her down, just because they needed somebody to pick on.

Taking a few more deep breaths, she folded her arms and walked closer to the group. It was important to appear as lucid as possible. "Go ahead, Bricks," She pointed at the papers, "Finish with the plan. I'm listening."

Bricks looked at her and then the crew. Not wanting to argue anymore he started. "Cool, we've already worked out our next move. But I think I ran into one of the Four Captains' crony last night and we have a bigger problem on our hands than I originally thought."

"Why?"

"Because they watching us. I had to knock her out just to get away from her. And if we don't be careful, they going to start plucking us off before we can get to them. Starting with you."

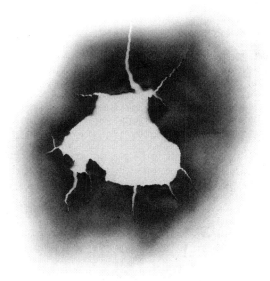

CHRIS

Yvonna eyed the pool in the backyard, as a little girl wearing a yellow coat, led them to the house through the rear. She was no more than ten and reminded her immediately of Delilah. In the back was a huge shed and she wondered what her friend Chris, who they were meeting, kept inside of it. Yvonna remembered being at his house before, when she first met him. Well actually, she recalled waking up on the ground, after almost dying in the pool due to a night filled with drinking. She was as reckless back then, as she is now, when it came to taking her medication.

Chris, who she came into contact with after needing a powder called Lidocaine, that could be used to make fake cocaine, was as hospitable to her now as he was back then. The young Matt Damon look alike, could not take his eyes off of the curves of her black body and what he considered the wildness behind her eyes. He was still a fan.

Chris' white skin looked bleached, as he opened the sliding glass door. He was wearing nothing but a black satin robe and blue satin boxers. His bare chest produced a few brown curly hairs that matched his head, and his piercing blue eyes stared directly into hers. He hoped that he could finish what he wanted to start some years back, with present company excluded.

"Thanks, Amber," he said, and the little girl disappeared into the house. Focusing back on the woman before him he said, "Yvonna Harris," he reached out and grabbed both of her hands. He was high off chronic and didn't bother looking at the people she had with her, particularly her boyfriend Bricks. "You know...I was afraid that after I gave you my card so many years back, that I'd never see you again."

After Bricks treated her like half a freak the night before, she welcomed his compliments, along with the attention. "Well it looks like you thought wrong. Here I am."

He licked his lips, as if she had just invited him to bed. "I am glad about that.' He eyed her breasts and Yvonna had to admit, the white boy could get the pussy if they were brought together under different circumstances. "So my beautiful," he kissed the top of her hand. "What brings you this way?"

When Bricks saw his blue boxers rise in the front, forming a tent, he interjected. "She's here for business." Bricks stepped between them.

"Nothing more and nothing less." Swoopes added.

Chris cleared his throat and said, "Of course," he stepped back and allowed the clan into his home, which was decorated expensively with cream and burgundy colors. "Come inside." He led them to the dining room. Ming, Swoopes and Yvonna took a seat at the cherry wood table and Bricks elected to remain standing. "You want to introduce your friends to me?" He sat next to Yvonna and looked around the table at the rest. He was suddenly nervous. And with Bricks standing over him like Tyson in a winning round, he had every reason to be. "I didn't know you were bringing people with you. I would've..."

"Gotten dressed?" Bricks finished.

"No."

"So what, you thought you was gonna get a little brown sugar? Is that why you naked?" Bricks barked. "You trying to fuck my girl, white boy?"

"No," he shook his head in a mousy fashion, "I mean yes." Bricks tightened the space between he and him. "I mean no." The scared host ran to the sink, grabbed a glass cup in the cabinet directly above it and turned the cold water on. When he placed it under the faucet, his hand was shaking so much he was barely able to fill it. When he captured enough, he placed it to his mouth and swallowed all he could, although most of the H2O ended up on the floor. He was messy and the crew looked at him in confusion. You would've thought that Bricks broke his jaw. Seeing how scared he was, Swoopes decided to ease the tension. Besides, they hadn't gotten what they came for yet.

"You need to relax, homie." Swoopes said to Chris. "That man ain't about to kill you."

Placing the cup in the sink he responded, "I know, I know. I'm just not use to having so many people in my home." He walked back to the table. "Can I get you and your friends something to drink?"

"No thanks, Chris." Yvonna decided to get right to the point before Bricks killed the man. "When I called you earlier, I asked if you still had access."

"I know," he sat down next to her until Bricks grunted. Then he jumped up and stood across the kitchen next to the sink. "But you never said what you needed access to."

"Explosives."

"Oh...well...uh," he scratched his head. "I can pretty much get you anything you need. You know that. Some of the stuff I have here."

"And now you know exactly what I need. Can you help us or not?" Yvonna said.

"Give me a second," he stole one last look at everyone before disappearing downstairs.

"You sure you can trust this white boy?" Swoopes inquired. "If he shakes anymore behind my back, I'ma drop his ass. He making me nervous."

"Please don't, Swoopes. He's not the enemy."

"Well how come he act like he ain't never done business with niggas before?"

"I don't know." She looked at Bricks. "Maybe somebody got him all confused."

"Don't blame me. These your people not mine."

"But you don't have to scare him either. He's on our side, remember?"

"Trust no one." Ming said, sitting on Swoopes' lap. They were getting cozier. "Fuck what you heard." Everybody looked at her sideways. Ming was always good for a surprise phrase every now and again.

When Chris returned, he had a large brown box in his hands. He carefully sat it on the table and took a deep breath. Since they had a pretty good idea that he had explosives in the box, everybody stepped back and hung against the walls of the kitchen. Alone at the table, he reached into it, and grabbed a block of what looked like white rubber.

"This is the best of the best, my friends. The king of explosives. The almighty." He held it up in his hands, as if everybody couldn't see it from where they cowered. "You can't get better than this I assure you."

"What is it?" Swoopes asked, wanting to keep the seven good fingers and one eye he had left. "And make sure you careful with that shit." He had visions of a soldier's death, but not like this.

"It's C4." He placed it methodically on the table before reaching into the box again. When his hand came back out, it was clasping a gold tube connected to a wire. "This is a blasting cap. Separate they aren't a problem, together they mean war." He stuck one into the C4 and everybody except Yvonna hit the floor.

"Fuck is you doing, slim? Bricks asked. "You trying to get us killed?"

"It's no fun when the white boy got the gun." He laughed, tagging him back for the fear he caused him earlier. "Now who's scared?"

"I'm not playing! Don't blow nothing up in here. You a little too comfortable with that shit if you ask me."

He continued to laugh until Bricks released his weapon from the hold it was in, cocked and aimed. "Seems like you have a problem with jokes. I can cure that for you if you want."

Chris separated the tube from the C4 and everybody relaxed. "Not that serious." He placed it on the table. "Just wanted to show you what we're dealing with." He took a piece of the C4 off of the edge of one of the blocks and flattened it." C4 can be molded so you can literally place it anywhere you want, like clay. But you need a detonator to blow shit up. Which is what I showed you before everybody hit the floor."

Silence.

"Can't we shoot the C4 and have it go off?" Ming asked. "Instead of the blasting caps."

"Why would you ask some dumb shit like that?" Bricks inquired. "You can blow your face off if you want to but I need mine."

"It wouldn't work anyway." Chris interrupted. "You can drop C4 and even put fire to it, but it will not explode by itself. However, the moment you introduce shock or friction, you have trouble."

"That don't make no sense." Swoopes disagreed as if he were an expert. "What has a harder impact than a bullet?"

"It needs electricity not fire."

"Yeah, whatever."

"It's true. That's another reason its good for transport because of its stabilizing elements. As a matter of fact, soldiers in the military sometimes use C4 to cook with. If you have enough, you can build a fire strong enough to prepare a meal."

"We not trying to cook a meal." Bricks said. "We trying to blow mothafuckas up."

Chris cleared his throat. "I didn't think so." He picked up the C4 and the blasting caps. "Put these together and it'll take care of any problem you have. Trust me."

"So where do we go from here?" Bricks asked, wanting to get down to business.

"There's the matter of the payment and after that, you can go wherever you please. Just leave me out of it."

THE EIGHT SECRETARIES OF TOLERANCE

A blast of sunshine surrounded the Walter E Washington Convention Center. Although it was winter, the large windows surrounding the facility, made it feel as if it were a great spring day on the inside. The center was swarming with sinners wearing their high hats, cheap perfume and holding their tattered checkbooks. Today was the best day of the year to some because AFCOG was holding its annual *'Give God Your All And He'll Do More'* convention. As always, the most celebrated evangelists of AFCOG, and some would say the Christian community as a whole, were present. This was not an event to be missed, although if the members knew their true intention, most would have.

Marge and her daughter Tyisha stepped off one of the twenty-five buses in the parking lot. She was hoping that the more services Tyisha went to, the higher the chances were that she'd rid herself of the lying lips she picked up without her notice. Although they had an agenda, they weren't alone. Other bible toter's wanted to get a glimpse of God's Eight, or The Eight Secretaries of Tolerance, as known by the secret society running AFCOG.

While chaos ensued in the convention, the Eight met in one of the smaller rooms to hold their meeting. In a red pencil skirt with a matching blazer, Dana Kellogg stood at the head of the table. The other seven remained seated; all hoping the day would be profitable and end without an issue.

Reading to begin the meeting, Dana directed her long black hair out of her face by a graceful swing of her neck. "I've spoken to Rufus a little under an hour ago. And he wants me to say that even with the death of Ron Max, he wants us to remain focused."

"It's easy for him to say," Elizabeth Hay responded, who along with Dana, also reported to Ron before his demise. "He isn't the one who has to wonder when or if this bitch will strike again." Like Dana, Elizabeth's brown skin was painted expertly with just enough makeup. "I'm tired of having to look over my shoulders every five minutes for this woman."

"Well don't look over them!" Charles Blaine responded. "And I would also like to add, that although you can demonstrate your heathen abilities outside of this convention, while handling any AFCOG duties, I request that you keep your potty mouth to a minimum." Charles, a black man in his mid forties, was just as scared of the legend known as Yvonna, but he refused to let them know. Besides, his leader Anna Livingston assured him and his peer Heather Randolph that they didn't have a thing to worry about. "We just have to remain focused and get the job done."

"I really don't think we have any other choice." Dana added.

"What else is Rufus saying about the matter?"

"He didn't say much about the matter after that."

"But I bet he said something about the money." Heather Randolph added. Heather was a drunk who didn't care. Most times she didn't bother anybody, but when her life was in danger, she could be quite the headache. "I know for a fact he had something to say about that. Didn't he?"

Dana placed her hands on her hips. "He did, but you shouldn't have a problem with it."

"Why not?"

"Because you getting paid just like everybody else in this room." She looked at the coffee cup in her hand. "How else are you gonna get the cheap shit you push down your throat every morning?"

Heather rolled her brown eyes and tried to minimize the embarrassment she felt on her face. "Whatever." She continued as she sipped her vodka, which was sprinkled with a little coffee. "I just want this shit over with."

"Like I was saying, Rufus has given me his hopes for the financial goal for the day. He suggests that whenever an opportunity presents, that we promote the special edition AFCOG bibles which are embroidered with his signature, the classes and future conventions. He said if we do these things, we should net at least a little over a million today. Couple that money with the girls we have on the streets, I say it is looking pretty good for us all." She placed her notes down. "I don't have to tell you how grateful he would be to us, if we are able to achieve this goal."

"And how will he show you his gratitude?" Elizabeth Hay, said, "By letting you suck his dick?"

The other ministers gasped and Dana's eyes attempted to snatch the breath from her body. "Now, now, Elizabeth," Dana picked up, "I would never think about coming in the way of his dick, because we all know you have that covered! *If* you could see it fit to keep your pussy shaved and wash up more often, I'm sure he'd choose you more."

"Stop it!" Hillary Webster yelled, as she jumped up from the table. "I hate these fucking events!" Everybody looked at her as they tried to figure out where she was going. "I don't think there's a person in here, who hates them more than me." She rolled the diamond bangles back up her arms and took a seat. Her light skin, loaded with freckles was dry and she looked older than thirty-two. The business of defrauding innocent people and selling children was not kind to her. "And just like you all, me and Patricia are also frightened." She looked at Patricia Parker who held her head down. She was twenty-five and caught up in something she never wanted to be involved in, the sex trafficking industry. "Our captain Ramona Cass assured us just like the others that we are safe, but we aren't stupid enough to believe that. However we don't have a choice. All we can do now is stop fighting each other and get this day over with. I just want to go home."

"You are too weak." Toni Upshur, who reported to Abel Pickling interjected. Unlike the other captains, Abel told her and her other direct report Susan Madison to be afraid. As a matter of fact, she suggested they be very afraid, to keep them on their toes. "We knew what we were doing when we signed up for this business. Judging by the diamonds in your ears and bangles on your arms, I don't think you are going without or suffering either."

Out of the blue Elizabeth said, "Why don't you stop lying to the team and tell them what Rufus said to you on the phone the other night, Dana."

Dana eyed her suspiciously. "What are you talking about?"

"I think you already know, darling." She focused on the rest of the team. "Basically he told her he'll make sure she has security around the clock and that the rest of us need to step up and provide security for ourselves if we want to survive. He said he didn't want anything to happen to his precious Dana, seeing as though she still has that baby face he loves so much."

In Dana's book, that was the final straw. Both pimps, who were moonlighting as reverends, lunged toward each other in an effort to pull out the other's throat. That was until Charles Blaine separated them both, by gripping a fistful of their hair from the back.

Yanking hard he said, "You know, I really am getting tired of this shit." He looked at their faces and maintained his hold, since it was obvious they weren't ready to be released. "Why must you two do this every time we come together? We're about money in this room! If you want it to be about anything else, handle it in the parking lot." He released them, forcing them forward. "Now let's get the fuck out there, preach the gospel and do what we came to do. We have that big shipment to handle later, don't forget." When they appeared to be moving for each other again, he asked, "Which one of you sluts do I have to hurt, to make myself clearer?"

Silence.

"Then let's get this money."

After the scuffle, Dana and Elizabeth straightened their clothing and put themselves mentally in the frame of mind to inspire. Although the rest hadn't been in a fight, they did the same mental exercises. The name of the game, manipulation. Their business? Selling hope. When they walked into the ballroom holding the main event, they took their place in one of the seven chairs on the stage, while their peer took the stand.

Susan Madison, who was born in Abel Pickling's breeding house, walked up to the mic first. It was her first major seminar, after being brainwashed in the AFCOG way for many years. Finally after she gave up all of her worldly possessions and moved onto Rufus Day's compound, he knew she was ready for the next level. That included seducing the innocent. Besides, her honest face and childlike voice, captivated worshippers and made them believers.

Camera flashes took up the first few moments before her speech begin. She looked back at the Secretaries and smiled. "You can do it, Susan." Dana encouraged. "We believe in you."

She turned back around and wrapped her small hand around the mic stand. She was about to speak into the mic, until she noticed it was too low for her five seven-inch height. She adjusted it accordingly and said, "Thank you for coming to AFCOG's fourth annual *'Give God Your All And He'll Do More'*, seminar!" her voice bellowed from the podium and sent chills up several members' spines. They needed to believe in something and the shifty organization gave them exactly what the doctor ordered. "Is God in the house today, or is God in the house always?"

"God is in the house always!" The crowd answered.

She smiled because already, she succeeded in winning them over. "Now I don't know about what you came to do but we," she turned to her peers who raised their hands in succession, "came to praise his name!"

She turned back around and faced the crowd with more confidence than ever. But when she looked upon the audience, she saw several wet faces and the guilt gut punched her. Deceiving people was not in her blood but she had a duty. This was wrong but what could she do? She shook her head and held onto the mic, unable to speak. The others immediately got nervous but Dana reacted and approached her.

Covering the mic with her hand she asked, "Can you handle this?"

Susan looked up at her and smiled. "I have it. Don't worry."

Dana patted her softly on the back and walked away. Looking at the crowd she took a deep breath and slowly parted her lips. "Good morning, worshippers. If you don't know me already, let me introduce myself. I am Susan Madison, one of the Eight Ministers for AFCOG." The applause erupted throughout the auditorium. "I am very pleased to be a part of your experience today. Before we separate for your seminars, I'd like to introduce Minster Toni Upshur."

Toni Upshur was just as beautiful as the other six female ministers. Her natural long hair hung down her back and swaggered with each step. Her hand accepted the mic from her peer and for a second she just stared at the crowd. She would show Susan how it was supposed to be done. The applause rose to the ceilings and simmered away like fog and she loved every bit of it. With one wave, she controlled the room and the only sound now was a few quick coughs.

She moved her red painted lips toward the mic and said, "I see thousands." Slowly she backed away from the mic as if they were dancing. Stepping closer, she observed the audience. "Thousands of believers who came to honor him." She continued, releasing the mic from its hold. "And I honor each and every one of you today. It's not easy to stand up for God. It's not easy being criticized just for being different. It's not easy giving fifty percent of your salaries to AFCOG, when your families mock and attempt to destroy you in the process. But you don't care." She pointed her red fingernail at them and walked to the other end of the stage. "You know why?" She paused only to build momentum. "Because you have bought your way into heaven and there you will be received." The roar of the audience lit up the auditorium yet again.

Once the audience grew silent, something different threatened to demolish the mood. "You a dead bitch talking!" Someone yelled toward the back. "A dead bitch talking!"

The angry mob turned to see who had spoken so harshly to someone they admired and adored. However the moment they bent their necks, the heckler was gone.

Toni was visibly shaken and she tried to pull it together. She looked at her peers and the looks on their faces didn't make her feel any better. They were stricken with just as much fear as she was. They knew who it was, without ever seeing her face.

With her hand on the mic, she smiled although her cheeks trembled. "Seems like we can't shake the devil even in the house of the Lord."

"Yes we can!" Someone suggested.

"Let's pray for them!" Another offered.

"It's certainly worth a try."

Two Hours Later

Dana and Elizabeth were finishing their seminar, which housed one hundred participants. The title was, *'Establishing Financial Security, In The House Of The Lord'*. Despite the heckler's outburst, which had all of them on edge, they were able to do their jobs. Things were uneventful, until one of their youth helpers walked into the class with an urgent message."

"We're getting ready to close, Fredericka." Elizabeth advised, not wanting her disruption. "We'll be out in a minute."

"I'll only be a second." She approached their desk, hurriedly handing the letter to Elizabeth. "Before I left I wanted to give you this envelope. It's from Rufus Day."

Dana stood up, eyed the envelope and said, "Thanks, Fredericka."

She walked away and Elizabeth moved closer to Dana. "What do you think it is?"

"I don't know. You know we don't have cell service in this building. Maybe he called the office." When she seemed hesitant she said, "Well open it up. See what he wants."

Elizabeth decided to address the participants first. "We hope you all have enjoyed our seminar. If you have any questions, please use our message board and enjoy the rest of your day."

When she finished with the chivalries, she and Dana walked into a corner to read the letter. Slowly Elizabeth took it out the envelope, which drove Dana, crazy because she was taking so long. The black letters on the white card caused her heart to thump.

Yvonna went to the police regarding Elika and Tata. Meet Abel in room 319 to discuss a plan of action.

Dana felt dizzy as she reached for a seat. She didn't make it.

Five Minutes Later

Dana and Elizabeth sprinted into the hallway, to meet with one of the Captains. They would've run faster but their high-heeled shoes slowed them down. On the way to room 319, they ran into Charles, Heather, Hillary, Patricia, Toni and Susan, who all received the same letters.

"Did anybody call Rufus yet?" Elizabeth asked as they approached the door.

"No. I wanted to wait to see what Abel was talking about first." Charles replied. "Plus the cell reception is on the half in this building."

"Well did she talk to either of you?" Dana asked Toni and Susan, her direct reports.

"We know just as much as you do…nothing."

They had to admit, something was off but curiosity was killing them. When they finally made it to room 319, on the empty hall of the center, Dana was the first to open the door, only to find the room completely dark.

"What the fuck is going on here?" Charles asked no one in particular.

The other seven followed them until the door slammed behind them. When they turned around, Ming was holding a gun in their direction. "Now, now, now. That's no way for a man of God to speak." Ming said to Charles. "We gotta do something about that mouth. Don't we?"

With raised eyebrows he asked, "Who are you?"

"Have a seat." Bricks demanded, causing them to face the other way. One light in the room suddenly lit up a section toward the front. Eight seats were lined up side by side, with no occupants. They were placed especially for the self-imposed ministers. When they didn't move quickly enough Bricks said, "Don't make me say it again. Have…a…fucking…seat." Reluctantly they took their seats and when they did, the locks on the doors were chained by Swoopes and Ming.

Yvonna remained silent. She was confused and didn't understand what was going on. Her mind was starting to fail her big time and she was trying her hardest to get it together. When everyone was in position Bricks waited for her command. "Squeeze." He whispered, nudging her with the butt of his gun. "We ready."

Silence.

He placed his hand on her shoulder. "Squeeze, go 'head. Let's get this shit over with."

She looked at him, her clan and then the Eight. Clearing her throat she tried to remember what it was, she needed to say. She decided to start with her name and go from there. "My name is Yvonna Harris." She walked closer to them with her team following behind. The moment she uttered those words, the Eight Secretaries knew their lives were over. "And today we have a problem."

"What are you going to do to us?" Dana asked. "I think you have the wrong impression about who we are."

Yvonna ignored her and a few more spots of silence filled the room. "My name is Yvonna Harris," she repeated, "And I am a victim of the bullshit you have been running for so long. You have ruined my life, my daughter's life and now my friends. I'm here to take revenge. I'm here to take your lives."

"I think you have the wrong people." Dana continued, trying to play hero. "We're with AFCOG, Adults For Children Of God. We would never do anything to hurt kids. We love them too much."

"A little too much if you ask Ming."

"I really think there's been a great mistake." Elizabeth added, doing her part to save their lives. "And if you turn your guns away from us, we can explain."

"There's nothing you can say to me, that I would be interested in hearing at this point." Yvonna advised. "Maybe if you would've stepped up when I was getting fucked in my ass by grown men as a child, I could hear you. But right now you're dead to me. All of you."

"Well I would still like to try." Charles said, with a stupid smile on his face. He was so use to talking his way out of drama, that he was feeling himself. "We are religious people. And like she said, we love children too much to cause them harm."

"You mean you fuck children too much!" Swoopes yelled.

"Wait a minute! We haven't fucked anybody!" Heather yelled, provoking a facial blow by Ming's shoe.

"And when they beg you, and the sick mothafuckas you roll with, to stop, you beat them until they love it." At that moment the team realized that they'd been there for a few moments and he hadn't killed anyone. This was the most self-control he ever had. "When you're finished with their bodies, you take every ounce of respect they have." He looked at the floor. "And when they grow to become men, you wonder why they're holding a gun to your face. But you forgot about one thing."

"And what's that?" Bricks asked, leading him into his moment.

"They forgot that children grow up. And when they do, they remember." His eye scanned over their fancy suits and jewels. "They remember everything."

"Exactly." Yvonna interjected before throwing Toni a phone. "Call your leader."

"What leader? Who are you talking about?" Toni said.

Without waiting, Swoopes shot her in the throat and the phone fell out of her hand.

"And then there were seven." Ming laughed, watching her body slump.

"We not here to play games." Bricks added. "Don't make us repeat ourselves again. Call Rufus."

When nobody else could move, Charles nervously picked the phone up and dialed a number. At first the call wouldn't go through until he powered it off and back on.

"Put it on speaker." Yvonna ordered, when she heard the call connect. "I want to talk to him too."

After three rings, Rufus answered. "What's up?"

"Mr. Day, you're on speaker." He swallowed air. "And we have company."

"Who is it?"

"Hello, Rufus." Yvonna said, giving him his answer. "It's me again. Do you know why I'm here?"

"I don't know, but let's see, to offer yourself up to my cause? Maybe sell a little pussy?" He was sarcastic, and not as scared as he was when she talked to him days earlier. She wondered what he had up his sleeve."

"I doubt it, bitch. I offered enough of myself up to you to last a lifetime." She could feel rage creep over her and she was getting confused again. "And it's because of you and this sick organization, that I could never have a life of my own."

"Am I supposed to care?" Yvonna didn't respond. "Listen here, bitch," he said startling his followers by his foul language. They'd never heard him talk so swiftly, but he knew the gig was up and he didn't want the moment to pass, before telling Yvonna how he really felt. "Before you met me, your mother Jhane left you to die. She chose to get high and she sold you to the highest bidder. That being your stepfather. You weren't bred in AFCOG, because if you were, you'd have more respect for what I'm doing. You're a degenerate. A worthless life and you should've been dead a long time ago. Look at your world. You don't have anybody in your bloodline who cares about you. Do us all a favor and kill yourself."

She felt like she wanted to cry. To hear how he reduced her life made her feel dirty. "And what are you doing with your world?" She managed to ask. "You're no better than me!"

"Oh no, darling, that's where you're wrong. I'm way better than you. I'm in the business to make money." He paused to let his words simmer. "And I could've seen you to one of them foster homes, but instead you were a pleasure to the men who paid for you and even a few women. Had it not been for me, you would not be here and I deserve a little more appreciation."

Bricks wanted to yank him through the phone. Instead he placed his hand softly on her shoulder. "Don't worry about it, Squeeze. That nigga's number is coming up."

"Who is that?" Rufus inquired. "Bricks? Or maybe it's Swoopes or your Chinese friend Ming." He had their full attention with the mentioning of their names. Prior to that moment, they always thought they were sidekicks as far as he was concerned. Now they realized he had their history too.

"What the fuck do you know 'bout me, homie?" Bricks yelled.

"Who are you?"

"Bricks."

He laughed. "For starters I know you have a son. A son that isn't biologically yours. A son from, what I gather, you love very much." He pulled his card and Bricks felt like someone gut punched him. But it was the next statement that had him seeing blue. "You know it's not too late, Bricks. You can always end this crusade and sell the boy to me for a fair price. I have quite a few men who would love to introduce him into the world, the proper way."

"I'm going to kill you for saying that shit!" He yelled walking up to the phone. "You hear me mothafucka? I'm gonna snatch your life wit' my bare fuckin' hands."

Rufus laughed again. "You can't kill what you don't know about, son. But I can." He continued. "I had a feeling you would go there, to the convention, so you're not as smart as you think."

"And you didn't tell us?" Dana asked, who had sucked his dick virtually everyday for the past six months. "I thought you would protect me."

"Don't worry, Dana. In your death you'll be appreciated even more."

She gasped.

"There…in front of you, you have people who work for me, Yvonna. People who to you, may seem ordinary, yet they have given their lives for me. I have that kind of power." The sounds of a few of the secretaries weeping made it hard to hear his voice. "For all you know, one of your friends may be under my employ right now. I mean, can you really say you trust them?" The four of them looked at one another because he succeeded at filling them with suspicion. "Here's my bottom line." He continued. "It will take more than just the eight people you have before you, to stop my flow. You could never stop me, nobody can."

"But...Rufus," Dana sobbed. "These people are going to kill us."

"At least you'll die with honor! And for the cause. For *my* cause."

"So you don't even care about us?" Patricia asked, focusing on the phone. "After everything we've done for you? Everything we've given up."

"Of course I care about you. And I'll tell the other members how you selflessly sacrificed your lives for AFCOG. You'll be remembered as heroes."

"Wow, you don't even have loyalty to your ministers." Bricks smirked. "I guess you truly are a bottom of the barrel type nigga."

He seemed irritated by his comment. "This is a billion dollar business. A BILLION!" He screamed. "There is no way on earth I can allow you or your friends to come in the way of that." His voice was filled with tension. "Now the Eight before you are soldiers. They were my soldiers. And as far as I'm concerned, they died in an act of valor."

"You going to see me soon, Rufus." Yvonna said slyly. "So I'm glad you know what I look like."

"Correct. I know you, but you wouldn't know who I was if I tapped you on the shoulder. I am the almighty, Yvonna Harris. I'm in the business of pussy, kids and dreams. I fulfill all fantasies. And with power like that, I can't lose."

"You going to burn in hell. And I'm going to see to it that you get there."

"Find me first." He taunted.

When the call ended Yvonna stepped back and watched Bricks, Ming and Swoopes shoot all but one of the ministers. They were preparing to shoot Dana next until she said, "You have to free the kids."

"We already know that."

She looked down at her hands and then up at Yvonna again. "I'm talking about the kids who are about to be sold. They are in a tractor-trailer in Bladensburg, Maryland. Near the old railroad tracks. There was an auction that was supposed to go down later today. We had to facilitate it."

"What the fuck? How many kids are we talking about?" Bricks asked, thinking about how cold it was outside.

"One hundred." She rubbed her runny nose on her jacket. "Ranging from the ages of five to fourteen. We cleared out most of the breeding camps to see it go down."

Yvonna felt her blood boil over. "How much were they worth?"

"A half a million."

"Shoot this bitch, I'm tired of looking at her." Yvonna advised.

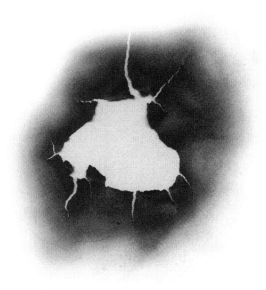

BILAL, Jr.

Bilal, Jr. was praying the car never came to a complete stop. He didn't want to do what he was hired to, partially because he wasn't built to be a gangsta. Still, if he turned back now, he would only make matters worse. Then there was this thing with his aunt. He'd beaten her so badly, she was unconscious and in the hospital fighting for her life. If she came to, he was worried that she'd be able to tell them what he'd done. And now, he was about to commit murder.

"You cocked and loaded right?" Laser asked Bilal, Jr., as they sat in a black stolen Caprice. "I don't wanna hear no shit when we get out this car."

Bilal, Jr. decided not to speak and instead he nodded his head. He felt anything he said, even if it was for the job, would show his fear and anxiety. He knew this was a test and to make Uzi proud, so he would have to rise to the occasion.

Laser gave him a once over and said, "You better be ready, nigga. Let's do this shit."

Parked on a tree-lined street, in a quiet neighborhood, Laser found an inconspicuous parking space away from their target. When they were ready, the brothers eased out of the car and approached the unsuspecting man. He seemed to be focused on the handful of ass cheeks he held, that belonged to a short dark skin girl with an expensive weave, instead of his well-being. The poor fool's life was on the line and he didn't even know it. Gearing up, Bilal, Jr. let out two quick breaths and inched slowly toward him, while Laser hung back, appearing to be accessing the surroundings.

Bilal, Jr. wasn't even sure how he got up on his prey so quickly. But the next thing he knew he was saying, "Main man, I know you ain't out here with your arm 'round my bitch." Although the words may have sounded hard coming from a gangsta, released from his mouth, it resembled a five-year-old frightened little boy.

Melvin turned around to address, whoever must have mistaken him for a punk, but the minute he did, his face was met with a barrage of bullets. He died so quickly; he seriously didn't know what hit him. Bilal, Jr. murdered Bricks' only living sibling and he didn't know the man.

Things moved so swiftly that he'd forgotten all about the woman he was with. Her scream reminded him that he'd just done the ultimate. He ran away, to separate himself from the crime. He was ready to leave when instead Laser said, "You gotta finish it, Bilal. You can't leave her alive. She saw your face."

Bilal, Jr. looked at Laser with wide eyes. "But...why? We got who we came for. Let's just go." He tried to move toward the car until Laser yanked his forearm.

"We not leaving until you finish."

He was confused. He didn't want to kill the one person let alone two. "Why can't you do it?" He boldly asked. He wasn't sure where his question came from but he wanted an answer all the same.

Laser stepped to him, frowned and asked, "You questioning me?"

"No."

"Then go back and finish what the fuck you started." He pointed. "Now, before she gets away."

Bilal, Jr. walked up to the woman, who surprisingly hung over Melvin's dead body, as if he would come back to life. When she saw the killer creep back, she suddenly wondered why she hadn't attempted to get away. When she realized it was high time to start moving, she took off like the speed of lightning. But he was younger and quicker, so he knocked her to the ground with a fist to the back of the head. She dropped, rolled over and looked up at him.

"Don't do this!" She sobbed with her hands covering her face. "You don't have to kill me. I won't say anything. Please!'""

"I'm sorry," he cried, wiping his tears, "But I do have to kill you." He fired his gun, took the ring off her finger and dashed to the car.

When they made it home, Bilal, Jr. rushed to the bathroom and dropped to his knees. He lifted the toilet cover, followed by the seat to release his stomach contents. Sprinkles of dried yellow piss dressed the outside of the bowl, but that didn't stop him from placing both hands firmly on the rim. Now as comfortable as he was going to get, he threw up everything he ate in the past few hours. He couldn't understand how his life got to this level of fucked up, but he wished he could change things. Bilal, Jr. was not a murderer and he definitely didn't want to kill people he had no beef with. He was confused, naive and troubled, all of which spelled danger.

Now that he was assessing the situation, he wasn't sure why the man had to die. He was told that someone name Bricks and Melvin crossed Yao in Vegas, but that was the extent. He didn't have a relationship with Yao to ask more questions and his brothers didn't volunteer the answers. None of it mattered now anyway, because he committed the ultimate crime, a double homicide.

"You aight, lil nigga?" Uzi asked knocking on the door. When he didn't answer he invited himself inside. Seeing his little brother on the floor, he dropped his head back and leaned against the doorway. "Don't tell me you don't have the stomach for this."

"I have the stomach." Bilal, Jr. wiped the vomit off his mouth with the back of his hand. "It's done ain't it?"

"I hear you but you gotta do better than this, man." He looked down at him. "Later for all this emotional shit. People aren't put on earth to live forever. You live and then you die, in that order."

Bilal, Jr. rose from the toilet and looked at himself in the mirror. He seemed frazzled and he didn't want his favorite brother to see him like that. Flushing the toilet, he said, "True."

Uzi placed a firm hand on his shoulder. "How 'bout you tell me what happened tonight?"

"I already told you," he grabbed his toothbrush. "It's done."

"I know that, but why didn't you pull the trigger?" Bilal, Jr. dropped his toothbrush into the sink and looked at his face to see if he was serious. "That was the plan, and I'm hearing you failed. Tonight was about you getting your stripes but you didn't earn 'em. Why?"

Bilal, Jr. didn't want to commit the heinous act in the first place, but since he did, he damn sure deserved his credit. "I'm confused. I...I did kill 'em. I killed both of 'em."

Uzi frowned and backed into the door. "Laser told me he put in the work. And that you ran and couldn't see things through. Did you run or not?"

"I did run but..."

"But what?"

Bilal, Jr. swallowed. "Laser lying, man!" Visions of how the dead bodies looked against the concrete reminded him that he was a murderer. He would have nightmares for the rest of his life, he was sure of it. "I killed both of them. With the gun you gave me. Not him."

"So why would Laser lie?"

"I don't know why." Bilal, Jr. said, shaking his head. "I guess it's like I been telling you all along. He doesn't like me. He may even want me out of this house and not around you. You heard him talking the other night to Gabe, telling him that it was my fault some niggas beat Easter when they tried to rob her, because I wasn't around." Although he was at fault for the crime, he used it to display his point that Laser couldn't be trusted. "From the moment I first met ya'll he

wasn't feeling me. I mean, I know he my brother, but you have to remind him of that because I don't think he likes it. It's not me."

"I'ma have to cut you short right there." Uzi roared and pointed a stiff finger into his chest. "My twin may have shit with him, but he wouldn't lie to me. We've never lied to each other a day in our lives. Just because you live here don't mean he'd start now."

Something Uzi said resonated with him. The word *Twin*. Suddenly it all made sense. He couldn't compete because although he was also his brother, Laser was his *twin*. That meant they lived in the same womb, came out of the same pussy and spent every day of their lives together. When it was all said and done, he was a newcomer. Blood relative or not.

Defeated, Bilal, Jr. said, "I don't know why he would lie either." He dropped his head. "But he did."

He pretty much gave up on trying to get through to him. Until he remembered the ring in his pocket that he'd taken from the girl. He was about to show him when Uzi opened the bathroom door and said, "Laser, come here for a second. I want to ask you something."

Laser walked out of the bedroom on his cell phone. A smile dressed his face until he saw the look on Bilal, Jr.'s. "Let me call you back, Tiffany." He placed his cell in his pocket. "What's up?"

"Who took care of the job tonight?"

Laser laughed lightly. "What you talking 'bout?" He looked at Bilal, Jr. and back at him. "I told you I put the work in." To his face he lied like it wasn't nothing. He was good at it too. Bilal, Jr. saw at that moment that although Uzi was thorough, he didn't have the ability to know when Laser deceived him. He was blinded. What he also discovered was that Laser was a punk who was incapable of going the extra mile, unlike him. "I know he not in here lying on me."

"You sure, man? 'Cause you know I wanted B to do that."

"I said I did it. Why...this little nigga said something different?" As if he really carried out the order, he stared Bilal, Jr. directly in the eyes. For a moment it appeared as if they were having a face off, until Bilal, Jr.'s head hung and broke the stare. He surrendered not because he was scared of him anymore, but because he was embarrassed to even be related to him.

Uzi allowed ten seconds of uncomfortable silence before finally speaking. "Naw he didn't say anything different. I was just checking." Laser nodded at his twin and smirked at Bilal, Jr. He left them to it, and got back on his call. "If you put the work in, why didn't you say it to his face? It was the perfect time."

"I gotta get some air." Bilal, Jr. moved for the door. "I'm so sick of this fuckin' shit." Not wanting to be in the house, he went outside. He walked five blocks up the street until he ran into a face he wasn't sure he wanted to see again.

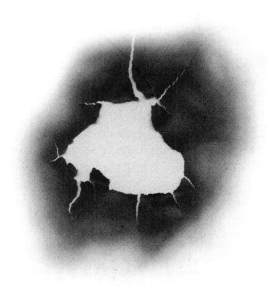

YVONNA

Bricks spotted a white tractor-trailer that seemed to be out of place, behind a warehouse in Bladensburg, Maryland. He brought the car to a slow crawl and parked thirty feet away from it. They needed to be careful before approaching. From the passenger seat, Yvonna looked around to be sure no one was eyeing the trailer, but it didn't appear to be manned.

"I hope nobody's in there." She looked at Bricks. "That would be one of the cruelest things they've ever done."

"You already know hope is lost whenever AFCOG's involved." Swoopes responded, looking out the window. "You heard the nigga on the phone, he don't care 'bout shit but money."

"This is a nightmare." Ming said, holding Swoopes' hand. "Ming knew people could be cold, but never like this."

When the coast was clear, the foursome stepped out of the car and strolled carefully up to the trailer. In case it was a set up, they needed to be careful. It appeared locked and they wondered how they would get in. The first thing Yvonna noticed when she was within a few feet were icicles hanging along the sides. Depending upon how long they'd been in there, they might not even be alive, as the weather was unkind that day.

"Move out the way, Squeeze." Bricks came from behind, holding some type of metal bar that he found. "Maybe this'll work." With the bar wedged under the lock, he pushed and pulled trying to get it to open. Nothing he seemed to do, worked. Ever so often they'd look behind them, to be sure no one was coming and luckily they maintained their privacy.

After five minutes of uncomfortable attempts, to everyone's surprise, Swoopes jumped on the edge of the trailer and assisted him. It was the first time Yvonna had seen them helping each other. With one last push and then pull, the lever dislocated and they pulled the door open.

Since Yvonna was outside, her eyes had to adjust at first to the darkness in the trailer. But when she looked closer, she saw a crowd of children wearing multi colored coats. The smell inside was atrocious, as they had nowhere to release their bowels. When she first focused on them, they had different faces. But after some seconds, they all looked like her as a little girl. And then they changed to Delilah. Sanity was slipping more each day.

"Oh my, God! They're all, Delilah!" She ran into the trailer and startled the children when she started to grab them. "What is she doing in here? And why are there so many of her?"

Bricks ran up to her, after she squashed the head of a boy who bared no more resemblance to Delilah than Whoopi Goldberg did to Halle Berry.

"Squeeze, this isn't Delilah." When he finally pried her fingers off the kid's face, she hit him.

"Get off of me! This is my baby!" She gripped his coat again and tears found their way to her face as she squeezed him harder. "This is my child and you don't know what the fuck you talking about!" She pointed at him. "Stay away from us! You hear me? Stay the fuck away!"

Bricks backed up and fell into the line up with Ming and Swoopes. They looked at her with pity, forcing her to review the child's face again. She released him after discovering that he wasn't her daughter. Startled, she backed into the wall, placed her hand over her mouth and sobbed.

"What is wrong with me?" She looked at the child who rejoined his trailer family and then back at her crew. "What's going on?"

Swoopes was the first to step up. "It ain't nothing." He smiled lightly. "For a moment you thought he was your kid. You tired, Yvonna, that's all." he looked at Bricks and Ming for support. "We all are."

"It could've happened to anyone of us," Bricks lied, knowing full well that only someone certifiably insane, could mistake a boy for a girl. "It's been a long day."

"It'll all be over soon." Ming kicked in. "Don't worry."

Yvonna looked at everyone with eyes so wild, they looked loose. "You're right." A half of moon size smile spread across her face. It crept everyone out, especially the kids. "I'm just tired." She wiped the tears and snot off of her face on the arm of her coat. "I just need some rest. Everybody gets exhausted sometimes. That's me right now."

"Yeah, that's it." Bricks responded, ashamed that in her current state, she turned him off. "Besides, you didn't hurt the little guy. He's fine."

Remembering the business at hand, Ming examined what AFCOG deemed as shipment. "Look at all the kids. What are we going to do with them?"

"Right, Squeeze. You have a plan?" Bricks didn't want to hear her idea but out of respect, asked all the same. "We not talking about a few kids. It's a hundred or more."

Everybody looked at her, almost as if they were waiting on her to fail. In the condition she was in, she was no leader and she knew it. Her team was aware too but they wanted her to bury herself, in the hopes that she'd realize that mentally she was no longer capable.

"Ya'll remember all those buses at the convention center?" Yvonna asked, thinking off the top of her head. "The ones parked out front?"

"Yeah. What we gonna do with them?" Swoopes inquired, wondering where she was going.

"Let's see if we can get our hands on two and get these kids out of here." She surprised all of them, when she actually came through with a good plan. Maybe she wasn't as far gone as they thought.

Three Hours Later

It was midnight when they found themselves in a hotel room. It was located in a remote part of Virginia. Thanks to Ming's rich ass, which everyone somehow forgot, they were able to secure rooms for everyone at The Comfort Inn. When the younger children were settled in their beds, they held a meeting with three of the eldest teenagers.

"Thank you so much," the teenager named Porter said, shaking their hands. The other teenagers stood behind him, with suspicious eyes. "What can we do to help you?" He was looking at Ming. For the first time she felt appreciated. "Anything, you just name it."

"You don't have to do anything to repay me back." She grinned. "Just be safe."

Swoopes grabbed her up and planted a kiss on her lips. "I'm proud of you, ma. You did good today." They were definitely a couple and it was obvious now.

"Thank you, baby."

"We'll try to be safe." Porter said, taking a moment to think about their lives, before they rescued them from the trailer. "I just hope they leave us alone. All we want is to live and be free to start all over." Knowing who Yvonna was, after hearing Ming speak about the legend on the bus earlier that day, he addressed her next. "What can we do to thank you?"

"Live your best life." She shrugged. "That's all I want."

"I will try!" Porter looked at his friends, "We all will and we'll do it in your honor."

"Don't do anything in my honor." She scowled, hating the attention. "I'm not who you think I am. If you do nothing else in life, I ask that you don't be anything like me."

He frowned. "I don't know why you are so modest, and why you believe you are unworthy of appreciation, but I will always thank you. And I will always remember your face." He looked at his friends again. "We all will."

"So what will you do from here?" Bricks asked. "You're a long way from everything. Do you even know where to start?"

"Right, because it's one thing to be free, and its another thing to have to take care of yourself." Swoopes added. "Not to be a bug in your juice but you need a plan if you want to make it out here."

"I managed to save a little money, without my master knowing. And thanks to the lady called Ming," he smiled at her, "which we will speak about always, we should be fine for a couple of days." He sighed. "After that most of the younger ones will probably go into foster care. A lot of the older kids, like us will seek jobs. When we're settled, we'll come back for as many as we can. I think that's all we can do for now."

"But if they go back in the system, are you afraid that AFCOG may find them?" Bricks said.

Porter grimaced. "I'm tired of being afraid. Tired of not being able to live my life. We have to fight now and thanks to you guys we can do that." Then he looked at the floor. "I do wish it was a way we could help bring Rufus to justice, but we don't know how."

"If things work in our favor," Swoopes interjected, "you won't have to look over your shoulder for too much longer. Just hang as low as you can, until we can get things straight. If shit move real good, you'll be free to do whatever you want in a matter of weeks."

"He's right. Once Rufus is done, you should be good." Yvonna responded. "Oh and there's a man name Reverend Dynamite." She reached in her pocket and handed them a number. "Apparently he's helping a lot of kids get on their feet, maybe he can help you too."

"It's worth a try."

When Bricks' cell phone went off, he stepped a few feet away to answer it. "Hello." Hearing his comrade's voice, he smiled. "What up, Kelsi? Everything cool with…"

Silence.

"What...what you talkin' 'bout?" Yvonna turned around to face her man. They all did. Judging by the tone in his voice, she knew something was off. "What you telling me, Kelsi? I'm not understanding what you telling me right now. Slow down, because...because I thought you just said..."

Silence.

The phone dropped out of his hand, and he fell against a soda machine, rocking it loudly against the wall. "What is it, baby?" Yvonna inquired, as she attempted to place her arm around him. "Who is that on the phone?"

Bricks started swinging and when he almost hit both of the girls, Swoopes ran to hold him back. "Fuck is up wit' you, slim?!" Swoopes inquired. "You wilding out on the girls!"

"Somebody killed my brother." He looked at him with glazed over eyes. "Kelsi just told me somebody killed my fuckin' brother!"

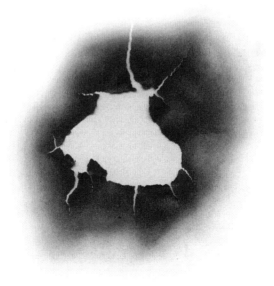

BRICKS

The hip-hop music didn't make a lot of sense to Bricks, as he sat at the bar with his head down. He tried to understand the lyrics to the rap song by Biggie that he rocked with many times in the past. Now when he attempted to remember the lines, all he could think about was that his brother was murdered and that they weren't on the best of terms before he died. Had he known it would've ended like that, he would've told him how much he loved him and how everyday of his life, he looked up to him.

When he gave up on the lyrics, he ordered two more vodka shots and a Corona, bringing his count to ten vodka's and five beers for the day. He was working hard for the eleventh, when Swoopes slid into the hole in a wall, after looking for him for hours.

Swoopes gave Bricks a once over and glided in the seat next to him, as if they didn't know one another. "Give me whatever he had," he examined Bricks' mental state and said, "and another for him too." He slammed a fifty on the bar. "That's it for now."

Bricks peered up at the bartender and then over at Swoopes. "What you doing here?" Bricks placed his head back down. "I don't feel like getting into it wit' you right now. I got a lot of shit I'm dealing wit', just get the fuck out." His breath smelled as if vodka coursed through his veins, in replacement of blood.

"I don't feel like gettin' into it wit' you either." Swoopes downed his shot and slammed it on the counter. "Pour me another." He told the bartender who quickly fulfilled his request. "You get any other information yet? On what happened to your peoples?"

Bricks lifted his head just enough, so it wouldn't slam back down on the bar. Twisting his neck, he observed the man who shot him not even a year earlier, resulting in his hospitalization. He was stupid for partnering with this dude and he knew it. Their beef was the pink elephant in the room that kept shitting all over the place, while everybody ignored it. He thought about YBM, the dudes he ran with at one point and time. And suddenly he understood exactly what was going on. Swoopes had set him up and killed his brother. From the inside he portrayed himself as an acquaintance but he was definitely foe.

"You, dirty mothafucka!" His words slurred and the extra drool which hung on his bottom lip, made him look pathetic. "You had something to do with this didn't you?" He tried to point a finger in his face but he couldn't lift it further than his chest. "You killed my brother."

Swoopes shook his head and felt empathy for the man. He was drunk, defenseless and unable to articulate at the moment. Swoopes' sorrow didn't last long, when Bricks summoned enough strength, to come down on his head with a Corona bottle.

Engaged, Swoopes jumped off the stool, gripped Bricks by the shirt and lifted him off of his feet. He was about to slam his fist into his hanging bottom lip, when Bricks' head nodded to the side. Although his eyes were open, the man was clearly at his limit. Instead of injuring him, he threw him back on the stool as if he were a hot bag of shit.

"Fuck this nigga!" He huffed, before grabbing a napkin, to tend to the wound on his head. Then he pushed out the exit. "If he want to wallow over spilled blood let him do it." He got halfway down the street when Bricks' bobble head came to mind. In the condition he was in, he was a sitting duck for even the smallest of predators. Turning back around he decided to make sure he got out safe. It was a good thing he did, because that quickly, someone was scheming on the cash Bricks had dangling from his pocket. Swoopes approached the crook and said, "Unless you wanna suck on this," he opened his coat revealing his weapon, "I suggest you step the fuck off." The man's scamper awoken Bricks who had nodded off yet again.

"What are you doing here? I said I want to be left alone."

As far as I know, this is a public bar." He looked at the bartender and grabbed another napkin to nurse the bruise on his head. "What you say, man? Is this a public or private spot?"

"Long as you got cash, membership has its privileges."

Swoopes chuckled and looked back at Bricks. "You see, champ. I got just as much right to be here as you." Bricks' head started leaning closer to the counter and Swoopes pulled the back of his coat, so his head would rise and hang backwards.

"Whatchu want wit' me?" Bricks asked, shaking him off. "Just go."

"Like I said, I'm chilling, but I wanted you to know, I ain't have shit to do with your brother's death. And I know you know that already."

Bricks wiped his hand down the front of his face, before it slammed against the counter. "I don't know shit."

"Yes you do. If you even thought I had something to do with it, we would've had that conversation the moment you got the news." He sipped on the Corona he didn't drink earlier. "And not after you got all drunk and busted either. I'm not the enemy. Not right now anyway." Since it appeared that at the moment, Bricks couldn't speak he continued. "And what happened between me and you, when I shot you was street business. Anyway, we both know when this shit is done, we gonna have our time if you got a mind to get back at me. But right now, in the name of something worse than anything we could do on the streets," he said thinking of AFCOG, "I called a truce and I hang by my word. I didn't have nothing to do with the death of your brother, but I'm sorry it happened."

"Whatever." Bricks slurred. His head appeared to be magnetized toward the counter, as it moved in slowly again. Swoopes countered that move by gripping him by the back of his coat again. "So you talk to your family...'bout what happened?"

Bricks' low eyes appeared to widen at the mention of his relatives. "Yeah...I told them to be watching each other's backs, because I don't know what's coming next." A tear rolled down his face and he turned in the opposite direction, to prevent Swoopes from seeing it. "He was my brother. One of my best friends." He looked straight ahead, at the liquor bottles on the mirrored shelf. "And I can't count a time in my life, where he hadn't been there for me." He looked at Swoopes and honestly asked, "What I'ma do without my brother? What I'ma do without my man?"

Swoopes looked down at his hands which were clasped together on the bar in front of him. "I know how you feel."

Bricks immediately shot him an evil look. "How you know what the fuck I feel like? You telling me you lost a brother?"

"I'm tellin' you I lost everybody." Swoopes corrected him. "Anybody who was ever 'spposed to love me." He sipped his Corona to give his painful thoughts a break. Emotions were the devil. "I know what its like to lose somebody close. I ain't a total monster, nigga." He pointed at his face. "'Spite the eye patch."

Bricks lost his emotions again as he thought about Melvin. The worst sound in the world was a real man crying. Bricks tried to stop it, but lost the battle. In the end he allowed a cry that sounded as if it poured out of heaven and rolled from his soul to have voice. If somebody wanted to blame him for breaking down, fuck 'em. "And you know the worst part about it," he looked at Swoopes with bloodshot eyes, "my little man was 'spposed to be wit' him, but I sent him to stay in Atlanta with my comrade. I remember hating Melvin, like I never hated anybody else for making me do it too. I...I acted like he never did shit for me in my life," he beat his chest, in an effort to relieve some of the pressure off his broken heart. "They killed him and it's all my fault."

When Swoopes felt a burning sensation rush down the middle of his forehead and toward his nose, he knew he was choked up. The last thing he was going to do was cry with another nigga at a bar. "You think AFCOG was involved?" He asked, in the hopes of discussing anything else.

"I'm not sure." He wiped the tears off his face with this dirty palm. "You heard Rufus...he said he was up on all of us. So I wouldn't be surprised." He waved the bartender for another round. But because he already displayed enough man emotion for the night, which brought some of the customers down, he acted as if he didn't see him. "If I were you, I'd call and check up on my people too." Bricks tried to get the bartender's attention again by way of hand flurries, but he was unsuccessful.

"I told you earlier, man, I don't have no people." Swoopes said. "They gone, all of 'em."

Silence.

"When this shit is all said and done, what you gonna do? I mean, where are you going to go?"

"I don't know, Bricks." He shrugged. "Shit been so fucked up for me, that I can't see that far into the future." He asked for another beer and a shot, while the bartender was in the serving mood. "When I was younger, I use to dream all the time. I use to wish I could be a surgeon, or a movie star." Swoopes smiled although he rarely did. "I just knew I was gonna be this big time person, but somebody snatched that dream from me." When he remembered all of them men who raped him in his life, he felt a blinding rage. When he got like this, he felt like hurting somebody. Anybody. With his switch on lunatic mode, he looked around the bar to find one person who was looking at him sideways. Shit, he'd even take the dude who was about to rob Bricks on his way back into the bar. He found nothing. No one. His mind was still flickering until Bricks' comment brought him back to reality.

"A doctor?" He laughed. "What makes you think somebody would let you operate on 'em?

"Why is that so fucking funny? I said it was a dream." Drunk or not Bricks was pushing limits.

"Not for nothing, but I can't see you being a doctor. Or no actor for that matter." He tried to get the bartender's attention again and again it was ignored. "You ain't fit to be nothin' but the street nigga you aspired to be. Live with it."

"Good thing I don't give a fuck about what you think, drunk." He smirked. "Niggas love kicking down dreamers. That's why so many niggas on some other shit. Can't get no support from their own people. Blacks!" He shook his head.

Bricks thought about what he said and felt the truth in his statement. "Look, I ain't mean that shit. For real, I probably don't make the best company right now. Maybe I should just be by myself."

"Naw...I'm hanging right here. Plus if somebody went after your brother, what's to stop them from coming after you too? Somebody gotta watch your ass."

"So you my bodyguard now?" He smirked, as he tried to mean mug him from top to bottom. But when his eyes came dangerously close to shutting for a drunk nap, he sprung them open. "Not for nothing, but I think I can take care of myself."

He looked at him and laughed. "I'm not saying you can't, moe. I'm just saying I'm staying right here."

Bricks didn't want to let him know, but for some reason, he appreciated the company from his adversary. "Why are you still here, man?"

"I just told you. Stop asking stupid shit."

"Naw. I'm talking about with Yvonna...and all of this shit she got going on?"

"Sometimes I think you don't hear nobody but yourself."

"That's not even true."

"I'm serious. I told you before we got history with this AFCOG shit. And when the bitch Gabriella, gave Rufus my name in Vegas, I knew I couldn't go back to my old life anyway, not that it was much of a life. He knew I was alive and he probably didn't know how much I remembered." He sipped his beer. "Plus I deserve revenge for what they put me through just like she do."

"So you never think about everything she did to you?" Bricks continued. "You never think about getting back at her?"

"I use to. As a matter of fact, before the situation at Ron Max's house with the YBM, I couldn't say if I trusted her or not."

"And now?"

He placed his half full beer on the counter. "And now I realize she's the only one I can trust. We alike in a lot of ways. And at least with Yvonna, you know where she's coming from."

"Sometimes." Bricks said, remembering their last fight.

"What you mean?"

He swallowed. "How you feel 'bout her talking to herself?"

Swoopes was just about to respond, when three dudes walked into the bar. Two of the three looked identical and the third favored them also but was younger. Since Swoopes had interaction with all three at some point, he recognized them immediately. "Look, we got company that we probably need to avoid. Now I'm gonna slide out first and if you want, you can follow me. Either way I'm gone."

"Who the fuck are they?" Bricks maneuvered his neck four times trying to recognize a face. He saw no one and true to Swoopes' word, he vanished.

YVONNA

The heat in the room appeared to be stuck on hell, despite Ming's attempts to reduce it. When she looked at Yvonna, she was turned to the opposite side of the room and she was mumbling. Ming was going to call down to the front desk to get the heater fixed, but they were on the run, and needed to keep their interactions with outsiders to a minimum. When the thermostat didn't budge, frustrated, she slammed down on the bed.

Startled, Yvonna sat up straight and looked at her friend. "What was that?" She asked with wild eyes. "That noise? You hear it?"

"Are you still sick?" Ming asked, as she returned to cleaning the barrel of her gun. Her eyes were always glazed over and the clan was getting nervous. "Because you don't look well, Yvonna."

The moment Ming asked the question many thoughts flooded Yvonna's mind. These days Gabriella and Bilal refused to leave her side. They hung in the shadows and never went away. They were with her always. So when she asked are you sick, for some reason, she thought Ming could see them too and that maybe she wasn't so crazy after all.

From the other bed she asked, "Why you ask me that? If I was still sick?" There was a mixture of hope and interest in her question. "You wanna tell me something? You can tell me anything, Ming."

Ming's jaw dropped when she noticed the way her eyes moved wildly from left to right. "No reason. Just asking."

"Ming, there is always a reason with you." She scooted closer to the edge, and Ming hoped she wouldn't jump on her bed, which was closest to the door. "You never just do anything. There's always a reason with you."

"Really, I just want to know if you okay. It's no big deal."

She sees them too. I know she does. Now if I can just get her to be honest with me, everything will change. "Tell the truth, Ming." Without an invitation, she shared her bed. "You see them don't you?" Her clammy hands covered Ming's. "It's okay. Just tell me."

Her eyes widened. "See who?" She looked around the room even though she was certain they were alone. "What are you talking about, Yvonna? I'm so worried about you. You need help."

"Ming, please. It's okay to be real with me. You have to understand, all my life people have been trying to tell me I'm crazy." She released her friend's hand and tapped the side of her own head repeatedly with her index finger. "Now you're my best friend. I never had a friend closer than you are to me." She pointed at Ming while sweat poured down her face. "I thought I was close to the girls who did me wrong when I was younger. You know…the ones I was telling you about."

"You mean Sabrina and Cream?"

"Yes." She nodded her head up and down, in disturbingly swift motions. "But now I realize they were fake. Just people in my life to do me wrong but you've been real with me from the jump. So just tell me the truth." She paused and looked at her with expectant eyes. "You see them don't you?"

"Yvonna…I'm scared."

Instead of understanding that she was the one creeping her out, she closed the small space between them even more. She figured if she sat closer, Ming could feel how much she meant to her and would no longer be afraid. "There's no reason to be scared." She reduced her voice to a whisper and looked out of the corners of her eyes weirdly. "They won't hurt you. They really are nice people, they just…well….they just don't show themselves to everyone. But if they're showing themselves to you, don't you see, Ming, it means you're special."

"So, you do see people?" She asked. "These are the same people who talk to you all the time in the bathroom?"

"This is not going to end well." Gabriella said. "If I were you, I would quit while I'm ahead. She's gonna tell you anything just to get out of her face."

"If you tell her you see people she's gonna think you've lost it, baby." Bilal added, appearing by her side. "If you decide to do it anyway, don't tell her shit about me. I don't want everybody in my business. I got niggas looking for me already."

She thought about what they were saying and decided to keep it real anyway. "Yes. I do, Ming. I see them all the time." She stood up and walked toward Gabriella. "This is Gabriella right here. She's been my friend for the longest." She rapidly shuffled toward the other side of the room. "And Bilal is right here. He's my boyfriend." She shook her head recognizing her mistake. "I mean he *was* my boyfriend." She looked into the ceiling because she was getting confused. "Wait...Bricks is my boyfriend now right?" Not waiting on an answer, she ran back to the bed and hopped on it. "So you see them?"

Ming's heart felt like someone had taken a mallet to it, and beat it repeatedly from the inside. Her friend looked like a mad woman with her wild hair and wheeling eyes. But to appease her, and in the hopes that this problem would go away, she nodded slowly. "Yes...I," she cleared her throat, "I see them, Yvonna. I see both of them."

An eerie smile unrolled on her face. "You do?" Yvonna placed a fist on each side of her cheeks. "Please don't play with me. It'll break my heart if you're lying, Ming."

"I do see them, Yvonna." She swallowed and looked toward the area where she was told Gabriella was standing. "Gabriella, how are you? I'm sorry she had to kill you in Vegas. I hope you aren't terribly angry with her."

Yvonna frowned and leaped back on her own bed. Her toes scratched the dirty carpet as she stared at her with dissension. "Ming, this Gabriella was always separate from the Gabriella you met. That other Gabriella was nothing more than somebody posing as a friend. You were right about her the whole time. I should've listened to you because she fucked Terrell and couldn't be trusted. No, this Gabriella right here is like a sister to me. Not exactly. But you get it right?"

"Oh, yes," she nodded oddly. "I get it. So this Gabriella was never murdered. She was totally different from the one you killed. Even though they look alike, I'm assuming, and are the same person."

"Yes." She clapped her hands together. "You get it!"

Happy to have scored high on the insanity board she said, "Okay...well hello, Gabriella. How are you?"

"Bitch, fuck you!" Gabriella spat, although she couldn't hear her. "You ain't nothing but a fake ass slut puppet."

Yvonna turned her head toward the empty space. "Stop being mean, Gab! She's being nice to you and you're being rude." She faced Ming. "Forgive her, Ming. Sometimes she can be a little cross. She means well though," she lied, "just as long as you stay on her good side." A sinister grin spilled across her face. "Which I know you will." After Ming told her she saw them, Yvonna was filled with confidence that maybe God did love her and she wasn't deranged after all.

"You know she's lying don't you?" Bilal advised. "She doesn't want to hurt your feelings but it's true. She thinks you're crazy, they all do."

Yvonna quickly turned toward Ming. "Did you hear, Bilal?" her eyes rolled around. "You heard what he said right?"

"Uh...yeah." Ming wanted to get the fuck out but the boys were gone with the car. Her homie was losing it more by the minute and she couldn't bare to watch anymore. "I told you I could see them. Stop asking me that shit."

"Well repeat what he just said."

"Yvonna this is stupid. I said I see them, so leave it alone."

"It's for his sake not mine. Please." She was off the chain. "Tell me...what did Bilal just say?"

Before she could respond, Bricks and Swoopes came through the door, smelling like a brewery. Bricks moved in slow motion, while he used Swoopes shoulder as a crutch. He looked worse than Yvonna ever seen him, then again, who was she to judge?

Seeing the despair on his face, Yvonna popped off the bed and approached him. "How are you, baby? Are...are you okay?"

"My brother's gone, Squeeze." He shook her off, removed his coat and threw it over a chair in the room. "I don't know how much better I can be." He flopped on the bed and kicked his shoes off, not caring where they fell.

"Is there something I can do?"

"Bring my brother back from the dead." The moment placed tension in the already small space. "Can you do that?"

"You know I can't."

"Then leave me the fuck alone." He flipped on the TV and asked Ming, "Did you have any luck locating the other Captains Of Pain?"

Ming grabbed the papers off the nightstand. "Yeah...we found out where Anna Livingston is about an hour ago. I say we hit her in DC and then go after Ramona Cass in Virginia before hitting Abel in Delaware if she's there."

Yvonna felt left out, as plans seemed to move on without her. "So when were you guys going to tell me that plans were changing?"

"You know now." Bricks shot back. He seemed to blame her for Melvin's loss and it was evident to everyone present. "We getting shit done, be happy for that. Since that's all you care about remember? You, yourself and Delilah."

"That's not fair, Bricks! Don't be mad at me like it's my fault what happened to Melvin."

"What about Rufus Day?" Swoopes inquired, trying to take some of the heat off Yvonna. "Did we find his address yet?"

"Yep," Ming nodded, flopping on his lap, before planting a soft kiss on his cheek. Instead of being irritated at her affections like he had in the past, he kissed her back.

"Ming, can you focus and tell me what's up?" Bricks asked.

"Oh...uh...yes, Yvonna's friend Chris was on point by giving us the information we needed. Right now, Rufus doesn't seem to have too much security at his compound in DC, so we shouldn't have a problem laying the C4, if we can get in. I think it should be the last move we make though. And then we can find a way to make it to the Philippines."

"Maybe we can ask Chris for his help with the passports. He seems to be able to get everything anyway." Bricks volunteered.

"It's worth a try." Ming responded, still sad Swoopes would not be going.

Bricks snatched the sheet Ming had in her hands. "Let's do what we gotta do. And I say we move tomorrow."

"Me too." Swoopes added. "For now, let's get some sleep. We all need it."

Everyone was in a deep slumber when Yvonna walked into the bathroom to talk to Bilal. After the way Bricks treated her, she had to admit, it was nice having him around again. She closed and locked the door and sat on the toilet. "Bilal, I know I haven't asked you this, but how am I supposed to help your son when I find him? I mean, exactly what am I supposed to do?"

"I want you to check on him for me. Until I escort you into your next life."

"You're serious about leading me to death?"

Silence.

"I don't know if you took a look at my life, but I'm not necessarily the best person to be checking up on anybody. Plus Bilal, Jr. is almost a man now." She looked down at her hands. "Even if I were to go see about him, he still hates me." When she remembered poisoning him with the Coca Cola she felt guilty all over again and shook her head. "How am I going to get through to him?"

A few thunderous raps at the door startled her. *Knock. Knock. Knock.*

"Yes?" She yelled.

"Squeeze, who are you talking to?" Yvonna whipped her head toward Bilal and again he was gone.

Frustrated at his interruption, she got up from the toilet and opened the door. Bricks trudged inside and although he slept some of his drunkenness off, he still looked heavy. Yvonna wasn't trying to be insensitive, but she couldn't deal with Melvin's death and everything else at the same time. Too many problems were the reason she was deemed insane to begin with.

"What do you want, Bricks?"

"You heard me, babes, who are you talking to in here? What's going on?"

"If I tell you, you won't believe me." She could feel the tears already stirring in her eyes. "And I want to tell you so badly but I don't want you to judge me."

"Squeeze, talk to me." His eyelids seemed to cover most of his eyes. "You been spending a lot of time in the bathroom alone lately." He opened the door wider and moved to leave. "Come to bed." He grabbed her hand and she pulled away from him.

"I gotta tell you something first, Bricks." She slammed and locked the door before plopping back on the toilet. "When I tell you, you have to promise not to say anything mean." He wouldn't respond. "You have to hear me out because that's the kind of relationship I want us to have, okay?"

"Yes, Squeeze. Go 'head." His head fell backwards before crawling forwards. "I need some sleep, it's been a long day."

"Bilal and Gabriella come to me a lot lately. And at first nobody could see them. But baby, today I found out that Ming can see them too."

He took a few steps back and looked at her as if she were an ingrown toenail. "Wait a minute, what you talking about?"

"Let me talk slower," She was so excited that she rushed her words. Taking two deep breaths she said, "Okay...remember when I told you that I was diagnosed with Multiple Personality Disorder with a touch of Schizophrenia?"

"Yes." It was all he could think about.

"Well I found out today, that's what the people wanted me to think. They wanted me to believe I was crazy, so they could overmedicate me. You have to remember that the money is in the drugs not in the cure." Sweat poured down her face. She looked at the door and lowered her voice. "But a wonderful thing happened tonight. I found out I'm fine, baby. I'm just as sane as you."

I hope not. He thought. "Squeeze, I hate to tell you this, but Gabriella and Bilal are dead."

"I know they're dead!" She screamed, causing him to jump back and fall into the fighter stance. Seeing his defensiveness she took three more breaths to relax. "I mean...I know...they...are...dead, Bricks, but they come back to me, because I can hear them." She pointed to her head. "In here and Ming can too."

Bricks wanted to break Ming's jaw for adding to the problem. "So you're saying they're like ghosts."

His ignorance was weighing on her. "No...they're real people!"

"But they can't be real and dead at the same time, Yvonna. That's what I'm trying to tell you."

"He's plotting against you to have you recommitted, Yvonna." Gabriella advised softly in her ear. "And if you don't kill him he'll succeed. Do it. And do it now."

Yvonna thought about what she was saying and looked into his eyes. She would kill him if she had to, she knew it. But she loved him so realizing he was her man and not her foe she said, "Baby, you have to believe me."

"Kill this nigga!" Gabriella screamed. "Waste no more time! Take care of it now!"

Yvonna pointed to the empty space. "You see her? She's right there."

He looked in the direction. "Yvonna, nobody's there."

"Why are you doing this to me, Bricks? I thought you loved me? I thought you wanted to protect me."

"And I do!" he defended himself. "But I'm not about to sit up in no bathroom and pretend to see mothafuckas who ain't there either! Now if you want to talk to walls, knock yourself out! But I just lost my brother and don't have time for this shit right now!" He walked out and slammed the door behind him.

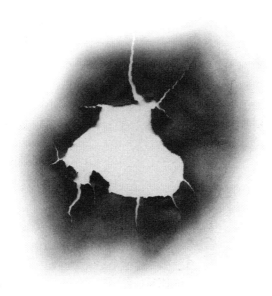

BILAL, Jr.

I t was warmer than the day's prior and Bilal, Jr. was thankful as he sat in a motel room alone. After Melvin's murder, he was given five hundred dollars to do what he willed. For him it was simple, grab a hotel, pay it up for a few days and kick back and relax. He wanted some space between him, his twin brothers and his aunt Easter who refused to die. As the second day rolled by in the hotel room, suddenly he felt lonely.

Remembering the person he hadn't seen in a while, that he ran into the other day, he decided to give her a call. Everything in his soul told him to leave her alone and that she was bad news, but he was young and would ignore his intuition. What was the worst that could happen if he spent a little time with an old friend?

After speaking to her on the phone, she agreed to keep him company. So he sent a cab to get her and waited impatiently for her arrival. He wanted to be with someone familiar. Someone who was all about him, even if only for the night. When there was a knock at the door, his heart beat faster and faster as he anticipated her face. She was beautiful the last time he saw her on that DC Street, but he could only imagine what she looked like now.

The moment he opened the door, Rozay extended her height by rising on the tip of her toes before throwing her arms around his neck. He changed each time she touched him, for the good, bad or indifferent. When they separated, he looked at her wide eyes and bright teeth. The girl was perfect. When she eased into the room, as he kept the door open, he took notice at the way her blue True Religion jeans hugged her curves.

"You gonna close the door or what?" She asked, knowing all the while he was worshiping her body.

"My bad," he closed the door, ran his hand through his curly hair and stood before her. She smelled so good. Like expensive perfume and a recent trip to the beauty salon.

"B, it's so good to see you!" His dick immediately hardened and he looked down, hoping it didn't show through. "You don't know how excited I was to see you the other day. For real, I didn't think you would call me though. I mean, what took you so long?"

"Life."

He was different and she was trying to figure out why. "Where do you live now?"

"With my brothers."

Her neatly arched eyebrows rose. "You got brothers? I didn't know that."

"Me either at first. They're twins."

"You look like them?" She dug deeper, hoping they would still have things in common to talk about.

"I guess so." He didn't want her inquiring too much about them, because he wasn't sure if he would stay around too much longer anyway. He dipped away from her and toward the spread of alcohol on a table next to the door, to maintain control of their meeting. "Everybody tell us that anyway."

Rozay walked closer to him and he realized he was wrong about her scent earlier. She now smelled like strawberries and vanilla. Maybe she mixed the fragrances to throw them off but it smelled so sweet. She still sported the black Chinese bang bob, which moved every time she did.

He thought about kissing her, until he recalled hearing some time back, that she was with southeast Tony. He was broken-hearted when he learned they got together after she broke up with him.

"You wanna drink?" He removed a plastic cup from its stack. "I got Ciroc and Henny."

She shrugged. "Ciroc is fine. You can put some coke in it too." He mixed her drink and she took it from him, gently touching his fingers in the process. Placing the cup against her lips, she smiled slyly. "Thank you." She paused. "So what you doing here?" She walked away and sat her purse on the floor. He saw it was a Louis Vuitton bag and wondered was it the one he'd bought her. "It look like you been in here for a minute." She looked around.

He made his drink and moved toward her. "I'm chilling."

"I see that...you back in school?"

"I'm not thinking about school right now. My mind is on my money." A wide grin spread across her face. "Maybe next year."

"Why go back to school at all?" She encouraged. "It ain't like nothing going on anyway." She sat on the bed and he joined her. "You really dropped out?"

"If that's what you wanna call it. For real I just decided I got other shit to do then to be sitting in class wasting time."

"So how much money you making now?" Her eyes grew wider, as her mouth fell into her cup. "Like a whole bunch? Or a little bit?"

"Enough to finally take care of you. If that's what I wanted to do."

She ended the fake game she was putting on her drink and downed it in a second flat. Then she placed her cup on the floor and threw her arms around his neck. "B, don't play with me." Her lips touched his ears and he could finally see her for the gold digger she was. It wasn't like he cared; to him some things were worth the high price tag. "I'm so serious about being back with you if you ready. I been wanting to get back with you for the longest, but you couldn't afford me at first." With a firm hold on him, she ran her hand through his curly mane. "That's why I had to leave you alone." She paused as she remembered an important truth. "Well, that and the fact that you let AJ and his friend Dirk break my fingers." She wiggled them to show they now worked.

He pulled back from her. "First off I didn't let anybody break your fingers."

"You didn't stop them either." She frowned, wanting him to accept responsibility. "I mean, how you think that make me feel, Bilal? I need a boyfriend who can take care of me, even if I do pop off every now and again at the mouth. But you didn't do that. You let some niggas come up in your house and hurt me and that was wrong."

"If we get back together, nobody will ever hurt you again." He looked into her eyes. "I promise."

"Whatever," she waved, wanting him to make his argument stronger. Whenever anybody promised to protect her, she got aroused. "I hear you talking but you not saying nothing."

Dead ass serious, Bilal stood up, dug into his coat and pulled out the weapon he used to kill Melvin and his lady friend earlier in the week. At first Rozay was scared, thinking he was finally about to shoot her for all the foul shit she said about him at school. But when he pointed the hammer the other way, she breathed a sigh of relief.

"What's that, baby?"

"You know what it is?" Bilal, Jr. grinned, for the first time, loving the power he felt with the gun in his hand. "You pretty but you smart too."

"That's yours?"

He looked at her. "What you think?"

"I think I'm in love."

He grinned a little and sat next to her. "Let's just say if somebody tries to fuck with you again, it won't be good for their health. And depending upon how I feel, it may not be good for their family either." He stood up and placed the gun on the table. Truth be told, it made him nervous if he kept it too close. Sitting next to her again he said, "you wanna smoke?"

She reached into her bag on the floor and brandished a fully loaded blunt. "You got fire?"

For five minutes they bandied the weed back and forth, until they were good and high. Now in a clouded haze, he felt more confident to ask the burning question. "You got a boyfriend now?"

She looked at him and laughed. "Boy, no. Even if I did I would leave him for you, B."

"Why would you do that?"

"Because from the first moment you came into class that day, I loved you. That's why I started flirting with you and stuff. I knew you were the one. You don't remember that shit?"

"I remember you had a lot of fans, that's about it." He smirked.

"Well I wasn't interested in nobody but you. But you were soft and that made me think twice about choosing you. I hear you when you say things changed though. And that you can protect me." She looked at the gun across the table. "You ever kill anybody before?"

"Why?"

She hunched her shoulders and wiped the hair from her face. "I just wanna know."

"I may have. But I wouldn't tell you about it if I did." He stood up and turned the TV on. "That way if the police came and asked you anything, you wouldn't know shit." He sat next to her when the channel rested on Rihanna's music video.

She turned toward him and rubbed his leg. "Let me shoot it."

"Shoot what?"

"The gun." She pointed at it on the table.

"Why?"

"I never shot one before. My brothers too afraid to show me how and it makes me mad. They be at the range all the time but never take me."

"Maybe you not old enough."

"I am, they just don't want me to go." She rubbed his leg harder. "Let me shoot, boo. Just once." When the current seduction setting wasn't working, she kicked it up a notch. "I'll make it worth your while. I promise.'"

Her eyes melted him. She was a weakness he had been hoping to free himself from for a long time. But now that she was in his presence again, all he wanted to do was please her. To make her happy. Wanting to play hero, he stood up and got the gun. Something told him not to but again he ignored his intuition. Slowly he handed it to her and said, "Okay, aim toward that wall. And fire."

"Won't it go through it?"

"First off a bullet won't go through a wall. So you don't have nothing to worry about. Second of all that wall leads outside so even if it did go out, you won't hit nobody. We in the back of the building. Ain't nobody behind there." He placed his hands over hers and said, "When you ready, aim and shoot."

He removed his hand and Rozay waited less than one second before busting off. The force of the weapon pushed her backwards and the sound scared the hell out of her. Ignorant when it came to guns, she dropped it and fell into hysterical laughter. "Oh, my God!" She yelled jumping up and down. "I can't believe I just did that shit!" She covered her mouth and looked at the hole and the small tail of fire around it. "That was so much fun!"

He enjoyed the fact that the smile on her face had everything to do with him. "Now you got it out of your system." He chuckled. "So you should be good now." He placed the gun in his lap and rubbed her back. It was time to fuck. "I like how you handled that shit though. Now it's time to see what you do with me."

In addict mode she asked, "Can I see it again?"

"Yeah…but no more shooting. You can only hold it. Plus that shit was loud as fuck and I don't want nobody to hear it and call the cops." He handed it to her and walked inside the bathroom. Realizing bullets were still in the gun, he quickly returned and took it from her. "I gotta take the bullets out first." He knew she was infatuated and didn't want her to do something like hurt herself. If that happened, he knew Uzi would kill him, especially since it was the gun used in Melvin's murder.

She laughed. "What you don't trust me?"

"It ain't even like that, I don't trust the gun." He took the bullets out and stuffed them into his pocket.

He tried to hand it back to her but with an attitude she said, "Fuck it."

Still high, he shrugged and sat it on the table. "That's on you, ma." He rushed to the bathroom to take a shit. Had he not been off the chronic and liquor, he would never have gotten so comfortable releasing his bowels with her in the room. From the toilet he yelled, "If you *want,* we can get something to eat when I come out. That jay got my head twisted."

She screamed, "I'm hungry as shit, where we going?"

"Wherever you want?"

"Wait…you have a car too?"

He laughed. "How I'ma have a car when I sent a cab for you? I got some paper though. We can just jump in another taxi." He paused and spun the toilet roll. "You have any ideas?"

Silence.

"Rozay, you have any suggestion on where you wanna go?"

Silence.

After taking a dump he wiped his ass, flushed and washed his hands. Then he moved toward the door. "Did you hear me, baby?" He opened it and when he stepped into the living room, he saw five guns aimed in his direction. Rozay was handcuffed, faced down on the floor crying softly.

"Come out slowly, son." One of the officers demanded. "With your hands up!"

He followed orders. "What's going on?"

"Put your hands behind your head and lay down, face first on the floor."

"Can you tell me what we did?" he was high and asking dumb questions. He knew full well what he'd done. Well, what Rozay did anyway.

"If I have to tell you again we gonna come after you. But if we do that, it's gonna end in pain. That's not what you want."

Bilal dropped to the floor and the cops rushed toward him. They forcefully placed one hand behind his back followed by the other. Soon after, the cold steel of the cuffs dressed his wrists. "Can you at least tell me what's going on?"

"Someone was shot. And the bullet came from this room."

"Fuck!"

ANNA LIVINGSTON

A nna sat on the floor in her mansion in Washington DC, with a glass of vodka in one hand, and a balled up piece of tissue covered in mucus and tears in the other. Her dark walnut colored skin was loaded with tearstains. She nervously shook the glass, causing the ice cubes to dance against one another. She was delirious and paranoid at what was happening to AFCOG as a whole. It didn't make her feel any better that their leader Rufus Day, played Yvonna's mission off as nothing more than a spoiled woman's attempt to shut their operation down. Although she was a millionaire, courtesy of the thousands of children she exploited each year, she now wondered if it was worth it.

When her phone rang, she dropped the tissue and rose from the floor, almost slamming her forehead into the table. On her feet, she snatched the gold handset off its cradle and announced, "Anna Livingston's residence."

"Did you hear about the eight secretaries? They've all been murdered." Ramona Cass, one of the other captains asked. "Shit is falling all apart now. I never thought it would go so far."

Anna paced back and forth before walking in an inelegant circle. "I don't wanna die, Ramona. If I have to, I'll meet with her and try to talk some sense into her head."

"What makes you think you can reason with her? She's a killer, Anna."

"Well everybody loves money!" She disputed. "And I don't know about you, but I'm willing to meet her and put up a million dollars to see her walk away." Although the idea sprung to her mind, she was actually looking for Ramona's partnership with her plan. The last thing she wanted to do was approach the legend known as Yvonna Harris on her own. "What is Rufus saying?"

She sighed and it was obvious she was frustrated. "He's saying it's an isolated event."

"What about Pastor Robinson? And Ron Max? This is anything but isolated."

"I agree," Ramona continued, on the verge of tears. "I don't want to go to jail. They'll kill us in there if they find out what we're in for. Everybody hates people who exploit children."

"I'll kill myself first!" Anna confessed. "But before I get to that point, you need to come over here and discuss my idea, to speak to her. You could put in five hundred and I'll put in the other half. We can arrange a meeting with her and everything." After walking herself dizzy she stood in place. "You think Abel will be down with our cause too?"

"Fuck no! Abel called me earlier today and said the first mothafucka who come through her door is getting it in the face. She hired some young boys to help. You know she part crazy. Between me and you, I think she's looking forward to the war."

Anna shook her head, disappointed that she couldn't shorten the upfront money she planned to use on Yvonna, by splitting it three ways. "Let it be her funeral." She sat on the high sofa. "You coming over or not?"

"I'll be there in an hour." She sniffled and with a broken voice said, "Oh my God, Anna. I think this is it. I think the shit we did in the dark has finally caught up to us."

"It doesn't look too good." She declared, "but we still have fight in us and money in the bank. With those odds, we should at least be able to come up with a plan. So hurry over, I'll see you soon."

Anna hung the phone back up on its cradle. When she threw her head back, she saw four people standing behind her, dressed in all black. She lost her voice in the middle of her throat and couldn't call for help that wasn't there anyway. Her temples throbbed and threatened to expose themselves on the side of her head. She tried to run but the moment her ass cheeks rose, Ming snatched her back in position, causing her neck to make a cracking noise.

"Don't get up again," Yvonna said, as she and her clan prowled toward the front of the sofa.

With barbaric eyes, she looked upon each of them. The bunch looked sinister no doubt, but she wasn't sure if one of them was the legend, or if they were a group of vagabonds who happened upon her home and made themselves comfortable. "Who are you? And what are you doing in my house?"

"You already know who we are." Swoopes said. "This is Yvonna and we here on some get back shit."

"I didn't have anything to do with no kids!" She sobbed, uselessly. "Honestly."

"You don't know shit about honesty." Yvonna laughed as she stooped down in front of her. She ran the nose of her gun from her kneecap to her inner thigh. Calmly she asked, "Where are the kids?"

"I don't have any kids. I think you've gotten me confused. I don't know what you're talking about." Ming stepped out of the line up, strolled up to her and stroked the side of her face before punching her in the abdomen. Anna balled up; covered her stomach with her forearms and coughed out blood. She turned a shade of red, that none of the clan had ever seen before, and two veins snaked to the middle of her forehead. "Please don't hurt me." She looked up at them. "I don't want to die."

"I wonder how the kids you sold to killers felt." Bricks said, eager to take the loss of his brother out on somebody. "Now we know about everything already. We know who you are and we know your position in all of this. So ain't no use in lying to us. I just lost my brother, don't make me take it out on you like you had everything to do with it."

The gig was up and she knew it. "They're downstairs." She pointed toward the only cherry wood door in the living room which was locked. "The keys are over there on the mantle, above the fireplace."

Yvonna grabbed her by the hair and escorted her to the mantle to retrieve the keys. Anna fumbled with them, in an effort to locate the correct one. She'd been to the dungeon she hosted more than ten times a day, and now she acted as if it were her first time. When the door finally opened, the crew with Anna and Yvonna in the lead, treaded downstairs. Swoopes on the other hand, chose to nurse his basement phobia and remain upstairs.

"I'll stay up here to stand guard." Swoopes noted. "I got ya'll backs in case someone comes in."

Knowing bullshit when he heard it, Bricks felt it was necessary to let him know. "Sooner or later you gonna have to get over your fear. It's stupid anyway."

Embarrassed he responded in the best way he could. "Like I said, I'll be up here."

The crew disappeared into the darkness of the basement. They went down three more sets of stairs which surprised them because they didn't realize it was so deep. Once they were at the lowest level, they came to another door which also had to be unlocked. Anna placed the key inside the knob and pulled the door open. Because they weren't sure about the reception, Ming and Bricks guns were trained ahead of them, while Yvonna kept a firm hold on Anna.

With a flip of the switch, they were stunned to see over twenty kids in the room ranging from the ages twelve to sixteen. All of them were partially naked, with the exception of the soiled underwear that covered their frail frames. Every time Yvonna saw one of the factories, it brought back horrible memories.

Angry at the world, Yvonna struck Anna in the mouth so hard with the butt of her gun, her gums split. She dropped to the floor and with gaping eyes looked upon her in shock. "You mothafuckas are the worst." Yvonna pointed out. "You don't care about nobody but your fucking selves." Then she looked at the children who, in her opinion, were her brothers and sisters in the struggle. "I'm the one they call The Legend but my name is Yvonna Harris," brief chatter rose throughout the room, "and these are my friends." Ming waved while Bricks nodded. "We're here to set you free."

The frightened children didn't seem to understand what was going on. Most of them looked at each other and maintained their positions against the walls, within the darkness. "Do you understand what we saying?" Bricks took over. "You can bounce. You ain't gotta stay in this hell hole no more."

It took the clan a second to understand why they weren't rejoicing like the others they freed. Anna was in the room, giving them nonverbal glares. One of the older teenagers stepped out of her shell and pointed at her. There was something about her vaguely familiar.

"What," she asked her, "you're afraid of this bitch?" Yvonna questioned, as she looked at Anna. They remained still.

To put them at ease, Yvonna kicked her in the gut and Ming, as always, got in on the fun. After the melee against Anna, the children finally realized what was going on. Their tormentor, the woman who kept them hostage all of their lives, forcing them to breed for money, afterwards stealing their children, was no longer in charge. Partially unconscious, Anna lay on the floor coughing up blood chunks.

"This woman will no longer bother you. You're free." Yvonna responded.

The girl said, "Thank you so much." It was then that Yvonna realized that she was Gabriella's daughter, the one that caused her to betray her. The one that they were using as blackmail, to complete the mission to kill Yvonna. She didn't respect her mother, so she wouldn't tell her she was dead.

Another male teenager stepped from the darkness. "My name is Clandus," he told them, "well that's the name they gave me anyway."

Slowly he approached Anna with rage in his eyes and vengeance in his heart. Hair covered the weirdest places of his body, including his forehead and back. The mucky briefs he wore, protruded a little more than what Bricks thought was necessary in the front. While Ming smiled in embarrassment. The cave boy stooped to Anna's level to address her. "You have taken everything from me!" He screamed, as his body trembled. It was obvious that although he was angry, he was still afraid. "When all I ever did, all we ever did, was try to love you."

With that, he gripped her by the hair and pulled her to her feet. "When I fathered my first child, I use to pray to God, that you would find it in your heart to let me and his mother keep her." He sobbed heavily, and Bricks recognized the pain all too well, with the loss of Melvin. "And when you took our baby anyway, I prayed that God would at least place it in your heart to let me keep his mother, because we were in love. But again my prayers were unanswered. When you took her anyway, my prayers changed again."

"Then I asked for the strength to get through each day. To just breathe and be the best man I could." He was shaking so much now, his motions resembled and earthquake preparing to rumble. "But you even took that from me when I was forced to lie with a twelve year old little girl so you could make your money!" His voice escalated, startling everyone in earshot. "When that child was killed while giving birth, I asked for one thing, and that was that you be delivered to me alive, so I could kill you myself." He looked at Yvonna and her clan. "Finally my prayers have been answered." What he did next was so horrifying, neither Yvonna, Bricks nor Ming could believe it.

Bending down, he took a bite out of her face and spit the chunk out on the floor. As if they rehearsed this a thousand times, the rest of the children closed in and did the same thing. They chewed different parts of her body, as if she were a full course meal. Her wails didn't stop or hinder their process because they meant business. Bricks, Ming and Yvonna backed up and looked at the horrid scene, while Anna's bloody hand extended from the crowd as she mouthed, *'Help me.'*

Wanting to bounce, and in the loudest voice she could muster Yvonna said, "All I want to say is this, do not leave her alive."

The leader looked up at her, with Gabriella's daughter by his side and said, "If I do nothing else in life, I will see to it that this bitch does not walk the face of the earth again."

With that, the clan trekked up the stairs to a waiting Swoopes. Yvonna quickly grabbed a pen and paper, with a number to record Dynamite's number. She placed it on the door with a knife, knowing they would see it.

When Swoopes saw the stunned looks on their faces he asked, "What happened?" No one could articulate it in the right way, fearing they wouldn't do the scene justice. "What the fuck went on?" he pointed at the door as if they didn't know where they just came from.

"If you stop being afraid of basements, you would've seen the most horrendous shit you've ever seen in your life." Bricks admitted.

"First off I ain't scared. Second of all…"

The knock at the door ceased all conversation. It was light at first before growing louder. The clan dropped to the floor to avoid being seen from the windows. "Anna open up the door!" She banged harder. "It's Ramona."

"Wait. That's the bitch we gotta get next." Bricks whispered.

"What you think she doing here?" Ming muttered.

"I don't know. But if she comes in, she'll make shit easier for us." Swoopes responded.

BANG! BANG! BANG!

"Anna! Open up the door! I see your car parked out front. I just talked to you on the phone so I know you in there." She paused for a quick second. "If you don't open up, I'm coming in!"

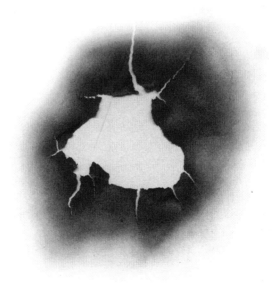

POLICE
STATION

Detective Connie Griswald sat in her chair, with her legs on her desk as she filed her nails. It wasn't in her nature to be lazy, but because her lieutenant was tired of her scratching up surfaces, which resulted in more work for his department, she was given a desk job. What a waste because truth be told, she was a great detective. However Lieutenant George South was more interested in maintaining a high closed case ratio, instead of finding out who actually committed the crime. He would put anybody behind bars, just to keep his impeccable, although flawed, record in place.

"Are your nails smooth enough?" Lt. South asked, hanging over her like a baiting storm.

She quickly placed her feet on the floor and threw her nail filer in the drawer. "Lieutenant, I was just…"

"Doing your nails." He attempted to smile, but years of trying to prove himself as a capable black lieutenant, didn't allow any signs of compassion to seep through. "Look, I'm not going to waste your time or mine, its time to go to work. And I need your help."

Her eyebrows rose. "My help?" She cleared her throat. "Is this some type of joke?"

He frowned and she wished she hadn't spoken to him as if they were homies. "Now why would you say that, Griswald?"

"Because you haven't needed my help in over a year."

"Well I need it now." He looked at her nails. "Or are you looking to make a career as a nail technician."

"No…no, I want to work." She shook her head rapidly. "Please tell me what I can do."

A manila file appeared from behind his back and he threw it on her desk. "Great. Now there was a mass murder at the AFCOG convention center some days back. Eight ministers were murdered in a ballroom. It was a brutal scene and the Christian community is in an uproar, believing God fearing people are being targeted by a mass murderer. I had Dunsen on it but as you know, he had a death in the family."

"What kind of monster would kill a minister?"

"Let alone, eight." He added. "Well, whatever monster responsible made it obvious that he isn't interested in what you or I think, which is why he needs to be caught."

"What makes you think it's a man?"

She was already reading further into things than he wanted her to. He would've never used her had his other detectives not been tied up. Lt. South didn't have a problem with her solving a case, just as long as she didn't spend too much time on leads, which went nowhere.

She eagerly picked up the file and skimmed through the documents. "Well?" he said looking down at her.

"What?"

"What are you waiting on? Get moving!"

She quickly grabbed her coat and headed for the exit. Turning back around she said, "I know this is far fetched, Lieutenant, but do you remember the reverend that was murdered some months back? I think his name was Pastor Robinson." She knew exactly what his name was, but often dumbed down her intellect to make him feel smarter.

"Yes." He dipped his head. "I recall that case. Why do you ask?"

"He was the same pastor that was involved in that case with the missing little girl many years ago. Remember, he was the last person who seen her at his church. The girl's name was Gabriella, and that case ended up being connected to Yvonna Harris."

His forehead wrinkled. "You mean the woman in the news for her multiple personality disorder?"

"Yes, sir. I think they made a movie on her life too." When he said nothing else she proceeded. "I know this is a lot, but I was thinking that the deaths of the eight murdered ministers and the pastor, may all be related some how." She hit a home run but his response made it seem as if there was no one in the ballpark to see it.

"Listen, Griswald, focus on the eight ministers. I don't want you adding murders to my department that don't involve me." She smiled and walked away. "Griswald!"

She stopped and faced him. "Yes, sir?"

"Remember what I said. Stay focused, unless you really want that career in the nail salon after all."

"I got it, Lieutenant. You can trust me."

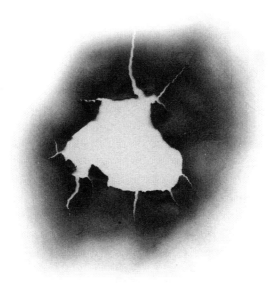

BRICKS

B ricks was in bed alone, looking at the bathroom door, which hid Yvonna inside. It suddenly had become her favorite hovel. Ming and Swoopes shared another bed and watched the TV, kissing on every commercial break.

"What we gonna do 'bout that, man?" Swoopes asked, although his eyes never left Ming's. "It's gettin' over the top now."

Bricks eyed him suspiciously. "Do about what?"

"You know what he talking about." Ming said, looking at the bathroom door. They could hear her having a good ole time talking to herself. "It's getting a little weird."

"It's *been* weird." Swoopes admitted. "And wit' the cops closing in on us, we need everybody on this team to have a leveled head."

Detective Connie Griswald had proven to be a worthy adversary. In the days since she was given the file, she had already questioned Bricks' family, his friend Kelsi, Ming's employees at the nail salon and even Swoopes' great aunt, whom he hadn't seen in ages, about where they were, and their possible involvement with the case and Yvonna Harris. How she knew the three of them were rolling together was beyond them.

"I'm still trying to figure out what the fuck ya'll talkin' 'bout." Bricks knew exactly what they were referring to, but he chose the moment to act ignorant. Anyway, he'd been to both of them separately about a plan of action and nothing ever came of it. Now the only thing he wanted to do was re-member his brother, kill rapists, and drink beer. "Anyway, I thought ya'll was 'bout to fuck."

The moment he said that, from the bathroom Yvonna said, "I don't want to hurt people! I'm tired of you making me do things I don't want to do." Ming and Swoopes urgently

looked at Bricks. He had to admit that the situation was esca-
lating. She was now talking about not wanting to hurt people.
The question was, which people?

Hoping she was talking to someone on the phone, although he knew she wasn't, he yelled, "Squeeze, who you
talking to? You on the phone or something?"

Silence.

"Uh...no, I'm not talking to anybody, baby. It must be
the TV in there."

Swoopes shook his head and Ming looked as if she
wanted to cry. "She's my best friend, and I don't know what
to do." She whispered. "I don't understand what this is. To
talk to yourself. She does it all the time now, and it's like she
loves it or something."

"Is it true?" Swoopes asked, Bricks. "That she got
schizophrenia or multiple personality disorder?" If she did, to
him it would explain the day she sucked his dick at Bradshaw's. If he knew it was the crazy person and not Yvonna,
he might have let her do it. "'Cause if she do, we have to take
charge of this operation. I want to see this shit through just
like the next person, but I don't want to die unless I have
too."

"So just because she's sick, you wanna kick her out?"
Bricks inquired with an attitude, although part of him knew it
would be best. "This was her idea to begin with not ours."

"I'm not saying that. But I am saying that we boxing'
wit' heavyweights. We can't afford to have her on the front-
line if she can't handle the fire." He focused back on the television. "Since she's your bitch like you so eloquently told me
more than once, it's your responsibility to take care of it."

Bricks knew he was telling the truth but he also didn't
want to tell his girlfriend that her opinion no longer mattered.
"From now on, I'ma be handling all aspects of this operation.
It ain't like I haven't been doing that anyway."

"You had help, nigga." Swoopes responded. "Don't act like you been rolling dolo."

"You know what I mean."

"And what are you going to tell Yvonna?" Ming asked. "She's not going to understand if we don't make her a part of the plans anymore."

"Allow her to think we still following her lead. I don't need the heat until I can figure out another plan. Just give me a few days."

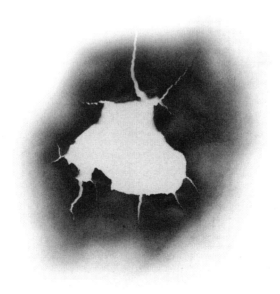

Shyt List V

BILAL, Jr.

B ilal, Jr. was lying on the bottom bunk, in his cell, while his leg unconsciously shook. He couldn't believe he was in such a fucked up predicament. He wasn't sure whom to fully blame. When he and Rozay were arrested because she fired the gun into the wall, per his request, the bullet penetrated a pedestrian's leg. And although the man was alive, it pierced his femoral artery and was threatening to take his life. At the moment Bilal, Jr. was being charged with the reckless discharge of a firearm, possession of a firearm and assault. If he died, the charge would escalate to manslaughter.

"Santana!" An officer yelled approaching his cell. "Rise and shine, youngster."

He stood up, brushed the back of his pants and said, "Yes, sir."

The correctional officer came into view. "You have a visitor."

His heart pumped wildly as the C.O unlocked his cell. When Bilal stepped out he said, "Turn around." He did and was dressed with a pair of silver handcuffs. He grabbed him by the forearm and led the way. "Right this way."

When Bilal, Jr. was taken to a grungy visiting area, he took a seat and looked at the glass separating him from the opposite side, as if it were a movie. Finally Uzi and Laser walked in. Disappointment covered him because the most ridiculous part of his soul, hoped it was Rozay since he heard she was released. Bilal, Jr. followed their lead and picked up the phone on his right.

"What happened?" Uzi got right down to business. "And why the fuck would you do something so dumb?"

In a less than audible voice he said, "It wasn't me."

"What you talking about it wasn't you? They found the gun with your fingerprints on it, Jr. Your fingerprints alone."

Bilal played the tapes back in his head. The last time he held his weapon, he'd given it to Rozay per her request and walked to the bathroom. When he remembered it had bullets, he returned, removed it from her hold and took the bullets out. He tried to give it back but she didn't accept. So at the very least, it should be two sets of fingerprints on the gun. "That can't be. Rozay pulled the trigger and..."

"Did she wipe the gun off before she handed it back to you?"

He scratched his head and his world spun. He knew she was sneaky but was she capable of such treachery? "I can't remember. I mean...I didn't see her do it." He had no idea that the young girl actually wiped her fingerprints off the gun the second Bilal stepped into the bathroom. She used the edge of the sheet. He was too ignorant to foresee or understand such things.

"Well you facing some serious charges. Plus," Uzi looked around, before peering into his brother's eyes, "They know about the other thing you did too."

He gripped the phone tighter and asked, "What other thing?"

Uzi laughed and sat back in the chair. "Come on, man. You know, the other thing." It finally soaked in. "It was the same gun, B, they already know about the dude Melvin and his bitch. And if the dude dies in the hospital, you got three bodies to concern yourself with."

Bilal saw immediately what was going on. The pain he felt in his heart was too much to explain. They were setting him up. "I don't know what you talking about."

"Come on, B." Uzi chuckled as Laser hung back and watched the show. "Stop fucking around. You know, the other thing you did."

"I thought you said it wasn't me." He swallowed. "I thought you said it was Laser."

"Look, lil nigga," Uzi said in a swift tone, "You not gonna try and put this shit on me or my brother." Suddenly it was as if they all weren't related. "Now it's your crime which makes it your time. Do you understand what I'm saying?"

"I don't even care no more."

Uzi laughed. "That's good, 'cause you gonna need that attitude to make it in prison." The smirk on their faces made him ill.

Bilal looked at both of them knowing it was over. Then he placed his fist on the glass so they could see his bruised knuckles. "It was me, who beat Easter to a pulp." He smirked. "I tried to kill that bitch but she had a head like a brick. If she ever wakes up, she should be brand new, minus the nonstop talking."

Uzi wasn't smiling anymore. "I'ma kill you, mothafucka! Do you hear me? You're dead!"

Bilal gritted on both of them. He was alone, and he reasoned that he had better get use to his new home behind bars. "It don't make me no difference, fuck both of you niggas. I'm out!"

RUFUS DAY

Beneath Rufus Day's compound was a fairytale world for kids. Colorful candy in red machines hung against the walls and brand new dolls with large smiles on their faces, waited for a little girl's love. So when Rufus led Tyisha downstairs, the grim look she once held was wiped away and replaced with a twinkle. She was in heaven within the crooked kiddie world.

"Oh my goodness!" Her eyes scanned the room and all the toys it had to offer. "It's beautiful down here." Like a puppy eager to play, whose master held him back, she trampled anxiously in place. "I never seen anything like it." When she first got there, she was worried about what he was going to do to her, because her spirit told her the man was off. All of that had changed because if this was how it was going to be, she would gladly spend a little time in his world. Ready to romp around the room she looked up at him and asked, "May I?"

He smirked having seduced yet another gullible and unprepared soul. "Yes you may."

On his command Tyisha took off quicker than an Olympic track star. First she hit up the candy machine and chewed two vanilla flavored balls in one breath. Then she tackled the baby dolls before boring of them quickly. On to the next thing, she hopped and flipped on the royal blue trampoline before moseying over to the pinball machine. He allowed her five minutes of uninhibited play, while keeping his lust at bay.

Approaching her from behind, he placed a firm hand on each side of her shoulders. An electric shock ripped through her, reminding her that something was deadly wrong. But she was a child, whose mother didn't arm her with the necessities, to spot a predator. With his leaky eyes, he looked down at her and noticed her body was already swaying. She should be, after all, he'd laced the candy she devoured with just enough Rohypnol, better known as the date rape drug, to make her high.

"You look like you're pretty good at this game." He praised. "Such a smart young lady."

She systematically pulled the left and right knobs as she continued to earn a high score. "I have a smaller version of this at home. But this one is bigger, it's like Disney World in here."

"No, sweetheart." He pruriently massaged the back of her neck. "It's better."

He sauntered away and sat on the huge yellow sofa. She was grateful for his absence but knew it wouldn't last. Although the game was the most important thing in the world, in a moment, all that would change. He had knowledge that the candy machine, which dispensed no more than two balls at a time, was just enough to get her high, while avoiding sleep. Besides, he liked his little girls awake and conscious.

"Tyisha, come sit next to me." He demanded.

"But I'm playing the game." She looked back at him and loathed the dirty look on his face. "I'm about to win."

"Tyisha, come to me now." With one last pull on the lever, reluctantly she trudged toward the sofa. He patted the space next to him, and she fell into the seat. "What's wrong? You don't want to sit next to your master? And keep him company? And please him? To put a smile on his face?"

She looked away and focused on the black life sized doll in the room. She wondered what things he'd done to her. "I do want to please you." She lied. "I think…"

He lifted her chin. "That's good. Because it's very important to make me happy with you. If you don't, I can make your life difficult and I don't necessarily want to do that. All I want to do is have fun." He raised his arms. "Look at this place. It's all for you."

She heard him but suddenly her mind floated and she couldn't get her thoughts in order. She saw strange colors. Some took on the shape of butterflies and flowers. While others resembled the devil, complete with horns, fangs and deep unsettling eyes. Frightened, she blinked twice and realized it was actually Rufus. What was happening to her? Her neck felt like rubber and she had trouble holding up her head.

She focused on the doll again. "Master, I feel sick." When she looked back at him, her head rolled downward and to the side. It was then that she noticed he was naked from the waist down. "What are you doing? You don't have any clothes on."

"Tyisha, get undressed, sweetie, and come over here to sit on my lap." In the past his face wore a warm expression, cunning yet inviting. Now his mouth hung open allowing his pink slick tongue to relax out the corner of his lips. Adoring the fear in her eyes, he groped himself until he was rock hard. As if it were not enough, he pulled her tiny hand and placed it around his clammy penis. She felt nauseous.

At this point Tyisha had seen and felt enough. She was mentally unavailable, yet she summoned the strength and courage necessary to run. Immediately he flew behind her. In this instance her height was a plus because she was able to shake him from right to left, throwing him momentarily off her trail. Angry that the kid was getting the best of him, he vowed to throw his weight on top of her body, to pen her down. When he activated his plan, he failed miserably. Instead, all he was able to do was push her to the floor. He grabbed her ankle but she kicked him in the face and dipped up the steps, leading out of the basement in a hurry. Before long, she faded into the rooms within his house.

When she made it to a small burgundy room with yellow flowered wallpaper, she closed and locked the door behind her. Once inside, she spotted a phone on the other side of a twin bed. Like a rabbit she leaped on top of it and gripped the handset. Her mind was starting to slow down even more and she was finding it impossible to remember her mother's number. It didn't help that from the outside of the room, she heard Rufus screaming her name at the top of his lungs in the house. For a moment she appreciated how big the compound was, because it gave her some time to shake him off her scent. After five more attempts to reach her mother, she was finally successful."

In a harsh whisper she said, "Mommy…he's…he's…"

"Tyisha, is that you?"

"Yes."

"Well what's wrong, baby? You sound out of it."

She looked at the closed door and breathed a sigh of relief. He hadn't knocked it down, so she still had time because he didn't know where she was. "Mommy, I want to come home. Please come get me."

"Why, what happened?" Before she could answer she continued. "Because you know this is a wonderful opportunity that the master has offered you. Don't mess this up, Tyisha."

Her memory had become more discolored and she was having trouble placing her words in order. If she could think clearly, she'd explain to her mother how for no reason, he undressed himself from the waist down. She would go on to explain that since she arrived at his house, her mind didn't feel the same. But as she felt her mother's energy, something told her nothing she said would have mattered.

"Mommy, please. Come get me! I want to go home."

Instead of support, her mother offered rage. Tyisha was so inappreciative and it made her sick. Rufus warned her about how she was acting lately. The program was for trouble kids and he explained that she would get worse, before she got better, and apparently he was right.

Besides, Marge needed the money more than her self-respect and pride. "Look, Tyisha, that man is trying to work with you so you'll be something better than what you are right now. Now either you respect him as our master and pastor, or I'll never talk to you again? Do I make myself clear?"

She swallowed the bitter pill of rejection, from the woman who was supposed to care for her. "Yes, mommy. You do."

Outside The Compound

Bricks, Swoopes and Ming sat in the car outside of Rufus's compound with a trunk full of C4 explosives. They left Yvonna in the hotel with her imaginary friends and she seemed to be okay with it. Bricks decided that it was best to attack Rufus first, since they believed he had a good idea of their M.O, which meant killing his captains first. His idea would catch him off guard. Plus with the heat the cops were bringing down, nobody wanted to get locked up when he was still out there. If that happened, it would be all for nothing.

"Look," Bricks pointed at a silver Benz pulling up to the gate at his compound. "That car might be what we need to get in.

"Ming hopes so! We been sitting out this bitch for four hours."

When the driver in a silver Benz punched a code into the keypad in front the gate, they inched closer. The moment the gate opened, they trailed behind her. They were halfway up the driveway leading to the house when the Benz abruptly stopped.

"What this bitch up to?" Bricks asked suspiciously. "It's not Rufus so he can't know what we're up to."

"Ming doesn't have a good feeling about this."

The car idled in the driveway for a few more seconds before Ramona; the car's captain, fired a nine-millimeter handgun out the window. The first bullet crashed into the rearview mirror on the driver's side but the others threatened to end their lives. They knew the white boy Chris said that it would take and electric current to detonate the bomb in their trunk, but no one was trying to prove him wrong.

So Swoopes and Ming fired back at her, crashing her back window followed by her trunk. Ramona continued to unleash as one bullet flew over Ming's head and into the keypad at the gate. She was clearly trying to kill her first. Thinking on his feet, Bricks speedily drove backwards out the driveway, before the entire car fishtailed to the side. On a mission Ramona continued to buck although she hit nothing but Rufus's mailbox. Luckily for them she was an awful shot.

Halfway down the road, Bricks slammed his fist into the steering wheel as his team looked out the back window, hoping she wasn't following.

"FUCK! FUCK! FUCK!" Bricks screamed. "We let that bitch get away! And she fucked up the plan for Rufus!"

"That shit was too close for comfort. We couldn't get rid of her now. Plus we gotta get to them kids in her camp." Swoopes confessed. "I ain't gonna lie though," he looked behind him once more, "I did think that was it." He looked at Ming. "Man I thought she almost hit you." He touched her face. "You gotta be careful about sticking your head out of windows and shit."

"Don't act like you give a fuck about me." She joked, lightning the mood.

"More than you know." He stated.

"When it's finally her turn, it'll be my pleasure to kill that bitch." Bricks admitted.

"No, Bricks, she almost killed me," Ming added. "Now this shit is personal."

Back At The Compound

Rufus came running out the front door when he heard all the commotion outside. It put him on edge when a hysterical Ramona fell into his arms. "What happened?" he asked as he held her up and looked over her shoulders. At first he thought she was involved in a car accident but now it looked like much more.

"They were on their way here, probably to kill you," she adlibbed, "so I fired back at them and they got away." She raised the gun in her hand. "This is getting to be so much, Rufus. She has to be stopped." She was saying shit he already knew. "She's killing everybody!"

Although they weren't successful, Rufus was furious. It was evident that the bitch and her crew weren't going away and they were smarter than he thought. He wondered if taunting them at the convention was a good idea after all.

"That's not all, Rufus. I had a meeting with Anna last night, but she didn't answer the door. So I came back this morning knowing she would be there. But when I walked into her house using my key, I found her mutilated body in her breeding camp, and all of the kids were gone." She ranted, gripping his arms. "I just know I'm next and then Abel. If we don't stick together, as you can see today, they're coming after you too."

Without a response, he dipped into the house but she followed. "No, you gotta go home, Ramona." He stopped her and she seemed confused. She just saved his life and this was how she repaid her? "I have a lot of things to do today. I don't have time for this right now. I'll call you."

"But what if they follow me?" She asked, wedging her body into the door. "I'm scared."

"You did a good job of defending yourself this time," he shrugged, "just do it again." He pushed her out by her face and slammed the door. Before finding Tyisha, he decided to call the hit man he hired to kill Yvonna. Surprisingly, he answered right away. "What the fuck is going on?" Rufus growled, as if he were a street nigga. "I gave you a job that apparently you can't handle. What are you, incompetent?"

"If you love yourself, never talk to me like that again."

As if he just had breakthrough therapy, he remembered he wasn't the go hard dude he portrayed himself to be. "I'm sorry, man. But this bitch is ruining my life." From where he stood he thought he heard Tyisha but he was wrong. "I need resolution like yesterday."

"And you'll have it. Just let me do my job. You on the other hand need to do your best to stay alive." Rufus hung up and didn't feel any better. When to his astonishment, Tyisha returned and stood in the living room.

In a weak voice she said, "Hi." She tried to keep her eyes open and maintain her stance in the upright position, but she was swaying like a withered bush. The candy she swallowed earlier was calling her name. "Looking for me?"

He grinned. "Yes, and you've been awfully bad, Tyisha."

"I know." She walked toward him and took his paw. "But I'm ready now."

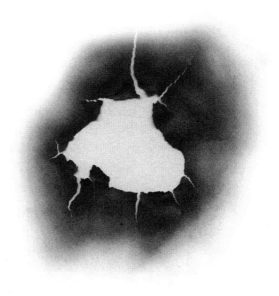

YAO

Yao and Charles Bank, sat in one of Yao's restaurants alone discussing business. In the world of killers, the best knew each other and so was the case with them. This is why when Charles reached out to Yao, in the name of learning his interest in Yvonna Harris, they decided to meet in the backwards part of Washington DC. It didn't take Charles long to investigate Yvonna's past and locate those she'd fucked over. She did a good job of leaving a trail in her wake, which lead him to the Chinese king pen.

"It's been a long time," Yao confessed, as they shared a table in the corner of the bistro. He sipped from the red merlot in his glass. "Even though it's been a while since we've been in contact, your legend stands strong." He placed his glass down. "That's why I was pleased when you reached out, I can always use a good man in my corner."

"My number hasn't changed in over 30 years." Charles, and immigrant from Jamaica, had been in America illegally for most of his life. His skin was the color of onyx and his eyes were dark and empty. He didn't have anything in his name, including a residence or car. Staying off the radar had become art for him. He moved within the underbelly of the criminal world, and only took jobs with the referrals of his most trusted friends. "And that's not why I'm here, although you are always free to use it."

"Yes," Yao grinned, "I'm quite aware that our past is not why you chose to reach out to me." He peered in his direction. "But it appears that we have the same person in common."

"You're correct. I have a relationship with Yvonna that has never received closure. She escaped me some time back, and I think about her most days since we last met." Since he didn't drink alcohol, he sipped from his coffee to mask his

frustration. "What have you done to locate her so far? Because if we are going to ban together to get this woman off the streets, I need to know everything you do."

"I'm ashamed to say that I haven't done enough." He forked the rice in his bowl and mulled over his failure. "If I had, I wouldn't feel the need to sit with you now." He wiped his mouth with the white napkin in his lap. "Together, hopefully that will change, because quite honestly, I have better shit to do with my day than to be meeting in secrecy about this bitch."

One moment he was pleasant and the next he was harsh. This was Yao's personality on a regular basis and people never knew how to take him. "You seem to have a problem with me right now." Charles responded. "I'm not the enemy you know."

"Never said you were." Yao pointed in his direction. "But asking to speak with me in private, without my men, makes me question your motives."

"There's no reason to distrust me. With me what you see is what you get. Plus, no one hired me to kill you, I told you who I want."

Yao didn't like his response. "That's great, because I'm going to ask you to do something you aren't prepared for." He poured more wine out of the bottle on the table and into his glass. Red dots splashed on the white tablecloth. "I need you to bring her to me, alive."

Charles creased his brow. He didn't know what Yao was about to say but he certainly hadn't expected this. "And why is that? Because as you know, I have orders to kill her. And there isn't a job I don't finish." He knew that wasn't totally true but after he got his hands on her again, it would be. She was the only person he let get away.

"Well you're going to have to leave this one alone. I need her to answer some questions the government has about the murder of Urban Greggs. Although she hasn't been formally charged, they suspect she's involved in the crime. And until she is found, they're taking their annoyance out on me because I was last seen with her. My fear is that if they dig further into my lifestyle, they'll discover some things I'd like to keep private. Not to mention I'm not able to operate my business the way I usually do, because I'm always surrounded by cops."

"I sympathize with your plight, but what you're asking me I simply can't do. I really hope you understand."

Angry, Yao jabbed a knife into the table and yelled, "You don't have a choice unless…"

The knife Charles wielded in Yao's direction, entered his throat, severed his vocal chord and took his life. Yao's arrogance caused him a horrible death. Yao said he knew the man before him and he was correct in that his legend preceded him, yet he went against his gut instinct by speaking to him so stridently.

Before their meeting, Charles didn't have anything against the man. Now that he was dead, Yao didn't have much against him either. But it was clear that they could not come together for the greater good, which was to rid the world of Yvonna Harris.

Charles was honest when he said he thought of Yvonna most days. The last time he saw her face, he was strangling the life from her body. He was hired to kill her when in a closed meeting, in a hotel room; he was given ten grand and a direct order. The discussion that night included Jona Maxwell, who was Yvonna's former psychiatrist. Lily Alvarez-Martin, Guy Samuels and Peter Jensen who were all sworn police officers and Terrell Shines, Yvonna's former fiancé.

At the end of the agreement, Charles promised to fulfill their wishes and kill Yvonna. The job was in the process when in the midst of taking her life by strangling her; he discovered she was nine months pregnant. Charles may have been a murderer, but he lived by a code and it was specific. *Never kill a child. Never kill and elderly person. And never kill a pregnant woman.* His motto was the only reason she

was alive to that day, but he had intentions on making that change.

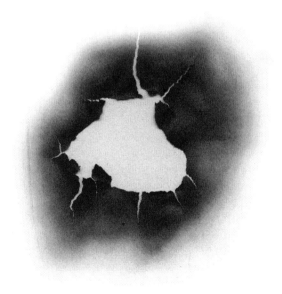

YVONNA

When Yvonna sat up in the bed of her hotel, she realized she was bored. The look on her face was mixed with exhaustion and pain. She was lonely, even though she had company.

"What's wrong with you?" Bilal asked sitting on the edge of her bed. "If you would've done what I asked you to do, maybe you wouldn't be so sad. Help somebody other than yourself. Go see about my son."

"I'm never that sad. Plus I wouldn't even know where to start with him. I told you that."

"Even I can see your wallowing in your own shit." Gabriella added, as she lay face up on Swoopes and Ming's bed. "Go out and have some fun. If they can why can't you?"

As much as she hated to admit it she was right. So, Yvonna decided to take advantage of the hotel pool, even though she was aware of the dangers of leaving the room. Yao was after her. The police were after her and as far as she knew, Rufus Day was after her too. She almost talked herself out of having a good time, until she recalled how her team treated her like an outsider lately. They would hold meetings in the bedroom, or speak outside in the hallway, anything to avoid her. Whenever she asked what was up, suddenly nobody had much to say. With the burner phone in her room, she decided to call Delilah before doing anything. She missed her and hoped she wasn't still angry with her for God knows what. The phone rang once before Jesse answered.

"Hey, sis." Yvonna sang. "What's going on?"

She sighed. "Nothing. Well, nothing unless you consider how Delilah cries nonstop. She seems so sad and I don't know what to do for her. Did something happen when she was with you, that you want to talk about?"

"I don't know why she's down, Jesse and it's been eating me up. One minute she was happy to be with me, and the next she was asking to be with you. I mean I needed her attention too but I guess nobody cares about that." Yvonna said selfishly. "I wish somebody thought about me sometimes."

"I am thinking of you, Yvonna. Always. I was just thinking the other day how much I miss you. One minute we were working on our relationship, and the next it was over." She sighed. "It makes me sad. By the way, how are you holding up? I mean, are you taking care of yourself?" She heard what she asked but she also understood what was really meant. "I worry about you a lot."

"Well don't." Immediately she regretted her snappy response. Jesse and her daughter were the only family members she had in the world. "Sorry, Jess, it's been rough lately."

"I know." She sounded annoyed. "Well let me get back to Delilah. Don't worry about her, you know she's in great hands."

"What are you about to do?"

"I have class after I take her to the playground. She also just started a new daycare program I enrolled her in." She laughed to herself. "She taking over it already. Anyway, take care of yourself, Yvonna. I love you."

"I love you, too."

Now she wished she hadn't bothered to reach out to her because she didn't get anything out of it. Taking Gabriella up on her advice, she decided to take a dip in the indoor pool. Since she didn't have a bathing suit, her underwear would have to do. She grabbed somebody's used towel from the bathroom, along with the key and headed out. A few women observed her with disgust but the men didn't seem to mind.

"I see you still got it." Bilal confessed, looking at her sexy curves. "You always knew how to turn heads."

"She'd be alright if she watched what she eats. If you ask me she should've did this a long time ago. Any exercise she can get will do wonders on them thighs." Gabriella commented.

"Fuck you."

When she made it to her destination she sat on the edge of the pool, placed the towel on the side and splashed the water with her feet. She loved the way the coolness felt running through her toes. Sprinkles splashed on her brown thigh and into her face and she realized this was just the stress reliever she needed.

"Jump in!" Gabriella encouraged. "You didn't come out here to sit around. Enjoy yourself."

Not being able to hold back any longer, she stood up, and dove into the middle of the pool. The moment she did she knew it was a big mistake. The first thing she noticed was that the water was unbelievably icy, but that seemed to be the least of her worries considering the stabbing sensation all over her body. Yvonna immediately felt panic and shock as she tried to reach the edge and climb out. Her energy was expended and within seconds; the breath seemed to be pulled from her lungs.

When she tried to gasp for air, she took in water instead. Not knowing what to do, she started thrashing about the water like a fish on land. Every now and again her mouth would open as she tried to call out for help. That's when she saw several people pointing in her direction with alarmed looks on their faces. Although Yvonna was an excellent swimmer, all of her experience was forgotten because now she was drowning. She looked at Bilal who was smiling. This was how she was going to die. Her life would end like this. She wasn't prepared. She wanted a little more time to make things right, but she knew in her heart, it was over.

Outside The Hotel

When Bricks parked the car at the hotel, he saw a large crowd surrounding the outside pool. "Why everybody at the pool? It's cold as a mothafucka out here. They having a party or something?"

"Right, what the fuck is going on?" Swoopes asked. "I could use a little fun if that's what's happening. Maybe grab me a bitch and the two of us can have a threesome." He continued looking at Ming. "What you think?"

"Don't get fucked up!" Ming said, elbowing him in the side. She focused on the disruption again. "I don't know, guys, but I have a feeling Yvonna is involved in this shit."

The moment she said that, they moved hurriedly toward the scene. When they could see through the crowd, Ming's theory was proven correct. Just as she thought, Yvonna's naked limp body was being hoisted out of the pool. A white man placed a towel on the ground, and hovered over her like a shadow. His lips quickly found his way over her mouth as he forced his breath into her lungs.

Not knowing he was performing mouth-to-mouth resuscitation, Bricks went into lunatic mode. "What the fuck that nigga doing on my bitch?"

Not thinking smart, he steam rolled toward the scene with Swoopes and Ming in his shadows. All three were ready for war but Bricks would've escalated to murder. It took all of five seconds for Bricks to elevate the rescuer by his coat, and throw him into the dirty pool in Yvonna's place. The man thrashed around, and a few onlookers switched their rescue efforts from Yvonna to him instead, to save his life. He could care less because with Yvonna in his arms, he knew it was time to bounce. Too many people had seen the four of them together and who knew if the police were already dispatched.

"We gotta go, slim." Swoopes said as he and Ming hung closely at his side. "I don't think it'll take more than five seconds for the cops to get here."

"I think you right." Bricks admitted. The foursome hit it to the car and sped away from the scene in search of another hotel. So Bricks could tend to Yvonna in the backseat, Swoopes took the wheel and Ming sat shotgun. Yvonna's head rested in his lap and her body curled up in the fetal position, as he stroked her hair.

"Is she okay?" Ming asked, with concern on her face. "She looks blue."

Yvonna's eyes opened at the sound of Ming's voice and her eyes rolled around. "What happened?" She placed her hand on her forehead. "I'm confused."

Bricks couldn't lie. He was happy that she was alive but angry that she placed herself and the team in such a fucked up predicament. "Squeeze, what the fuck were you doing? Don't you realize you could've killed yourself? You trying to leave me like that?"

Swoopes tried to multi-task by looking back at her and at the road ahead. "Yeah, what you trying to do, get us hemmed up? You know we got people looking for us."

Yvonna's eyes circled around the car before resting on Bricks. She was shivering and he massaged her shoulders over the towel to get her warm. It was easy to see why she was cold; she didn't have on anything but panties and a bra. "I wish somebody tell me what happened." She stated in a breathy tone. "I feel like somebody kicked me in my head."

"You jumped in an outside pool in the middle of winter! That's what the fuck happened!" Bricks yelled, harsher than he intended. "Now answer my fucking question! What were you thinking?"

"What you talking about?" She examined his eyes. "I was in an outdoor pool? I thought it was inside."

Bricks, Ming and Swoopes looked at each other. Yvonna's condition was quickly deteriorating and they could no longer deny it. Even if they didn't have this mission to accomplish, they needed to get her help. Outside of her young daughter, and a sister who had her own life, they were all the family she had. She was their responsibility and she couldn't take another incident like this, because the next one could mean her life.

Before going to the new hotel, they stopped by a department store to purchase her some clothes. Bricks remained in the car to keep an eye on her, while they went inside. When he saw Swoopes and Ming trekking back to the car, he realized that for the moment anyway, he was grateful for them. After grabbing a few more items, mainly liquor, they checked into a new hotel. Once Yvonna was asleep and nestled under five blankets, the three of them stepped out of the room to talk in private.

"That shit was close," Swoopes said swirling the Hennessey around in his cup. "I ain't never see no shit like that. She was actually about to drown to death."

"Me either." Bricks leaned against the wall before taking a sip of vodka. He seemed heavier than he already was and his mood didn't go unnoticed. "I don't know what I would've done if something would have happened to her, man. I appreciate ya'll for being there too."

"She's my friend too." Ming said, leaning on her man. "I'd do anything for her."

"How you holding up otherwise?" Swoopes asked. He might not have been his comrade, but he did a good job of checking on his well-being when it came to Melvin's loss. "You know, wit' your brother?"

He sighed and held back the tears that wanted to flow. Besides, he spent most nights crying in bed when the three of them were asleep anyway. There was no need to subject them to more of his sorrow. It could certainly wait. "I'm good, thanks though."

"You need your cup refilled?" Ming asked, pointing at it.

He sipped what was left and handed it to her. "That'll be nice."

Ming disappeared into the room and Swoopes moved closer to him, so only he could hear his whispers. "You know what we gotta do right?"

Bricks was confused. "Do about what?"

"Yvonna."

"Naw. You got any suggestions?"

"Better than that." He pointed at him. "I got a plan."

Later That Night

The room was pitch black as Bricks lay next to Yvonna in bed. He couldn't go to sleep if somebody knocked him out, too much was on his mind. Melvin...Chomps and this thing with Yvonna. He was crawling around in his head when Swoopes and Ming's sexual murmurs grew louder. Normally when they fucked they'd keep the TV on out of respect, but he reasoned they didn't care now. Good sex was a stress reliever so they had the best idea. While they got their life, he thought about Swoopes' plan. If they did things right, it would be exactly what was needed and hopefully he could get his girl back.

He was about to attempt to get some rest, when he heard Ming's soft moan grow louder. It was obvious that she was doing her best to mute her sound but like a dog in heat, he felt her sexual tension. He tried to go to sleep again until he heard the soft squishy sound of Swoopes going in and out of her wet pussy. It was then that he realized that it had been a while since he had sex.

He took one look at Yvonna's sleeping face and released his dick from his boxers. He wouldn't bother her because he wasn't interested in being with her in that way at the moment. Ming's moans grew louder and if he didn't know Swoopes was in the bed with her, he would've sworn she was playing with her own pussy. She sounded so sweet and her calls of ecstasy caused him to harden up. Closing his eyes, he thought of her tiny breasts and the thick manufactured ass. He stroked himself to a thickness he could've stabbed someone

with. For some reason, he remembered how much Ming begged to be fucked on a consistent basis and reasoned she was probably a freak in the bed. Her whorish natured caused him to throb as he worked himself harder.

He was almost about to cum, when Yvonna moved, opened her eyes and stared directly at him. Bricks didn't know if he wanted to run or slam his eyes shut to fake sleep. He knew she couldn't see his thoughts but he was sure he still looked guilty. The whites of Yvonna's eyes shined in the darkness and gave him no meaning. To say he was caught with his dick in his hand was an understatement.

When she disappeared under the covers, he thought she was going back to sleep. That was until the tip of her tongue found it's way on his chocolate stick. It slithered alongside his pole before she enveloped him inside of her hot mouth. Bricks was panicky and turned on at the same time. He knew she wasn't well, but the way she was sucking his dick, it was obvious her illness had nothing to do with her head game.

When he was positive she was handling business, he continued to focus on Ming's voice and body in his mind. It was wrong no doubt, but he knew he wasn't the only nigga on earth who imagined fucking his girl's best friend, nor would he be the last. Before he knew it, he poured his load into her mouth and she swallowed it all. Yvonna stayed down for a few more seconds, to lap up all of the milk he spilled.

When she came back up, she looked at him, at first without saying a word. When she finally spoke, a chill ran through his body. "Yvonna's a lucky girl. Her man is so sweet." With that she closed her eyes and went to sleep.

Bricks stayed up for the rest of the night.

RAMONA

Ramona was in a surplus store, in a mall, stocking up on items she needed to survive no matter where she went into hiding. She threw an item from her shopping cart, a North Face backpack, on the counter. When she heard something drop, she looked around where she stood to be sure she wasn't being followed or watched. The coast was clear and she took a deep breath. She needed to get as far away from Virginia as humanly possible.

When her phone rang, she answered when she saw it was Abel. Lately she felt she was all alone especially since Rufus shun her, and Abel seemed to be preparing for the final showdown, instead of offering support. In her opinion it was best for her to drain her bank accounts and move to a warmer climate, instead of fighting Yvonna Harris. Fluent in Spanish, she had Mexico in her sights and couldn't wait to get there.

"Hello," she added a first aid kit to her purchases, "where have you been, Abel? I've been calling you non stop."

"I met with some people who can help me sort some things out."

"What do you mean?"

"Where are you?" She asked suspiciously. "Maybe we can meet up and talk about it in person."

"I can't right now, Abel. I'm at a surplus store."

"A Surplus store? Where you going? Camping?"

"I'm going away." She explained as she placed the last of her items on the counter. "And if you were smart enough, you would too."

"Cash or credit?" The white male cashier asked.

"Cash." She thumbed through her money bundle. When a bill dropped out of her hand, she was about to yell at the person who picked it up, until she saw his face. It was the same man who she was firing at, back at Rufus' compound. It belonged to Bricks.

Suddenly the purchases on the counter seemed unimportant. She dropped everything and ran urgently through the mall to save her life. She didn't want to die. She wanted to live. But when she turned behind her she saw Bricks and Swoopes were still hot on her trail.

"Help!" She yelled. "I'm being robbed. They're going to kill me!"

Her cries for help seemed to have a different reaction then she intended. People avoided her like the plague as they ran in the opposite direction. Since it was early, the mall was virtually empty. Ramona was about to dodge into a cosmetic store, when Bricks fired in the doorway, impacting her path. She ducked, fell down and crawled a few feet before getting up to run again.

"Don't kill me! Please! I don't know what you want! I didn't do anything!"

She tried to run out the door leading to the garage but Swoopes fired at that exit too. Instead she dipped into the woman's bathroom and surprisingly, they didn't pursue. Out of breath, she looked under the stall to find an empty one. Since they were all vacant, she flung open the stall door closest to her and hopped on a toilet simultaneously releasing the 25-millimeter she had in the holster on her waist. Then she waited. Waited for the violators to come inside, so she could put them out of their misery.

And it seemed like forever. She discovered that in her case, the anticipating was worse than anything else. When someone walked in, she looked through the cream slit to see who it was. She couldn't see a face as they disappeared into the stall next to hers. She looked down at the black heels the woman wore and deducted that they seemed too stylish to commit a crime. And then she remembered, Yvonna adored fashions too. Maybe the legend herself had come to finish her off. Maybe cornering her in a bathroom was all a part of the plan. When she finally saw the beautiful Chinese woman exit the stall and walk to the sink to wash her hands, she was relieved. She didn't recognize her. So she tucked the weapon back out of sight, so that the woman wouldn't be afraid.

Ramona hopped off of the toilet, opened the door and walked up to the woman. "I don't mean to scare you, but someone out there is trying to kill me. I can't go out there right now or they'll get me. I need your help. Can you please go and tell the police?"

Ming tilted her head. "Why would they do that?" Her response seemed out of order considering what she just said. "I mean, what did you do to warrant your life being taken?"

She realized her mistake. Ramona backed into the stall and Ming followed her. She tried to reach for her weapon but Ming had already pierced her intestines by way of stab to the navel. She didn't stop there. To be sure she was dead, she slit her throat. Injured, Ramona slid face down on the soiled toilet bowl, until the last breath spilled out her body.

When the deed was done, Ming quickly exited the bathroom, ran into the mall and out the exit. When she got outside, she didn't see Bricks or Swoopes and immediately felt a sense of abandonment. It wasn't like they hadn't plotted in the past to get rid of her before. At one time they claimed she was too irritating and not as smart as they were. Maybe this was their opportunity. She was glum because she thought she was finally getting through to Swoopes. Thought he finally realized how much she loved him. What a fool.

When her phone dinged, she looked down at it and saw a message that changed everything. *"Throw me in the trash. You are about to run into an outsider."*

Ming's eyes gaped open and she tried to catch her breath and remain calm at the same time. It was code for somebody was on to them, probably a cop. Although she was scared, it felt good to have an answer for their dismissal. Swoopes didn't abandon her.

Quickly she located a storm drain, threw the phone down and kicked it inside. When she was done, she walked deeper into the parking lot, knowing they probably needed her

to get away from the mall to be rescued. She didn't make it too far before detective Connie Griswald pulled up in front of her.

With major attitude, she parked her unmarked police car and eased out. Flashing her badge she said, "Ming Chi, I've been looking all over for you."

Ming placed her hands on her hips, leaned forward and spit in her face. "You found me, pig! Now what?"

Griswald was ensued with anger. Not only had she disrespected her badge, she disrespected her body with her fluids. It was obvious that the only thing she understood was pressure. Griswald forcefully grabbed Ming by the forearm, slammed her against the car and slapped the cuffs on her wrists.

"What are you doing, Pig?" Ming laughed. "I hope you know you're about to end your career! You haven't even read me my rights!"

"Whatever you say, sweetie." She retaliated. "But until then, I'm taking you downtown to answer for the death of your uncle Yao. And the Eight Ministers of AFCOG."

RUFUS

Rufus' compound was surrounded with large trees and acres of land that went on for miles. Originally it was created to conceal what he was doing on the premises, selling young girls for profit. Now he appreciated the serenity, as he tried to think of a way out of the nightmare he got himself into.

Over the past few days, he beefed up security to a level that almost made it difficult for even him to do his dirt. Ten security guards surrounded the gate leading into the property, five shielded the front of the compound and six safeguarded him inside the premises. For extra protection, vicious attack dogs patrolled the grounds looking for anything or anybody who wasn't supposed to be there. The way he had things running, there was no way Yvonna or her clan could infiltrate the property, without causing themselves bodily harm.

He was watching television in the living room when he got a call from Abel Pickling. She said she was in front of his property but could not enter because his goons denied her access to the premises. He started to confirm their decision, since she showed up without an invite. Eventually he changed his mind because she and Ramona were the only upper level management people alive, who worked for AFCOG. Yvonna systematically managed to pluck everyone off one by one.

"Let her in." He told the guard on the phone. "It's okay."

"No problem, sir. She's on her way up."

He hung up and addressed the guards inside of the house with him. "Give us some privacy."

"You sure?" One of his men asked.

"Positive." He nodded.

They immediately left him alone and Rufus paced in place. Something about Abel rubbed him the wrong way. On second thought everything about her rubbed him the wrong way. Abel Pickling was an unbalanced individual with hunched over shoulders, baggy eyes and a face resembling a bulldog. Although she was by far the most unattractive woman on earth, she was serious about her money. That alone made Rufus trust her because she was just like him. There wasn't a thing she wouldn't do no matter how grimy it was.

Once he asked her to deliver a child to a pedophile in South Dakota. The man was just released from prison and was banned from being anywhere children roamed and that included the local malls. Since he was sure police were watching him at all times, he requested the child be brought to a car he rented. Parked in a warehouse district, Abel delivered a twelve-year-old little boy to him in the car. She sat in the front seat while he raped him without and ounce of remorse, as she read the newspaper.

When Rufus opened the door, he shivered. No matter how many times he saw her, he could never get over her grim appearance. Wearing a long black coat with a wide hood, she looked like a witch. "Finally you meet with me," she said as disdain masked her voice. She pushed past him and stood in the middle of his living room. "I've been waiting to see you, since it's obvious that you've been dodging me."

With Abel it was important to maintain control of the situation, or else she'd run all over him. "First of all you aren't to talk to me like that."

She walked up to him and slapped him in the face. Before he could fire back, she smacked him on the other cheek. "Ramona's dead. They found her in a public bathroom at the mall and it's all your fault." She pointed her decrepit finger at him. "Had you protected her, had you protected all of us, none of this would have happened."

Rufus didn't know whether to be livid that once again, Yvonna succeeded at picking off a member of his crew, or the fact that she placed her clammy hands on his face. "Abel, I don't know what's gotten into you, but if you ever put your hands on me again, there's going to be problems!"

"If you don't listen to what I have to say you'll have problems anyway." She threatened. She made herself comfortable on his couch without an invitation. "Get over here, Day. We must discuss a plan of action. It can no longer wait."

It was clear that the control he had over AFCOG was over. She didn't fear or respect him. Wanting to get her out of his house, he wriggled his body in the recliner and stared at her. "What do you have in mind, Abel?"

"I've had my assistant follow her. She follows her in the darkness and reports back to me daily. Which is how I was able to tell you about her friends." She coughed and a yellow piece of phlegm flew from her mouth and fell onto her coat. "Tissue?"

Disgusted he pointed to the end table next to her. "It's over there."

She grabbed a few pieces and said, "Like I was saying, my assistant Grey is really good, which is how I was able to tell you about her friends Bricks, Ming and Swoopes, as well as provide you with their pictures." She rubbed the mess off of her clothes and threw it on the floor. "But we've since lost her and don't know where she is. Anyway, she has a kid. Her name is Delilah and right now she's staying with her sister Jesse." She coughed again. "She delivered the kid to her some time ago." She was an ugly woman but she certainly wasn't dumb. "If we kidnap this child, I'm sure we can get Yvonna to come out of hiding, and when she does, we can finish her off."

At first he was certain that nothing Abel said, would make him feel better, but he was wrong. Even though he had Charles Bank on the case, if he could coax Yvonna to turn herself over to him by stealing her child, he could save some money and some energy in the process.

"What if it doesn't work?" He crossed his legs. "You're assuming she has a heart and that she cares about the child."

"She loves her. If you remember, that's what got all of this madness started in the first place. Maybe you should've left them alone. She came after you because she's afraid that as long as you live, she won't be able to lead a fulfilling life with her child. Let's make sure she's right." When Tyisha walked into the living room, with a man following her, Abel looked at Rufus. "I see you're still making money, by any means necessary."

"Not as much as I use to." He stood up and walked the pedophile to the door. The freak handed him five hundred dollars and left without as much as a bye to the girl. Tyisha not knowing what to do stood in front of him. Her eyes were heavy and she seemed despondent. "Go wash up, and when you're done, get in my bed. You need your rest."

When Tyisha walked away Abel said, "You love testing the goods don't you?"

He nodded.

"One day that nasty trait is going to get you killed. I promise."

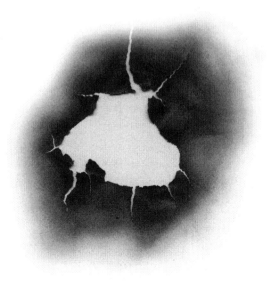

BRICKS

J ay Z's latest CD played on the car stereo, as Bricks and Swoopes sat in a stolen black Caprice. They were on a mission. After following Terrell Shines for twenty minutes to a strip club, that he waddled inside half drunk and out of his mind, they were waiting for him to reappear so they could attack.

When Swoopes told Bricks his idea included kidnapping the doctor in an effort to help Yvonna, at first he wasn't interested. The last thing he needed was getting caught by the cops, and risking an opportunity to finish what they started. But Swoopes was persuasive, and he convinced him that unless they were taking Yvonna to be committed, she would get worse before she got better.

"Why you think Yvonna would get wit' a nigga like him?" Swoopes asked, leaning back in the passenger seat, smoking a blunt. When it entered his left lung, he hit his chest and coughed. A puff of smoke flew out of his mouth and disappeared into the air. "Seems like a square to me."

"She probably wanted something from him." Bricks dug into the large Cool Ranch Doritos bag in his lap. "Why would any bitch of Yvonna's caliber fuck a square?" He licked his finger to get the seasoning off.

Swoopes looked at him and shook his head. "Man, them the gayest chips to ever be made."

"Fuck is you talkin' 'bout, cuz?"

"Any chips that you have to lick your fingers to enjoy," he pointed at his hand, "is a bit soft if you ask me."

"Nigga, stay the fuck outta mine and worry 'bout you." Although he hated the comment, he would refrain from finger licking for future references. "Oh, and next time you and Ming decide to fuck all hours of the night...don't."

Swoopes was in mid smoke when Bricks made his comment. "Look, nigga, don't get mad at me because you outta sorts with your shawty." He placed the blunt against his lips and pulled. "The way we been cooped up, ain't nothing left to do but fuck."

Bricks laughed. "You right about that shit." He ate a few more chips. "So ya'll official? You and Ming."

Swoopes passed him the smoke and leaned back. "I haven't had a girl in months."

"What you talkin' 'bout, you was dealing with that broad Crystal in Vegas."

Swoopes recalled her face. "Crystal was around but she was weak. She didn't have her own mind, that's why I didn't give a fuck when she got slumped." He watched a stripper rush to her car with two bodyguards following her. She must've been a star he thought. "If she was strong, I could've seen myself with her for real, but she wasn't. At the end of the day, she lost herself in me." He thought about Ming and how she needed something from him. "Ming is a different story. I get the impression that she wants love, because she deserves it, not to please me. I respect that. I respect her. "

"You crazy."

"I *am* crazy." Swoopes announced. "And I'm use to it now. At first I'd get into my feelings when people said that shit about me but now I shrug it off as truth."

When they saw Terrell hobble out of the strip club with his keys in one hand and a stripper's ass cheeks in the other, Bricks and Swoopes eased out of the car. He was so busy laughing it up in the dancer's face, that when he came up for air, he didn't see the knuckles coming at him full speed ahead. When he finally realized his fate, he dropped to the ground and the female with him took off running in the opposite direction. In a joint effort, Bricks and Swoopes picked him up, popped the trunk and threw him inside. Terrell was dizzy in the darkness trying to figure out what was happening and why. He wasn't even sure who accosted him because in the frenzy, he didn't see their faces. But when he finally saw them, he wasn't happy about it.

"What the fuck do you niggas want?" He screamed the moment the trunk popped open. They were in the driveway of his home. Although it was in a residential neighborhood, the other homes were not close by, allowing them to hide under the night's cover. "This shit is gone too far!"

With the absence of words, Swoopes stole him in the face silencing him momentarily.

Terrell pressed his bloody lips with his hands and looked at Bricks. Maybe he would be more reasonable. Removing his hand from his face he asked, "Do you want to tell me what the fuck is going on?"

This time Bricks took the liberty by slugging him in the eye. Terrell placed one hand over his swelling eye and the other on his protruding mouth. If he had a third hand he would've placed it over his crotch because they were liable to do anything at the moment. It didn't take the good doctor long to realize who was in charge and it damn sure wasn't him. "You know what's going on, nigga." Bricks advised, shaking his hand. The last blow pressed his knuckles in the wrong way. "You being kidnapped."

"And don't even bother asking why because we bet you already know." Swoopes added, peering at him.

Taking his hand off of his mouth, in a submissive tone he said, "Can I talk now?" Bricks nodded once. "Why you doing this?"

"Because when we asked for your help," Bricks advised getting angry all over again, "you didn't give it, so now we taking it."

"Well what you need? Because whatever it is, you don't have to do this shit." It was a miracle! Suddenly the doctor was on some Good Samaritan shit. "Whatever you do, please don't hit me anymore."

"We need medicine." Bricks responded, looking around. "And we need it tonight."

"How am I going to get medicine this time of night? I'm not a pharmacy."

Swoopes was about to hit him again until he flinched, and protected his eyes. When he let his guard down, he stole him in the mouth again instead. "Can you please stop hitting me?" He yelled. "That shit hurts!"

"When you stop fucking around, you can go 'bout your business." Bricks responded. "Now we out front of your house and I know you got a prescription pad in there somewhere." He observed the glazed over look in his eyes. "You probably using the shit for your personal use. We don't give a fuck. All I care about is you writing one up for Yvonna, enough to last her a long time. And then we gonna go get it filled, together."

"Even if I do that…"

"You mean when you do that." Bricks corrected him.

"When I do that, Yvonna is not going to take her meds. And if you gotta go this far, you already know that. I was with her for years and she never did what was good for her." He tried to reason with both of them but all he was doing was making them angrier. "I'll do it if you want, I'm just letting you know."

Bricks hated to admit that he had a point. Immediately he thought of another plan.

"Don't worry 'bout why the cow goes moo." Bricks advised as Swoopes looked at him sideways. "Just go in that mothafucka and get what the fuck we askin' for."

Without another word, they grabbed him out the car by his ears, and pushed and pulled him into his house. They found his prescription pad in his office and watched him scribble several prescriptions for her. Bricks and Swoopes didn't know what was needed, so Terrell could've faked them out and gave them anything. But it was obvious that the way he looked through his medical reference book and referred to her chart, which was still in his office that he cared. When he was done they drove to a 24-hour pharmacy and Bricks went inside while Swoopes guarded Terrell. Thirty minutes later, he had the medicine they needed.

Once Bricks climbed back into the car, from the back seat Terrell asked, "So are ya'll gonna let me go now?"

"Yeah," Swoopes, who was sitting in the backseat with him, responded. Then he reached over Terrell's body, opened the car door and shoved him out with his Nike Boot. "Get the fuck out." Terrell rolled out into the street, missing an oncoming car by inches.

When he was gone, Swoopes locked the door and climbed back in the front, as Bricks continued to drive. "I got one question and one question only for you."

"Shoot." Bricks said, merging onto the highway.

"Did you really tell that nigga not to worry about why the cow goes moo?"

"Nigga shut the fuck up!" Bricks laughed.

The Next Day

When Yvonna woke up, after being drugged with two Benadryl's and a healthy glass of Merlot, she was sitting in a dark room on the floor, with Bricks, Ming and Swoopes standing over her. "What's going on?" She asked rubbing her head. "And why are ya'll looking like that?"

Bricks stepped up to her. "We have good news and bad news."

"Well since I'm scared right now, give me the good news first."

"Yao was murdered and he's no longer chasing us. He's not a problem anymore."

Ming dropped her head, and Swoopes pulled her into his body. Although she knew he was a despicable man, she loved him anyway and the news hurt. It didn't make things any better that the detective told her in anger.

"Are you serious?" She looked at the three of them. "He's really gone."

Bricks smiled. "Dead serious." He swallowed. "Now that's the good news, the bad news is, you've been relieved of duty, Squeeze. For now anyway."

"What?" She looked at them strangely and when she tried to stand up, noticed her ankle was chained to a wall. Somebody was always treating her like an animal, maybe she was. "What is this?" She tried to move her leg but it was securely locked. "Why are ya'll doing this?"

"To protect you and keep you safe." Bricks responded.

On the table in front of her was a cloudy glass of water and some crackers. "What is all of this? And where am I?"

"You're at a safe location. And you gonna be here for the next couple of days, until we sort some things out and get rid of AFCOG."

"Bricks, don't fuck with me. My head hurts right now and I don't have time for this shit."

"I'm not playing with you. And I haven't been this serious in a long time." In a loving voice he continued. "You not well, Squeeze and we want you to get better."

"By chaining me to a fucking wall and feeding me dirty water and crackers?"

"Don't worry, if you drink this water and not waste a bit, you'll get a better meal. We not leaving you here forever, just until we work things out."

Focusing on Ming she said, "Don't let them do this to me. Please."

"I'm sorry, but we're doing this because we love you." She said in a low voice. "This is not meant to hurt you."

"Ming, if you let them do this to me, I never want to talk to you again. Do you hear what I'm saying? Never!"

"I'm sorry you feel that way...but I can't."

Looking back at Bricks she said, "I hope you know I'm never going to talk to you again after this shit. I would never have done something so foul to you, Bricks. This is wrong and you know it."

"Well for an opportunity to make you better, that's a chance I'm willing to take."

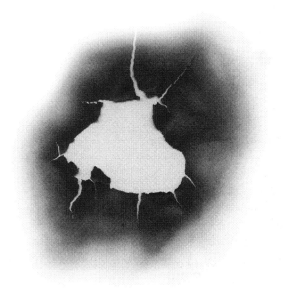

Shyt List V

CHARLES BANK

harles sat in his white Subaru, across from a daycare center, watching happy kids play outside. He was surprised at how lax the staff was at, '*With Love Daycare Center'*. The white woman with a red updo allowed most of the children to play next to the open gate, as she preoccupied herself on the phone. This had been the third day in a row Charles followed Delilah, and he trailed her whether she was with her aunt Jesse or not. Although watching their love for one another took his mind off of his murderous lifestyle, it wasn't his intent.

He was waiting on Yvonna Harris to show her pretty face, so he could finally put her out of her misery. When his cell beeped indicating his battery was running low, he bent down to plug it into the charger. When he rose, he saw Delilah being walked away by a man he had never seen her with before. He knew Jesse had a boyfriend, but that he was away at Florida State. He also knew Yvonna was involved, but Bricks, who he could identify, was on the run with her. The man who held Delilah's hand was definitely a stranger.

Although the child seemed not to mind going with him, something about his gait told him something was wrong. He watched, as the man looked both ways as he led Delilah to the sidewalk and toward his car. To be sure he wasn't losing his mind, he looked for the woman who was supposed to protect the kids. She was involved in a heavy conversation and was not tuned into the scene. What a dumb bitch.

"You can't be serious!" he said to himself. When he saw the stranger open the passenger side door, place her inside and jog to the driver's side, he knew what was happening. Delilah Harris was being kidnapped in broad daylight. If the abductor were successful, there would be no need for Yvonna to check on her only child. This would do nothing but make his job more difficult. He needed Delilah's life to remain in tact because she was his bait.

When the man pulled out into traffic with Delilah in tow, Charles followed behind them, doing his best to avoid being detected. The moment he turned on a residential street, Charles rammed his car into the back of his vehicle. The man's wild eyes through the rearview mirror told Charles he knew it was done on purpose. The stranger sped up, in an attempt to get away but he was rammed a second time. Again the wrongdoer was able to regain control of his car. But when he made a left turn on another block, Charles plunged into him so hard, he went flying into the stop sign a few feet before him. The hood popped open and the glass shattered the man's view. Smoked poured from the car and it looked like it was seconds from blowing up.

Charles instantly hopped out of the car, leaving his door open. He zoomed up to the kidnapper's vehicle, flung his door open and pulled him to the ground. Briefly he looked inside at Delilah who was in her seat belt and alive. "Who the fuck are you with?" He asked the abductor.

The man was off balance because he was just forced into a stop sign without his seat belt. His head was split open and his own blood poured into his eyes. Stealing him in the face again Charles asked, "Who the fuck are you with? Answer me!"

"I...I don't know what's happening."

Charles released his gun stuck it in his open wound. "This will be the last time I ask you." He looked around and saw a woman open her door with a phone in her hand. She had already activated 'Run Tell That' and the cops would be there in a minute flat, so he had to hurry. "Who are you with?"

"Rufus Day and Abel Pickling. Of AFCOG." He placed his hand on his stomach. "They hired me, to kidnap her for ransom. Now can you please get me some help? I'm think I'm dying."

Tiring of him quickly, Charles stood up, tightened the silencer on his nine and shot him in the body followed by a blow to the head. The man jerked once before closing his eyes permanently. With him dead, Charles dipped to the passenger side, grabbed Delilah out the car and picked her up. She kicked at first but she quickly realized she was no match for his strength. None of this shit was in the plan and he was heated. He threw her in the car like a rag doll and jumped in the driver's seat before speeding away.

Angry he looked over at her. "What's your name?" Although he knew it.

"Delilah." She responded softly.

"Why would you go with somebody you don't know, Delilah? Without screaming? Don't you realize he could've hurt you real bad?"

She shrugged and looked up at him. "He said he knew my mommy. And I wanted to see her again."

"Well he didn't!" He focused back on the road. "Some men do evil things to little girls. And if you don't watch out, they're going to do evil things to you too." He felt he wasn't getting through to her and decided to go deeper. Since it was obvious that the staff was incompetent, he wanted to drive his point home, in case there was another attempt on her life. At least until he got a hold of Yvonna, then she could do what she wanted. "There are a lot of bad men out here. Who'll take a little girl like you and make her do all kinds of things that will hurt badly. So the next time a man grabs your hand you don't know, you better scream to the top of your lungs. Or else he'll kill you." He parked in the same place he was before he pulled off. "You understand what I'm saying? It's for your own good." She nodded.

Before he stepped out, he looked across the street at the daycare employee who was still on the phone. She was so oblivious to her surroundings and that a child was stolen under her watch that she carried on like all was well with the world.

Frustrated Charles got out of the car and walked around to Delilah's side. When he opened the door she hopped down and placed her hands on the ground to break her fall. Standing up straight, she dusted her fingers off on her clothes and looked up at him. He could tell she was scared and although he was irritated, he understood she was a child.

"Go 'head." He pointed at the daycare across the street. "Look both ways and then cross."

When he walked to the driver's side, he noticed she hadn't budged. Before getting in, he looked around again, approached her and asked, "What are you doing?" He pointed toward the street. "Go ahead...there aren't any cars coming."

She shook her head. "My mommy said don't cross the street by myself."

"I bet your mother told you not to go with strangers too, but you did anyway!" He yelled. After all, the child was being ridiculous. "Didn't you?"

She was about to cry until he said, "Please don't." He observed his surroundings once more. Little girls crying crept him out. She was draining all of the life from him and when he was done with her, he was going to call it a day. "Don't cry, Delilah. I didn't mean to yell at you." He put his hands out in front of him. "Please, stop, I'll go with you across the street."

He grabbed her hand to lead the way. When he did, she let out a blood-curdling scream. She chose now to follow his advice to yell whenever a stranger grabbed her. In his opinion it was the worse timing but what was a killer to do? The lady across the street finally recognized she was a child short and dropped the phone on the ground as she headed toward the gate. Charles flew into his car and left the scene, observing the woman in his rear view mirror. When he was far enough away from getting detected he shook his head and said, "I'm getting too old for this shit."

CONNIE GRISWALD

Connie Griswald drove speedily down the highway at midnight, half tired and afraid. Her lieutenant said a crime occurred at his home and he needed her help. When he first called, she was hesitant about answering, when she saw his number on the caller ID. They had an argument earlier in the week when she arrested Ming Chi, after tailing her without authorization. Lt. South tore her a new pussy when Ming was brought into the precinct and Ming's attorney threatened to sue the entire department and their mothers too. Not to mention she was distraught over hearing about the loss of her uncle Yao in such a hostile manner.

Griswald knew it was a bad idea when she arrested her, but Ming sent her over the edge when she spit in her face and she wanted to implicate her in the crime. In the end Lt. South determined that Ming Chi had no more to do with the AFCOG murders, than President Barack Obama. He certainly didn't see where she was going with her insinuations, by assuming that Yao's death was related to the minister murders. But Griswald thought differently.

She believed that because Pastor Robinson was murdered not to long before the AFCOG ministers, that there was possibly a link to Yvonna and Yao too. It was a long shot but one she gladly took. She would've preferred to interview Yvonna but could never find her. It was as if she fell off the face of the earth. Ming on the other hand, was easy to locate because of her weaknesses. The need to see her son, Boy, who was staying with one of her aunts in Maryland and her reckless use of the phone. So when the time was right, she followed her and it ended up being her latest mistake.

When she pulled up at his residence in an upscale city in Maryland, he was standing in the doorway wearing grey slacks and a matching grey sweatshirt. He didn't seem happy to see her even though he extended an invitation. He opened his door wide and said, "Come in, Griswald."

Griswald pulled out a pen and pad. "I got here as fast as I could, lieutenant. I'm sorry it took me so long." She closed the door behind herself. "Did you contact the local police first? Or am I the first one on the scene?"

"I didn't contact them. I need your help instead." He walked toward the back of the house. "I know you have a knack for solving a case under a case." His tone was off and it made her uncomfortable. "So I figured this would be right up your alley." He looked back at her. "Follow me, it's right this way."

When he walked down the hallway and stopped at the door, she followed suit. Until they were standing in front of a bathroom. "What is it, sir? The suspects were in here?"

"Yeah, and they left something in the toilet that I wanted you to check out."

She laughed until she saw he was dead serious. "You're joking right?"

"No I'm not, Griswald. Look in the toilet," he pointed, "the evidence is there."

She stepped inside and saw yellow water and brown stool floating in the bowl. "Sir, what is this? I'm not understanding what it is you'd like me to do. I'm not a forensic scientist. I'm a detective."

"I know who you are, Griswald, although you forget at times. Like I said, the evidence is all right there." He smirked. "Now I have some gloves under the sink along with some plastic bags. Get them out. You'll need them to be sure you're following every lead."

"Sir," she laughed, waiting for him to say he was kidding, "What lead can this possibly tell me?"

"I guess you'll find out after you remove it."

She laughed from embarrassment more than comedy. "I can't do this."

"You can and you will."

She could tell by the look in his eyes, that he was not backing down from his request. She needed her job. Not because she had bills, or a child or even responsibilities. She needed to be a cop because without it, she was nothing. So she did what she had to do. Following his orders, she grabbed the gloves and a plastic bag. And then she turned her head, reached into the toilet and felt for the log. When she found the shit she grabbed it and threw it inside the bag, before tying it in a knot. She placed it down on the floor because she couldn't bare to have it in her hands, and removed the gloves. Tears fell down her face and she was humiliated.

"Sir...I...I don't," she took two quick breaths to prevent crying, "I don't understand what this is all about." She looked at the bag.

"You came here to do a job. And I pointed you to the bathroom so you could follow the lead. What is there to understand?"

"You said the perp left evidence in your bathroom." She threw the gloves in the trash. "And then I find stool. Like I said, I'm not a forensic scientist. There was virtually nothing I could do about this. I'm not even sure what happened. You haven't told me anything."

"You are absolutely correct. You were asked to collect evidence without knowing the facts. You were given a job," he stepped closer to her, "and I made shit out to be more than what it is, just like you, Griswald." She held her head down, having gotten his point. "Don't look so sad, Griswald, if I can take your shit, you can definitely take mine."

"I'm sorry, LT."

"What?" He leaned his ear closer to her lips, to hear her better.

"I said I'm sorry, lieutenant." She said louder. "I get where you're going with this. I'm an idiot for bringing Ming Chi to the precinct, without having evidence that she was guilty. Forgive me."

"I know you're an idiot, but that's not why I'm *not* going to fire you. I'm going to give you another chance because you're young and dumb, and too smart to realize when you're ahead. I'm not going to fire you because despite your fuck ups, you're a good detective. But the next time you disregard my orders, it will be over for you. And when that happens, taking my shit will be the least of your worries."

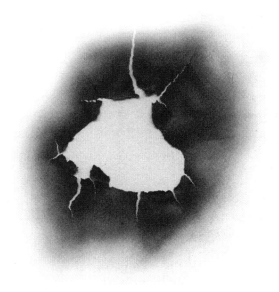

Shyt List V

ABEL PICKLING

Bricks, Swoopes and Ming followed no more than three cars behind Abel Pickling on the Maryland highway. They knew this was the last kill before moving onto the man of the hour, Rufus Day. Originally they went to Delaware to find her, before she was spotted in Maryland. They were partially anxious and eager to put this AFCOG shit behind them.

"Where the fuck do you think she's going this time of night?" Swoopes asked, wiping his fingerprints off the bullets before placing them in his gun. "We've been trailing this bitch for hours."

"You don't think she knows we're following her do you?" Ming asked, sitting in the back seat, behind Bricks. "And telling people we're following her? They say she's the most dangerous out of the four. We have to remember that shit."

"Naw." Bricks guessed. "That old bitch is looking for something. Eventually she'll stop driving and when she does, we'll put something in her head. I'll be glad too, because it's time to get at Rufus, once and for all."

They followed her for another fifteen minutes. Shit was groovy until she turned off the highway and onto a dark rural street. The only vehicles on this street were Abel's, theirs, and two other cars.

"Be careful over here, man." Swoopes observed, looking out into acres of dark land that appeared to go on forever. "It looks like they be lynching niggas over here."

When she made a right into a lot, they observed the sign on top of the entrance. It read *Pumpkin Face Haunted House*. "This the joint Tata was telling us about." Bricks added. "She owns this spot."

"But why come over here now?" Swoopes inquired. "It's gotta be closed for business."

When she turned into the lot suddenly they were all alone. If they didn't know before, they knew now. She had to be fully aware that they were following her. And outside of the taillights on Abel's car and their headlights, it was completely dark. Just when things couldn't get any wilder, she sped up and killed her lights. They tried to speed after her but they didn't know nor could they see where they were going. As she mashed on the gas leaving a dust cloud in her wake. Before long, all they saw was pitch-blackness and a puff of dust from their own wheels.

"Let's get the fuck out of here, man." Swoopes suggested, looking out into the night. "This shit is a set up and we can't see shit. This is her battlefield and we walked right into it."

"I don't feel good about it either." Ming said, looking behind her. "Please, get us out of here, Bricks! I'm scared." Considering she was never frightened, it was not necessarily a good thing.

"We gotta get this bitch now and get it over with." Bricks advised keeping up with his high-speed car chase. "I'm not trying to be chasing this bitch back to Delaware, Ming. Either we do it now, or let her get away. And I didn't come this far to let her go. Did you?" He looked at Swoopes and back at Ming, she was visibly shaken but she had to man up. They were playing in the major leagues.

The moment he said that, three sets of car lights turned on. They were parked on the side until they gave chase behind them, so they didn't know they were there. "I knew it was a fucking set up!" Swoopes yelled, cocking his weapon. "It's time to show and prove now!"

"They gonna kill us!" Ming cried, heavily. "I don't want to die! What about my son?" She responded, tears pouring out of her face. "I don't want to leave him. I'm not ready to leave him!"

"Ming, cut it out! You my bitch ain't you?" She nodded yes. "And my bitch is thorough right?" She nodded again and smiled, as her body shifted from left to right because Bricks was driving so fast. "Then man up."

"Yeah, we got this, Ming." Bricks said, more confident than he felt. "Ain't no need in you throwing in the towel already. Just cock your weapon and get ready to handle your business though."

Swoopes and Ming knew what that meant. It was time to go to war and they had a method too. They always sat on the opposite side of the car so that if they had to fire, they wouldn't be in each other's way. Soon as they rolled their window down, Ming leaned her upper body out of the car like she did back at Rufus' compound. She fired twice before ducking back inside when Bricks hit a bump.

"Can you be careful? You almost made Ming fall."

"Ming, I'm trying to save our lives. You just do what you gotta do to keep them dudes away from us."

Swoopes got some good hits on one of the oncoming cars but Bricks needed him to knick the driver.

Being inspired by how her baby looked on the money she said, "Let's do this shit! I'm Ming Chi, the baddest bitch in Maryland."

"You sure are!" Swoopes agreed. "Now buck them niggas, babes."

She placed her head out of the car and the moment she did, she was hit with a shot to the body. She dropped down over the door and fell out of the car. "Oh, my fucking God!" Bricks screamed, when Ming was no longer behind him. "Please tell me they didn't get her."

Swoopes was so overwhelmed, that he slunk back in the car and looked out at the road ahead of him. Then he looked back at the place the love of his life was once sitting. He was always the type who didn't realize a good thing until it was too late, so he was heavy with remorse. They killed the first girl he could say without a doubt, that he was in love with. In a monotone voice he said, "Bricks, pull up and park. We gotta handle this shit right here. I'm not running from these mothafuckas no more."

"What?" Bricks looked at him and then the haunted attractions he kept circling, to elude their chaser. "We can't pull over, we have too many people after us." He looked in the rearview mirror. "Take a look."

Swoopes peeped over at him. "You did what you wanted to do and now my girl is not here. I wanted to leave remember? But we did what you wanted and now she was gone." he said in a soft but hard tone. "Just do it."

Bricks could tell by the expression on his face that he was grieving, but he also knew he wouldn't suggest something so foolish unless he had a plan. He wasn't sure what the plan entailed, but he knew he had one all the same. Remembering Abel and how they needed her dead, he took a good look at the road ahead. When he had a good visual picture, he sped up real fast and killed the lights on the car. Then he dipped to the left, and fell into the darkness. Within five seconds, just as he thought, two of the cars crashed into each other, before blowing up in flames. Now they had one car to worry about plus Abel Pickling, who was some where on the property.

In the confusion, Bricks and Swoopes ditched the car and decided to take their chances on foot. "This way, man." Bricks said, barely able to see ahead of him. He dipped into a haunted house some feet ahead of them, with Swoopes right behind him. Since it was December, the attraction was closed until next fall but that didn't make it any less creepy. "I can't believe we lost shawty. Yvonna's gonna lose it. This is all my fucking fault!"

"We can't think about her now." Swoopes said, wanting his mind clear. Everything in him desired to grieve but he knew what could happen if he didn't get his thoughts together. He was at war and it was the last place you needed to be if you had heart. "We have to keep focused and get out of this."

When they walked into the house, it smelled stale and old. The floor creaked as they moved into the darkness. They didn't know if the scent was on purpose, or if the haunted house was actually on its last leg. "You got a phone on you?" Swoopes asked. "I can't even seen my hand before my face."

"Yeah. Give me a second." He took it out his pocket and pressed the enter button to turn it on. It gave them enough light to see three feet ahead of them, and nothing more. "Let's hide in that hole, beneath the house." They could hear footsteps outside and two voices moving closer.

"What, behind those monsters?" Swoopes whispered, like they were going to come alive and eat his dick. "What are you crazy?"

"Nigga, stop being scared and hide! I told you, you had to get over your fear of basements. Now is the time." Bricks climbed down the steps and stood behind the Freddy Krueger prop, while Swoopes slowly followed and stood behind the Jason prop. "They coming in now."

Swoopes felt dizzy being in such a dark clammy space. He thought about how he use to defecate himself in the darkness, when they didn't allow them upstairs to bathe. He avoided basements with all he had, and now he was standing in a smaller version. Remembering Ming's face, he grew stronger. When they heard footsteps leading in their direction, Swoopes mumbled, "You ready?"

"Fuck yeah." He whispered.

Bricks heard the two men walk into the house. Their footsteps could be heard clearly over their heads. "You think they in here?" One of the outsiders asked the other. "I saw them run in this house."

"I don't see why they wouldn't be here." The other responded. "But prop that footstool in the door, so we can see what's going on. It's too dark in here." There was a little commotion before the door was held open. A line of light spilled into the haunted house, but Luckily the light would not extend to where they hid. "Where you think they hiding?" The outsiders' breaths were heavy. "I just want to get the fuck out of here and get it over with. We should've never gotten involved with that bitch!"

"You didn't say that when we took the money." The other responded. "I'm not getting it with Yao no more, he gone. We gotta switch up to take care of ourselves. Now shut the fuck up and help me look for them."

From Bricks' vantage point, he could see through the slats above his head, the fog coming from their mouths due to the frigid temperature outside. Analyzing the situation, he felt he had a good shot. But he also knew if he aimed wrong, he would reveal their hiding place prematurely. When he was good, he aimed and fired.

"Fuck! I'm hit!" One of them said dropping to the floor. "I think that shit came from down there!"

His partner fired wildly into the floorboards but Swoopes was time enough for him. He hit him with precision and so did Bricks. They quickly came out of the hovel and finished the job. Their shots were professional and on point as they landed into their bodies. At first the two men were wounded, until Bricks fired on one of them, killing him instantly.

"I'ma get other nigga," Swoopes proclaimed.

The man was moaning and they slowly walked toward the sound of his voice. He tapped the light on his phone and noticed that they were identical twins. As far as Bricks was concerned, they were two unlucky niggas but Swoopes knew their names and faces well.

"What the fuck!?" Swoopes responded looking at the one of them who was still alive. "Uzi, what were you doing here?"

"You know this nigga?" Bricks replied, gun still trained on him.

Uzi barely had enough strength to open his eyes. But when he did, he didn't like what he saw. "It's you!" He looked at Swoopes. "You, dirty mothafucka!" Uzi was about to raise his hand and attempt to shoot Swoopes, when Bricks fired into his chest. His eyes slammed shut permanently, along with his brother.

"Now they're together." Bricks replied thinking of his sibling. "Where you know them from?"

"It's a long story." He bent down and dug through their pockets until he found a cell phone. When he scanned through it, he got exactly what he wanted. "Check this shit out."

Bricks took the phone and read the text. *"Murder them black niggas and meet me in my office. When you do, we have more business to discuss."*

Bricks wiped his fingerprints off the phone and said, "I bet you any kind of money her office is here."

"If you think it, I'm with it."

"Let's go!"

Abel Pickling was sitting behind the large black desk in her office. She was watching the door as if she were expecting company. Although she was disappointed, she wasn't surprised when she saw Bricks and Swoopes stroll in with their guns, instead of the hired help. Her dark face formed a row of perspiration on her forehead. "Hello, Fellas." She smiled, with a face only a mother could love. "I see you've found me."

"That we did." Swoopes replied, looking around. Something was up and he could feel it. "Out of all of the places to come, you picked here to die, Abel?"

"What can I say? I love my money. I might as well die with it, that's if I got to go."

"You got somebody else wit' you?" Bricks asked. The office was too small to have someone hiding in the darkness but he could never be sure. "If you don't you a fool to be here by yourself."

"We're alone, but you already know that." She laughed. "After all, you killed my men."

"How did you find Uzi and Laser?" Swoopes asked.

"Yvonna left a trail of people behind her. Her hate fan club is one of the largest I've ever seen in my life." She coughed, covering her mouth. "It was easy to locate them, and for the right price, they joined my team. Pretty little boys, weren't they?"

"You is one ugly ruthless bitch." Swoopes advised.

She laughed. "You know, I've been selling pussy for twenty years. And in all my years of supply and demand, I've never seen juicer bitches than you two." She stood up. "If only you could've came to me at another time, I could've put you on." She moved toward them. "Gave you something to do with them nice firm asses instead of sitting on them all day."

"Don't move, bitch!" Swoopes yelled as they both trained their weapons on her. The fact that she thought it was okay to talk to him that way, made his blood boil. "I'm not fucking around wit' you."

"I know you're not." She bent down and pulled Ming up by her hair. "But you need to know that I'm not fucking around with you either." Ming's body looked limp in her hand, as she kept her up by her hair. Blood and dirt covered her chest and her eyes were partially open. "Look what I found on my property," she ran he finger over her lips, "I think this is somebody you know."

"Ming!" Swoopes yelled, wanting to bum rush Abel and save her life. "I thought you were dead, baby." It fucked him up to see her doing so badly. "Why do you have her like that?" he looked at the wound in her body. "You hurting her."

Abel looked down at her and said, "She's not dead yet. But of course that remains to be seen."

"What do you want?" Bricks asked, hating that they had to possibly negotiate with her. For the minute anyway. "Let's get down to it."

"I want you to let me go."

"Okay, put her down and you can bounce." For the first time ever, Swoopes was ready to compromise. "We won't fuck with you on your way out and you don't hurt her. Agreed?"

While they were discussing the arrangement, Ming's eyes closed a little and she gripped her hair hard, causing her eyes to flap open. "Owww!" Ming cried. "Please let me go. I can't...I can't breathe."

"Look, we said you can leave! Just put her down!" Swoopes begged, growing anxious.

"I'm not done, mothafucka!" Abel yelled. "Like I said, I want you to let me go, and I want you to tell me where Yvonna Harris is. You do that, and I'll release her right now."

Bricks frowned. "Yeah right, bitch! Picture us taking you up on an offer like that. We have the guns, not the other way around."

"Either you take me up on my offer, or she's dead. I'll break her neck right now just so you won't have her." She looked at Swoopes and could see the love in his eyes. "She doesn't have too much longer, son. If you love her like you say you do, you better show her now." She looked down at her. "She's losing a lot of blood. Don't let Bricks keep you from what you want. And don't for a moment think that he wouldn't do the same for Yvonna."

Bricks looked at Swoopes. He could tell he was considering betraying him for Ming, and he knew the feeling. He was in love too and would've gladly given up anybody for Yvonna.

Seeing the tension between her teammates, on some gangsta shit, Ming closed her eyes as if she were dead. She was still alive but she knew she was going to die. She didn't want them getting into a fight over a life that was over. In her opinion, there was no use making a deal with the devil for a dead soul. "What you gonna do?" Abel asked, not knowing Ming had tapped out.

When they saw her closed eyes, Bricks and Swoopes raised their guns. "Ming, are you with me, baby? Please say something!"

Silence.

"Ming, don't die on me!" He screamed looking at her face. "Please!"

"She's gone, man." Bricks advised. "Let's finish this bitch."

Swoopes looked at his partner, took a deep breath and said, "On second thought," he wiped the lone tear that fell down his face, "fuck you and your offer you ugly bitch."

"So you're telling me you won't let me go?" she frowned.

"I'm telling you, that you can eat this shit and die!" Swoopes said, seeing Ming was gone.

Bricks and Swoopes fired into her face, causing her to drop to the floor and release Ming. When she fell, Swoopes rushed over to Ming and dropped to his knees. He held her head in his lap and her eyes opened.

"Hey you." Ming smiled. "Why so sad?"

"I thought you were dead. You did that on purpose didn't you?"

She smiled. "It's over, Swoopes. You and I know it."

He shook his head. "The first time I fall for a bitch, she up and dies on me." He looked up at Bricks. "Can you believe this shit man?"

"Ming, how you doing, sweetheart?" Bricks asked looking down at her. "You gonna make it?"

"Naw, you gotta get Swoopes out of here."

"She's right." Bricks responded. "Let's get her and get the fuck out of here." Bricks responded, looking out the window. "I don't trust this creepy ass place."

"Help me lift her."

When he moved to pick her up she said, "I'm not going to make it, Swoopes. Please let me stay, I'm in so much pain." Blood poured out of her mouth and he continued to try to lift her until she pleaded harder. "Please...Swoopes, it's over," she dug into her pocket and handed him Boys' picture. "Tell him, I...tell him everyday of his life, he made me happy. And that I was blessed to be his..." She closed her eyes but this time, they would not reopen. He didn't even know all that she wanted him to tell her son.

"Fuck!" Swoopes cried into the night. "I can't believe this shit!"

"We gotta go, man!" Bricks said touching his shoulder.

In anger he looked up at him and said, "I'm not leaving without her."

"And I'm not leaving without you"! He confessed. "Now she's gone. And the best thing we can do is pay the mothafuckas back responsible for this shit. Getting ourselves killed won't help the situation, Swoopes." In a concerned voice he said, "Let's go, man. It's over."

For the first time in a long time Swoopes cried. His tears fell on Ming's face as he kissed her softly on the forehead. Realizing there was nothing left to do, he placed her softly down and stood up. Taking a deep breath he said, "I want this nigga's head. It belongs to me."

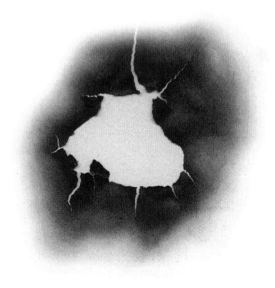

YVONNA

Yvonna was kept hostage for days in solitude. Her living conditions were comfortable, but she wanted to be in the know. The first day Bricks and the team checked on her, but after that, they seemed to be more interested in AFCOG matters. She didn't mind at first because she had people to keep her company, or so she thought. One minute she was sleep and speaking to Gabriella and Bilal, and the next minute they both were gone. She didn't know who provided her with food, but she did know every morning when she'd wake up, she'd have it available for the day. And that mentally, she was doing much better.

When the door opened around two in the morning, Bricks and Swoopes trudged inside with sour looks on their faces. Having experience in sorrow, she knew immediately something was off. "What ya'll looking all crazy for? I'm the one who's being held against my will." She turned the television on. "Oh...and thanks for the TV. You two bastards really know how to treat a hostage." She was being sarcastic but they didn't respond.

"Squeeze, we took care of Abel Pickling." He sat on the couch next to her. "She's gone."

Although she was pissed with them, hearing the news was like music to her ears. "Really?" She beamed as she looked from him to Swoopes. "So why the long ass faces?" A coldness crept over her body when she counted who was in attendance. "Wait, where's Ming?"

Swoopes hung his head low and stepped toward the door. "I can't do this shit, man." Bricks didn't appreciate handing the bag of shit to her alone, but he would do what he had to do.

"What's wrong with him?" Her question was calm but her heart beat thunder. "Why he storm out like that?" She started playing with the remote and aimlessly flipping channels. It was obvious she knew what was about to be said, before it was. Fidgeting was her way of not dealing with the inevitable. "Ming!" She screamed into the open doorway from where she sat. The last thing she said to her was wrong and she couldn't get it out of her head. "I'm not mad at you no more, bitch! Get in here!" She laughed to herself. "I know they put you up to this hostage shit too! And when I'm free, we gonna fight."

"Squeeze..."

"Ming! Can you stop fucking around and get in here!"

Bricks moved closer. "Baby, she's gone."

Her eyes widened and her chest hardened. "What you telling me?" She looked at him and then the floor. She focused back on him and then the wall. Her eyes could no longer concentrate and things looked blurry. It was then that she realized she was crying. "Where is she? Where is my best...my friend...my..."

"They killed her, baby. They shot her when we were handling Abel." He placed a soft hand on her thigh. "She died on the battlefield. I'm sorry, Squeeze, but she ain't coming back."

Yvonna couldn't move her face. It was temporarily paralyzed with grief. Her heart rate elevated and she couldn't control her limbs either, she went limp. This scared Bricks and he started rubbing her arms and shoulders rapidly. "Squeeze, talk to me." She didn't respond. "Come on, baby. Say something." Yvonna's eyes focused in the space before her, while her heart roamed in hell. She lost her best friend and after she treated her so cruelly. There would be no apologizing to her this time, it was over.

Not knowing what else to do, she let out a cry that cracked the heavens. "My friend! I lost my best friend!" She sobbed. "I lost the only person who loved me other than my daughter and you. Take it back, Bricks! Take it back!"

"I know, baby. I'm sorry." He paused pulling her closer. "I'm so fucking sorry."

Two Hours Later

Yvonna requested to be alone after the news. Since there was no need to keep her hostage, they unlocked the shackle but she didn't leave the room. Instead she stayed where she was and thought about her life. She came into the world wanting love and ended up being born into hate and confusion. She wanted to do something noteworthy. Something that would make her worthless life matter. She got the answer when she turned on the television and saw that Bilal, Jr. was facing some serious time for the deaths of Melvin White and Diana Burke. He was also charged with the reckless shooting of James Madison.

"Oh my, God!" She placed her hand over her mouth. "Melvin was Bricks' brother." The moment the words left her lips, she knew she could never let Bricks know. She wasn't sure how quick it would take his family members to tell Bricks who was involved, but she prayed they'd be in the Philippines by the time the news broke. Bilal, Jr. wasn't a killer, just a child pushed into a world he wasn't prepared for.

At some point she couldn't hear the newscaster anymore because she knew what had to be done. She wasn't hearing his father or Gabriella's voice anymore either, courtesy of the tainted drink given to her daily. But she still felt a sense of responsibility to the teenager. In her mind if she didn't do right by the first person she wronged early in his life, she was no better than AFCOG and would not be able to rest. Loving Ming the way she did made her see the error of her ways. It was time to grow up and love strong.

Later that day she placed a call to an attorney and made arrangements to give him a retainer large enough to work on Bilal, Jr.'s case for the next five years. If he needed more, she would meet with him once she made it to the Philippines, electronically. Something told her getting the lawyer wasn't enough, she felt she needed to see his face but for now it

would have to do. When she finished with her calls, she was surprised to see Chris walk into the room with a turkey burger and homemade fries.

She smiled lightly and looked at him with suspicious eyes. "Hold up, what are you doing here?"

He placed the food on the table and sat next to her. "You're at my house. In the shed in the back."

She didn't see that coming and shook her head. "Please tell me how they convinced you to keep me here?"

"They said you were sick and they needed my help." He looked into her eyes longer than he intended, until she looked away. "I would never pass up on a chance to help you, even though I didn't understand why we had to keep you shackled in here. I guess when some time passes, you can explain it better to me."

The old Yvonna wanted to unleash on him because she felt his loyalty should've lied with her, not Bricks. But in the scheme of things, she realized he did it for her. And with the amount of time she was spending in the bathroom talking to the walls, it was for the best. "Thank you." She smiled. "I really appreciate everything you've done."

He leaned back. "Wait a minute you must be still sick because you never apologize."

"It's a first time for everything." She grinned. "Plus I'm realizing a lot about my life and the people in it. It takes too much energy to hate." She thought about Ming again and wanted to sob but she held it together. "I just want to be happy, Chris. I want to take care of my daughter and be happy. You know?"

"I get you." He paused, thinking about the blunt he left burning in the ashtray in the kitchen. "So what are your plans when you leave here?"

Deciding to keep it real with him she bared her soul. "I'm a wanted woman, Chris. I have to get out of the country."

"I figured as much." He seemed saddened.

She frowned. "How would you know that?"

"Because you and your team seem to always be in thought. And you move like time is not on your side." He paused and looked at the television for no reason. "I'm in business with people who move in the night, so it was easy for me to figure it out." He looked back at her. "So how are you going to get away? You know they real strict with planes and things now days. If you're wanted, you're probably in every system around the world."

She looked down. "I don't know what I'm going to do." She observed him. "But I do know I'm going to give it all I can."

"What did you guys do with the C4? I haven't heard about any explosions."

"We're saving it for one person, who appears untouchable right now." She looked out into the room. "I don't even know if that's a good idea anymore." She looked back at him. "I'm so confused."

"Nobody is untouchable. If you think hard, you can discover a way to hit him where it hurts." He smiled. "But let me help you, Yvonna. With everything else."

"I'm listening."

"I have a private jet in Essex, Maryland. You and your friends are free to use it. And if you want, I can hook you up with some passports. The jet won't be able to get you but so far, because I don't have authorization to fly internationally. But at least if you're away from this area, once you get on the west coast with the fake passports, you should be able to catch an international flight out of the United States."

She tried to conceal her excitement; this was the break she needed. Still there was the thing about money. "What do I owe you?" She already promised to meet Bilal, Jr.'s attorney later that week, so she wasn't sure how much paper she'd have left. "I'm hard up for cash."

In a smooth tone he said, "Don't play with me, Yvonna. You know I'd do anything for you, including putting a few bucks in your pocket."

She threw her arms around his neck. "I can't thank you enough, Chris. I don't know why God brought you into my life, but I'm grateful."

When she tried to pull away he held her tighter. "Thank me by giving me a call if you ever get rid of your man." He looked intently into her eyes. "I have a feeling that I can treat you better if given the chance."

She smiled and held him tighter. For what he was doing for her she allowed him to maintain his embrace. Would even give him a little pussy if he asked. "Maybe I'll take you up on that offer." She said in his ear, although she knew it would never happen. Bricks held her heart, and with him was where she wanted to stay.

One Month Later

TYISHA

Tyisha looked at her customer across the room. His white back was crammed with brown moles and tight curly hair. He was sitting on a chair naked, snorting powder up his nose. Tyisha was use to seeing drug use now. Over the past few days, Rufus nurtured her growing addiction by giving her heroin and weed on a consistent basis. She needed it most days to get out of bed, and without it she could not function. He succeeded in breaking her down emotionally and physically and all that was left was the little girl she used to be.

The John turned around and looked at her. "You get down?" He held a plastic tube in his hand and wiggled it for effect. "I have a few more lines if you want. Don't mind sharing just as long as you make it worth it for me later."

She always needed *something* to do what they wanted from her. So she eagerly slid out of bed before he changed his mind. Wearing nothing but what she was born with, she made her way in his direction. Her toes nestled into the dirty motel's carpet and she stood behind him with a glazed over look in her eyes.

"Here you go."

She snatched the tube out of his hand and inhaled the last three lines. When it made contact to her organs, the tube dropped out of her hand and immediately she felt tingly. It was amazing; suddenly all was right with the world. When her legs gave out, and she was about to fall, he lifted her up and placed her in position, on the bed. Crawling next to her,

for a moment, he looked at her young face. "How you get into the business, sexy?"

She grinned. "Why you ask so many questions? Let's do what brought us here. I'm about pleasing you," she pointed a stiff finger into his chest, "and getting my master's money." Rufus warned her about speaking to the clients about anything other than how they wanted it, so she was trying to change his focus.

"Aw, come on, beautiful. I just want a little conversation before we get down."

"I really can't. I'm sorry."

The last time she disobeyed Rufus and talked to a client about life, she lost food for two days straight. Although this was her life now, it wasn't always the plan. Originally he was going to break her in a little longer, but with the threats of losing AFCOG all together looming in the air, he had to put her to work now. The only problem that faced Rufus where Tyisha was concerned, was Marge. Suddenly she called everyday wondering how her daughter was fairing in the program, when at first she didn't seem to care. He explained to her that she had run away, and he hadn't seen her in days. Everyday she'd call and ask about her, never calling the police, because Rufus said he had it covered. What a stupid ass bitch.

"I just want to get to know you, sweetness." He pinched her undeveloped breast. "No need in getting all uptight."

She felt like she was about to cry. She'd done this in the past whenever they said more than what they wanted her to do to them. When she couldn't bring herself to stop the tears, they would always complain to Rufus that she was bringing them down, when it was usually their fault. Thanks to Rufus she was a machine, not to be nurtured and loved. "Please, I just want to do my job." She smiled although a tear escaped her eye. "Okay?"

The client wasn't feeling the situation and would tell Rufus about his experience when he was done. He mostly complained for a discount on the next girl but also because he enjoyed the workers in the past that although young, could hold a conversation with him when sparked. He needed to see them more mature, to get aroused, often yelling at them afterwards because they were acting too grown.

"How 'bout you get yourself cleaned up first." He was talking about the worthless tears on her face. "And then we can get started."

High and disoriented, she hopped out of bed with a bed sheet wrapped around her naked body. He thought it was odd because he already seen her nude, but allowed her to do whatever floated her boat. After fifteen minutes of looking at the ceiling waiting for her, the coke had him wanting to satisfy his desires.

"What you doing in there, girl?" He yelled stroking his dick from the bed. "I'm tired of waiting on you now! Come on!"

Silence.

"You hear me in there, bitch? Bring your ass on! I paid my money just like the rest."

Silence.

Irritated, the obese man slid off the bed and ambled toward the bathroom. First he placed his ear against the door in an attempt to hear her on the other side. When he heard a soft bump at the bottom of the door, at first he thought it was her, but discovered it was his erect penis knocking against the wood. He was so high he was tripping to the highest degree.

Banging on the door with a hard fist he yelled, "Bitch, get the fuck out here! If you and your pimp fucking with my money, I'm not gonna be so nice! You need to know that! Now I want what I paid for! Get out here now!"

When she didn't come out, he took a few steps back, and rammed the entire right side of his body into the door like a bull. When it fell down, his eyes roamed around for her. When he did, he saw Tyisha's naked body hanging from the

shower rod. She hung herself by the neck and her eyes were wide open. She looked petrified, as if she didn't know dying that way would be so hard.

"Oh no!" He backed away. "Oh fucking no!"

He tramped around the room in delirious motions. A young girl was dead and suddenly he felt the need to protect his family. This would kill his wife, their newborn son and his career as a doctor; if it ever got out that he fucked a twelve-year-old prostitute in a hotel room. First he tried to wipe his fingerprints off of everything he touched and then he realized he didn't have his clothes on. Deciding it was best to get dressed first; he grabbed his things and got the hell out of dodge before the cops got there.

****

Marge was sitting in her living room, as her friends tried to console her during the loss of her daughter. It had been days since she got the news, but everyday she woke up, without her in her life, it was as if she died all over again. She was a horrible mother and she knew it, but hindsight was twenty-twenty.

To make matters worse, the media tried to make her out to be a drug sick twelve year old when she knew different. Tyisha may have been troubled, but she wasn't a monster until the streets got a hold of her. Luckily Rufus Day was there to defend her good name. Still, whenever she analyzed the situation, she always blamed herself. She failed her only child and now she would never see her face again.

"How you holding up, Marge?" One of her church friends asked, placing a soft hand on her right shoulder. When Tyisha died, Rufus dispatched them immediately. "Can I get you anything? Anything at all?"

She looked up at her, with red eyes and said, "No. Unless you can bring my baby back."

The other women in attendance felt her sorrow and made a promise to do all they could to lift her spirits. "You know," she started sitting next to her, "Reverend Day is having service this Sunday. And I'm not supposed to tell you this, but I found out that the topic is about facing adversity when dealing with death."

Marge hadn't seen the reverend since her daughter died. That didn't stop him from taking care of her bills and having people clean her home when she couldn't find the strength. She thanked God for him every day. "You know what, that may be what I need." She was hopeful as she looked up at them. "Rufus Day always knows what to do to put me in a thankful mood. Thanks, Denise."

"Don't thank me." She declared. "Thank Master Rufus Day."

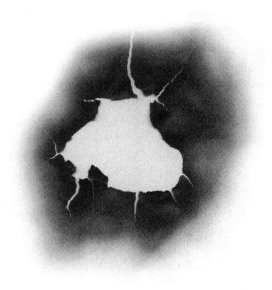

YVONNA

The sun was very seductive as Yvonna, Bricks and Swoopes sat in the parking lot gazing at AFCOG church. Members flooded inside wearing their Sunday's best in the hopes of receiving an encouraging word or two from their immoral minister. All Yvonna and her team could think about, was the fact that they failed. That they tried everything possible, to kill Rufus Day but he had proven to be a worthy adversary. Wherever he went, security was kept at presidential heights.

When he was at the compound, security guards and guard dogs kept him safe. When he went shopping, which he did less than he had in the past, he had armed men with him at least three. Even when he was at church, he was protected by two security guards, although they were not allowed inside the sanctuary because he didn't want to give the message, to his congregation, that being around him was unsafe.

"We're never going to be able to get to him." Yvonna looked at the large bus which pulled up with more members inside. "I don't know what else to do." She shrugged. "I gave all I can give and it feels like it ain't enough."

"Maybe we should just leave, Squeeze." Bricks said to her from behind the wheel. "Thanks to Chris, we got the hookup on the jet and I'm not trying to pass up on the opportunity because we running after this dude." He touched her leg. "You gotta know when to fold."

"But I don't know when to do that!" She screamed, as tears filled up her eyes. "I wanted him to answer for what he did to me. For what he did to all of us." She looked back at Swoopes.

"And he has, baby. But we have to think smart too. If we walk in there together, we not coming back alive. It's not worth it." He taught. "Plus I already made arrangements to pick up Chomps from the airport in two hours from Kelsi." he looked at his watch. "You gotta go get Delilah and we still pushing it just to be on time. It's over, baby. Let's go to our new home."

"If we leave, I'll feel like we failed."

"I wish you stop saying that shit. We didn't fail!" he stabbed his fist into his palm. "If anything, we let this nigga know we not to be pushed over." He assured her. "We came a long way with this shit. We freed all of the kids in the breeding camps and we took out his captains and secretaries. He never gonna be able to move the way he use to. We did good, Squeeze." He looked back at Swoopes. "What you think, man?"

"I think I want to break that nigga's jaw." Swoopes confessed. "But he's right, Yvonna. Going into that church now would be like a suicide mission." He laughed to himself as he looked out the window.

"Isn't that what you wanted?" Yvonna asked. "Don't think I don't know that all the times you got into it with people, was in the hopes that somebody would kill you." She pulled his card. "Remember...a blaze of glory?"

"You right, but I'm wondering if that was a mistake." He looked at the church again. "Who would've thought you could die going into a house of God. Then again, that ain't no house of God...that's hell."

"See what we saying, babes. It's over." Then he looked back at Swoopes again. "You did everything you gotta do so we can bounce, Swoopes?" he dug into his pocket and threw a passport in his lap; he'd already given Yvonna hers back at Chris' house. Although it possessed a picture of his face, the name was different. "If you didn't we not gonna be able to wait on you when that jet pulls off. We'll have to get up with you another time."

Swoopes reviewed the document in shock. "Wait, how did you get my picture?"

"We stole the fake ID in your pocket when you were

drunk. I gave it to Chris and he made it work." Bricks laughed. "You shouldn't sleep so hard."

He tried to hide the smile on his face. "But I thought I couldn't roll."

"That was then and this is now." Bricks responded seriously. "If you wanna leave wit' us you free to do it. But I ain't 'bout to hold your hand either."

Swoopes couldn't believe it. Prior to now he didn't have a clue as to where he would go when it was all said and done. He didn't have a girl. He didn't have family. He didn't even have a friend outside of them. But thanks to Bricks, all of that changed. Bricks didn't invite him for what he could do for him; he invited him because he wanted Swoopes around. But the nigga in him wouldn't allow him to show his full appreciation, not yet anyway. "I guess I can bounce wit' y'all." He shrugged. "I ain't got no other plans, after all, who else gonna protect you?"

Bricks nodded, oddly delighted he was still with them. "Good." He focused back on Yvonna. "So you ready, Squeeze? We not gonna be able to hit this cat." He looked at the church. "It's over. Let's get our family and get on that jet."

She looked at both of them with disappointment. The plan although near perfect was faltered in her eyes. "If we leave without confronting that bastard, everybody who died including my best friend would have died in vain." She touched his hand, remembering the sad way Boy looked, when they told him his mother was never coming back, but that she loved him. "It's not enough to just walk away, Bricks. To me that's cowardly and it's not my style, you know that about me. We have to handle this all the way and we gotta do it now, before we leave."

Frustrated he sat back in the seat and shook his head. "I don't know how we going to get in there. He keeps two security guards in the front of the sanctuary, so the moment they see us, it's gonna be a problem."

"We could go in there blasting. Hitting up any and everybody in the way." Swoopes suggested. "I damn sure don't have a problem wit' it."

"No. I can't do it like that anymore." Yvonna interjected. "If you can get the guards off the door I can do the rest. I just want him to see that after everything he did, I'm still alive. To me that'll be better than killing him."

"If you say so." Swoopes doubted. "I think he needs four extra holes in his face. Then again, that's just me."

Bricks threw his head into the headrest and looked at the road ahead, it seemed grim. Everything in him said to leave and leave now. But if Yvonna wasn't going with him, he didn't want any part of it anyway. He raised his head and looked at her. "If you insist on doing this shit, then I got an idea."

Bricks and Swoopes stole a jacket and shirt from Wal-Mart to look the part. It didn't take them long to realize that they could've saved themselves the trip, because the moment they walked through the church's door, the two security guards moved in on them like they were soul mates. Neither of them expected them to come at them so quickly, but they didn't have time to think, either. The situation only allowed for reactions. Luckily nobody was in the lobby area of the church because service had already started. So this was perfect because they were going for the element of surprise when they got at Rufus.

In an attempt to make as little noise as possible, Swoopes stole the man in the face before crawling on him to slice his throat. Bricks dropped his opponent as well, before climbing on him to cover his mouth to jab a blade inside his chest. When the murders were complete, Yvonna ambled inside and through the sanctuary door. Swoopes and Bricks, who were covered in blood, followed.

Rufus Day was so engaged in deception, that he didn't see them, so they melted in the wooden back row pew. With hostility in her heart, she looked at him behind the pulpit. He looked sicker than she imagined. His mannerisms mirrored a snake and it took everything in her power to contain herself. When she looked around at the congregation, something to her seemed off but she didn't know what. And after listening to him for two minutes, she knew it was almost time to stand up.

"You're not going to always get your way when it comes to the Lord." Rufus preached to his members. "You're not going to always get him to give you what you want. But as sure as my name is Rufus Day, he will most certainly give you what you need."

"Will he *really* give you what you need?" Yvonna yelled, rising from her seat. Bricks and Swoopes hung behind her like a cape. "Because as I remember, all I needed was peace and to have a family who loved me." She laughed to herself as she slowly walked toward the front of the large church. "Instead I endured a lifetime of pain and hurt when I was just a child. Under your reign and for your financial gain."

The color seemed to drain from Rufus' face. He looked behind them at the door, for his men, although he knew they were not there. The situation was futile and he guessed it wouldn't end well for him. In an attempt to maintain his composure, he cleared his throat and said, "You aren't the only one who dealt with pain, my child. Most of the members in my congregation have too. But it is how you handle it that builds character." He hit his chest for effect.

"You really do believe that shit you be saying don't you?" Yvonna spat, stopping where she stood. "You are so sick, that you convinced yourself when you're here, that you really are a reverend."

He was flushed at the disregard she had for his church status. "Young lady, this is a house of worship and I am the leader. If you can't respect it, you can just leave."

"Fuck this house and don't call me young lady! You know exactly who I am! My name is Yvonna Harris and I am no longer a victim! I'm no longer your sex slave! And although bruised, I am finally free!" She hit her fist into her palm and tears rolled down her face. "And the only place you can lead these people to is hell!" Her voice sent thunder throughout the large sanctuary. "I was a child. And all of the children you sold were too! But you didn't care! You don't care. The only thing on your mind is money and getting your rocks off! I represent everyone you abused, everyone you took advantage of and everyone you exploited."

"I don't have time for this…"

"You don't get to do anything but listen to me." As if they planned this, Bricks and Swoopes hopped on the pulpit and grabbed his arms. "You aren't worth the bones your body is being held up with." Her head dropped, and a flash of her past troubled her again. "I was coming here to kill you today. To take your life, like you tried to take mine. But you know what, it's not my job anymore." She shook her head. "Instead I wanted you to see my face and know that you did not win. You are not able to make me feel worthless anymore. And I wanted you to know that no matter what, I have my life back. And you can have what's left of yours."

"He's not going to live, Yvonna." A teenager said standing up. It was Porter, the same teenager she rescued from the tractor-trailer. He was cleaned up and looked handsome. "We're here to see to it."

Yvonna looked around the church and saw all of the children she rescued. That's what seemed off to her when she first walked in; most of the congregation seemed too young. They smiled in recognition and she covered her mouth in surprise. This wasn't the plan and she wondered how they pulled it off.

"I don't understand." She looked at everyone. "What are you doing here?"

"We knew we could never have a life until he was murdered." He looked up at Rufus. "And we're here to do just that."

"Why didn't you tell me?"

"We didn't know this was the plan so it's a coincidence that you came today. We thought of this when we all met at Reverend Dynamite's house in Virginia. It was last minute." He smiled at her. "You've done enough, Yvonna. You're free to live and it's our time to take it from here." He turned toward the congregation. "If you don't want to witness what's about to happen next, I suggest you leave now."

There was a flood of people who at first, sat in shock because they couldn't believe their eyes, running out the church. When he gave them a warning, most took it and bolted out of the church to save their own lives, unless they were with him. One member however, chose to finally stand up for her dead child.

"So it's true!" Marge yelled, walking toward the front. "You...you had something to do with my baby dying?"

"Marge, don't listen to these people." He tried to pull away from Swoopes and Bricks who maintained their hold. "They're crazy!"

"We're not crazy but you are!" Clandus responded, his bones protruding from his face. "You took our kids, and made us have more, all while you raped the girls! And I have been dreaming of this day ever since." She met Clandus at Anna's house when he ate her flesh.

"Tell me what happened to my baby!" Marge interrupted them. "You're about to die, the least you can do is tell me what happened to my child!"

Realizing he really was about to die, he told her how he felt. "You are what happened to her! Had you watched her, she would've never been subjected to my ways." He grinned and licked his crusted lips. "And my rules. I gave you fifteen thousand dollars and you sold her to me but you know what, I could've given you less and you still would've taken it. Any person, who doesn't watch their child and they're raped, is just as guilty as we are. We can't get to your children unless you hand them to us."

He hit a nerve. "But I trusted you! You were my pastor!"

"And whose fault is that?"

When he said that, the children of AFCOG converged on the pulpit. Bricks and Swoopes hopped down to get out of the way. "Thank you so much, Yvonna." Porter said holding her hand in the midst of the drama. "But you need to leave now. We have it from here."

It turned out that seventy percent of the church was filled with the children of AFCOG. And the rage on their faces expressed how she felt inside. She knew then that they would finish the job, without her having to lift a finger. It was finally over. She would get to live the life she always wanted, in peace.

"Let's go, Squeeze." Bricks said, gripping her hand. "The cops are on their way."

Yvonna took one last look at the melee behind her and decided it was time to bounce. On their way out, they passed detective Griswald, who was walking up the steps.

"Yvonna Harris! Don't move!" She went to draw her weapon but they ran away before she could shoot, disappearing into the flock. Not to mention the crowd in and around the church didn't allow her to get a clear shot. "Freeze!" When they didn't obey, she called for backup and focused her attention on the confusion inside the church instead.

The three of them jumped into the car with three police vehicles in pursuit. They knew if they were going to have a chance to get the kids and avoid the cops, they needed to split up.

As the police sirens blared from behind, Bricks looked through the rearview mirror at all of the flashing lights.

"Squeeze, I'm gonna shake 'em but when I do, I need you to go to the jet strip." He dodged in and out of traffic. "Me and Swoopes will scoop the kids." He dug in the console and pulled out a phone. "I got a few minutes left on that. Call Jesse right now and let her know I'm on my way."

Reluctantly she made the call and when she was done, threw the phone on the floor. "I don't think it's a good idea, Bricks." She looked at the cops who were still on their trail. "Stay with me. Please. I got a bad feeling about this."

"I can't, baby I won't be away long though. We just have to split up for the moment. I don't want nothing stopping us from getting on that jet and out of the states. And if we not there at the time we told Chris we would be, they might not take us later. So you have to go, to tell 'em we coming and to make them wait." He smiled although it was obvious he wasn't sure about his decision. "Just do what I'm asking." He looked at the road and back at her. "Please, Squeeze. For once in your life," he placed a free hand softly on her face and said, "trust me."

Yvonna had a bad feeling, but since she wanted to see Bilal, Jr. before she left anyway, to apologize for ruining his life, she figured it would be best if they separated and got back together later. "Alright, Bricks. I'm gonna trust you."

"I think you did it, slim." Swoopes observed, looking out the back window. "I don't see them behind us no more." Yvonna never seen him smile so high before. "Just pull up over there." He pointed to a busy strip mall. "I know we can get a couple of cars with no problem there."

Bricks eased into the parking lot checking their surroundings first. They piled out of the car and Bricks grabbed Yvonna after seeing her sour face. "I don't like how you looking at me right now, Squeeze. You gonna jinx me."

She tried to look up at him, but the sun was blinding her view. "I'm not trying to, baby. It's just that I never get to have the life I want. Ever."

"You deserve it now, Squeeze. And I don't know what's going to happen with those kids at the church, but you gave them their freedom. What they choose to do with their lives after that is up to them." He kissed her forehead. "Just do what I'm asking right now and prevent that jet from leaving without us okay?"

"Okay." She hugged him tightly.

"Come on, slim." Swoopes said anxiously from the sidelines. He observed their surroundings. "Shit gettin' thick now."

"Yvonna, go straight to the jet strip. I know something is on your mind, but I need you to stick to the plan. I'll see you later." Before separating to get the cars, Bricks planted a passionate kiss on her lips. It tasted sweet to her and she reminisced how it would be waking up to him every day. She could tell then, that they were going to lead a great life together.

When the chivalries were over, they converged on two unsuspecting preys in the search of two new whips. With two quick surface wounds to their victims, they had stolen cars in their possession. They waved at each other once more, before fading away.

When she got behind the wheel, she thought about what Bricks said. If she went straight to the jet strip, she wouldn't be able to speak to Bilal, Jr., which was something she wanted to do for a while now. If she didn't see him and stayed on mission, she could make a quick stop first to buy Delilah a new doll. She didn't know what to do and she needed help deciding.

Alternate Endings

*In celebration of the first Shyt List, where you got to choose
your ending, we are allowing you the honor again.
But choose at your own risk.*

OPTION ONE
Have Yvonna visit Bilal in jail.
Hint: Possible Happy-Sad Ending.
Go to Page 298:

OPTION TWO
Have Yvonna go to the mall to buy Delilah a new doll.
Hint: Danger. Danger.
Go to Page 304:

OPTION THREE
Take the Surprise Route
Hint: Expect the unexpected
Go to Page 307:

Option One

The Jail Visit

Yvonna was nervous as she waited for Bilal, Jr. to appear on the other side of the glass. She was wearing a long brown wig, large black-rimmed glasses and zero makeup. She always kept a fake ID on her so it was easy to see him without being detected, not to mention he hadn't been transferred to prison yet. She couldn't believe how skittish she was, he was just a child.

The moment she saw his face, she couldn't get over how much he looked just like his father. As a matter of fact, since he was older now, he looked exactly like Bilal did the last time she saw him. When he picked up the phone, she followed suit.

"Thanks for retaining my lawyer." He looked at the table under him. "But I'm confused on why you did it." He faced her. "One minute you trying to kill me and the next you want to help me out. Why?"

"I know it's confusing, Bilal. I don't understand a lot of this either. Just know that you and I are connected in more ways than you realize. And it was my responsibility to help you get out of here. And to right a few wrongs. In all of my life, you're the only one I truly regret hurting."

He frowned. "Why you say that?"

"When I was younger, I murdered your father. I didn't know until years later, that it was triggered after I overheard him talking to your mother on the phone. She wanted him to leave me. He just proposed to me and I must've been consumed with jealously. So I took his life, and I'm so sorry, Bilal. I truly am." She sighed. "When it happened I thought it was my father who committed the crime, but it was actually me. I'm sick, sicker than a lot of people realize, and I'm just understanding why."

"I'm confused."

"I suffer from multiple personality disorder. It's plagued me all of my life." She swallowed hearing her truth. "And the night of your father's death, I was so dead set on revenge that I didn't think about how life would end up for you." Tears rolled down her face. "It wasn't enough for me to murder him. Mad at the world, I murdered your mother and your grandmother too." She looked into his eyes. "And for the first time in my life, I want to say I'm sorry. The way your life ended up is my biggest regret."

Bilal, Jr.'s cheeks trembled and his eyes were red and teary. "You left me with nobody." He balled his fists up and stared at them. He could still see Easter's teeth prints on his fingers. "You left me with nothing."

"I know. And I'm sorry." She looked at him intently through the glass. "I did to you, what they did to me." Her watch beeped indicating she had thirty minutes to make it to the strip, or risk getting left. "Look, I know you can never see it in your heart to forgive me, but I hope you'll try to accept my apology. I just wanted you to know that none of the things that happened to you was your fault, including being in here. It's all mine."

"Did you kill my twin brothers too?"

Bilal and Swoopes told her about the situation, but for some reason, she didn't want him to know they were involved. "No." She lied, holding her head down. "I didn't have nothing to do with that."

Silence.

"I've been waiting to talk to you alone. I wondered what I'd say to you and how I would feel." He confessed. "And now that the time has come, I don't have the emotions I thought I would." He paused and focused on the ceiling. "I don't know what to say to you, Yvonna. I'm confused…"

"Say whatever you feel."

He sighed. "Okay," he swallowed and tapped his knuckles on the desk. "I would like to say thank you for paying for my attorney, because when I get out of here, I'm going to spend the rest of my life looking for you." He pressed his finger against the glass, leaving his sweaty print behind. "You haven't seen the last of me, bitch so I hope you're a good hider. Now get the fuck out of my face." He got up, dropped the phone and left her alone.

Bricks and Swoopes were at a light waiting on it to change. They were five blocks from Jesse's house when all of a sudden; Swoopes' eyes widened and anger covered his face. Bricks saw the look before when they had beef, and immediately went for his gun, thinking he was about to turn on him. Before Bricks could react, Swoopes pressed his weight on the top of his body and bore down.

Seconds later, shattered glass from the driver's window covered their bodies. Still in control of the car, Bricks pressed the gas even though he couldn't see ahead of him. When the car was in motion, he shoved Swoopes off of him, and fired at the driver who was obviously trying to take his life, all while driving. When he got a look he saw a dark skin man, with heavy lines on his forehead and face. He didn't know it then but his name was Charles Bank. But when Bricks was done with him, he would be identified as John Doe.

Halfway up the block he was finally able to catch his breath and speak. He murdered a man he didn't know wanted him dead. The car was dead silent, but thoughts of how close he came to dying ran through his mind. "Man, can you believe that shit?" Bricks asked, focusing on the road. "Niggas don't wanna see us survive!"

Silence.

Fear crept over him. He knew he was gone but was in denial. "So when we get on the island, don't be bringing no bad ass Filipino bitches around us who got sisters. I ain't trynna get killed fuckin' around wit' you." He laughed. "You the type of nigga who loves to do shit in abundance. And Yvonna would kill me."

Silence.

"So you did it just like this huh?" he shook his head. "You went out like you always wanted, in a selfish blaze of glory." He was overwhelmed with the loss of yet another close friend. "We came so far, Swoopes!" In a lower voice he said, "We came so far."

When Swoopes saw Charles about to fire at Bricks, he saved his life and he would never get to ask him why. He did it for a few reasons but it was mainly because Bricks had Yvonna and Chomps, and he had no one. He wanted to die after he did something good, before he had a chance to fuck up his life again.

Bricks couldn't believe what was happening to him. A lot of soldiers had fallen just to bring AFCOG down. Melvin, Ming and now Swoopes. Although he never planned on it, Bricks couldn't deny that he connected with a man who at one time was his sworn enemy. Slowly he looked at Swoopes. His eye was wide open and a gaping hole lie in his neck. Brick was filled with rage and confusion but knew he had to push forward. He pulled over on the side of the road and pulled Swoopes' body outside. There was a large tree in a patch of green grass and he sat him against it.

"I'm sorry, man. I didn't mean for you to go out like this." One tear fell down but he wouldn't allow anymore. "At least you got to smoke some crazies." Quickly he dipped back into the car and out of sight.

Yvonna made it to the landing strip on time. To her surprise the pilot had been given orders not to fly out until they had Yvonna's approval. She called Chris and thanked him again but he told her to remember their promise. He was serious about filling the void in Yvonna's life, if Bricks ever fucked up. She allowed him to have his dream but there was no other man for her, she was sure of it. And even if Bricks did fail, she could never come back to the states. She had to make it work with Bricks, and she was looking forward to life with him. Which is why when he was an hour late, she felt impending doom.

She was just about to call Jesse to see if he made it to her, when a red car sped onto the landing strip. It was different from the car he'd stolen earlier and she wondered what happened. When he parked, Chomps and Delilah hopped out without a care in the world. As instructed earlier by Bricks, they held each other's hands as they moved toward the jet. She saw the happiness in their eyes, but she also noticed the mournful look on Bricks' face and that the fourth car door failed to open. *Where was Swoopes?*

"Mommy!" Delilah cheered, having gotten over her fear of her. "I miss you so much!"

"I missed you too!" She avowed, stooping down and opening her arms. Delilah ran into them and she appreciated the embrace. When she was filled up with love she said, "Okay, baby, get on the jet. I'll be up in a second."

"Yeah! We're going to fly!" She sang, running up the steps with a new doll in her hand. When Yvonna saw it, she realized she didn't need to buy her another one anyway.

"You go with Delilah," Bricks said to Chomps. Yvonna touched him softly on the head as he passed her by. He had gotten cuter since the last time she saw him. "Hey, Squeeze."

"You came back to me." Her tone was sad but unassuming. "But it looks like you're alone."

Bricks held his head down. "He didn't make it."

She looked out into the open and tears poured from her eyes. "So you finally killed him."

She was joking but he had taken her seriously. She knew then that she loved him. "He died defending me, that's payback enough."

"So I guess it's just you and me huh?"

"You gotta problem with that?"

She smiled. "If I had to pick one person to spend the rest of my life with, I wouldn't want it any other way." She grinned a little. "Even at our worst, we're still doing better than a lot of people aren't we? At least we have each other."

"You know it."

"Have I told you thank you, Bricks?" She asked, already knowing the answer. She didn't express her gratitude enough because she took him for granted, but that would be changing. "And how much I love you for giving up everything for me? And that I'm nothing without you and that your love made me a better person?"

"No, but I don't have nothing to do on the way to the Philippines." He kissed her. "You can start telling me all," he landed a kiss on her lips, "the way," he planted one on her nose, "over there." He continued as they got on the jet.

A lot happened that day. Rufus Day was murdered by the hands of those whose lives he destroyed and Clandus and Porter were arrested. They weren't concerned when a hot shot attorney, eager to be a part of the high profile case, agreed to represent them in court. It was definite that they would get off.

Some weeks later, AFCOG was finally recognized for what it was a modern day slave operation, which specialized in the exploitation of children. Of course all great things were attributed to one woman, a fugitive from the law. Some said the authorities knew where she was but after everything she and her team went through, they deserved a chance at life. Not to mention the world was embarrassed that it allowed AFCOG to mislead them into thinking they were legit for so long.

Sitting closely together, they gripped each other and kissed passionately. As the jet glided through the air, Yvonna looked out at the window at the sky. It was icy blue, and she knew it represented her future, which was very bright.

THE END ONE

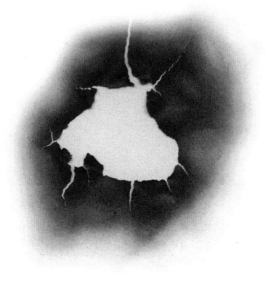

Option Two

The Doll

Yvonna decided that before going to the jet strip, she would buy Delilah a new doll. She could already see the smile on her face when she handed it to her. It would be her gift, for how she treated her the first night they reunited. So she drove a few miles out to a mall she knew was in the area.

Knowing time was not on her side, she parked in a handicap space and stepped out of the car. The moment she did, she felt a stinging sensation rip through her shoulder and arm. She fell forward and leaned on the car for support before another bullet pierced the flesh of her back. She couldn't reach the weapon in the car and it wouldn't matter anyway. Because the next bullet traveled through her ear, forcing her to the ground.

She looked up at the sun, realizing her life could've been different, had she stuck with the plan and went straight to the landing. Bricks would be so hurt and Delilah would be so sad without her in their lives. How stupid! Still focusing on the sun rays, they were momentarily blocked when she saw her sister's beautiful face.

"Jes, Jesse..." She couldn't speak, her lungs were punctured and life was slipping away from her. Still with her eyes, she asked her why.

"I'm sorry, Yvonna. But I can't let you do to Delilah, what you did to me." Tears rolled down her face. "She told me about what you did, when you slapped her at her father's house. And I can't have my niece going through what I did, when I was a kid, with you. I really am sorry, Yvonna. But the world is better off without you. Please know that I love you." Jesse ran away leaving her alone.

Something weird happened when she left. The bright sun now resembled an eclipse, as she passed out.

The doctors thought Yvonna Harris was unconscious. Thought she couldn't feel a thing, but they were wrong. This was a nightmare. She felt extreme pain as a scalpel sliced the flesh of her arm, to remove a bullet that pierced one of her arteries. It was the most excruciating pain she'd ever experienced in her tumultuous life.

Whoever shot her three times in the upper body, and once in the ear, wanted her dead. They wanted her stopped. And judging by the amount of blood she'd lost, they were going to get their wish. Yet a little girl by the name of Delilah, needed her to survive. And that same little girl, born to a woman plagued with a mental disease, would not understand if she didn't keep her promise, to come back to her in one piece.

Yvonna did enough dirt to see death row ten times over, yet as she lay on the top of the operating table, she was asking the one with the final decision, to spare her the death penalty. In the past, dying was not a fear but that was before she experienced unconditional love.

Trying to get her mind off of the bullets occupying her body, her thoughts flashed to those she murdered. As if they were standing before her on a jury, she could clearly see their faces - Bilal Santana, Bernice Santana, Cream Justice, Sabrina Beddows, and Dave Walters. Sure there were more, but in her opinion, when she took their lives, it was the beginning of her demise.

Remembering the prayer Pastor Robinson recited before she killed him some months back, she wondered would it work for her. *Our Father, who art in heaven. Hallowed be thy...hallowed be thy...*

She couldn't finish the prayer because she was enveloped in pain once more, thanks to the relentless effort of the doctors. This time the feeling was so incapacitating, that she saw flashes of light under her closed lids. She tried to part her lips to speak once more, to let them know that they were making a mistake, but nothing on her body moved, not even her mouth.

Screaming from the inside she yelled, *I can feel you! Please stop! You're hurting me!* There was a brief pause before she felt the rest of her clothing being torn from her body. *What are you about to do now?* The moment the thought entered her mind, a scalpel ripped through her trachea.

She died instantly and so did the legend of Yvonna Harris.

<u>THE END TWO</u>

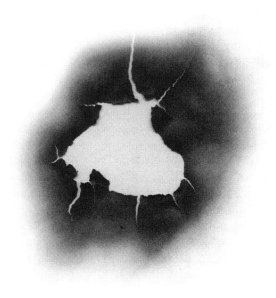

Option Three

Crazy Walls

Yvonna sat on a bed, in an all white padded room, with her arms held closely to her body by a straight jacket. Her hair had grown wild and longer than what it was before she first committed herself. She'd been there for years, shortly after Charles Bank strangled her, in an attempt to take her life. Had it not been for her pregnancy, she would've been dead. Her voluntary stay ended up being involuntary, when she grew more violent each passing day. She was high all the time, and could never get her thoughts together. Although she'd been on many medications, Yvonna was by far the most complex patient Dr. Connie Griswald was ever assigned.

When the door to the room that kept Yvonna hostage twenty hours out of the day opened, in strolled Dr. Griswald and Gary Manes, an orderly who was at her side pushing a wheel chair. "Hello, Yvonna! Your family is here to watch television with you for an hour." She walked closer to the bed but stopped short. Just because she was bound by the arms didn't mean she wasn't dangerous.

One fall day Dr. Griswald found out when she approached her without assistance. Yvonna hopped out of the bed and lunged on top of her, in an attempt to chew the side of her face off. Gary Manes saved her just before she nibbled on her jugular vein. He'd been with her whenever she approached Yvonna ever since. "Are you ready for your visit?" Dr. Griswald always spoke to Yvonna as if she were sane, although she never answered properly.

"There's a conspiracy." Yvonna looked at them both with wild eyes. "There's a conspiracy with AFCOG. You need to let me go so I can help! There are children. Lot's of them who are being sold to movie stars and pedophiles for sex. I can help them! I know who's involved."

Dr. Griswald looked at Gary who shook his head. "Yvonna, AFCOG is a reputable agency, sweetheart. They do a lot of charity work for the community. I assure you you're greatly mistaken." She knew Yvonna wouldn't understand but every now and again she got a kick out of antagonizing her anyway.

"You don't know what you're talking about!" She yelled, as Gary lifted her and placed her securely in the chair before strapping her in place.

"Sure I do. You've seen AFCOG on TV, and you're confusing it with other programs you watch." Yvonna seemed to hallucinate more when she watched television, which resulted in Dr. Griswald stopping her TV privileges last month. She ended up changing her mind when Yvonna's family claimed she was so inconsolable and sad during their times together, that without it, the visit wouldn't be worth it. "Everything you see is not real, Yvonna. You're a very sick, sick woman."

"You a liar!" She looked over at her. "You're all liars." She looked at Gary. "You're part of the conspiracy. You're part of AFCOG!"

Gary pushed her slowly to the TV room with the doctor following. Once there, Dr. Griswald removed the keys from her pocket and opened the door to the family room. She stepped back, allowing Gary to wheel her into the area first.

Inside the room sat Penny, Jesse and her daughter Delilah, who always had a new doll in her hands. It was the only thing Yvonna remembered about her, because the dolls' faces always seemed happy.

When she came into the room, her family wore hopeful looks upon their faces. They hoped she would speak to them. Hoped she would be sane. And hoped she would know how much they loved her.

"I'm going to leave you alone now," Dr. Griswald said, "she may be a handful today. Just warning you." She and Gary walked out closing the door behind them.

"Yvonna, how are you?" Jesse asked softly, from where she sat. She was afraid of her although her arms were bound to her body. "You look pretty." She lied. "Your hair is growing longer every month we see you." Yvonna looked deranged and out of order. She was anything but attractive at the moment. "I love you, sis, and I wish you would just talk to me." She wanted to comb her hair but last time Yvonna tried to bite her.

Immediately Yvonna shot an evil look at her. "You shot me!" Her eyes rolled around in her head. "You tried to kill me but it didn't work! Who are you working for? AFCOG? Is that it?"

"Yvonna, nobody tried to kill yous, baby." Penny said, with Delilah on her lap. "Yous had a rough life and you're a little confused. That's all, chile!"

"Turn the TV on!" she screamed, rocking back and forth. When no one fulfilled the request she yelled, "Turn it on got damn it! They transmit information to me from the TV! They all do! If it's not on I won't get my mission. And I need my mission!"

Jesse looked at Penny. "Turn it on, chile." Penny ordered. "I guess its betta to have her screamin' than to not have her at all."

Jesse did as she was told using her prosthetic arm, and Yvonna stared at the television. Rufus Day, a renowned reverend, was preaching from the pulpit like he did every day. She frowned immediately. "Turn the channel!" She begged, rocking heavily. "Turn it to my show. They have a message for me." By the show she meant the soap opera, *Turning Corners*. It was about a group of friends who plotted to take down a profitable child sex ring by themselves. Yesterday she watched the season's finale, in which Diamond and Tony got away on a jet headed for the Philippines, after killing the leader of the organization.

Reluctantly, Jesse turned the channel and sat in her seat. These visits were always harder on her because she wanted her to do well. To be better but it never happened.

Five minutes into the program, which was a rerun, Delilah hopped off of Penny's lap and ambled in her mother's direction. "Mommy, you okay?"

"Yes..." She didn't take her eyes off of the show. It was as if Delilah wasn't even in the building. *Turning Corners* drew her in and she would retain as much as possible, knowing that after the family hour, she would be alone with her thoughts in her room, so she could decipher the message. "What do you want? Watch TV, little girl."

"I love you. Do you love me?"

"Talk to her, Yvonna." Penny advised. "She is ya only chile."

At first Yvonna's wild eyes seemed to fill up with irritation, but when she looked at Delilah's face, her expression softened. She wanted to tell her something that would help her in life. Something that would make her cautious of the people she came in contact with. "Mommy loves you." She smiled weakly, tilting her head to the side. "But you have to be careful who you cross, baby. You never want to end up on somebody's shit list."

THE END THREE

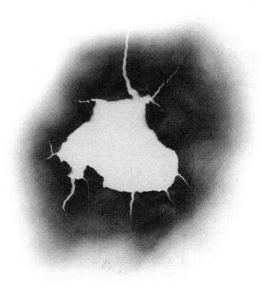

CARTEL PUBLICATIONS
PRESENTS

The Cartel Collection
Established in January 2008
We're growing stronger by the month!!!
www.thecartelpublications.com

Cartel Publications Order Form
Inmates ONLY get novels for $10.00 per book!

Titles	_Fee_
Shyt List	$15.00
Shyt List 2	$15.00
Pitbulls In A Skirt	$15.00
Pitbulls In A Skirt 2	$15.00
Pitbulls In A Skirt 3	$15.00
Victoria's Secret	$15.00
Poison	$15.00
Poison 2	$15.00
Hell Razor Honeys	$15.00
Hell Razor Honeys 2	$15.00
A Hustler's Son 2	$15.00
Black And Ugly As Ever	$15.00
Year of The Crack Mom	$15.00
The Face That Launched a Thousand Bullets	$15.00
The Unusual Suspects	$15.00
Miss Wayne & The Queens of DC	$15.00
Year of The Crack Mom	$15.00
Familia Divided	$15.00
Shyt List III	$15.00
Raunchy	$15.00
Raunchy 2	$15.00
Reversed	$15.00
Quita's Dayscare Center	$15.00
Shyt List V	$15.00

Please add $4.00 per book for shipping and handling.
The Cartel Publications * P.O. Box 486 * Owings Mills * MD * 21117

Name: _____

Address: _____

City/State: _____

Contact # & Email: _____

Please allow 5-7 business days for delivery. The Cartel is not
responsible for prison orders rejected.

Made in the USA
Columbia, SC
01 September 2021